PENGUIN BOOKS

THE KING'S WAY

Françoise Chandernagor, who lives in Paris, is a
legal adviser for the French Council of State. This is
her first novel.

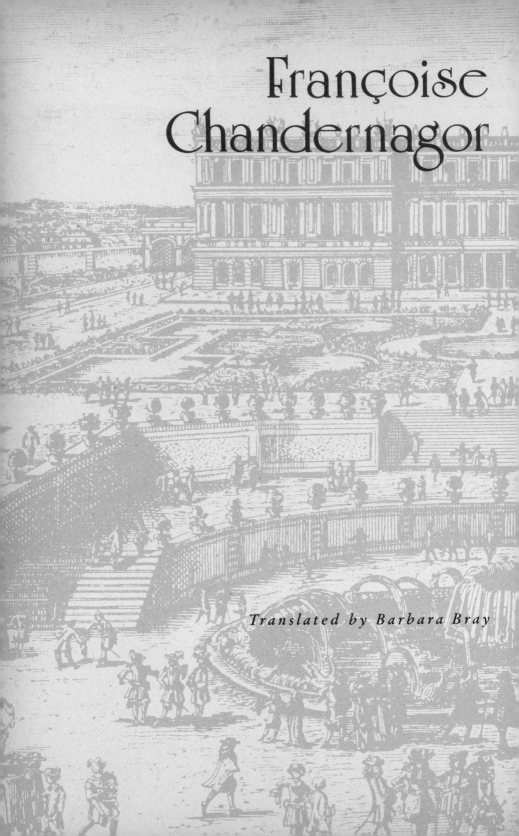

Françoise Chandernagor

Translated by Barbara Bray

The King's Way

RECOLLECTIONS OF
FRANÇOISE D'AUBIGNÉ,
MARQUISE DE MAINTENON,
WIFE TO THE KING OF FRANCE

A NOVEL

PENGUIN BOOKS

PENGUIN BOOKS
Viking Penguin Inc., 40 West 23rd Street,
New York, New York 10010, U.S.A.
Penguin Books Ltd, Harmondsworth,
Middlesex, England
Penguin Books Australia Ltd, Ringwood,
Victoria, Australia
Penguin Books Canada Limited, 2801 John Street,
Markham, Ontario, Canada L3R 1B4
Penguin Books (N.Z.) Ltd, 182–190 Wairau Road,
Auckland 10, New Zealand

First published in France by Editions René Julliard under the title
L'allée du Roi, 1981
This English translation first published in the United States of America by
Harcourt Brace Jovanovich, Inc., 1984
First published in Great Britain by William Collins Sons and Co. Ltd. 1984
Published in Penguin Books 1985

Copyright © Editions René Julliard, 1981
English translation copyright © Harcourt Brace Jovanovich, Inc.,
and William Collins Sons and Co. Ltd., 1984
All rights reserved

LIBRARY OF CONGRESS CATALOGING IN PUBLICATION DATA
Chandernagor, Françoise.
    The king's way.
    Translation of: L'allée du roi.
    1. Maintenon, Madame de, 1635-1719—Fiction.   I. Title.
PQ2663.H314A7913   1985   843'.914   84-26566
ISBN 0 14 00.7699 9

With the author's approval, Chapter 12 of the original French version has
been omitted from this translation.

Title page illustration: Garden and castle of Versailles, copper engraving by
G. Perelle (1600-75). From the collection of The Bettmann Archive.

Printed in the United States of America by
The Book Press, Brattleboro, Vermont
Set in Garamond

I SET NO LIMIT TO MY DESIRES.

—*Madame de Maintenon,*
in a letter to Godet-Desmarais

The King's Way

One

For Marie de La Tour,
when she reaches the age of twenty.

The walls of my retreat will be the walls of my grave.

Blurred features, eyes that weep without cause, a body like a skeleton with clothes hanging on it—while my weariness reminds me I am mortal, the mirror tells me I am already dead.

Just now I walked over to the window. I could see the little ones, the Reds, little girls between five and ten, running and frolicking about in the snow in the Green Courtyard, red ribbons flying loose over their brown frocks. You, my spoiled darling, were trampling the muddy paths with all the earnestness of seven years old. Beyond the bare flowerbeds, through the windows of the refectory, I could see the Yellows and the Greens, the girls from eleven to thirteen and from thirteen to seventeen, finishing their dinner in silence. The silver cutlery and their white caps reflected back through the casements more light than they received. From the chapel behind me, I could hear the singing of the big girls, the Blues, between seventeen and twenty years old, as they and their teachers joined in the midday office. Their voices rose through the chill air as pure and searing as a flame.

Could I have chosen a sweeter refuge than this house full of children? And yet I feel like someone walled up alive.

I used to think the soul wore out at the same time as the body and that when the hands grew too weak to grasp, the spirit itself let loose the passions and vanities of this world. But now this gaunt body holds a heart more eager, more restless, more thirsting for love and the absolute than the heart of my youth. The tight prison of my flesh, the silence of the convent stifle me. My child, I am dying of drought rather than of old age.

In the days when I was pretty, I knew every pleasure. I was liked wherever I went, I spent years among people of intellect, I won royal favor, experienced human glory. Yet all this only left me with a dreadful void, an uneasiness, a lassitude, an insatiable desire for something else. At Court I was desperately unhappy despite unimaginable success; God's help alone kept me from death. When the King died and I shut myself up in Saint-Cyr, I brought with me a burning thirst and the hope of an affianced bride. I was glad to renounce a world I did not love. In the first week I sold my horses and carriage, dismissed my servants, gave away my gowns, my toilet articles and my perfumes. I even cut down on my food. I resolved never to quit the cloister again.

Nowadays, I go from my room to the chapel and from the chapel to the garden. From the garden to the classroom, and from the classroom back to my chamber again. I hear mass twice a day. I see no friends save a few relatives, whom I receive as seldom as possible. I have even renounced the pleasure of correspondence, though I used to write twenty letters a week. My vigil takes no account of time or date. I have given myself up unreservedly to God.

And God, for whom I abandoned everything, abandons me. The one I sought eludes me, deserts me in my wilderness. I cannot even pray as well within the peace of these walls as I could amid the tumult of Versailles. My cry is left unanswered, my useless ardor unappeased.

If only I still had an interest in the affairs of France, or the conversation of those engaged in them, to distract me from this spiritual emptiness. But however intelligent a nun may be, she knows nothing of that which used to fill our lives. Most of them were brought up here, and the rules of the convent are all their learning. I have to resign myself to doing without company.

Everything is lost to me at the same time, everything betrays me, afflicts and wearies me, everything within me fails, except my feeling for you, my child, and for my poor duc du Maine. If they open up my body after I am dead, I fear they will find my heart as dry and twisted as that of Monsieur de Louvois.†

Sitting by the window in my bower of blue damask, I can hear you laughing in the garden. What are you up to now? Have you put a flower pot on your head? Are you eating holly berries? Or cutting the lace off your petticoat to dress up your doll? You know all too well how I dote on your pranks. I overlook more than I would if I loved you for yourself alone. But you are dear to me as a caged bird is dear to a prisoner in his cell.

Just now, when I was teaching you your alphabet, you looked at me with all the gravity you can muster, which is not much, and said, "I know you are a queen, Mamma." I looked as stern as I could and answered, "Who told you that, my pet?" When you saw my frown, you drew back, the corners of your mouth drooped. You bravely fought back your tears.

After all, what do you know about this old woman who has appointed herself your governess, who teaches you tapestry work, has you sleep beside her at night, and lavishes on you gifts as useless as they are magnificent? And is it really you I give them to? Sometimes, looking at your fresh cheeks and bright eyes, I see the shy face of that undernourished little girl who lived in such poverty she dared not let herself even wish for a ball or a necklace. Through you the wife of the King of France showers sweets and toys on Françoise d'Aubigné. But she was too hungry a child ever to be satisfied.

†References are to notes for the English-language edition of *The King's Way*. See pp. 489–97. —TRANSLATOR

TWO

I was born the 26 or 27 November 1635 in the prison at Niort in Poitou. My father, Constant d'Aubigné, lived in the jail attached to the Law Courts there. He had been imprisoned in Niort for about a year, after sampling the cells of Paris, La Rochelle, Angers, Bordeaux, La Prée and Poitiers, not to mention a few houses of detention outside France. In later years he claimed to have been at home in every kind of prison, having spent nearly twenty years of his life in them. None he knew came anywhere near the comforts of the Bastille, which he was sorry not to have been able to judge for himself; none had been anything like as disagreeable as the Conciergerie at Niort.

The Conciergerie was housed in the Hôtel Chaumont, which may still be seen by the tower near the rue du Pont. It is now very dilapidated, but even then it was neglected and insalubrious, and so cramped that its inmates were forced into indecent proximity.

It is therefore uncertain whether I was actually born in my father's room. My mother, Jeanne de Cardillhac, had probably taken lodgings with one of the warders in the prison yard, as the wives of inmates not belonging to the town usually do. Since she became pregnant during my father's imprisonment in the Hôtel

Chaumont, I conclude that husbands and wives were not kept too strictly apart there.

I cannot say, then, whether I first opened my eyes on the bare walls of a cell or on the scarcely more attractive ones of a hovel occupied by the gatekeeper Bertrand Bervache or some other prison officer. At all events, they were not the walls of a palace or even an ordinary house, and I surmise that my mother was none too pleased at giving birth to a third child when it was already as much as she could do to feed the other two.

She had met with none of the help she expected when she asked for my father's transfer to Niort. Bereft of support from her own family, she had looked for assistance from her husband's parents and relations. My grandfather, Théodore-Agrippa d'Aubigné, had lived for many years at Maillezais in the part of the Marais† near Niort. My grandmother, Suzanne de Lezay, had first seen the light of day only a couple of miles from the town. My father and his sisters were all born either at Le Chaillou or at Mursay; both houses were quite close by. So my mother had thought to find many friends and connections in that part of the world. But their presence proved of no appreciable help. In Niort as elsewhere, everyone had heard of the vices, crimes and betrayals of Constant d'Aubigné. The fact that my grandfather had cursed his only son as "destroyer of the family's prosperity and honor" was also only too well known. A father's curse is in any case a terrible burden for a son to bear, but when the father is a famous poet and anathematizes his offspring in print, then private misfortune soon turns into public hostility.

During the year she was in Niort, my mother had received more good words than good offices, and I came into the world amid such penury I might almost be said to have been born in a stable. But no wise men hastened to greet me.

I was baptized 28 November by a priest called François Meaulme. Though my d'Aubigné grandfather had been a very ardent Protestant, my mother was a fervent Catholic and my father a complete atheist. It was his habit to turn Papist or Huguenot according to circumstance, never omitting to extract some financial gain from his

5

recantations. He always arranged for the church or chapel concerned to hold a collection in aid of the new convert. Toward the end of his life he even planned to go and turn Moslem among the Turks, hoping the conversion of a Christian would bring in a handsome sum. Death prevented that escapade and he died, as he had been born, a Huguenot. However, when I came into the world, this unbeliever did not object to my mother's having me baptized a Catholic like my brothers. Perhaps, seeing he was in a royal prison, he thought it more seemly to pretend to be a Papist. Anyway, the day after I was born, I was received into the Church.

Ever since 1660, when I had to produce it for legal inspection, I have kept an extract from my baptismal certificate among my papers. Later on the parish register came into my hands, and there I appeared between Françoise Laydet, daughter of a clog-maker, and Catherine Giraud, daughter of a fuller. At least I was offered up to God in better company than they. My godfather was François de la Rochefoucauld, son of Benjamin, lord of Estissac and cousin of the author of the *Maxims.* My godmother, Suzanne de Baudean, then nine years old, was later lady-in-waiting to the Queen and wife of the maréchal de Navailles, with many claims to fame. She was born the daughter of Charles de Baudean-Parabère, governor of Niort and my father's jailer. A more intimate bond between the two men was that Baudean had been my father's childhood friend, and subsequently his boon companion in unruliness and riotous living. Whether the protection of the powerful Parabère family was more effective at Court than that of the d'Aubignés, or whether Baudean himself settled down more quickly into respectability, the two friends' present situation showed that their lives no longer had anything in common. Different as their fates might be, however, the governor of Niort still remembered their early comradeship well enough to lend me his daughter for as long as it takes to utter a couple of responses. Perhaps his kind deed also owed something to his being married to Françoise Tiraqueau, baronne de Neuillan, who was related by marriage to my father's mother. Because of Mademoiselle de Baudean's tender years it was the baronne, who by Poitou custom counted as a kind of aunt to me, who was intended as my real godmother. They named me Françoise after her, thinking her patronage might be useful to me in time of need.

Those high and mighty seigneurs—Madame de Neuillan, the governor and the Rochefoucaulds—put in the same sort of appearance at my christening as is granted to the children of servants or poor relations: they came as a favor. As for the godfather and godmother themselves, their combined ages did not add up to twenty, and they doubtless had no feelings at all about the infant they held in their arms, as unadorned as a foundling in its plain swaddling clothes. But I was forgetting—my father was there too. He signed the certificate of baptism. The prison at Niort might be dreary, but it was not hermetically sealed.

Yet however lax the restrictions, my mother could not get used to them. She dreamed of a more ordinary existence and longed to leave the gloomy cells in which she had spent all her life. For she herself had been brought up in the Château-Trompette in Bordeaux, where her father was governor. She had lived there until she was sixteen, when she met and married my father, who had set up temporary residence in a cell there. Eight years later, wandering and want had finally wearied her of gates and bolts—and of her husband. So shortly after her confinement she sought another home, less damp and less connubial.

I do not know if she can be said to have succeeded. The Regratterie or huckstering district, where I believe she found a modest lodging, is still close to the Hôtel Chaumont, and the air is just as foul. It lies below the level of the river and is invaded by water and rats in season and out of season. Whenever it rains, the cellars of the houses in the rue Basse and the rue Mère-Dieu overflow and flood the pavement, and the smell of mud vies with the odor of decay wafting up from the market. My mother's new abode was neither cheerful nor even respectable.

Yet she remained there for two or three years with my two brothers: Constant, who may have been five or six when I was born, and Charles, who was still in long frocks and could only just toddle. Did I live there with them? I do not know. I think it likely my mother put me out to nurse, perhaps in Niort itself. There were

7

plenty of wet-nurses then, and their milk cost next to nothing. War, religious persecution, highway robbery, the silting up of the river and the diversion of trade away from the port—all these had increased the numbers of the poor. Half the people in the town survived only on the oat and barley loaves given out three times a week by the prior of Notre-Dame. Women unable to hire out the work of their hands sold their milk or their bodies. I do not know to which of these unfortunates my mother entrusted me, nor if she employed her at home or sent me away.

As my later experience often confirmed, I think my mother already resented my existence. Her way of life, the poverty and loneliness to which my father's excesses had reduced her, the uncertainty hanging over the future—all combined to drain away her strength and leave her only enough feeling to love two of her children. Naturally enough she was much attached to her first-born son, and by summoning up all her reserves, she managed to take some interest in the younger boy. When it came to a third child, there was no room left in that heart shrunken by misfortune. She may even have been so indifferent as to neglect my health, for when my father's youngest sister, Arthémise de Villette, came to see us one day—Madame de Villette lived less than five miles away and sometimes lent her sister-in-law small sums of money—she was so alarmed at the state she found me in under my nurse's care that she asked my mother if she might take me home with her immediately and place me with a woman in her village. My mother gladly agreed.

While I was on my way to Mursay and my mother was wasting away in a life of privation which cost her what remained of her youthful beauty, my father was turning his prison into a gambling den. He had always had a rare talent for cards, and his studies in that art at the Protestant university in Sedan in his youth, and later in Paris and London, had made him into a formidable gamester. Despite his fall from grace, his manners were still quite urbane, and the warders and sergeants-at-arms soon learned to bring their purses to his table instead of to the inn, and to prefer his company to that of the carriers and dockers from the port. His tolerance of their ways and skill at cards earned him enough to pay his expenses in jail, as well as to slip Bervache and the turnkey a few pistoles to let him out occasionally. The beauties of Niort were not shy, and with them the aging gallant, despite his grey hairs, kept up the reputation he had earned in the past by certain whirlwind abductions.

Had my mother known about these escapades when she married him? Did he think fit to tell her of the fate of Anne Marchant, the former wife he had dispatched into a better world with seven dagger thrusts, after magnanimously allowing her to say her prayers? I fear she was so swiftly and completely captivated by her father's prisoner that she did not want to know, and that she disregarded other people's warnings and her own family's opposition. Moreover, I have in my possession a letter dating from that time in which she admits she must endure her husband's irregularities with patience, having been so heedless as to deserve the treatment now meted out to her. At the beginning of their relationship, before she attained that melancholy resignation, though, she loved him with a passion so intense and blind I can scarcely imagine it. True, my father was a well set-up fellow, but when they met he was three times her age. He was a spirited reciter of poetry and wrote verses of a kind himself; he could play the viol and the lute; but he was penniless and publicly dishonored. He had gamed, drunk, cheated, stolen and quarrelled so freely that word of it must have spread to Bordeaux and all Aquitaine. He had rumpled so many skirts and rifled so many corpses that his fame shone out beyond his native province. Could my mother, merely because of the civil wars and the noise of the guns, and despite the celebrity my grandfather himself had lent his son's vices, really not have known that Constant d'Aubigné was a counterfeiter, a turncoat, a traitor to his King and several times a murderer? He had been sentenced to death, and only circumstance had saved him from having his head cut off. He was posted up as "wanted" at many a street corner. In short, he was a notorious ne'er-do-well. And worst of all an unlucky one.

Some women are attracted to this type of man, and perhaps Jeanne de Cardillhac owed her first love to a weakness for losers.

But she made so complete a recovery that from the day I was born to the day my father died, my parents never lived together again except briefly and by chance.

At the time of which I now speak, I knew nothing of what had passed so long before my birth. Nor did I learn of it while I lived with my aunt de Villette, who loved her brother dearly and regarded his most terrible crimes as mere peccadillos. Only my mother's complaints, later, gave me some hints. There was one advantage to the ignorance I was kept in until I reached or even passed the age of reason, namely that it allowed me to respect a father I could see no cause to love and who showed me no kindness. The most I can say for him as a parent is that he was always fair: he divided his indifference equally among all his children, and my brothers too enjoyed their full share of it.

Madame de Villette lived to the north of the town, on the edge of the rolling Gâtine, in a large country house surrounded by lands she had inherited from my grandfather. The château of Mursay with its eight towers and three drawbridges was then very handsome and quite new, having been built by my father's great-grandmother, Adrienne de Vivonne. It is set in delightful surroundings, with the river Sèvre running through its moats and murmuring sweetly day and night. The valley, enclosed by wooded slopes, opens gently to let the green and peaceful waters flow out toward Niort and the sea. The steeple of the church at Siecq can be glimpsed through the trees on the hill facing the château, and behind the house lies the village of Mursay itself, girdled with vineyards and walled gardens.

My uncle and aunt lived there modestly enough off a not very extensive estate, which amounted to hardly more than a quarter of the legacy my grandfather had bequeathed to his children. It consisted of a few stretches of woodland, five or six fiefs of vineyard, some swampy water-meadows, a farm, a fishery, some barns, a mill, a common oven and a few mixed tithes. By good management Monsieur and Madame de Villette produced enough from this small property to feed and clothe their four children, three daughters—Madeleine, Aimée and Marie, who were already past infancy —and one son, Philippe, who was only three or four when I came to Mursay and was to be my chief childhood companion.

My aunt handed me over to Louise Appercé, her farmer's daughter-in-law, who had been foster-mother to my cousin Aimée seven or eight years earlier. She had just lost a baby, and was so glad of an opportunity to relieve her full breasts that she would take no payment for me until I had to be weaned. Then, when I was on slops and bread and milk, my aunt gave Louise small sums to cover my food, while making herself responsible for my clothes and handing down my cousins' frocks and caps. So I grew up on the farm at Mursay, running about with the hens, playing with the dogs, and speaking only the local patois. I still understand it well, and love it as if it were my mother tongue.

I came to be three years old and could be left with a foster-mother no more. My father was still lodged at the King's expense, my mother still left to the charity of neighbors. She had obtained a separation order enabling her to administer her own affairs and had recently started a lawsuit designed to let her children enjoy some part of their father's squandered inheritance. This required her to go to Paris. Now more than ever she wished to be rid of me. Perhaps she might have taken the trouble to come and pat me on the head before she left, had the coach to Paris passed through Mursay. But it did not. I saw neither her nor my two brothers before she left Niort for ever.

I remained with those who had taken me in and who now installed me under their own roof, and who loved me as if they were my real father and mother.

Three

L ife was very quiet at the château of Mursay. I say this not
so much because of those early days, of which I remember little,
but because I spent several more years there with the Villettes later
on. Life was peaceful at Mursay, austere but tranquil.

My uncle Benjamin watched over the crops himself, counting
the sheaves and faggots and tramping all day long across the fens.
No one else was allowed to sell his livestock; he himself directed
all building, oversaw the mill and the oven, kept exact accounts and
visited all his people regularly, reconciling husbands and wives,
tending the sick and succoring the poor. With amusement tinged
with pride, he would show how the corridors of his château were
full of hay and wheat, its park planted with fruit trees and its
courtyard strewn with bales of straw in which the dogs made their
kennels. He used to say my grandfather wisely decreed it should
be so, and that even in his day the place was more like a farm than
a nobleman's residence.

Beneath a severe exterior, Monsieur de Villette was tender-
hearted and benevolent. Though he rarely troubled to speak, when
he did so he spoke with such skill and sobriety that he showed his
wit without meaning to. Of course, it was not until much later that

I discerned these virtues. All I can remember from my early years at Mursay are the black gaiters which encased his legs and formed a kind of shell above his sabots. Too small to see any higher than his knees, I reduced his whole amiable person to two leather tubes and a few buttons. But those tubes showed me such fatherly kindness that I loved them passionately.

As for my aunt, she is for me a model of all the domestic virtues I aimed to promote at Saint-Cyr. She rose early and ruled the whole house. Though in her youth she had received a very thorough education, and her father had spared no pains to make his "one little girl," as he called her, a woman fit for the highest responsibilities, she presided in person over both pantry and poultry yard. Every afternoon she would sew or spin with one or two maids; she never had many servants. My cousin Madeleine, who was then sixteen or seventeen and not yet married to Monsieur de Sainte-Hermine, helped her in her work.

Parents and children alike were punctual in their religious duties. As dedicated Huguenots they read the Bible together morning and night, sang Protestant hymns and went to chapel in Niort every Sunday. Every day my uncle preached a short sermon based on one of the Psalms or on some other passage from the Old Testament.

As I was a Catholic, they did not oblige me to take part in their observances. But just as, hitherto ignorant of French, I learned to speak it from listening to them, so also, from seeing how they lived, I learned from my earliest days to think of God as they did.

I was given a nursemaid, Marie de Lile, a peasant brought up to be my aunt's chambermaid and now in charge of me. It was she who washed me, though seldom enough; she who did my hair as I sat on the floor with my head in her grubby apron. She dressed me up as smartly as she could and was always telling me to stand up straight. Apart from that she let me do as I pleased. I was amazingly fond of her, and when my cousin Aimée taught me my alphabet and I could read from the Bertram Bible and the *Christian's ABC,* I taught Marie how to read and write, and whenever I misbehaved she would say, "As a punishment you shan't show me how to read today." I would weep bitterly. I also used to comb her hair. It was long and greasy, but that did not deter me; I would have done anything in the world to avoid being deprived of that pleasure. I was always very attached to Marie, and thirty years later I brought her to Court and made her son my butler.

My cousin Marie taught me a few songs, and from Philippe I learned addition and subtraction, multiplication and division. All I did apart from these intellectual exercises was trail after my uncle or Marie de Lile all day. I could soon milk a goat and card wool, and, even better, roll in the hay or jump off the straw bales. I would spend whole days bolting flour into a bin, perched on a chair so that I could reach. Three times a year Monsieur de Villette took me to the fair in Niort, and it was he who taught me how to get the best possible price for a calf. This knowledge stood me in good stead twenty years later when I was spending the summer in the country with Madame de Montchevreuil. As her farmer was ill, I took it upon myself to sell a newborn calf. I got fifteen or sixteen livres for it, and because the buyers had no better coin, I had to bring the price home in pennies. This was almost too much for the strength of my apron, and altogether too much for its cleanliness, but Madame de Montchevreuil's cousin, the marquis de Villarceaux, thought it a charming sight, and his delight in it produced consequences affecting my life for a very long while.

At Mursay I went about everywhere dressed like a little peasant girl in petticoats of blue drugget and fustian jackets. At home I wore sabots; they gave me proper shoes only when there were visitors. My aunt said a pair of shoes cost the same as a sheep, and I would only have spoiled them running about the fields. And true it was that in those hard times I often saw our poorer folk going barefoot, carrying their shoes in their hands so as not to wear them out.

When I was a little older, my cousin Marie and I, who were about the same age, used to spend part of the day looking after my aunt's turkeys. Turkeys were still rare and valuable in those days. They made us wear masks over our faces so as not to get sunburned, and they gave us each a little basket containing our lunch and a book of Pibrac's verses. We had to memorize a few pages every day. We each had a long stick to stop the turkeys going where they should not. The common folk of Mursay were fond of their little turkey-girl and like my cousins always called me "Bignette," after the Poitou habit of making nicknames out of surnames. I would often hold forth to them, and because of my youth my sayings were elevated into witticisms. I was, moreover, what is called a good child, and my aunt's domestics doted on me no less than did the villagers. But this did not save me from being chastised when I deserved it. I remember being whipped two or three times with long twigs from the verbena that grew in the courtyard. One day Philippe and I had the bright idea of stripping off the branches to prevent the natural renewal of this scourge, but my uncle then used the wood from the stems, and we had occasion to long for the former state of things.

This pastoral may seem insipid to sophisticated tastes. Nothing is more tedious to contemplate than happiness and virtue. Yet I was happier then than at any other time in my life, and had I disposed of but half the dowry bestowed on my cousins, I would gladly have carried on the same existence in some neighboring château, marrying like them a Monsieur de Fontmort or de Sainte-Hermine.

But God had another fate in store for me.

My days slipped by peacefully, divided between the local fairy tales told me by my nurse Marie and the religious and secular history recounted by my aunt. I liked reading, and since there were no books save works of piety at Mursay, I pored continually over them and was able to produce many an apt quotation. My cousins applauded, and my uncle fondly judged me clever beyond my age.

For all this praise, I was not spoiled. Monsieur and Madame de Villette treated me as a daughter, but as a daughter who was poor. They knew I was not destined to great wealth, and like provident parents avoided giving me habits of ease or even comfort which I might later find it difficult to discard. I was loved as much as my girl cousins, but despite my youth I was not so well housed or clothed as they. I had no fire in my bedroom unless I was ill, and I washed in cold water regardless of chilblains. I was never allowed to indulge in whims and fancies. One day when I turned up my nose at a bit of dry bread, my aunt said gently, "You will be less particular, my child, when you have been the rounds of your lands."

On two or three occasions she spoke to me at length about my situation, and as I really was a sensible child, I readily shared her views. Lacking neither the moral and material sustenance necessary for my survival, nor the kindness and caresses which for a child constitute luxury, I rightly considered myself completely happy.

The Sunday visits to Niort were my only afflictions. As I have said, the Villettes went regularly to worship at the Protestant church. I was meanwhile left at the prison to see my father. I chafed at these visits. It may be that my father, bereft of any company but that of his jailers, looked upon the encounters with his "innocent," as he called me, as a consolation. But I, even if I had felt anything more for him than a mechanical deference, would have regarded it a chore to have to talk to him for two or three hours on end. What could a gallant of fifty-five and a shepherdess of seven find to say to each other? After the customary kiss and the opening civilities, neither he nor I knew how to make conversation.

If he tried to dispel my boredom with some small talk, his wit could not measure itself to mine, and his bent for sarcasm and licence completed my embarrassment. If I made some pious allusion, as I was in the habit of doing with the Villettes, he would stand me between his knees and say gravely, "I cannot bear to have you told such stuff, Bignette. Can you, with your intelligence, possibly believe what they teach you in your catechism?" With no spiritual communion to make up for the disproportion between our minds, our words were bound to be at odds.

I would sit in a corner on the floor and watch him writing letters, playing cards with the soldiers and his fellow-prisoners or feeding the birds in the little aviary he had set up by his bed. Not knowing what to say to or do with me, he soon found me burdensome and sent me out to play in the yard with Bervache's little girl. But this liberation only brought a new torture, for the turnkey's daughter was unmannerly and unkind. She played roughly, and I hated to hear her call my father "Constant" in my presence, as if they were intimates. It is true she stood higher in his favors than I.

One of her father's prisoners had given her a set of doll's furniture made of silver, and when I praised it, hoping to win her over, she answered that, judging from the way I was dressed, I had nothing like it of my own. "No," I retorted, "but I'm a lady and you're not." I was proud by nature. My pride was all I had.

My father hated the prison in Niort even more than I did, and with more reason, and urged my mother, while she was in Paris, to get Cardinal Richelieu to have him transferred to the capital, or better still freed altogether. My mother may not have sought his pardon with too much zeal: she had plenty to do without that, and she was not anxious to have such a husband too close to her again. But she did see the Cardinal and test the wind. He said she must not think of winning the prisoner's freedom; his reputation was very black, and besides "you would be very glad if I refused." He then asked her if she was not my father's second wife, and what he had done with the first, and other similar questions, so she decided to drop the subject.

This setback did not deter my father. Not only did he think fit to discourse to me about his wife's desertion every time I went to see him—it did after all provide a subject for conversation—but he also lodged a complaint against her with the Law Court at Niort, saying that she was using his money for her own purposes in Paris, leaving me without food and maintenance and him without the wherewithal to live and pay his jail fees. By a strange coincidence my father's petition arrived on the very same day that the Parlement† in Paris pronounced judgment in my mother's case, stripping her of what little she still possessed and forcing her and her two sons to live on charity in a convent.

Shortly afterwards Cardinal Richelieu died, and Cardinal Mazarin, who succeeded him, released many prisoners, including my father. He left Niort, and to make up for the lack of movement of the past few years began to rush from pillar to post. He went to Paris, but not for long, then equally briefly to Lyons, and after that to Geneva. Then Paris again, Niort, La Rochelle and Paris once more. He posted hither and thither, night and day, wearing out boots and horses. No one knew, he least of all, whither it all tended.

Meanwhile I, lulled by the kindness of the Villettes, thought my happiness would never end.

But at the beginning of the year 1644, my mother crossed the drawbridge at Mursay, and within the hour had carried me off to another life.

Four

By the same evening I was in a hovel in La Rochelle, where I made the acquaintance of my brothers.

Constant, then about fifteen, was a melancholy young man clad in a suit of scarlet velvet and lace which he had outgrown. He seemed kind and gentle, though devoid of wit. My mother loved him passionately—one might say she loved only him. Nor was he unworthy of this exclusive attachment: he never forsook her through all her trials and had earned her preference by the solicitude and loving care with which he surrounded her.

Charles, only a year older than me, was more amusing. I liked him at once. I had just left Philippe de Villette, to whom I had become attached with all the ardor of early feeling. For this and even better reasons I considered myself inconsolable. Charles taught me that one can get over anything at eight years old. Three funny faces and a couple of japes and my sorrow seemed less. The younger d'Aubigné brother was handsome, bold and endowed with a Parisian wit that was reckless but irresistible. Though both in Niort and in Paris he had lived through days of tears and sorrow in the company of a suffering mother and a gloomy brother, his good humor was unimpaired. In two days he won my heart, and no matter what pain he caused me later, I was never quite able to forget that first impression.

Those days in La Rochelle also enabled me to know my mother, whom I had scarcely seen since I was born. At first I could not get over my surprise that she kissed me but twice, and then only on the forehead, after our long separation. Little did I guess that those two kisses were the only ones I would receive from her in my whole life. I found her sharp-tongued and impatient with the helpless laughter inspired in me by Charles's tricks. I could tell she did not like me. "By no means a pretty child," she said one day to my brother Constant in my presence. "She's all eyes—it's quite ridiculous!"

It was only a few days after my arrival that my reservations about her turned to outright aversion. The change arose because of the way she took me to church. I had never attended mass, and the idea of going inspired me with curiosity rather than hostility; although I had occasionally gone to chapel with the Villettes, I did not regard myself as a Huguenot. My mother took me to church as if she were dragging me to prison—with threats, and her hand gripping my wrist. I could be got to do anything by reason and kindness, but I was not naturally docile; there was a rebelliousness in my character which was immediately awakened by the use of force. The result of my mother's method was that as soon as I entered the church I turned my back on the altar. She gave me a box on the ear which I bore bravely, proud to suffer for my religion.

As far as mass was concerned, my resistance was groundless and did not last, but I never got over the dislike for my mother which this incident inspired.

Time went slowly for me at La Rochelle. I could not tell what we were waiting for. My father did not share our small lodging, and we rarely saw him. I do not know where he lived—perhaps on horseback, for he was as restless as ever and rode unceasingly about the Saintonge region accompanied by one Tesseron, a servant he treated as a friend. My mother was often out, taking her elder son with her, and Charles and I were left in the care of a hideous pigeon-toed old woman, our only domestic. This did not mean, however, that we were free to do or even to speak as we pleased. Madame d'Aubigné left us with a large volume of Plutarch to study, and with orders to talk to one another about nothing else while she was away. Far from regarding this restriction as vexatious, my brother and I, for want of better amusement, took great pleasure in it and greatly enjoyed comparing the deeds of the characters. I had a predilection for the heroines and would point out the ladies who in my opinion had excelled the men. My brother would maintain that his heroes were the more wonderful, and, each stoutly supporting his or her own argument, we spent several agreeable weeks preoccupied with Athens and Rome.

When we had finished with Caesar, Scipio and Alexander, we learned what lay behind my father's ceaseless expeditions and my mother's visits to the merchants and lawyers in the town. Constant d'Aubigné had decided to leave France and take his family to the isles of America, there either to hide or to repair his misfortunes. In those days France used to send to her colonies all poor vagrants, convicts, female foundlings and the black sheep of respectable families. My father would not be out of place among them. Sometimes these unfortunates were joined by a few decent young fellows who could not find work, as was often the case in Poitou, or by the sons of merchants eager to seek their fortune. My parents agreed with some of this sort to found a settlement in the colonies. The cost of the voyage they borrowed from the Ursuline nuns of La Rochelle and from a tailor.

In April 1644 my father and mother concluded before a notary an agreement whereby Hilère Germond, a wealthy ship owner, was to take them on one of his vessels to Guadeloupe, together with their three children, a manservant—Tesseron—and a maidservant. Germond also undertook to bring them, on another ship, a "volunteer" soldier, a trunk and a cask of brandy. The bargain was concluded for 330 francs in cash. I found the document among the papers my mother left to my brother Charles when she died.

So at the beginning of the summer of 1644 I embarked on the *Isabelle de la Tremblade,* together with my parents, my brothers, my father's manservant and the old maidservant. I was delighted to leave and to see new things; the world seemed to expand before my very eyes. I knew something of the harbor at Niort from having dallied to watch the carriers loading the barges and lighters with salt and wheat and cloth when I was sent on errands, but that bore no comparison with all the activity in La Rochelle.

Before our own ship set sail, I looked on in wonder at the loading of several others about to leave for Acadia, England, Portugal or the coast of America. With an interest not unmixed with impatience, I thus watched the departure of the *Merry Martha*, the *Charity* and the *Judith*. At last, at about four o'clock in the morning, the captain ordered the gun to be fired, a sure sign of our imminent departure and a warning to the passengers to come on board. During the next hour the crew slaughtered several sheep on the quay and stowed them away to provide fresh meat for the first part of the voyage. Then the *Isabelle*, under the command of master mariner Mathurin Forpe, set sail, and we moved off from the coast. We did not touch land again for sixty days.

The voyage was far from being as pleasant as it had promised. In those days the captain of a ship did not adapt the number of his passengers to the size of his vessel. The *Isabelle*, a two-hundred-tonner, carried some three hundred people—men and women of all ages, ranks and nationalities; they were also of various religions, though Protestants were in the majority.

The ship was so full of cargo of all kinds that there was scarcely room to lie down properly among the casks of salt and bales of wool.

Our party, being among the "free passengers," was not so badly off as some. We were housed as crew between-decks and slept on straw mats, while my father was accommodated Caribbean-style in the pilot's cabin, where he had a sort of suspended cradle called a hammock. We were quite free to go up and rove about on deck so long as we did not get in the way.

Not so the poor "volunteers," of whom there were a good two hundred. These were penniless peasants and laborers, forced by the poverty prevailing in France to go and seek their daily bread in the colonies. They could not pay for their passage, and before setting sail had engaged their services for three years without wages to an employer who defrayed this expense. Because of the length of time for which these unfortunates had parted with their liberty and turned themselves into slaves, they were known as the "thirty-six monthers." They were shut up below-decks without air or sufficient change of linen and with no fresh water to keep themselves decent. They became covered in vermin, and, heaped up together amid the dirt and filth, they infected one another with various diseases, the stench and corruption of which rose up between-decks. Their discomforts were such that more than fifty of these unhappy creatures died of fever during the voyage; that is to say, nearly once a day, one of them was thrown into the sea after the firing of the gun.

I too suffered, though less materially, from the lack of cleanliness. The captain had arranged for several barrels of fresh water to be placed about the deck for people to wash their shirts and drawers, but the liquid in these tubs soon became so disgusting that I washed my frocks in sea water. In other words, they remained dirty. I caught lice, which I passed on to Charles, and always in my hair or clothes I had one or more of the prodigious horde of bugs that inhabited the ship and could be seen swarming up and down the rigging in thousands, like sailors.

In this state of neglect, food brought little consolation. When we had finished the fresh meat and vegetables brought on board before we set sail, we, like the volunteers, were given nothing but dried cod, very salt and smelly, hard dry biscuit and gruel. All we had to drink was cider, watered down every day to make it go farther, then, after two or three weeks, tepid water which had "gone off" and tasted nasty. And not much of that. Fortunately my mother had brought with her some syrup of vinegar which she mixed into the water so that my brothers and I could drink it without too much distaste. Nonetheless, throughout the voyage I suffered torments of thirst, made worse by the heat of the sun when we were off the coast of Africa.

These not inconsiderable inconveniences apart, I, unlike my mother and my brother Constant, had the good fortune to be a good sailor, and this enabled me to witness many scenes that were new to me, and not to suffer too cruelly from the restricted space imposed on us.

I was much entertained by the fish. One day I saw a whale, only a musket-shot away, blowing water up into the air like a great fountain. Another time the sailors caught a big fish which they called a "requiem" or shark. The captain had had a lump of bacon impaled on an iron hook at the end of a long rope and slung over the side as bait. When the fish took the bait it was hauled up on deck by La Battrie, Bellerose and Vent-en-Panne, three merry sailors who had made friends with Charles. The "requiem" is a most dangerous fish. As soon as it was laid upon the deck it began to thrash about, snapping with its jaws. Bellerose, a bold fellow, came up behind it and dealt it a good thump on the head with a mallet, then, taking advantage of its surprise, kept on striking until the animal's fury abated. This is the only safe way to make friends with wild beasts.

Usually the sailors kept the fish they caught for themselves and fried them to enliven their ordinary diet, but they soon were so taken with Charles's impish tricks and my good nature that they invited us to share their feasts. My mother, still abed between-decks, got to hear of this and forbade us to frequent them any more.

Fortunately we had other, perhaps more innocent, friendships at our disposal. I had become attached to a poor young volunteer called Jean Marquet, who was thirteen years old. He had been so grievously ill at the beginning of the voyage that, seeing he was just a boy, the captain had had him taken from the hold and put to bed in a longboat on deck, covered with a tarpaulin. He stayed on there after he got better and came to join in with us in our games. He was from a respectable family, his father one of the rich merchants of La Rochelle. For some reason or other he had pledged Jean to a surgeon who was to take the boy to the islands, make use of him and let the father hear no more of him. Jean was very unhappy at being abandoned thus, and wept for his country if not his parents. I do not know what became of him, for I heard a year later in Martinique that the surgeon had died there soon after he arrived, and no one could tell me what had happened to the gentle lad who had been my companion in all my amusements and discoveries aboard the *Isabelle*.

With him I had gazed, albeit from a distance, at the coasts of Madeira and the Canaries and the Cape Verde Islands, though wind and tide kept us from putting ashore. A few days later we had an even more exciting diversion, when we narrowly escaped being captured by pirates. Round about the fortieth day out, we spied an English or perhaps a Turkish ship making toward us at incredible speed. It fired a shot at our rudder by way of greeting, but God turned aside the ball which would otherwise have meant the end of us, and we sent off two balls in answer, one of which seemed to pierce the pirate ship's side. In a trice all except the topsails were furled and everyone was on deck, expecting to be boarded and prepared to conquer or die.

Mathurin Forpe, the captain, observed the ceremonies usual in such encounters. He took a glass of wine, turned toward the enemy and threw both the glass and its contents into the sea as a sign of contempt for their skill and strength. Then everyone, my father and Jean included, seized a cutlass and took up positions on the poop. The Capuchin father who usually said mass exhorted the passengers to make true acts of contrition for having sinned against God. The Creator having been satisfied, it was now necessary to satisfy His creature: to put heart in the men, the casks of wine awarded for crossing the line where rolled out on deck.

While these preparations were going forward, my mother busied herself dressing Charles and me in the best clothes we had, attaching to my belt a long rosary she usually wore herself.

"At least we shan't be with her any more if we're taken prisoner," I whispered to Charles.

But we were not taken prisoner. Either because the enemy judged a fight not worth the trouble or because he thought he was not strong enough for us, he disappeared in a flash, showing that he was as good at avoiding battle as at attacking foes he thought weaker than himself. A common tactic, and not restricted to ships.

We dropped anchor in Martinique at the beginning of August. As we approached land I grew more and more astonished that people could ever have come to live there. The island seemed to me nothing more than a frightful mountain riven with precipices. Nothing about it pleased me except the green vegetation everywhere. A few Negroes came on board; I had never seen any before, and I thought them very black. Many bore whip-marks on their backs, which aroused pity in the passengers who were unaccustomed to such sights. But one soon gets used to it. Jean Marquet took leave of us with tears, and the *Isabelle* set sail once more for Guadeloupe, where we arrived two days later. We went ashore in the longboat to the town of Basse-Terre.

When I set foot on land after so long at sea I felt dizzy and fell in a faint outside the warehouse of the merchant captains. Still far from well, I was taken across the town to the fort, where my father was to meet Monsieur Hoël, the governor. I was lodged there in a clean enough room and looked after by a Negress, while my parents and their two French servants moved into a little house in the town. When I had grown used to dry land and was cured of a fever probably due to grief at having said goodbye for ever to my beloved Villettes, I was able to join my family. My father had already left the island. He planned to go and live on Marie-Galante, a few hours' voyage away.

Marie-Galante, which unlike the other islands of the region is not mountainous, was then cultivated by the native Caribs, and it was thought that all sorts of plants could be acclimatized there. My father, accompanied by Tesseron and some other passengers from the *Isabelle,* had decided to set up a plantation. My mother, my brothers and I, together with a volunteer who had come from France on the other ship belonging to Hilère Germond, followed a few weeks later.

Even after so short a time we found a house prepared for us which was quite handsome by local standards, that is to say it looked very much like a barn. It was of wood, with a roof of palm leaves; though fairly long, it was divided into no more than two or three rooms, and these were separated by half-walls so that the air might circulate freely. Around this building the gentlemen and their indentured workers, together with a few slaves, had started to grow things. They had cleared the ground not only for native fruits and cereals, such as manioc, sweet potatoes, yams and bananas, but also for certain French root crops, like carrots, turnips and beets. They had planted tobacco and indigo too, hoping to trade in these commodities. The natives had so far offered little opposition.

I spent a few months of great freedom on Marie-Galante, leading a life not very different from that of the red-skinned Caribs around us. My mother did try to make me resume the study of Plutarch when the book arrived in her trunk, but she did not succeed. She was too busy providing meals for the colonists and ruling over the slaves to be able to reimpose her former discipline over her children. My brother Constant botanized to his heart's content, only occasionally helping to build a hut or pick some fruit. Charles made friends with the native children and learned to catch turtles and shoot with a bow and arrow. I collected shells and made them into necklaces, hoping that one day I should be able to present them to my cousin Marie.

I remember little about my time on Marie-Galante. Life there must have been very different from anything I had been used to, but children are never surprised at anything. I found it quite natural to eat turtle and sea cow, to drink orange juice and stroll among snakes and "cocodiles." There are only two incidents which I recollect clearly. The first was the severe public chastisement my mother administered to Charles one day when he came home to our village naked from head to foot and daubed with red like a savage. The second was an interview I had with my father.

One night when it was dark I went down alone to the seashore. The Caribbean is even warmer and more balmy at night than in the daytime. I sat down on the beach and gazed at the stars' reflection in the water; I thought they must be diamonds washed up by the sea. As I was dreaming thus, my father came and sat down beside me. I do not recall what he talked about at first—the islands, the oceans, the stars. He always liked grand subjects, especially when he was tipsy. Then he looked at me for a while and said I was growing quite pretty, was no fool, and with these advantages might, if I did not hamper myself with principles, have a life which would end more happily than it had begun.

I noted his prediction, while doubting if I ought to follow his advice.

That was the only time in the whole of my childhood when one of my parents spoke to me in a way that made me think they loved me.

Admittedly the illusion did not last long. Monsieur d'Aubigné ended the conversation by informing me he was soon to leave us.

"The great thing about being in prison," he said, "is that if you cannot do what you want yourself, at least you are not obliged to do what someone else wants. Your mother often makes me wish I was back in prison."

At the beginning of 1645 he went away, accompanied by Tesseron and leaving my mother and Merry Rolle, another of the passengers on the *Isabelle,* in charge of our little colony. He said he was going back to France to ask the West India Company to appoint him governor of Marie-Galante, but although, as I learned later, he obtained the governorship in March of that year, he did not return to Marie-Galante. He had soon seen how difficult it would be to establish a settlement on that primitive island, and once he had got his warrant to be its governor, he was quite happy to lead a life of pleasure divided between Niort and Paris, without bothering to let us know what was happening.

My mother no longer had the strength, on her own, to deal with the crowd of adventurers and poor unfortunates who made up our community. Many began to overindulge in rum and other liquors produced in abundance in the islands. The fields were neglected, the crops we counted on came to naught. Some of the slaves ran away and vanished into the forests. Merry Rolle decided to return to Guadeloupe with his workers, and without him no one knew what to do with the indigo harvest. To crown it all, the threat of an attack by the Irish made the colony break up in the course of a few months.

My mother had no choice but to leave the island and take refuge with us in Martinique, where she hoped to have news of her husband. The news duly arrived, I do not know how. He ordered her to set herself up in style, because he had certain new arrangements with the Company in Paris of which he had the highest expectations. My mother therefore rented a large house and some land in the Le Prêcheur district in the west of the island and, with a loan from a merchant, purchased, at a very high price, about twenty slaves to be our servants. The worker we had brought from France had already left us, either he had run away or he had died of fever. As for the servant from La Rochelle, I imagine she must have died at about that time of dropsy, a sickness which afflicted many of the white people who came to the islands.

Nor did the air there agree with me. I caught a malignant fever which affected me for the rest of my life; every so often it would recur, and the only cure was a little opium and much patience.

Quite apart from this, I had little cause to enjoy our stay in Martinique. My mother had nothing to do and kept me under greater restraint. I was not allowed to go out and spent all my days in her room. As the only servants left her were little slaves who were clumsy and did not know how to do her hair, she taught me to wait on her. I had to climb on a chair to comb her hair, but even so I combed it long and well, having nothing else to do.

Hair-dressing, the catechism and writing were my sole employment, and the only education I got too, in the isolation forced upon me by a mother who was always melancholy and bad-tempered. Every day I had to copy out a chapter from Plutarch or the New Testament, while Charles, who because he was a boy was left as free as air, enjoyed himself picking up lemons from the paths, catching canaries—the little birds found on the island—or stuffing himself with guava jam.

"You copy out my letters," he would say to me, "and I'll go and get you some oranges."

Seeing him able to take advantage of the marvels of America, I grew all the more impatient at being restrained, and I looked back with regret on the liberty of Mursay, of which the post occasionally brought news.

The only consolation I had in my loneliness was the company of Zabeth Dieu, one of my mother's twenty-four Negresses, who had been appointed my governess. My own special "doudou" dressed me and watched over my games, but taught me nothing since she knew nothing herself. She was, however, a very good singer, and from her I learned songs in the coarse local language that I remember still. I sing them sometimes when I am alone, with great pleasure, though I fear my voice is not sweet enough to give much delight to any listener. One of the lullabies I liked best was a sad and gentle love-song which went: "Why you leave me like this? Ain't no woman pretty as me. You gonna miss me bad—you'll see." I thought it must have been written for my mother.

I also liked to amuse myself with a little Negro boy called Biam Coco, who had been given to me as a playmate. He was the cause of a cruel punishment inflicted on me by my mother. One day I followed him into his hut and watched him playing with some other little slaves, aged like him about nine or ten. No doubt, since Negroes are naturally licentious even when young, their games were not altogether innocent. I did not know I was doing wrong. When my mother learned what had happened, however, she had me brought to her room, where without a word she took off my cap and started to comb my hair so roughly that she drew blood. She then sent me out into the midday sun and told me to stay there in the middle of the courtyard. As she intended, mosquitoes and other insects, attracted by the blood, came and attacked my head and neck. My cries did nothing to appease her wrath, and I had to stand exposed there for two long hours.

Biam Coco's punishment was no less severe. She had Deafy, her overseer, flog him till the blood came. This so grieved him that he ran away, but he was recaptured and chained up, which gave him a large ulcer on one leg. There was talk of amputation, and he began to eat earth, partly from despair and partly out of the belief, common to all Negroes, that if he died he would return to his own country. He did die, and if I had shared his belief, I would gladly have eaten the mud of Martinique so as to find myself, dead or alive, back in Mursay.

The months went by without event, except for mass on Sunday and occasional visits by travellers from France. One of these was a handsome man of ready wit come to botanize among the islands for the King. His name was Cabart de Villermont, and he was the son of a lawyer in the Parlement. I paid no attention to him at the time but saw him again often thereafter, and as both my marriage and my fortune originated with him, I think it fitting to mention him here.

Soon after Villermont's visit our house burned down. I do not know if, as Madame de Montespan maintained, fire is a sign of happiness for a child, but I personally wept bitterly.

"What!" said my mother sternly. "My daughter cry over a house?"

I was not really crying for the house so much as for my doll, which I had just put to bed in its little cot with my cap for a canopy, and I could see the flames creeping toward the place where I had left it. But how could I explain that to a woman who worshiped Plutarch!

Constant d'Aubigné had been away for more than eighteen months, and his wife had had to be mother and father both to us children, when at last we had news. The West India Company had authorized him to be governor of some desert island of his choice if his colony on Marie-Galante failed. As it had indeed failed, he had decided to settle temporarily on Saint-Christophe and was now recruiting associates there to join him in establishing some new venture in an unknown part of the island. He wrote to bid us join him in the capital.

But we had lived by borrowing on Martinique and could not leave without paying our debts. My mother sold the slaves. Luckily some of the women had had children in the meanwhile, and since they sell for more with their babies, we got back more than we had paid for them, and my mother was able to pay all she owed. I was sorry to leave Zabeth Dieu, as I had been to leave Marie de Lile. This time, though, I did not cry. I was beginning to get used to leave-takings.

On the voyage to Saint-Christophe I asked my mother if Father meant to make us visit all the islands of America. My only answer was a box on the ears. My mother, quite rightly, would not allow us to criticize our father no matter what he did.

Saint-Christophe was the most beautiful of all the French Antilles, and the earliest one to be settled. The colony then consisted of about three or four thousand whites, and there were real towns with streets and a few houses of brick and stone. The governor was Captain de Poincy, who was also governor-general of all the French Antilles. We stayed with him at Sandy Point, where my father already was, and where we were glad to find Monsieur de Villermont, who was making drawings of the local plants. This time he made friends with me and let me go with him on some of his expeditions to the savannah.

My time on Saint-Christophe was made pleasant by the comfort of the Big House, the governor's residence, where the servants did all they could to anticipate our wishes. I amused myself taming monkeys, of which there were many, and teaching a parrot to talk. I had soon had enough of this diversion to prevent me from seeking the company of such creatures later on, as did all the other ladies at Versailles. Having found parrots' conversation somewhat limited when I was a child of twelve, I could never understand how it could satisfy marquises of forty. But they say birds of a feather flock together, and I am not too surprised that some of those ladies recognized their own kin.

I do not know what my father was doing all this time. My uncle de Villette later gave me to understand that he was intriguing with the English, but he put on the airs of a colonist and empire-builder. However, after a few months he took leave of us, saying he needed some new document from the Company and must go to France to fetch it. We never saw him again.

For all the first half of 1647 we awaited his return. My mother was embarrassed at our having to impose so long on the hospitality of Captain de Poincy, and I myself was getting old enough to feel the discomfort of living on someone else's charity. My elder brother, too, was now old enough to bear arms and wanted to be a soldier; inactivity weighed heavily upon him. All these considerations, together with my father's silence, finally made my mother resolve to go back to France. Cabart de Villermont lent her a little money toward the journey, and she raised the rest by selling an assortment of shoes my father had brought over on his last voyage.

As shoes were very rare in the islands, and people of all ranks usually had to go barefoot, this consignment was worth a small fortune.

During the summer of 1647 all four of us embarked on a cargo ship bound for La Rochelle.

The return journey was about as agreeable as the journey out, with the odd storm, the odd pirate, and my mother and Constant heaving their hearts up between-decks. This time I was even more ill than they. The fevers I had caught in Martinique returned with such severity as a result of the poor food on board that I lost consciousness and lay speechless and lifeless. I was given up for dead and was about to be tossed unceremoniously over the side when my mother wanted to see me one last time. She detected a pulse still beating and saved my life by saying, "My daughter is not dead." Warming me with some spirits and with her own body, she revived me at a moment when my case was so doubtful the gun was already waiting to be fired. One day I told this story at Court, and the bishop of Metz, with his usual flattery, cried, "Madam, one is not brought back from the brink for nothing!" At the time, however, I was none too pleased.

We landed at La Rochelle in the early autumn of 1647, our only possessions a trunkful of clothes, a missal and a copy of Plutarch's *Lives*. My clothes were not suited to the season: all I had was a meager frock of grey calico, and I went barefoot as on the islands. The wind and rain of Poitou chilled me to the bone. I had to make do with this wardrobe, however, until the arrival of my aunt de Villette, whom my mother had advised of our return.

During those few weeks, which seemed like months to me, we depended on charity for our food and lodging. A worthy chairmender, a kinswoman of the old servant who had gone with us to America, let us live in a small room without windows or chimney under the stairs of a dilapidated house she owned near the harbor. Uncomfortable as this lodging was, my mother never left it for fear of meeting La Plume, the tailor, and others to whom she still owed money borrowed to pay for our voyage three years earlier.

So it fell to Charles and me, whom the people of La Rochelle could not recognize, to go out begging to support the family. Charles accepted this errand quite lightheartedly, but for me it was torture. Every other day I took an earthenware jar to collect some soup from the porter's lodge of a Jesuit college where my mother had a slight acquaintance with Father Duverger, one of the masters. The porter, though the situation had been explained to him by Father Duverger, dispensed his charity very ungraciously, handing over the bread and soup with grunts and grimaces. One day when I was warming myself by his fire as he filled my jug and did not notice soon enough that he had finished and I could take my dole and go, he gave me a stinging slap on the face to wake me up and growled, "Take yourself off, ragamuffin!"

You may almost die of hunger or cold, but if you survive you forget. Yet if you suffer just one day from shame, you go on dying of it all your life. No paint has ever effaced the mark of that slap or the burning cheeks caused by the scornful or pitying looks I encountered as I carried the soup home through the streets, barefoot, dirty, my hair wet with rain.

At last my aunt came and rescued us. Everything was arranged in a trice. On her way through Niort she had seen my half-godmother, the baronne de Neuillan, and together they had decided that Charles, whom my mother had long wished to make a page, should go to La Mothe-Saint-Héray and enter the service of the comte de Parabère, governor of Poitou and the baronne's brother-in-law. Madame de Neuillan also offered to take my mother to Paris to join my father; from what he had told us when he left, we thought him to be there, negotiating with the gentlemen of the Company. As for Constant, he was to go to Mursay; my uncle de Villette planned to find him a place in a garrison. I was to go with him and spend the winter in Mursay, to give my parents time to complete their business and return to Niort.

But it pleased God to overturn our designs. We did not know that even while we were making our plans, my father had already been dead for two months. He had not been to Paris. After leaving us, he had gone to London, then to Flanders, Lyons and lastly Orange, where he died while using an assumed name and intending to go to Constantinople. I think the poor man really suffered from a disease they call *penaque* in Poitou, a malady that prevents its victim from remaining peacefully in any one place.

Nor did we know in October 1647 that my brother Constant, that melancholy youth, had only a few weeks to live. Or that I would never see my mother again in this world.

Even had I known at the time that I was an orphan, I doubt if I should have been very distressed. I felt no sadness as I watched Madame d'Aubigné disappear along the road to Paris. Instead of a vainly hoped-for farewell kiss, all I had received from her was the advice to go through life "fearing everything from men and hoping everything from God."

Five

I found Mursay changed. I was very different myself.

The rains of America, which make the plants grow faster than the sun of France does, had made me shoot up too. I was still only twelve, but I looked old for my age and was nearly half an inch taller than my cousin Philippe, three years my senior. What I had gained in height I had lost in manners. At an age when a child is scarcely able to understand things, I had in the space of three short years seen so many places and been through so many experiences that my mind was left troubled and uneasy. I had become reserved and rude. Though as a small child I had been playful and talkative, I now smiled rarely and spoke little. I was indifferent both to people and to events. I had learned to expect everything except happiness, or rather—for I was not always unhappy in the Indies—I no longer hoped for that tranquil happiness in which body and soul are at peace.

Feeling as I did, I could at first find nothing to say to my cousins. Could I tell them that the house and village and family I had missed so much during the years I was away now failed to measure up to my memories and expectations? What I remembered was a green landscape, a house full of light, a group of lovely little boys and girls. Now it was the beginning of winter, and the countryside was cold, dark and muddy. The walls of the house ran with damp, and the village was no better than a swamp. My girl cousins were still unmarried and seemed to me very old, provincial and ugly. As for my uncle, who had never travelled farther than Marans and knew nothing of the world outside his Bible and his account-book, I decided, after receiving a few words of reproach, that he was the most narrow-minded of Protestants.

The death of my brother Constant, who was found drowned in one of the castle moats only a few days after our arrival, added the finishing touch to my distress. I still do not know how it happened. I have wondered since whether the poor child might not have been so unhappy that he killed himself. The fact that I could never discover where he was buried, or even if it was in consecrated ground, lends some weight to this idea. But if I did not know where, I did know when he was buried, though I found out only by sheer chance.

On the second evening after the accident, I was in my cousin Marie's room looking out the window toward the woods on the other side of the river. I saw three men below me loading a coffin on to a flat-bottomed boat. Then, together with my uncle, they got into the boat and slowly crossed the river toward Siecq. When they reached the other side, the three men hoisted the coffin on their shoulders and disappeared into the woods. For a long while I watched the lantern with which my uncle guided them shining through the trees, then it vanished into the darkness, together with the memory of my brother. No one ever spoke to me of him again.

I stayed leaning at the open window staring into the dark. I stood there so many minutes, or perhaps hours, that I got chilled to the marrow without noticing it. When Marie found me and roused me out of my reverie, I could not move my fingers. For several days I was ill with fever, but I asked no questions and hid my tears.

I was sure I should not find the peace I longed for at Mursay, and that I was born to endure every kind of misfortune, desertion and bereavement. I prayed God to be merciful and remove me from this world as quickly as He had done with Constant.

But as people rarely die when they want to, and never from the death of others, I survived my first despair. My aunt took advantage of my state of health to begin the reconquest of a mind which she had been the first to form and which had belonged entirely to her for seven or eight years. With wonderful skill and kindness she built up the broken edifice again stone by stone, and this time she made sure it would stand for ever. She never seemed to take offense at my silences or snubs or at the hurtful words I sometimes uttered, but by a combination of affection and firmness, a subtle mixture of kisses, reason and religion, she managed to open the gates of a heart which had been closed and to calm the troubled spirit which had been given back to her.

She filled my empty hours and kept me from boredom with a variety of occupations: dressmaking, embroidery, tapestry, even basket-making. She made sure I always had some handiwork to do. My empty heart she filled with the love of God, having soon decided that our Heavenly Father would return that love more faithfully than my earthly one, and that He at least would not desert me.

During my first stay at Mursay she had taught me the ethics and elementary practices of religion. During this second stay she taught me faith. Every day, in the course of one of the charming and stimulating conversations she had such a talent for, she would find an opportunity to speak to me of the warmth of divine love and of the light of hope. She told me it was possible to pray as naturally as one breathed; all one had to do was bask in the radiance of God. She had me share in her good works, and it was through my hands that every week, at the end of the drawbridge, she gave alms to the poor of the neighborhood.

Lastly, she did not doubt that the distress of mind in which she had found me called for regular religious practice. The only kind she could offer me was that of the reformed religion, and without hesitation, not bothering with the scruples she had observed before I went to America, she included me freely in her own devotions. I not only went with her to church on Sunday but learned Pastor Drelincourt's catechism, sang Calvinist hymns and psalms, read books written by heretic ministers and joined my voice in prayer with theirs.

Little by little, under the influence of this good woman, I recovered the will to live and the ability to love. With summer, wild flowers and the games of childhood returned. I sported in the hay with Philippe and Marie. Hide-and-seek, blindman's buff, tag, prisoner's base, ninepins, knucklebones—all of them kept us amused. I proved a champion at pick-up-sticks, where the winner draws the king. I did not realize this was prophetic.

In Paris my mother had learned simultaneously of the death of a husband she hated and of the only child she loved. There was nothing now to connect her with Niort. She no longer wrote, and we should have thought her dead if my aunt had not heard, by the remotest of chances, that her sister-in-law was living in dire poverty in lodgings in the parish of Saint-Médard. She was reduced to doing menial work to earn her living, her only support being a pension of two hundred livres a year. She did not wish to be dependent on anyone. Nonetheless, my aunt sent her a small sum of money through Madame de La Tremoille.

Though I was deeply grieved when I heard of Madame d'Aubigné's troubles, in general I worried no more about her than she did about me. I regarded myself as a member of the Villette family and wanted only to forget the years spent away from Mursay.

As for my brother Charles, who lived only a few leagues away in the château of La Mothe-Saint-Héray, I was glad to have news of him from time to time. His health was good, his behavior less so. Deprived of the family care and authority he needed, he was fast following in his father's footsteps. The mischievousness of the child was already turning into outright knavishness in the page of fifteen. This made me sad, for I was fond of him, but as distance and my own youth prevented me from remonstrating, I merely prayed God to show him His mercy.

More than a year went by. I had become Bignette again, the little Francine of the old days, lively, merry, popular. I was thirteen, as unconcerned about the future as the lily of the field or the birds in the sky. I would sit on the floor in the great hall at my aunt Arthémise's feet, resting my head on her lap and burying my face deliciously in her apron, while all around me they discussed my cousins' marriage plans. I looked forward to their weddings and to being able to wear a pretty gown of grey lace that had grown too short for Marie. I was already imagining myself in it, dancing the Poitou brawl, at which I was becoming quite skilful, when in an instant I was prevented from ever becoming perfect in its measures and, more irreparable still, was torn away for ever from the affection of my beloved Villettes.

My self-styled godmother, Madame de Neuillan, whom I had not seen since the day of my baptism, having heard through certain mischief-makers that my regular attendance at chapel and my earnest hymn-singing set an example to all the Protestants from Niort to La Rochelle, decided it was her duty to remove me from that pernicious influence. She thought I was an orphan, remembered she had been charged to watch over my salvation and, pointing out that I had been baptized a Catholic, petitioned Queen Anne for a *lettre de cachet.* † Because of the influence of the Parabère family, and the fact that her daughter Suzanne was lady-in-waiting to Mademoiselle de Montpensier, the Regent's niece, she obtained the royal signature without delay.

And so, the very day before my birthday, an officer and a handful of guards presented themselves with great solemnity at the gate of the drawbridge. My uncle and aunt were dumbfounded, but how could they resist the orders of the King? They had to hand me over within the hour to the men-at-arms, who surrounded me as if I were a thief and took me to Niort to the house of Madame de Neuillan, who was thenceforth entrusted with my education.

I wept sorely at first; I never did things by halves. But as no one attempted to console me, I dried my tears and checked my sorrow, resolving to be strong and wait for my mother to make her wishes in the matter clear. The hope I nourished was cruelly disappointed. Madame de Villette could not find my mother in Paris; we did not know that Madame d'Aubigné had already left the capital and gone to live in Saintonge, where she still had some relatives. There she paid no more heed to the fate of Charles or myself than she had done before. She knew nothing of my latest misfortune, and there was no one to tell her of it. I remained in the power of Madame de Neuillan.

Her grasp was neither gentle nor generous, but she soon relaxed her grip. She discovered before long that the responsibility to which she had laid claim so vehemently was beyond her power to fulfil. I showed no readiness to be converted and answered my benefactress's "kindnesses" with a rebellious insolence she found very discouraging. She soon tired of dispensing threats and punishments. She had other fish to fry besides this little chit of a girl: Court duties and the pleasures of the town required her presence in Paris for several months of the year. So one fine morning she deposited me in the rue Cremault with the Ursuline nuns.

This community, which had not been in Niort for long, did not take in the daughters of the best families in the town—they were still sent to the Benedictine nuns—but those of the middle class. No doubt Madame de Neuillan considered an education suited to a merchant's daughter good enough for a penniless orphan fresh from a nest of heretics.

The Ursuline convent is in the parish of Saint-André, in the highest part of the town. It overlooks the Regratterie, the market and the Notre-Dame district and backs on to the ramparts. The building which then housed the boarders was not very large. There were four rooms downstairs which served as classrooms, six rooms above providing dormitories for the sisters and for ourselves, two court-yards and two big gardens where we were allowed to run about during recreation time. It all was very clean and fairly comfortable despite the lack of space.

I was taken to the older girls' bedroom, where I put my clothes away in a cupboard. It did not take long. I could count my wardrobe almost as quickly as my lands in those days: two taffeta caps, two plain wool frocks, three aprons and a kerchief formed the whole. The kerchief had been given to me by my aunt, and I shed some tears as I locked it away. But I knew I must dry my eyes and keep my chin up. In the new surroundings where fate had thrown me,

I would have no guide but myself, and I needed to see clearly.

The superior and the head teacher then handed me over to a young nun called Soeur Céleste, who despite her youth was in charge of the oldest class. She owed this privilege to her intelligence and her talent for teaching, and for some reason I at once became extraordinarily attached to her.

Perhaps it was her beauty that attracted me. Though I have often repented of it later, I have never been able to help feeling favorably disposed when I meet with great beauty in a woman or a child. Even now, whatever I do, I am still irresistibly won over by a graceful figure, a fresh complexion and a pair of large eyes, while I am always suspicious of a twisted body or a cast in the eye.

Soeur Céleste, whose beauty would have stood out in a Court, was quite dazzling in a convent. She deserved even more credit since the Ursulines' habit is not at all becoming. In their little caps, like cheese puffs with broad strings hanging down on either side, the other sisters looked like elderly peasants. Beneath her cap, Soeur Céleste's complexion was of the most brilliant white, the shape of her face was fine and she had the prettiest mouth in the whole world. Her eyes were tender, her carriage noble, and to these attractive looks were added a sprightly wit and great liveliness of character. Her distinction drew you to her, and the charms of her conversation won you over.

She soon saw I was not to be managed by force. The harsh and cruel methods of Madame de Neuillan, guardian of my body rather than of the soul she could not reach, had not drawn me back toward the true religion. Worse, they had made me eschew the modesty suitable to a young girl of my age; instead I delighted in being rebellious and obstinate. Soeur Céleste used neither threats nor promises but only reasonable persuasion. She did not force me to go to mass, for which I had conceived a strong aversion: I might have caused a scandal, fond as I was of repeating my grandfather's maxim that "my horror of the mass cured me of my horror of the flames." I believed it was idolatry to worship Christ in the Eucharist and would have died rather than kneel in front of an altar. Soeur Céleste did not make me go. She allowed me to eat normally on fast days and did nothing to interfere with my religion. All she did was give me books that might open my eyes to Protestant error and wait for the grace of God to do the rest. When I left the convent at Niort I was just as much a Huguenot as when I went in, but at least I was a less recalcitrant one.

I do not know if it was Soeur Céleste's skill alone that softened my temper; my love for her and her affection for me were no doubt even more influential.

To sacrifice myself in her service was my greatest pleasure. As I was very advanced in my studies, I was made monitor of my class, and whenever she left the room, I would see that the rest of the girls got on with their reading, writing and arithmetic, learned their spelling and played quietly. I was happy to help her in her work, with no other reward than that of pleasing her. At night I packed the other girls off to bed so fast they scarcely knew what was happening. That way I was able to collect candle-ends which I made the girls use for a whole week so that I might have the happiness of presenting my teacher with a whole candle for her nighttime reading. My love for her grew so intense that when I left the convent a few months later, I thought I should die of grief. For two or three months I was simple enough to ask God every morning and evening to let me die because I did not think I could live without seeing her.

This love, which had the intensity all feelings acquire from loneliness, ended only with her life.

The happiness of the rue Cremault did not last long. Madame de Neuillan, who was avarice incarnate, hoped to be able to bring me up without expense, and she asked the nuns to apply to my aunt de Villette for the cost of my board and lodging. My aunt declined, with good reason, to pay for me to be given a Catholic education. The dispute between my true and false aunt dragged on, and not a penny was paid into the convent funds. At first the nuns shrank from objecting. Madame de Neuillan was the widow of one governor of Niort and the mother of his successor, and claimed to be the protector of the convents of the city. The ladies of the rue Cremault wanted to keep on the right side of her. But at last, after a few cautious remonstrances followed by more vigorous warnings that proved to be equally vain, they resolved to ignore Soeur Céleste's entreaties and turn me out into the street. Despite their professions of charity, the sisters preferred reprobates who could pay to virtuous souls who must be saved for nothing.

At the beginning of the summer of 1649 I found myself back again under the roof of Françoise de Neuillan. They did not kill the fatted calf for my return. As a matter of fact, there was never much feasting done in that house. Madame de Neuillan, since she was obliged to feed me, decided to do so only on condition that I could be made useful, so she gave me the keys to her granary and made me responsible for measuring out oats to her horses and corn to her hens. I did not even feel this humiliation, so afflicted was I at having left my worthy Céleste. In any event, if one had to learn to command, why not begin in the poultry yard? The only thing that troubled me was that the baronne, through meanness, left me practically naked. I had grown so fast that the two miserable cheap wool skirts I had brought with me from the convent only just covered my knees, but Madame de Neuillan decreed that there was nothing wrong in a girl of my age showing her legs and that my present wardrobe might last me out the year. Apart from the small problems of clothes and the services I was expected to perform in the stable, I was not treated much worse than my cousin Angélique, younger sister of my godmother Suzanne and later comtesse de Froulay. The baronne had given up trying to convert me, and though she dressed me like Cinderella and had me sleep with her maids, she did not confine me to the servants' quarters. My life actually was not very different from that of her own children.

Though its mistress kept the opposite of an open table, the hôtel de Neuillan was always full. Family connections, the great beauty of Suzanne, the still unmarried elder daughter, and the Court atmosphere prevailing there attracted people of wit from all over the province. Contact with them gradually made me more tractable. I abandoned my schoolgirl ways and peasant caps and attempted to polish my own hitherto rough wit, more fitted to theological controversy than to polite badinage.

My chief instructor in the social arts was Antoine Gombaud, chevalier de Méré, who owned a small estate near La Mothe-Saint-Héray but spent most of his time in distinguished company in Paris. He was a very small man, most elegant and highly perfumed, who liked to set himself up as an arbiter of breeding and fashion. After a few campaigns at sea, he had abandoned the sword for the pen and now confined his valor to the conquest of salons. He was friendly with Pascal, Balzac, Ménage, Clérambault and other men of letters, and had himself written treatises on True Honesty, Eloquence, Delicacy of Expression and Social Intercourse. At the time I met him, he was interested in the education of children of quality, on which subject he thought of writing an essay. I helped him in his experiments, and he delighted in introducing me to ancient authors he himself knew well and in teaching me geometry, in which he fancied himself the greatest expert, geography and the use of the globe. All this was spiced with bits of Greek and Latin. He also lent me novels, which made such a lively impression on me that I have never been so excited by my own adventures since as I was by those of the imaginary characters I read about then. Madame de Neuillan noticed that I was indulging in this dangerous pastime and ordered me to give it up. I obeyed scrupulously.

I was very struck by the idea of the passions, however, and the feelings which nourish them found a way into my heart, though they had no definite object. True, they might have fixed on the chevalier himself, and it was no fault of his that they did not. For Monsieur de Méré had fallen in love with his fourteen-year-old pupil, as he let me know in verses which, because of my visits to the islands, celebrated me as the *belle Indienne.* From that day forth I was known in Niort by no other name, and I thus acquired a reputation for beauty which I suspect was not then entirely deserved.

But I was not at all drawn to Monsieur de Méré. Apart from the fact that he seemed to me rather old, I found him slightly ridiculous, and I was irritated to see him so afraid of using common expressions that both in his conversation and in his poetry he would draw out his thoughts and envelop them in such obscurity that he became quite unintelligible. Still, I was flattered by his preference. Our first and last conquests are those for which we are most grateful. So I endured his compliments and was not displeased that he should sing my praises to all the booksellers in Niort and La Rochelle. I was grateful to him, too, for teaching me, between a lament and a languishing look, the rules of grammar and of polite behavior.

My education had reached that point when Madame de Neuillan, who had to go to Paris to finish the winter there, decided to take me with her. She travelled in a coach and six with my cousin Angélique, while I rode pillion on the mule that carried the luggage and the food for the journey. In this fashion, which did not trouble me, for after all the King's ships are no more comfortable, I made my entry into the capital. If I was not afraid of seeming provincial, I would say my first impression was of many houses and many people. My second impression was that the streets were very dirty and that the mud smelled most disagreeable. My mule only just kept my legs from being splashed by the black spray which spurted up at every step. The din of the coaches and the shouting and yelling of those who went through the streets selling herbs, cheese, old clothes, sand, fish, water and a thousand other necessities, completed my confusion.

I did not come to myself again till I entered the courtyard of the town house where Pierre Tiraqueau de Saint-Herman lived. He was Madame de Neuillan's cousin, and majordomo to the King. The baronne kept one whole floor of the mansion for herself. It was in the faubourg Saint-Jacques, near the porte Saint-Michel and across from the back of the Palais d'Orléans.

The regime there was no more liberal than that in Niort. Madame de Neuillan and her daughter Suzanne, my godmother, who between them carried stinginess and pettiness to a degree beyond belief, went so far as to forbid the servants to light a fire. There was just one very small brazier in the baronne's bedroom, around which the whole household had to come and warm itself.

As for meals, they were not worth thinking of. The baronne no longer brought her cook with her to Paris: she was vexed with him for having asked for larding needles.

"You see, Françoise," she said to me, "how great families are ruined? Larding needles indeed! They've cost my brother-in-law twelve hundred thousand francs! Larding needles! I prefer to have the concierge do the cooking!"

And so he did, and the food, which was meager enough to begin with, became quite horrible. However, here as in Niort there was a great deal of company, and company of the highest quality.

I had little opportunity to profit by it, for scarcely had I alighted from my mule than the baronne took me off to the Ursuline nuns in the rue Saint-Jacques.

She had been able to let me play the Huguenot in Niort, but she could not show me in Paris in such a role without appearing ridiculous. Not wishing to admit at Court that she had failed to make her pupil see reason, she handed me over to the nuns, not so much to change as to conceal me. She did not dare tell me she was about to shut me up in a convent, so she pretended I was just going to visit a relative of mine there and to greet her at the gate. I realized on the way that I was to be left there, so as soon as the gate was opened, instead of wasting my time greeting my kinswoman, I darted straight inside so as not to have to be told. I might not be mistress of my fate, but at least I could show I was not taken in by such tricks.

No sooner had I shot like a cannonball into the cloister than all the nuns, who had already been told of my heresy, put on their separate little performances. One fled, making the sign of the cross. Another told me, "The first time you go to mass, dear, I'll give you an *agnus* medal or a candy." I was already quite grown-up by now, and I found them so silly as to be unbearable. I could take neither their alarms nor their promises seriously, and I was not interested in either their holy pictures or their sugarplums.

Nevertheless, the result of my stay in the rue Saint-Jacques exceeded Madame de Neuillan's hopes. I began to tire of the troubles my resistance brought me. My steadfastness during months of unequal combat had been due more to pride than to conviction, and since I had got to know Méré and other versifiers, I had learned to prefer worldly triumphs to the glories of martyrdom. When I thought about it, I did not really care what language I prayed in so long as I could be sure God would hear me when necessary. This excellent philosophy was not very far from outright freethinking.

Thus when the nuns in the rue Saint-Jacques began the familiar routine of admonition and reprimand, punishment and reward, they were surprised to find their work already half done. I realized I was not being asked to do anything very extraordinary. Unlike a convert, I was not obliged to abjure another religion. All I had to do was voluntarily renew the vows made at my baptism and accept mass and the Catholic Communion. The affection I still bore my aunt de Villette was countered by the love I now felt for Soeur Céleste, so my heart was no longer directly threatened by the outcome of this theological battle. All I asked was that I should not be obliged to believe my aunt Arthémise was damned. This was agreed, and I accepted everything else that was asked of me.

The nuns of the rue Saint-Jacques took the credit themselves for this unexpected success and were so pleased with me for having thus enhanced their prestige that they would gladly have kept me there for nothing. But fortunately Madame de Neuillan decided she could now introduce me into society without harming her reputation, and as soon as I had made my First Communion, she withdrew me from surroundings which had no appeal for me whatsoever.

Preceded by my reputation as the *belle Indienne,* which Méré had imparted to the duchesse de Lesdiguières, the Chevreuses and the Rochefoucaulds, and confident in what the chevalier assured me was my extraordinary intelligence, I was sure I had only to appear in society to make a conquest of it. I was already intoxicated by the few flatteries offered up to me in the provinces, and my arrogance would have continued unbounded if I had met with a quarter of the success I expected. Luckily, however, wherever I went I was considered awkward, rustic and stupid.

Admittedly I was very badly dressed, all I had were my cheap grey frocks about twelve inches too short. My hair was no better. When we were in the islands, my mother used to apply her scissors to it practically every time she saw me, so as to make it grow thicker. She achieved her end: I had—and have still—a mane that is both thick and long, but it was so springy that in those days I could find no way of doing it that would keep my curls in order. I must have looked like a fugitive from the madhouse. In addition to which I was too tall, too thin, had no bosom and did not know what to do with my arms. My appearance did not create a sensation in the drawing rooms.

My mind worked no wonders either. I was much too eager to repeat what I had recently learned and did not know how to tell a story or express myself clearly. One day I decided to recite a tale I had learned in the morning to the first gathering I found myself among the same afternoon. I rehearsed it several times before I went out, but when I got there and tried to begin, I muddled part of the story and forgot the rest. My performance was so badly received that when I left, I heard my hostess say, before I had even left the room, "What a stupid little thing!" Nor had I yet learned polite manners. I still thought it ladylike to lean against the back of the chair and go through a door first. In short, I was judged to be badly brought up and not very clever and was made well aware of this opinion.

After some fairly severe humiliations, I suffered tortures during all the visits Madame de Neuillan and my godmother Suzanne forced me to make, and I became painfully shy. I blushed whenever I was spoken to, could not utter two words together and even wept one day when I was seated by a window and thought myself exposed to the eyes of everyone present. I had fallen once more into the black depression which occasionally seized me and which had already afflicted me on my return from America, my departure from Mursay and my separation from Céleste.

I was in this somber mood when one evening Cabart de Villermont, my botanist from America, suddenly arrived at Monsieur de Saint-Herman's. He recognized me with transports of joy and begged Madame de Neuillan to let him take the *jeune Indienne* to see his friend Monsieur Scarron, who planned to journey soon to the islands. I might be able to instruct Monsieur Scarron in the geography of the place, the customs of the natives and how to set up a plantation. The truth was that Cabart de Villermont, who had spent only a little time in the Indies, knew much more about all these things than I, who had no more than a few childhood memories of them. Nonetheless I went to the hôtel de Troyes, where Cabart de Villermont shared a lodging with Monsieur Scarron.

I do not know what frightened me most of what I saw in the little yellow room in that great mansion. Was it the future traveller abroad, who was so badly paralyzed he could scarcely move anything but his eyes and tongue, and of whom all that could be seen was a greying head and two humped shoulders emerging from a little box carried about by a couple of servants? Or was it the crowd, so large and so brilliant, that surrounded this unfortunate creature, laughing uproariously at his slightest witticism? Whichever it was, no sooner had this half of a man asked me a single question about America that I burst into loud sobs, much to the amusement of the company.

I returned home despairing of my own foolishness, of Paris and of life itself, and I was heartily glad when Madame de Neuillan decided soon afterwards to go back and take up her summer residence in Niort.

My only regret was having to leave behind Marie-Marguerite de Saint-Herman, Pierre Tiraqueau's youngest daughter, with whom I had begun to strike up a friendship. I wrote long letters to her as soon as I got back to Poitou, trying for my own satisfaction to reflect all the wit I had been unable to express in speech. But as I was addressing a child, there was no pedantry in my letters, and I revealed myself with childlike innocence. I wrote of Soeur Céleste with ardor, of the citizens of Niort with scorn, and of Monsieur de Méré's love affairs and Madame de Neuillan's virtues sardonically. I wrote a thousand trifles to Mademoiselle de Saint-Herman and they pleased her so much she showed some of them to Cabart de Villermont. He, in order to vindicate the favorable judgment he had long ago formed of me, and also to challenge my lack of success at Monsieur Scarron's reception, showed him one of my letters.

So one day I was surprised to receive a note from Monsieur Scarron which read as follows: "Mademoiselle: I always suspected that the little girl who came to my room six months ago in a dress that was too short, and then for some reason burst into tears, was really as clever as she looked. Your letter to Mademoiselle de Saint-Herman shows so much intelligence I am vexed with my own for not having recognized the merit of yours quickly enough. To tell the truth, I would never have believed anyone could learn to write such fine letters in the islands of America or with the nuns of Niort. I cannot imagine why you take as much care to hide your wit as everyone else takes to exhibit theirs. However, now that you are discovered, you cannot refuse to write to me as well as to Mademoiselle de Saint-Herman. I shall do my utmost to produce a letter as good as your own, and you will have the pleasure of seeing that I am far from equalling you in wit. Now and for ever, Mademoiselle, your faithful servant."

Reading this missive, I was beside myself with happiness and pride. Ugly and infirm as he was, Monsieur Scarron was nonetheless the most celebrated author in Paris and considered one of its greatest wits. He had had several successful plays produced, and it was said they had won the favor of young King Louis as well as of the general public. He had just published a burlesque romance, *Le Roman comique,* of which everyone spoke highly. He let loose on Paris a flood of epistles, odes, elegies and stories, and it was fashionable for wits, courtiers, officials and anyone of talent or distinction to go and visit him. He was not in a position to go out and seek such company for himself, but his intelligence, learning and imagination, together with his extraordinary cheerfulness amid all his woes, attracted everyone of note in France. To have caught the attention of such a man, on top of that of Antoine de Méré, restored my confidence in myself.

With Madame de Neuillan's approval, I answered Monsieur Scarron's letter, and over the ensuing months we exchanged some letters; mine, I flatter myself, were as neatly turned if not as gallant as his. Monsieur de Méré, for his part, still gave me lessons and assured me that I was making progress.

So when the following year Madame de Neuillan, who herself travelled in a different style, put me on the box of the coach to Paris with my little yellow serge dress, some hardboiled eggs and a bit of black bread, I looked forward to making a better impression in the capital than I had done on my first trip eighteen months before. The innkeepers and wagoners I met on the way seemed not insensitive to my new charms, which were probably not entirely spiritual. I experienced the pleasure, dangerous but delicious at first, of having to defend myself a little. Cabart de Villermont came to meet me at the stagecoach office, and the eloquence of his welcome confirmed me in the notion that I had grown in beauty as well as in intelligence, and that at any rate I was a child no longer.

In novels it is usual at this point to paint a portrait of the heroine who is about to make her entry into the world. I might be all the more tempted to follow this custom in that such a portrait could well be more flattering than the one I painted a little while ago of the convent miss up from the country. But out of good breeding rather than modesty, for I am vain by nature, I shall say nothing myself about the young person who got down from the Niort coach in the autumn of 1651. I shall leave that to others, who then or in later years wrote a few lines about me that I have been conceited enough to keep in the little secret books which have gone with me everywhere since I was quite young.

This is how Mademoiselle de Scudéry,† then very famous as a novelist, described me in the character of Lyriane in her *Clélie:* "She was tall and of good stature, with a smooth fine skin and pretty light brown hair. Her nose and mouth were well shaped, her carriage noble, mild, lively and modest. And what made her beauty more perfect and dazzling still, she had the loveliest eyes in the world—black, brilliant, soft, passionate and full of intelligence. A gentle melancholy would sometimes appear in them, together with all the charms which usually accompany it; then gaiety would break through in its turn, bringing all its own attractions . . . She did not put on the airs of a beauty, though she was a beauty beyond compare."

Somaize† also presented me, as Stratonice, "the most agreeable and witty of young *précieuses,* who has both beauty and grace. As for her intelligence, public opinion testifies sufficiently to that." Another flatterer was more precise: "A fine figure and noble movements; a beautifully shaped countenance, with great sparkling black eyes, a large mouth and splendid teeth, a proud expression, subtle, sometimes teasing conversation."

Monsieur Scarron depicted me as a charming and promising Iris:

> *No mere verse can e'er relate*
> *All th'allurement of her face,*
> *Or the modesty and grace*
> *Which the while they subjugate*
> *Ravish from the heart its power . . .*
> *If the treasures eye can see,*
> *With that captivating air,*
> *Wound men's souls beyond repair,*
> *Sure the charms that hidden be*
> *Far surpass that passing fair.*

The satisfaction I get today from quoting these foolish compliments, together with what I felt sixty years ago when I first carefully copied them out, shows me all too clearly that even the women who seem least concerned with their own charms really care more about them than they think. But at least I fancy I have the excuse that you have known me only in my old age, and if you were not told I was famed for my beauty before I won royal favor, you would never be able to understand my story.

Did I really possess all the attractions lent me by those fulsome pens? My admirers swore I did; my mirror was not always sure, but mirrors are so fickle. I shall therefore confine myself to those features which seem to me certain. When I made a successful entry into society, I was much above the average height, I had very large black eyes, regular teeth and long chestnut hair which I managed at last to dress in the fashion.

Anyhow, such as I was, I was found pleasing, and with Monsieur Scarron my person completed what my letters had begun. He was so affected he began to worry about my future. I had no dowry and no parents, so it was unlikely that a man would ask for my hand in marriage or that a convent would accept me. I myself had not given much thought to this sad situation. I was only sixteen and entertained high hopes of the future. Although by nature anxious and provident, I was intoxicated by the novelty of my recent successes. I bowed to myself in looking glasses, danced alone in my room, hummed a tune in the street. In short, for the first time in years I lived without giving a thought to the future. But I was well aware that my presence, and especially the fact that I had to be fed once or twice a day, was beginning to irk Madame de Neuillan. She had brought herself to give a drop of soup to a soul on the road to perdition, but considered the effort unnecessary in the case of a soul that was saved.

Monsieur Scarron, realizing how odious my position was, suddenly offered either to give me a dowry so that I could go into a convent or to marry me himself. Madame de Neuillan was both surprised and delighted at this unexpected opportunity to get rid of her burden. She accepted Monsieur Scarron's offer with alacrity but thought that, young and rather romantic as I was, I would not choose to marry a man of such monstrous appearance. She advocated the convent. The Ursuline nuns in the rue Saint-Jacques would be happy to have me: I had already been a monitor in Niort so I would certainly make a very good teacher in Paris, and with a little luck and a good deal of hard work, I might even hope one day to become director of studies in some convent in the provinces.

But she was reckoning without my dislike of the cloister and what was then my very great liking for the world and the pleasures of secular life. Above all she left out of account my already strong interest in my own fame and reputation, which far exceeded my interest in salvation. I might have agreed to be the founder or mother superior of a convent, but I could not at all see myself as an obscure, unheard-of nun.

As for turning down the offer altogether, I never considered that for a moment. I had inherited from my father a love of wagers and the power of making quick decisions, and I bet without hesitation on Monsieur Scarron.

He was ugly, of course, and a cripple, and people said he had no money. Even so I preferred marrying him to going into a convent, and I persuaded myself that his wit might make the marriage tolerable.

I had conceived an aversion for the passions, having seen in my mother the state to which they could reduce a woman and a family, so I was positively glad I did not love Monsieur Scarron, and, upon reflection, actually pleased that he was infirm. He would not abandon me at every opportunity, like my father; he was said to be incapable of consummating a marriage. I should have to bear neither his assaults nor his mistresses. All was for the best. In my bitter innocence, I was not far from thinking Heaven had given me an ideal husband.

On 4 April 1652, while France was being ravaged by rioting and civil war, the notary drew up the contract for my marriage to Paul Scarron, in the presence of Cabart de Villermont, Pierre Tiraqueau de Saint-Herman and François Tiraqueau, his cousin. Two days later the wedding ceremony took place in the little private chapel of the hôtel de Troyes.

The altar cloth was a petticoat belonging to Madame de Fiesque; the instruments of the mass stood on its bold yellow flowers. This mixture of poverty, gallantry and religion was a perfect miniature of what my life was to be for the next twenty years.

Six

———

I had expected a marriage in name only. A *mariage blanc*. But it was not white, it was grey. I learned later that two days before the wedding, when a friend jestingly asked if he thought he would be able to exercise his marital rights, Monsieur Scarron answered that while he would not play me any dirty tricks, he would certainly teach me some. One day in my presence he said that because of his state of health he had long hesitated between a woman without honor and a girl without fortune; having decided at last on the second, he resolved he must get from her the same concessions he would have obtained from the first. Though he did not teach me the things a husband usually teaches a wife, he did teach me others I would have preferred not to learn. It is difficult to imagine how far some husbands can carry authority; wives sometimes have to submit to almost impossible demands.

I was only sixteen. I had no female relatives or friends. I was his wife in the sight of God. So I submitted. From the first day of our marriage to the last I obeyed him in everything, but not without an inner resistance and disgust with regard to certain matters. My revulsion was all the greater because I had gone to the altar with no other instruction as to my duties than vague memories of the

Carib natives and the unseemly diversions of my little black play-mate.

I soon began to ponder the reasons that had led Monsieur Scarron to marry me. No doubt they had been very mixed. First, there was the noble and generous pity of which I have already spoken, which made him spontaneously offer to pay a dowry for me to go into a convent. Perhaps there were two or three less disinterested considerations. For some years he had been at law with the children of his father's second marriage. He had made over part of the estate to them in return for an annuity, and certain lawyers had led him to believe that if he married, the gift would be cancelled. Another motive concerned his idea of going to live in the Americas, where he hoped the climate would restore his health. The expedition was due to leave Le Havre in May or June of this same year, 1652, and Monsieur Scarron, its promoter, thought my experience would be of use to him in this dangerous venture. To crown all, there was the sudden liking he took to me personally. The amusement of watching a still childish mind awaken turned into a keen interest in my physical attractions, which were at least fresher than those of Céleste de Harville-Palaiseau, his old mistress, who for the last ten years had lent herself to his ecclesiastical whims—Monsieur Scarron was a canon—and whom he aptly rewarded by making her a nun.

When I was a child on Saint-Christophe, they used to repeat the English proverb, "God says take what you want, but pay for it." I had wanted this marriage, as an unhoped-for piece of luck for a girl without dowry or distinction of birth, who normally could not have aimed higher than life as a gentleman's lady or a lady's maid. I paid dearly at the beginning for the advantages I derived later on from this marriage. At any rate, the price seemed to me so high I felt I owed Monsieur Scarron no gratitude. The world considered he had done a good deed by marrying me, but I soon decided I had sufficiently repaid the gallant by my obedience and the invalid by my care.

The nights I passed with the invalid were no more disagreeable than those inflicted on me by the so-called husband. I do not know what disease Monsieur Scarron suffered from, nor what sin his sufferings expiated, but I am sure that poor cripple went through his Hell here on earth. His body was twisted into the shape of a Z, with his knees drawn up to the stomach; his head was bent over his right shoulder and could not be held upright; his arms were paralyzed down to the wrist; he spent all day propped up on a sort of pan in an armchair. If he wanted to eat or write, two iron bars could be pulled out of the arms of the chair and a tray rested upon them. At night he could only turn from one side of the bed to the other. To this discomfort was joined the great pain which in the daytime he succeeded in concealing with laughter and jesting, but which at night made him cry aloud and prevented all sleep. He took large quantities of opium, though this scarcely diminished his torments.

I used to help his valet, Mangin, wash and dress him, get him up and put him to bed. I prepared his medicines myself and spent most of my nights sitting beside him, keeping watch and trying to distract or soothe him. At such times, he was often ill humored and would confess himself "miserable as sin" or "melancholy as the grave." Still, I preferred his complaints and invective to the badinage he indulged in on the nights he was free from pain. I pitied him, though, and he was grateful to me for my patience and devotion. As I greatly admired his wit and learning, and the company that visited him was considered amusing, I would have accommodated myself to the situation if, since he was unable to be a husband, he had been content to be a father to me and had treated the whole matter with discretion. But if ever there was a man in the world wise enough to accept the fate Heaven sent him and keep quiet about it, Monsieur Scarron was not the one. He caused me even more pain by his words than by his deeds.

The yellow apartment in the hôtel de Troyes used to be full of people all day long. Soldiers and politicians now mingled with men of letters, for this was the time of the rebellion against the authority of the King and of Cardinal Mazarin. Sedition filled people's heads, and their hearts were aflame with revolt.

The King had been driven out of Paris, and Turenne was

besieging the capital, where the prince de Condé had taken refuge with his *frondeurs*† and his Spaniards. The gun at the Bastille kept going off, men cut one another to pieces at the city gates, at every crossroad a passerby would find himself stopped by some Andalusian gallows-bird or German trooper. The poor peasants from the surrounding regions had fled into the city, thinking they would be safe there while the armies devastated the countryside. Their cattle died where they stood for want of food, and when their beasts perished, they themselves perished soon after. Children followed their mothers into the grave. Once, on the Pont Neuf, I saw three infants huddled over the body of their dead mother; one of them was still trying to suckle. The Parisians themselves ate little and badly, since supplies no longer came into the city; they made up for it by drinking deep and talking a great deal.

Monsieur Scarron was in the center of all the tongue-wagging, for he had just published his *Mazarinade.*† It was later, not surprisingly, to cause him trouble, but for the moment it was a windfall for its Dutch printers and a triumph for its author. The poem, which vilified Cardinal Mazarin in a manner more obscene than burlesque, delighted the Gondis,† the Condés and other lesser conspirators who all but lived in the hôtel de Troyes. This *succès de scandale,* together with the respectful reception accorded to his last play, *Don Japhet d'Arménie,* made Paul Scarron the man of the moment.

His marriage was the crowning touch. All Paris talked of it as if it were his latest comedy: they marvelled, they jested, they applauded. In taverns and salons people laid bets as to his ability to consummate the marriage and beget children. Loret, in his weekly gazette, confidently predicted the birth of an heir in the near future. In June he announced that "this comic author, notwithstanding his weakly body, has become a progenitor, for a friend of his maintains that his wife is three or four months pregnant and more—so now say he's a cripple!" The Queen was more skeptical, and when she heard of the marriage exclaimed that a wife was the last piece of furniture he needed.

Scarron soon saw this dubious fame might be made to add to his notoriety. People already came to see him as much for the strangeness of his life and physique as for his reputation as a writer. He said he was "as famous as a lion or an elephant at a fair." When he realized how he might exploit his marriage, he took himself for his subject. He began by writing verses about the "fast" he imposed on me. Then he went further and mounted a little play in my presence. His valet, Mangin, was one of the characters, and the first performance was given with his friend Segrais† as audience.

"It is not enough," Segrais said to him one day, "to have married your wife. You should at least give her the pleasure of having one child. Do you think you could?"

"Do you think I should have that satisfaction?" answered Scarron. "Here is Mangin, my valet—he could stand in for me perfectly."

Then he called Mangin.

"Mangin," he said, "you'd give my wife a child, wouldn't you?"

"Certainly, sir," answered the other at every performance. "If God wills."

The audience guffawed. I wished the earth would open and swallow me up. But I survived, shyer than Agnès in Molière's *Ecole des Femmes* and blushing to the roots of my hair at the ribald gibes of my husband, who was like Molière's Arnolphe from the neck up but fit for nothing below. My embarrassment only added to the laughter. Monsieur Scarron knew the truth of the matter, but for everyone else I was still only a pretty face. My silences and confusion, which should have been ascribed to a streak of modesty deserving praise rather than scorn, was put down to foolishness. In Parisian society it is not done to have true feelings in false situations.

My only consolation was to write regularly twice a week— Wednesday and Sunday—to my dear Céleste. I could not do better since the post for Poitou did not leave more often. But as she was a nun, I had to conceal the main point. Even if I had been able to confide in her more freely, I doubt if I should have done so. In those days, living with a husband who played the buffoon, I had come to prize dignity and discretion so highly that my rule was to keep up appearances in all circumstances. I never departed from that rule afterwards.

Not long after my marriage I heard of my mother's death. She had stayed on in Bordeaux. I had not seen her for four years and had not loved her during the short time we had been together. Still, I did shed some tears. I do not remember where they came from. Probably from a heart less affected by its loss than vexed by the position in which its own foolish calculation had placed it.

The tide of battle fortunately changed the course of a life which was far from pleasing to me. When the *frondeurs* were defeated and Condé was hooted out of Paris, the Queen and the young King were able to return to their capital, and Mazarin's arrival was said to be imminent. So by the time the Regent and her son passed in triumph through the gates of Paris in October of that year, the all too celebrated author of the *Mazarinade* had already decided to make himself scarce. He did not fancy swinging on the rope his poem had promised the Cardinal.

By September we had left Paris, Monsieur Scarron in a sedan chair and I by coach. My husband used as an excuse the famous voyage to America which he had gone on talking about to the gazetteers and the wags of his entourage, though he never could resolve to join the expedition he had promoted. The ships had left Le Havre without him in the early summer, but he had hinted to friends that he would embark at Nantes and overtake them.

"I am off to court the daughters of the Incas and sleep in hammocks," he joked as he left the hôtel de Troyes. He had told others it was shortage of money which forced him to leave Paris for a country retreat where he could live cheaply. The reason he gave me for this sudden departure was that he had to visit the family estates which had come to him through the conclusion of his lawsuit. These properties, in houses and land, were situated somewhere between Amboise and Tours. He said he wished to assess their revenues himself, since he had pressing needs for money.

And so we found ourselves at La Vallière, a little manor house between the slopes of Nazelle and the hill of Amboise. It belonged to Monsieur Scarron's only sister from his father's second marriage, with whom he was on fairly friendly terms. After that we spent five or six months in his own properties at Les Fougerets and La Rivière, where it was very cold and far from gay. Three years of civil war had devastated the country. The people, worn out with want and looting, lived on roots. The fields were strewn with dead bodies from which the flesh had been stripped for food.

Nevertheless, I was delighted to get away from Paris, and I took advantage of our isolation to try to explain to Monsieur Scarron how I resented the way he made me look ridiculous before other people. I pointed out that such treatment was hard for a respectable woman to endure; that it might make me desperate, and thus try my virtue too far; and that since I respected him as I ought, he might in return spare my modesty. He was too intelligent and, when there were no spectators, too kind not to be touched by what I said. He promised to do as I wished, and he kept his word. As a result, we lived together on quite good terms while we were at La Rivière.

He even agreed that I might go to Poitou to see my relatives, though in fact I went to see my beloved Céleste. I travelled fifty leagues just to be with her, though ostensibly to see my family, and I did take the opportunity to visit my kind aunt de Villette. I found her very pleased that I was married, though she did not quite know to whom. I said nothing to her about the disadvantages of the match, partly to avoid giving her pain and partly in obedience to my own new rule of secrecy. Besides, I thought I was old enough to get out of my difficulties by myself or else to sink under them without causing this saintly lady more trouble. Madame de Villette touched on the subject of religion: she had heard of my conversion and was very grieved about it. She thought my marriage, by freeing me from the influence of Madame de Neuillan, would bring me back closer to the Huguenots again, but I disenchanted her on that score, saying I did not intend to change my religion every other year, as I had seen my father do all his life and as circumstances had made me do from my birth until now. She was wise enough not to revert to the subject. And she loved me no less. We took leave of one another with many embraces and promises of further meetings.

Scarron had made use of my absence to write a number of tales and try to go on with his *Roman comique.* When I returned, he read me every evening part of what he had written during the day. To keep me occupied while he was writing, he gave me various good books to read, which he liked to discuss with me afterwards. He also had me learn a little Spanish and Italian, judging an acquaintance with these languages indispensable in a woman of taste. What with all this reading, keeping the accounts of the two farms and looking after the poultry, I almost fancied myself back in the happy times at Mursay, and I hoped, without really expecting it, that we might remain in Touraine for a long while.

But while this almost amorous tête-à-tête pleased Scarron the lover of salons, it did not satisfy Scarron the lover of taverns. He missed his boon companions from the Pomme de Pin and the Fosse aux Lions, the young lawyers who were connoisseurs of girls and wine and the freethinkers of all kinds who made up his usual company. So in February 1653, having abandoned for ever the journey to the islands and given up the idea of managing his own estates, and having found out that the Cardinal was inclined to clemency, he decided to return to Paris to expedite the publication of *Don Japhet.*

We no longer had the apartment in the hôtel de Troyes, and had to take refuge with my sister-in-law, Françoise Scarron, in the Marais.† After a number of racy adventures, she now depended on a single but well-chosen protector, the duc de Tresmes.

If ever a man could justly be said to lead a double life, it was he. He carried the love of duplication farther than anyone I have ever known. He had given the three bastards he had with Françoise Scarron the same names—François, René and Louis—as his legitimate sons; his mistress's chamber was furnished the same as his wife's apartment; and the puppies born of the bitches in the home of his official family were brought up in the house of his unofficial one. Thus, as he went continually from the rue du Foin, where the hôtel de Tresmes was, to the rue des Douze-Portes, where his mistress lived, from the ménage at the front to the ménage at the rear, he scarcely seemed to change his surroundings at all. But everything in the second house—wife, dogs and children—though very like everything in the first, was a generation younger than in the original, so that by crossing the street the duc made himself twenty years younger as if by a magic wand.

It was off this visionary, or at least under one of his roofs, that we lived for the first few months after our return to Paris.

Scarron's stay in the country had in no way lessened his fame, but his usual associates were scattered and his finances had not improved. His brilliant *Mazarinade* had lost him the pension formerly paid him by Queen Anne, whose "illustrious invalid" he used to proclaim himself. He had sold his canonry at Le Mans the previous year to Ménage's secretary and had frittered away the proceeds. The money he had put into the American expedition was accounted lost, for the worst possible news came from the colony. The abbé de Marivault had been drowned, Governor de Roiville had been murdered by his own men, the settlers were slaughtering one another, the natives were in revolt and famine and disease were decimating those who had been spared the Indians' arrows and the executioner's axe. As for Scarron's books, they were committed to several printers, and it would take him months of work just to cover his publishers' advances. In order to eat and have some sort of roof over his head, he would have to sell his farms in Touraine or ask for charity.

He did both, beginning with begging, for unlike the little *Indienne* from La Rochelle he never had the least objection to cadging.

Dedications became his livelihood. Honor where honor is due —he began with the young King Louis, to whom he dedicated the printed version of *Don Japhet,* suggesting that the monarch would do himself no harm if he did the poet some good. At the same time he brought out a very courtly little epistle in which he made fun of his erstwhile friends. But both the King and the Cardinal had had enough, and neither of them would loosen their purse-strings any more for the rhymester. He had to lower his sights. Everyone, great and small, was laid under contribution: "It is no crime for me, ill and without means, to ask a little help." Gaston d'Orléans, brother of Louis XIII; Mademoiselle de Hautefort, lady-in-waiting to the Regent; maréchal de Turenne, the great captain who had won back Paris for the King; Fouquet, Mazarin's financial secretary; Elbeuf, Sully, Vivonne, his cousin d'Aumont—each in turn was applied to and dedicated to. So as not to tire the grandees, he also included the small fry: councillor Moreau, financier Fourreau, treasurer Dupin, even the despicable comte de Selle won immortal eulogies in return for a few crowns or a meat pie. Fouquet† was the most generous: he handed money out by the fistful to his flatterers, just as he helped himself to it from the King's coffers. As he was fond of mock-heroic poetry, he paid Scarron a pension of sixteen hundred livres a year, and he often sent an occasional gift through his secretary Pellisson. Gaston d'Orléans also put Scarron down on his list for twelve hundred crowns a year.

These various gifts, together with the proceeds from some new essays, permitted us to move out of Françoise Scarron's apartment at the beginning of 1654. She had a tendency to put on airs with her involuntary guests and to make us well aware of what her hospitality cost her. My only source of pleasure in her house had been young Louis Potier, the last of her sons with the duc de Tresmes, a delightful lad whom Scarron called his nephew "à la mode du Marais." He was three years younger than I was, full of intelligence and passion, and already, unwittingly, slightly in love with the too youthful aunt whom chance and poverty had brought under the same roof as himself.

On 27 February we leased, for three hundred and fifty livres a year, part of a mansion on the corner of the rue de Douze-Portes and the rue Neuve-Saint-Louis. The main part of the house was let to the comte de Montresor, and we had an annex which was entered through a single small gate and a narrow passage. The passage led into a dark courtyard looked out on by the kitchen, pantry and storeroom. The first floor consisted of an apartment made up of two bedrooms and a clothes closet, which was assigned to me. The second floor had two more rooms and was taken over by my husband. The whole place, though new, was extremely modest and would have been disdained by a humble haberdasher.

I was enchanted with it, however, for I did not have to share it with anyone. No catty sister-in-law; not even a Cabart de Viller-mont, as at the hôtel de Troyes where, though he had been very civil, I had to put up with his servants, his moods and his everlasting frangipani tarts. Now I was mistress in my own house. Only those who have had to do without can really appreciate things, and I was transported by my four rooms and six fireplaces. I revelled in my yellow saucepans and my turnspit. I was enchanted with the Vene-tian mirror that Catherine Scarron, duchesse d'Aumont and my husband's cousin, had given me as a tribute to my good manners and prepossessing appearance, which were much better than she had thought possible in the wife of her ludicrous relation. I con-gratulated myself on the ebony cabinet inlaid with scenes from the Bible which Elbène had lent us. I gloated over my silver dishes, my firedogs, my candlesticks and my ewers.

The yellow damask hangings from the hôtel de Troyes were reinstalled in the first-floor bedroom, together with the fourposter bed, the two armchairs, six chairs and six folding stools. I hung my Venetian mirror on one wall, a portrait of Mary Magdalen on the wall opposite and an Old Testament tapestry on the third; I then considered my show bedroom completely furnished. I made the adjoining room my real bedchamber and bought a big fourposter bed hung with red brocade for it. My maid and my dressmaker slept in the passage beside the clothes closet.

The larger room on the second floor was our reception room. I thought everything was quite sumptuous: the six-legged walnut table, the two large cupboards which housed Monsieur Scarron's library and above all the Ecstasy of St. Paul, which Monsieur Pous-sin had painted for his friend four years earlier. Behind this salon I fitted up the poet's own room, again with yellow damask, for I do believe that before our marriage he had purchased enough of it to furnish ten houses.

I considered my house quite magnificent, and perfectly worthy of the fine company I hoped to attract there. What with my initia-tion into the office of nurse, the course of reading prescribed for me by Monsieur Scarron and the settling into our new house, I had never in fact had time to go into society, and I knew nothing as yet

of the real splendors hidden behind the brick facades of the aristocratic hôtels of the Marais.

In this modest setting, which Scarron with his usual tact immediately named the Hôtel Impecuniosity, I made my debut as a
hostess, with the object of surrounding the crippled poet once again
with the company the failure of the Fronde and our absence in
Touraine had dispersed.

It was not too easy a task. The most illustrious of the *frondeurs,*
who had graced the hôtel de Troyes in its heyday, were still in exile.
As for the supporters of the King, they did not wish to jeopardize
their victory by hobnobbing with the "illustrious invalid" whose
name their henchmen were still dragging through the mire.

To give him his due, Scarron bore all their insults head high
and with supreme contempt for the authors. Nevertheless, such
writings were not likely to attract the men and women most in favor
to the rue Neuve-Saint-Louis. So to begin with we had to be content
with the society of the topers, grubby pen pushers and dissolute
priests who had first frequented Scarron ten years earlier.

Paris no longer showed any trace of the troubles of the civil war.
There was plenty of everything again—meat, drink and light
women. Life had resumed its easy tenor, and any kind of inclination
seemed permissible. According to a friend of those days, "agreeable error was not called crime, and refined vices were known as
pleasures." By this reckoning, pleasure was well represented within
Scarron's initial circle.

The little abbé de Boisrobert, more famous for his witticisms
and his morals than for his books, stood for the pleasures of the
flesh, on condition that the flesh in question be of the same gender
as his own. The corpulent Saint-Amand personified the pleasures of
the belly, though when I first knew him the old drunkard was
beginning to lose both his teeth and his wits. Alexandre d'Elbène
figured forth all the pleasures of the table in one person: when he
was not stuffing down sausage rolls he was attacking fat pullets and
capons. Gilles Ménage represented the pleasures of conversation,
as understood in Paris; that is, of scandal-mongering, for you could

not mention anyone to him without his immediately shooting them down.

The gallery would be incomplete without a portrait of Raincy, a dandy from the realm of finance, dripping with coins and perfumes, gold and jewels. He was always so covered in ribbons and brocades he looked like something out of the procession on Corpus Christi day. Admittedly he was sometimes mad enough to go to the opposite extreme: on certain nights he would lurk about the place Royale and confront ladies out late with a revelation of his extensive charms, either to frighten or to allure them.

Thus, in order to re-create a suitable circle of visitors for Monsieur Scarron, I was obliged to start with Boisrobert, Raincy, Saint-Amand and others less well known and more unsavory. I did not find it as disagreeable as I might have expected. True, I was not very pleased when our suppers degenerated into drinking bouts, with everyone shouting and bawling and the guests making hats of their napkins and drumming on their plates with their knives. Nor did I care for blasphemy, and I would pretend to eat a herring at my end of the table when the master of the house and his friends ostentatiously ate meat on fast days. Apart from that I enjoyed myself. People were beginning to appreciate my repartee: the months of compulsory reading were bearing fruit.

Moreover, as I often noticed later as well, I was a different person in the society of other people. Though melancholy and withdrawn when I was alone, I became lively and talkative as soon as I was in company. In those days I used to cry myself to sleep every night. My husband's importunities, bitter memories of a not very happy childhood, loneliness and a vague desire for something else —everything contributed to my sorrow. But as soon as the midday meal was over and the first hats came through our gate, as soon as the parquet sounded to the tread of boots and heels and the yellow chairs in Scarron's room disappeared beneath cloaks and folds of lace, then I became self-assured, cheerful and gay again, and the smile of the afternoon rose to my lips as easily as the tears came to my eyes at night.

It soon became known that despite the *frondeurs'* defeat there was always plenty to laugh at at Scarron's. People also started to say that the girl the ludicrous poet had married was turning out to be as witty as her husband as she grew older, and was at least more pleasant than he to look at.

There were no longer many gatherings in Paris devoted to wit, so boredom and curiosity attracted back to Scarron's room some of those whom the civil war had driven away. To begin with there were his family—his cousin the duc d'Aumont, and the duc de Tresmes, his unofficial brother-in-law, both of them happy to come and relax in the invalid's company, excusing themselves at the Louvre† on the grounds that they must spend some time with their family. The greatest names at Court and the largest fortunes in the city, however, still held back and failed to put in an appearance in the rue Neuve-Saint-Louis. But in Paris, if you do not succeed in attracting men of the sword and the law as well as men of letters, you may have a circle of wit but you do not have a salon.

Strangely enough, it was to the faithful but ridiculous love which the old chevalier de Méré still bore me that Scarron owed his social restoration. In just a few months his former glory was surpassed.

Méré had made friends with a young *frondeur,* the comte de Matha, when the latter, exiled by the King, took refuge in the country near his own estate. Matha preferred ladies' drawing-rooms to fields of battle, and Méré had no difficulty, when he promised him wine, song and the conversation of an "Indienne" as vivacious as she was beautiful, in luring Matha to the rue Neuve-Saint-Louis. Especially as the comte was little thought of by the King and notoriously detested by the Cardinal, and had no more reputation to lose.

Matha enjoyed himself at our house, and when he returned, he brought with him his inseparable companion, the chevalier de Gramont. They lived together in the same hostelry, both were of good birth but poor, both lived, unsuccessfully, on their wits. Gramont, an incomparable gambler, earned most of his wherewithal at the table of his relative the comte de Miossens, the maréchal-duc d'Albret and master of a magnificent new town house in the heart of the Marais, on the corner of the rue des Francs-Bourgeois and the rue Pavée. Since Gramont saw the maréchal every day, he naturally mentioned to him Scarron's drolleries and the agreeable society one found in the poet's room just a few steps away from the maréchal's own house. As Miossens loved wit and women and hated pedantry and bigots, he decided that was the place for him. So one fine day, we saw a splendid carriage draw up outside, and from it step down, more gorgeous still, César d'Albret, comte de Miossens and maréchal of France. From then on, Scarron's house was back in fashion.

César d'Albret owed his field-marshal's baton to his loyalty to the young King and to the courage with which he had served him during the Fronde. At the height of the rebellion this young man from Gascony, a mere captain, had had the courage to arrest Condé and the insurgent princes on the King's order and take them to the tower at Vincennes. Neither the threats nor the promises Condé lavished on him during the journey could make the young gentleman swerve from his duty, poor though he then was and despite the fact that the fate of France seemed to be trembling in the balance. The King was not ungrateful, and in return for a service which had saved his throne made Miossens's fortune. The new maréchal's fine presence and munificence added a final touch, and Miossens met with no refusals from the ladies, still less any enemies among the men. César d'Albret's presence in the rue Neuve-Saint-Louis told everyone that anathema was a thing of the past and that it was possible to be in favor and to come see Scarron at one and the same time.

Following his lead, people pressed to be admitted to our afternoon receptions, and every day princes, ducs and officers of the Crown were turned away. Both at Court and in town, people became desperately anxious to belong to our little circle; all the gentlemen of the Louvre wanted to sup in the yellow room.

I had to be on the alert all the time to see that the maids brought one guest something to drink and placed a chair for another; to halt political satire with a smile or blasphemy with a look; to link jest with profound thought, quip with controversy, art with philosophy, in such a way that everyone, whatever his humor, might find satisfaction and pleasure in the rue Neuve-Saint-Louis. Who would have thought that the poor little orphan from Poitou, the erstwhile shy Protestant, would one day find herself queen of this brilliant and rakish company? And yet I was an enormous success. My extreme youth, my artless airs, my sprightliness, my swift repartee and the way I tried to please servants no less than princes, these won everyone over. But of all those who acclaimed me, only one interested me. That was the man to whom Scarron owed the triumph of his salon, César d'Albret.

I find it strange, when I come to think about it, that without Méré I would never have met d'Albret, and that without d'Albret I would never have met the King. So the thread of my fate follows exactly the sequence of my amours, from the gallant I had when I was fourteen to the last of all my lovers. And d'Albret was not the least of the links in that chain.

Although he had but a modest fortune, he was of excellent birth. He had borne witness to the valor of Gascony in war both at home and abroad, and when I met him, his victories in love surpassed even his victories in the field. He who can easily vanquish is bound to attack, and he was always in pursuit of new conquests. This "Miossens so terrible to husbands, so vulnerable to love" was the first man I looked upon with tenderness.

When he came to the rue Neuve-Saint-Louis, I surrounded him with attentions as instructed by Monsieur Scarron, who knew that the fortunes of his salon depended on the maréchal's protection. But as I tried to please him, he grew to please me, and my heart was overwhelmed when I least expected it.

It is true I had been struck from the outset by the pleasantness of his face and a certain nobility of aspect quite different from anything I had yet encountered. He seemed to me as much above other men by his bearing as Soeur Céleste was above other women by her beauty. Unlike my sweet friend in Niort, however, he spoke very poorly, though he was intelligent enough. All his successes had not made him any less timid and shy than he had been when he left his native Béarn, and a sort of stutter which afflicted him in the presence of others prevented him from communicating his thoughts freely in company. Sometimes his speech was so confused that it was impossible to understand what he was trying to say. I thought a fault so noticeable and so public would act as a brake upon my feelings. I did not yet know that the more imperfect the objects of our affections are, the more attached to them we become, and that in love a marked defect through which one hopes to resist will sink one as surely as will a stone around a drowning man's neck.

At first I used to sit near him out of duty and thought it very creditable when I managed to get a couple of sentences out of him. I was longing to leave him to his own devices and go and laugh with Raincy or philosophize with Segrais. Out of duty, however, I summoned up gentler looks and kindly smiles, and I tried to talk to him on subjects which amused him. I took care he should be neither too hot nor too cold, neither hungry nor thirsty. I watched for the slightest frown, the least sign of impatience, secretly fuming that all these attentions kept me from my friends. Then, after four or five visits, one day when he had played a game of omber with Matha and the chevalier de Méré and had gone away promising to come again before the end of the week, I found myself hoping he would return the next day. I asked myself the reason and told myself he was a man of wit and breeding. Then, examining why I considered him witty and trying to recall what I had heard him say that afternoon, all I could remember was "gano," "three matadors" and a few other expressions used in the game of omber. I was horrified by this discovery, for though I had not yet experienced love, I feared this unfounded esteem might be its forerunner.

I persuaded myself I only wanted to see him again in order to check quite calmly how he could have deceived me thus as to his wit. When he came again three days later and I decided to look upon him with a completely cold eye, like a judge without any emotions, what happened was what anyone with more experience might have foretold: I saw in him infinite wit, wide reading, feeling, gaiety and even—so easily in such cases does one find what one wants to find—an underlying vein of piety which completely reassured me as to his intentions. It was as well I could count on that underlying vein, for the surface was entirely atheistical.

In short, his ideas struck me as clear and lively, and his expressions noble and simple, without studied phrases or affectation. His ruling passion for war, and his interest in all connected with it, convinced me that he possessed the ability as well as the appearance of a commander. Having thus reassured myself about his worth, I persuaded myself that the new pleasure I felt in his company derived from a well-founded respect and not, as I had at first feared, from some deviation of the heart.

As a result of this splendid argument, I gave up the struggle and sank a few degrees further into passion. I did not realize my imprudence and the true nature of the feelings which had taken hold of me until a few months later, when it was too late to think of resisting. I then supposed there was nothing I could do but hide what I felt.

I doubt if I succeeded. At least, it is highly unlikely that a man as subtle and as adept in gallantry as the maréchal d'Albret did not know quite well, and probably sooner and better than myself, what I felt for him. At first he gave no sign, just continued to seek out my company in preference to any other when he came to the rue Neuve-Saint-Louis and to give me an occasional apt word of advice about my dress.

Méré and Scarron had trained my mind, but without a suitable woman to teach me the art of adornment, I must have dressed less well than I should. I was living entirely among men. But Miossens, who spent all his time among women, was quite expert in the rules of fashion, the right length for a petticoat, the best color for a ribbon, the address of a good perfumer. He advised me what to buy, and, to help me in my purchases, he sent Raincy with me. Raincy was so sensual himself that he knew all the ladies' dress shops in Paris and Saint-Germain as well as any wanton wench. I was careful to do just as the maréchal told me.

So, accompanied by Raincy and, as was then the fashion, wearing a black velvet mask to protect my complexion and conceal my identity, I would go to Guilleri's in the rue de la Tabletterie to buy real Cordova water and essences from Nice. I went to the Toison d'Or for the almond soap I used to wash my hands. At the sign of the Grand Monarque I got a squirrel muff for only twelve livres. I bought lace from Perdrigeon, satin from Gauthier's, Spanish gloves, and was to be seen at Champagne's, Renault's, the Perle des

Mouches and the Soulier d'Or. For a few weeks I lived in such a frenzy of gowns and mantles that ever since I have made the greatest allowances for the same kind of folly in girls and young women. It does not last long with sensible people, but in order to die to such refinements you have to have lived through them first. The same might be said of other passions.

Now, in the evening, after the merrymakers had gone home, I no longer wept. I had something better to do. First I undressed for Monsieur Scarron, who could make no other demands just then because a new attack had paralyzed his hands and his every limb felt as if it were being stuck with pins. Then I ran to my room to hide, for I felt sullied by being looked at by him, and, locking the door, quickly put on my stays again and, over them, fancy petticoats and gowns of watered silk. I put all kinds of beauty spots above my lips and on my brow—the "passionate," the "coquettish," the "gallant." I rolled my hair in curl-papers and spent hours admiring myself in the mirror without ever getting tired. I tried out smiles, I experimented with glances. One day I even went so far as to put lemon juice in my eyes to make them sparkle. And I do not know whether it was the lemon juice or something else, but certainly all the visitors to our salon soon noticed that my eyes were brighter than before.

When you are in love you seem more attractive to others, and, even if your love is not requited, those you have disdained see qualities in you which they never suspected before. After a month or two, everyone around me was, to use the language of the time, either a "prisoner" or a "sufferer" or "dying of love." My charms and my glances suddenly inflicted more wounds in the Marais than all the campaigns in Flanders.

Barillon, later ambassador to England, was the first victim. He moaned about it in little notes which he slipped into the pockets of my apron. I started by telling him it was better to be respected as a friend than ill used as a lover, and that he would gain nothing by trying to change from one to the other. But he would not listen. Whenever we were alone, he would break out in fervent protestations, and when I declined to hear them, he would try to persuade me of the violence of his passion by dashing his head against the wall. However, I noticed he took care to do so where there was an open door or a window recess behind the hangings. This greatly reassured me as to the extent of his madness and the depth of his feelings.

La Mesnardière was smitten at about the same time. He informed me of the state of his heart by sending me a bouquet every day. These offerings were chosen and varied skilfully according to the language of flowers, which this alleged doctor and so-called poet, a habitué of the literary salons, prided himself on speaking better than anyone else in the world. It is true he was more likely to get a hearing in that language than in genteel parlance, in which he was entirely unskilled.

Guilleragues, who was later ambassador to Constantinople, was the next. He was not the most constant of lovers, and it was while doing the rounds that he came to me, affecting, truly or otherwise, a grand passion. Transports, doubts, jealousies, reproaches—nothing was lacking. And everything was so well acted that the drama became quite interesting. Guilleragues later became the friend of Jean Racine, and his love-letters, the best I ever saw, were almost as fine as the poet's verses and amused me greatly. They already showed all the nobility and despair which were to be seen ten years later in the famous *Letters from a Portuguese Nun,* which Guilleragues published as a translation, denying he was its author. I do not know if his feeling for me was genuine or if he thought fit to try out on me an experiment he meant to carry out later on a larger audience, but I confess I was flattered to be loved with so much perseverance and wit by someone I did not care for and whom I never deceived as to my own sentiments toward him.

François d'Harcourt, marquis de Beuvron, later lieutenant-general of Normandy, was the youngest and best of those who were "dying" for love of me. Nor was he the least comely. He had black eyes, long, thick, dark brown hair and a fine figure. And though he was not one who shone in conversation, he was intelligent enough.

One day we found ourselves alone together.

"If," he said, "I only wanted to let you know I love you, I

should not need to speak; my looks and my attentions have already told you of my feelings. But as it is necessary, Madame, that you should one day respond to my passion, I must disclose it to you, and at the same time assure you that whether or not you love me, I am resolved to love you all my life." For a long while I kept this most gentle and honorable of lovers under my sway, and later succeeded, by prodigious skill, in turning him into a friend. I never forgot him, and when I rose to favor took advantage of my own position to shower benefits upon his family. I even had his sister, Madame d'Arpajon, appointed lady-in-waiting to the wife of the Dauphin.

In addition to Beuvron and his distinguished predecessors, several lesser planets also gravitated around me: Charleval, Ménage and Beauchateau all took me for their sun. I scarcely gave them a glance, and my "cruelty" was soon so famous that my husband boasted everywhere that his honor was safe with my virtue. Neither my trusting husband nor any of my admirers guessed I had eyes for no one but Miossens, and that it was this fondness as much as my chastity that explained the severity which they deplored.

The only one who had any inkling was Louis Potier, my nephew "à la mode du Marais," who, young as he was, became suddenly more advanced in the knowledge of the heart than all those great wits, perhaps because he was more sincerely enamoured than they. He used his privilege of being with me at all hours of the day to remonstrate with me about my partiality for the maréchal.

One day, taking me aside in a window recess, he said:

"Really, Aunt, I wish you could see yourself when Miossens speaks to you. You positively wilt! I don't know what you see in such a fop—he has no wit. Besides, he doesn't love you. To please him you would have to be a courtesan like Ninon or a great lady like Madame de Rohan, and, as you are neither one nor the other, you are wasting your time. Anyway, everyone in Paris except you knows where he is paying court at the moment."

He mentioned a name I did not know, and I remember that at the same time as he pierced my heart by uttering it, I was gazing at the white cloth on the table. In the confusion into which his words plunged me, all I could think of was that there was a big wine stain there between the tray of oysters Beauchateau had just sent and the glazed meat pie Elbène had brought with him, and that I must see to it without delay if I was to keep my reputation as an efficient housekeeper. Since that day, I have never seen a red stain on a white cloth without thinking I was losing my heart's blood.

I pulled myself together, and Louis noticed nothing.

"Last but not least, Aunt," he went on, "he's an old man, fifteen or twenty years older than you. I wager he is grey-haired underneath his wig."

"Very well, Monsieur," I said. "Moderate your wrath. As far as I know I have not yet cast any slur upon your uncle's honor, which I presume you are now defending. As for my admirers' ages, I suspect you would wish me to prefer youth to experience. If so, why not introduce me to some friends of your own age, some champion at ninepins or the hoop?"

I left poor Louis all discomfited and went to my room saying my head ached. There I cried my eyes out, though more from vexation than from love, for the jealousy I thought I felt was only the turmoil resulting from pride meeting with humiliation on all sides.

The passion I felt for d'Albret was in fact what is known as love in the head, and I really had no wish for it to lead me too far. I had no doubt thought of letting him hold my hand if it came to that, but I had too much dislike for the sort of relationship Monsieur Scarron had imposed on me for the last three years to contemplate a real mutual love with anything but dread. Nevertheless, though I did not wish to be Monsieur d'Albret's mistress otherwise than in poetry and song, I should have liked to shine in his opinion as much as I shone in that of all the little marquises who haunted the rue Neuve-Saint-Louis. I should have been pleased to have Miossens imploring and enslaved like Beuvron, and content, like him, with mere hopes. Resolved as I was to resist both commands and entreaties, I would have been wounded by too great and too long an indifference on his part. The revelation of his preference for another completely prostrated me.

I suffered a violent recurrence of the island fever which sometimes attacked me, and my only consolation in my sickness was a curt little note from the maréchal concerning my health. Though I kept it under my pillows and looked at it twenty times a day, I could not by any means construe it into a mark of love.

Fortunately I soon had other cares to distract me from this first sorrow.

Monsieur Scarron, taking the for him unusual step of going through his accounts, found that we were heading straight for bankruptcy. The suppers we gave, the gowns and powders with which I dazzled our visitors, our ill-supervised and dishonest servants, our whole way of living, modest though it was, was ruining us. Moreover, my husband, who always had more than one wild project in hand, had taken it into his head to manufacture potable gold and other equally plausible products. He had obtained a license and set up a large workroom beside the pantry, where, surrounded by flasks and retorts, my flowery-tongued gallant La Mesnardière and our new servant, Jean Brillot, indulged in curious feats of alchemy.

Gold certainly melted there, not as a result of their concoctions, but rather because of an insatiable appetite for rare volumes and costly books of spells, for lead and mercury by the bucketful and for huge logs to keep up a blazing fire night and day. An unending series of new and heterodox experiments took place, all unsuccessful but all to be paid for in fine gold crowns manufactured solely by the King.

The arrival of my brother, Charles, was the last straw. I had not heard of him for some years, and now he was twenty, handsome, wild and of course penniless. He asked his brother-in-law to lend him four thousand livres to set himself up to join a regiment. In view of the state of our finances, Scarron hesitated to fulfil his family obligations, but I argued forcefully that he might well sacrifice four thousand livres for my only brother when I was sacrificing my youth and beauty to his age and infirmity. In any case, it was only a matter of a loan for one year. I still believed Charles capable of paying his debts. I did not know how much this brother of mine, for whom I had the partiality not only of a sister but of a mother too, was a perfect miniature of the vices and failings of his father.

In the end my husband gave in to my protests and complaints. But in order to pay our rent, meet our bills and acquit himself of certain old debts, he was obliged, after helping Charles, to sell his properties on the Loire.

Even this was not enough, and Scarron decided he would have to part with the picture Poussin had painted for him. He sold it to Jabach, a rich connoisseur of painting who promptly resold it to Richelieu, in whose apartments I often saw it after we became friends. It was a painful sacrifice for my husband, and I suffered too when the picture was taken down from the wall in his room and I saw him shed tears which, because he could not move his arms, he was unable to wipe away. I was ready to leave my wretched brother to his fate and beg the poor poet to keep the canvas he loved. But I put it off till the evening, and it was well I did, for at supper Monsieur Scarron seemed quite consoled, and he guzzled so heartily with Elbène and made so many jests with his friends that he nearly died laughing, and I had to leave the room to avoid seeing and hearing more than befits a respectable young woman. Anyhow, even if I had allowed him to keep his picture, the potable gold or the philosopher's stone would have forced him to sell it before long.

The round of booksellers and dedications began again. "We must pass round the hat with the quill," said Scarron. He set to and wrote two odes a day and three sonnets, which Brillot took at once to the great noblemen to whom they were addressed, so as to bring in some immediate petty cash. Wretched as these occasional verses and poems written to order were, they still brought us a fair amount of money, and when I complained to Scarron about the suppers he gave and pointed out that we could not keep open house all the year round, he answered that even if we did entertain his friends and patrons, "you must agree, Françoise, they pay us back handsomely." It was true that without their gifts we would often have gone hungry.

I did the best I could to help put our family finances in order. Economy and even privation meant less to me than the fear of going through the miseries of La Rochelle again and having to beg for my bread. So I cut down our staff, keeping only the new manservant and four maids. I was glad of the opportunity to dismiss that great fool of a Mangin who was so ready to "give Madame a child." I omitted the midday meal and saved up my hunger till supper time, a system which had the advantage of preserving my figure. I bought no more petticoats or perfumes, and wore farandine instead of taffeta and brocade. I abandoned such finery without regret, seeing that the display of fabrics and jewels indulged in at the instance of the one man whose opinion I valued had in fact done me little good with him. I resolved to be beautiful despite fashion, and I think I succeeded. With an elegant figure and the face of a twenty-year-old, you do not need money to appear to advantage everywhere.

Lessening my wardrobe did not lose me any lovers; I even gained a few. To be truthful, I was an out-and-out coquette, and glad of it. I liked the image reflected in looking-glasses and in the eyes of my lovelorn swains. My mind was dazzled by its own light, and as for my heart, while I did possess one, it was divided up into four unequal parts, the first three for my aunt de Villette, Soeur Céleste and my brother, and the fourth and largest for my handsome maréchal.

Clearly God came into this scarcely at all. Not that I forgot my religious duties, but I performed them only out of pride and to show my independence vis-à-vis the freethinkers surrounding me. Nothing but a mania for being different made me go to church. A fine motive, and it produced fine results. I went to mass as if going for a stroll. I got out my best lace, and having no servants went alone, and if some gentleman on horseback stopped to speak to me, I would chat and laugh with him till we reached the very place of worship. So much so that one of my neighbors, a pillar of the church as inveterate as her male counterparts who prop up tavern counters, felt it her duty to come and point out that smiling at men on the way to mass was an imprudence which might one day cost me dear.

I was ashamed at having exposed myself so thoughtlessly to her criticism, and I resolved thenceforth not to go out without one of my maids. I was careful to cover my bosom, too, but I could not bring myself to give up taking the collection. In those days, lady worshipers engaged in a strange kind of competition. Every Sunday a different one of them took the collection, and their charms were measured by the amount of money they brought in for the parish, just as women of the streets measure theirs by their daily earnings. Thus church services would be troubled with smiles and preening and languishing looks that were much out of place, though of course all was for the greater glory of God and the relief of the poor.

In truth my main concern at that time was not my salvation but the winning of Miossens's heart. He was said to be "so light in all his loves that he always changes and always will," and trusting to that reputation, I thought his latest passion for some little duchesse would not last, and that his fickleness might one day turn to my profit. In order to hasten the process, I determined to make him jealous, as if one could really use this goad on someone who is indifferent. So while I became a little more virtuous in church, I was much less so at home and in town, where I was then beginning to go about to amuse myself with my lady friends. These were but three, for few women came to see Scarron apart from actresses and writers like Madeleine de Scudéry.

I had a casual friendship with Gilonne d'Harcourt, comtesse de Fiesque, who was known as "the lovely Amazon" because, like Mademoiselle,† she had fought like a man during the Fronde. I never got far in her good graces, but all I wanted from her friendship was a carriage to ride in.

My feelings were deeper for Madame Franquetot, who was always called Kind Heart because she was so generous with her lovers. The fact that Raincy professed to love us both equally created a bond between us: we always received the same verses, and he bestowed on each the same protestations of passion.

The last of my three friends, Madame Martel, was a very handsome widow whose many charms I much admired but who, it must be admitted, did not have a good reputation. She was somewhat free in her ways, and the chevalier de Méré used to compare her to an open city.

So it was with the eccentric Gilonne de Fiesque, Kind Heart and Madame Martel or their friends that I was to be seen every afternoon in the Cours-la-Reine.† The Cours was already a fashionable meeting place, though people did not then dance there at night by the light of torches, as some young madcaps see fit to do today. Those who frequented the Cours in my time were content to stroll, chatting merrily, in the shade of the elms, or to be driven to and fro, smiling graciously through their carriage windows at ladies and gentlemen they did not know. Women selling sweets went up and down among the carriages, and for a few pence would deliver lovers' notes. Everyone passed in review before everyone else, noting the flow of a cloak and the cut of a gown, discoursing at length upon a smile, improvising epigrams and compliments. At five o'clock everybody went home to change, then came out again to go hear an opera or applaud the Italian actors† in the theater in the Marais. So I too might be seen in the Tuileries Gardens at nightfall. I liked those long walks where one sometimes passed one of the young Mancini ladies† prancing down the avenues. I hoped to catch a glimpse of the young King, who was just eighteen and said to be very comely, but I was not yet vouchsafed that happiness.

It is true I had others: a cloak spread at my feet to spare me from having to step in the mud, a helping hand when I alighted from my carriage, the offer of an arm if the path grew hilly, nimble fingers to loosen the laces of my gown when I complained of the heat. For I consented to mitigate the tortures of the poor martyrs who followed me around the gardens, escorted me along around the Palais† and joined me in exclaiming at the marvels of a ballet. I tried not to notice too soon the hand that stole round my waist or rested on my shoulder on the pretext of showing me the way to go. I permitted stolen kisses when someone shared a bunch of grapes with me or drank from the same fountain. It may be that I did not punish as I should have certain more daring attempts. But if, to use the language of the time, I allowed one or two of these gallants to win some minor outworks, none could claim I had let anyone storm the citadel. I wore an air of gallantry, but it was only an air and not the song itself. I was hoping these appearances would be enough to attract César d'Albret.

Unfortunately it had quite a different effect. Seeing the freer manners and excessive gaiety I now affected in company to wound the object of my passion, Monsieur Scarron, whose health had improved a little, was seized with an access of desire. When I had just left my powdered and perfumed dandies and was confronted with the shrivelled and deformed body of an elderly husband I did not love, I had plenty of time to reflect upon the state of a wife. And I assure you my thoughts were not cheerful ones. Even today at Saint-Cyr, when I see your comrades giggling into their aprons at the mention of the sacrament of marriage, I think they would do better to cry—as they certainly will when they go through the experience.

The second result of my brilliant policy was of greater conse-quence. It was soon the talk of Paris that I was a scatterbrain, and that I had suddenly changed from the greatest reserve with my admirers to the greatest intimacies. The salons of the Marais were as quick to tear you to pieces as to praise you to the skies, with as much reason in either case. One lampoonist wrote an epigram that was very well received: it was addressed to Scarron and pointed out that those he thought came to see him for his conversation came for something very different.

Monsieur Scarron did not appreciate this pleasantry. He com-plained to Fouquet, who had the lampoon seized but could not stop people repeating it. My husband then remonstrated with me severely, for although, according to him, he was not jealous by nature, he found himself to be very sensitive on the subject of conjugal honor. He even went so far as to reproach me for my imprudence in the liveliest terms before other people. I asked him, through Ménage, to keep such mortifying strictures for when we were alone, but he would not hear reason and I was forced to endure several of these humiliating public scenes. I was all the more indignant because I did not consider a little harmless coquetry a very great offense and did not think there could be any sin where there had been no pleasure.

One day, tired of being castigated thus in the presence of others, I answered boldly, "Perhaps, Monsieur, if you had not spoken and written so much about your marriage, people would not have believed I might have to seek abroad what every wife hopes to find at home." Thereupon he turned on me and rebuked me so violently that I ran away weeping to my room.

D'Albret came there to console me. He told me all our friends knew I was virtuous, and that Scarron's rages should be set down to his illness. He was so affectionate and full of solicitude that when I should have been most on my guard I relaxed my severity somewhat. I thought he too seemed less distant than usual, but he soon collected himself.

"I have been fond of duelling in my time," he said. "All too fond, for I had the misfortune to kill my dearest friend over some foolishness which mattered to neither of us. I do not wish to fight my friends any more, nor have I ever thought it became a gentleman to challenge a man weakened by illness. Scarron is my friend, and an invalid, and I will not fight against him on any ground. So it will be wiser for you and for me if I do not visit here for a while."

Having thus lost Monsieur d'Albret for a time which I thought, wrongly, would last for ever, I also lost the love of Monsieur de Guilleragues, with whom I had lost my credit through my coquettish tricks. It was in the following manner that I discovered the waning of his feelings. When I went to see Madame de Fiesque, where I often found him, I usually returned on foot, and he never failed to offer me his hand to escort me home through the place Royale. But while, at the beginning of our acquaintance, he used to go around the sides of the *place,* I observed that after all my follies he went across the middle. I therefore concluded that his love had decreased by the difference between the diagonal and the two sides of the square. This desertion, which should not have affected me since I did not love Monsieur de Guilleragues, upset me more than I would have thought possible.

On top of all these sorrows I had the anxiety of the unpaid rent, the old unpleasantness of patched petticoats and leaking shoes and the knowledge that my brother was entangled in some gambling troubles in his garrison and was in no position to repay us anything of what he owed. All these troubles and aversions, added to a humiliating situation and an impossible and painful love affair, filled me with a horror of life. My desire to be done with it almost overcame all the reasons against such a course, and I could resist the temptation only by turning more seriously to religion. To soothe my own sorrow, I went and visited those with woes greater than my own. I spent every other day tending the sick at the Hôtel-Dieu, and several times went to see the prostitutes at the Salpêtrière.† This restored my reputation somewhat, but I was too sincerely unhappy to have calculated it.

One morning one of my servants, Madeleine Croissant, told me as she was scrubbing the floor of my room that Mademoiselle de Lenclos was back.

"Just think, Madame," she said. "Last winter I bet my brother, who's coachman to Monsieur de Pomponne—a very good place, by the by—I bet him we'd see Mademoiselle Ninon back in the neighborhood before midsummer this year. It wasn't natural that she stay with the same lover all those years. So I've won ten crowns, which won't do me any harm, because as Madame knows I'm still only living in hopes of my wages . . . Well, it seems that everything is over this time between Mademoiselle Ninon and Monsieur de Villarceaux, and the marquis has come back to Paris and the poor marquise, who's said to be a very worthy lady with four children. He abandoned her for four years to run around in Vexin with that rake of a Ninon, who has neither religion nor morals but is as beautiful as the devil. The marquis is handsome too, very attentive to the ladies and a great lover, according to Monsieur de Boisrobert's footman."

"I wouldn't trust to the opinion of Monsieur de Boisrobert's footman on such matters," I replied.

"Well," she went on, "it's true Monsieur l'abbé's footmen are different from most. As I often say to Dumay, there at least are some footmen who are not gallows-birds like the rest—they need only be afraid of the stake!† . . . Anyhow, the abbé's pet must know something about Villarceaux because the marquis and his master

85

live in the same house, near the porte de Richelieu. And he assures me that the marquis . . ."

"That's enough, Madeleine," I said. "I do not care for gossip. Moreover, I don't know either Monsieur de Villarceaux or Mademoiselle de Lenclos, and I don't want to."

The next day Ninon came into the yellow room in the rue Neuve-Saint-Louis, and into my life.

Seven

It was the spring of 1656 and I had turned twenty that winter. I must have been dressed that day, as usual, in a watered silk skirt with a pattern of white and yellow flowers and trimmed with lace, and a black velvet bodice. My bosom was covered with a kerchief of Genoa point, as was my habit since I had been called a flibbertigibbet, and, beneath my white lace cap, my hair was curled in the current fashion. My eyes were the same as ever, black and somewhat languorous, for however hard I tried, in order to escape calumny, I could never succeed in making them smaller and more forbidding. Sitting on a folding stool beside my husband's plinth, I was turning those over-large eyes on each of my "martyrs" in turn, taking care not to let them linger on any one in particular. Beauchateau, son of the famous actor at the hôtel de Bourgogne,† was sitting on a chair beside me, trying to slip me a note, which I affected not to see and which finally fell on the floor.

At that moment our footman-cum-alchemist announced, as triumphantly as if it had been the finding of the philosopher's stone or the elixir of youth: "Mademoiselle de Lenclos requests an interview."

There was a stir of surprise, a murmur, exclamations, and all eyes turned toward the door. I swiftly picked up my admirer's note, tore it into little pieces and gave it back to him. When I looked up again, Ninon was standing there in front of me.

Was she as beautiful as the devil, as poor old Croissant had said? I cannot tell. But I never saw a princess or a queen with so much dignity and presence.

She must have then been about thirty-five years old. She was thus past her first youth, and I do not think she had ever been pretty, if prettiness is taken to mean fineness of countenance and complexion. Her features were rather large, with a nose almost aquiline and eyes piercing rather than melting. But she had such grace withal, her whole aspect was so intelligent, her figure so supple, her bosom so lovely, her hands so white and her manners so prepossessing that you could not help being enamored of her on sight.

"So this is the new sovereign lady of Paris," she said, examining me with a smile. "But she is just a girl! Look, she's blushing at a compliment!"

My cheeks had indeed flushed, not at what she had said but with surprise at finding her standing in front of me sooner than I expected, and also because I feared she might have seen the exchange between me and Beauchateau.

"So, my friend," she added, turning to Scarron, "you have taken advantage of my absence to get married. Do you realize I could resent your infidelity?"

"Ninon," he answered in the same bantering tone, "when you leave us we do not know what to do to console ourselves."

"Well, I forgive you your treachery because of your choice, which is not at all bad," she said, looking again at my curls, my figure and the lace on my skirt.

Boisrobert soon freed me from this embarrassing examination by throwing himself at her feet and crying:

"My goddess, how I have missed you!"

And he kissed her hands.

"Come now, Monsieur l'abbé, for you to miss me you would have to change—or I should have to wear livery!"

She had taken command of the conversation quite naturally,

introducing new subjects, ending arguments with a word, making everyone laugh with her own well-timed contributions.

Seeing her put both myself and the master of the house in the shade, I might well have felt some jealousy, but her natural kindness, her incomparable wit and the good breeding and nobility of all her ways left me with nothing but admiration. Not one of her smiles or sallies escaped me that first evening; I drank in every word and all the graceful gestures which accompanied them. I had met my master in the art of coquetry and the science of savoir-faire, and I could take neither my eyes nor my mind off her.

When she left the rue Neuve-Saint-Louis, escorted by the finest talkers and the most assiduous beaux present, she asked me to visit her the next day in the new apartments she was fitting out in the rue des Tournelles.

I was there at four o'clock. She was alone, lying on her bed in a simple gown. She received me with transports of friendship, drew me out about this and that and then declared that in bringing me out into society, her friend Scarron had produced his greatest masterpiece. She crammed me with preserved fruit and hot rolls, and said many pleasant things in such a way that I could not tell if she spoke in jest or in earnest. She wanted me to take home a necklace which she had tried on me and which she said went with my gown. She gave me a bracelet. In short, she covered me with comfits and caresses, like someone trying to win the affection of a child.

"I was expecting your friend Raincy this afternoon," she told me, "but he takes so long to dress and powder and perfume himself that one must not expect to see him anywhere till well after six o'clock . . . I have been back in Paris only a fortnight, my dear, but I know already that you have robbed me of some of my admirers: our beribboned gentleman for one"—she meant Raincy—"and Charleval, and even the foolish Beauchateau, who passes a lady a note as discreetly as if it were a playbill."

I blushed to the roots of my hair. She laughed.

"You must have your doctor let your blood more often, my child, for if you blush like that people will take you for a simpleton.

Besides, you won't be able to dissemble, and you have to be able to dissemble if you are married . . .

"So! As for my 'martyrs,' I hand them over to you." Her "martyrs" were those she allowed to adore her without giving anything in return.

"As for the 'payers' "—these were the financiers who kept her and whom she honored with occasional favors—"I rather fear competition from virtuous women like you who give themselves for nothing. But the world is full of bankers!

"It is my 'caprices' who concern me slightly." She was referring to those she loved. "I am not too anxious to see you hanging around them with that twenty-year-old face of yours. If, as I hope —for I like you—we have the same friends, let me be first with those I fancy, if not from generosity at least to respect the order of seniority. Anyhow, I never keep my lovers long, and you can have them afterwards to your heart's content."

This way of talking was new to me, I confess, and I did not quite know how to take it.

I was about to protest that I never looked at anyone but my husband and that if people had told her I had admirers they were lying, when the door was suddenly thrown open, without any announcement, by someone who must be on intimate terms with my hostess. And when he took off his hat and cape I beheld none other than the handsome maréchal whom I had expected never to see again. He seemed confounded to find me chatting by Ninon's bed as if we were friends, and I was no less surprised to see him. My astonishment was redoubled when I heard what Ninon said.

"Hello, Françoise, here's one of my caprices in the flesh! More flesh than anything else, to tell you the truth. I have not made much use yet of this little caprice, have I, d'Albret? But I think I shall remedy that a little, long enough to create a new circle and meet a few fresh people . . . You have begged me so constantly to accord you something, my friend, that I am going to answer your prayers. I grant you three or four weeks of passion—for me that's infinity, for you eternity."

It was undoubtedly a piquant situation. Miossens was torn between happiness at his sudden restoration to Ninon's favors and the embarrassment caused by the derision with which she bestowed them in my presence. I myself was divided between wanting to laugh at Ninon's cavalier manner with this lady-killer and wanting to weep with jealousy. I finally decided in favor of laughter, which was kinder to my vanity and allowed me to disabuse Miossens as to the depth of my feelings for him. I had resolved on this policy since the scene in my room, preferring to see César d'Albret as a friend rather than not see him at all. So I added my irony to Ninon's mockery.

But although I pretended to be merry, I had several reasons for finding the conversation irksome, and Raincy's arrival was a relief. As soon as he came the laughter was concentrated on his latest gew-gaws: over a voluminous shirt covered with lace and ribbons and tasselled bands, he wore a crimson waistcoat embroidered with golden butterflies. The flounces adorning his breeches below the knee were ornamented with silver birds; plum-colored fish swam on his gloves; his little red slippers were invisible beneath a froth of blue rosettes. He looked like a rainbow falling into a box of sugared almonds. We amused ourselves at his expense, and when d'Elbène and Gramont arrived and joined in, I took advantage of the general hilarity to go home.

But Ninon, either out of excessive consideration or from pure mischief, insisted that d'Albret accompany me to my husband's house. It was impossible for him to refuse, so we left the rue des Tournelles together. He walked along without saying a word, more embarrassed than I; and this small triumph gave me the courage to speak. My first subject was the beauty of the night, but since this was not yet far enough away from the subjects I wished to avoid, I rose from earth to sky, and flung myself into the ordering of the universe. I held out in these heights until we reached the rue Neuve-Saint-Louis. D'Albret, relieved of his anxiety, had entered into the spirit of the conversation, which though lofty in subject had been treated very lightly, and I could congratulate myself on feeling that he now thought himself to have been mistaken about my attitude toward him. This gave me a delicious pleasure unknown to those who cannot resist the promptings of their hearts.

From that day on the maréchal no longer avoided me. He

started to visit Scarron again and showed once more the esteem and affectionate interest he had bestowed upon me before. He spent no more than the prescribed four weeks in Ninon's arms, after which she turned her attentions to the marquis de la Chastres and two or three other beaux. Not to be outdone, Monsieur d'Albret took up with what he found ready to hand, namely Madame d'Olonne, who had been found ready to hand by many another.

I sometimes went back to the house in the rue des Tournelles, where against a background of the stern Priam painted by Le Brun and shepherdesses wreathed in roses by Mignard, Ninon received everyone of consequence in Paris. Scarron himself, who no longer left the house, had himself carried there two or three times on his plinth, at great inconvenience.

"I thought until now you worshiped no divinity," I said to him one day as his chair was being carried down our stairs, "but I was mistaken. Ninon must be your God, since she makes lame men walk and raises people from the dead."

But the temple in which that idol was adored did not compete with the churches for long. In April that year, on the orders of Queen Anne the goddess was taken to the convent for repentant prostitutes, though she was really neither a prostitute nor repentant. This was at the urgent request of the Company of the Holy Sacrament,† who were shocked by Ninon's fame and the scandals that surrounded her. From there, since too many people still came to see her, she was removed outside the city to the Benedictine nuns at Lagny, where she had almost no visitors.

"I really think," she wrote from there to Boisrobert, "that like you I shall end up loving my own sex."

The free-thinking Marais was in despair. As naive in some respects as La Fontaine's mouse meeting the cat, I too was afflicted at losing so diverting a personage, and one who claimed to base her friendship for me on such strange foundations. But on reflection, after a few weeks had passed, I was glad the "goddess" had been taken away and that her passage through my life had had the brevity as well as the fury of a whirlwind. Having foolishly acquired the reputation of being a flibbertigibbet, I would not have gone up in respectable people's estimation by entering into an intimate friendship with Ninon. I had neither the strength nor the inclination to defy criticism; moreover I could see that Scarron was old and ill, and I knew that should I find myself a widow, without money or relatives, I would have nothing to live on but what my friends would provide. There are only two ways for a woman forced to live as a parasite off the rich and powerful to enlist their help and avoid dying of hunger: either out and out immorality, which brings in plenty of gold, or discreet respectability, which may be worth a pension. Whether from fear of God or lack of fire, I inclined toward the second solution.

As my fits of devotion, which closely followed my fits of melancholy, lasted scarcely any longer than they, I decided I must change my friends in order to gain the good reputation my superficial church-going could not ensure. My policy was based on that attributed to Marie de Sévigné,† who made a point of going to hear a sermon the day after a ball or masquerade. In order to enjoy myself without harming my reputation, I decided to make friends with four or five prudes in whose company I might go anywhere. People see less what you do than who you are with, as I had learned when my outings with Kind Heart and the Belle Martel earned me a reputation for gallantry which went far beyond my real essays in dalliance. I saw it was possible to combine pleasure with virtue provided one chose to be bored with certain women instead of being entertained with others. All you had to do was establish yourself as very correct by ostentatiously declining to participate in some public excursion, then secretly and with no word said join in four or five private ones.

Having settled on this strategy, I was indebted to César d'Albret for the power of putting its principles into execution. Ever since he had thought me indifferent to his charm and occupied solely with things of the mind, he had somewhat repented of the unfair way he had treated me by absenting himself for months from the rue Neuve-Saint-Louis, and I sensed I might ease his conscience by giving him an opportunity to make amends. So I told him that because of her distinguished reputation I was dying to meet and become friends with his wife. He was surprised, for the maréchale's wit was far from being as highly praised as her virtue, which was thought to be great; but he did not like to refuse me a favor which by its nature reassured him still further about my feelings toward him.

It was thus I became the close friend of Madame d'Albret, a woman of merit and outstanding piety. Her only defect, for all that virtue, was that she was a little too fond of wine, which was all the more extraordinary because in those days women never drank at all, or at least only wine and water. I remember being there one day when she looked at herself in the mirror and finding she had a red nose said to herself, "Where in the world could I have got that nose?" Little Matha, who was standing behind her, muttered, "From the sideboard." I had much trouble not to laugh and thus jeopardize weeks of patient truckling. The haziness caused by wine, added to her natural silliness, prevented Madame d'Albret from being a very agreeable companion, and after spending some whole afternoons with her I understood better what it was the maréchal sought elsewhere.

But I held to my resolution, cost me what it might. I sewed tapestry with her for hours on end, practically without uttering a word. I went with her to see plays: the poor woman could never understand anything that was happening on the stage and needed me with her to explain what was going on before her very eyes. I accompanied her to vespers and to hear sermons, for she required me as an interpreter if she was to have any inkling of what the priest was saying. In short, I constantly did my best to please her, and this charmed her, for she was not used to such attention either from her husband or from his friends. Thanks to the friendship she conceived for me I was soon able to go to the best houses in the Marais and was admitted into the circle of virtuous, well-bred women whom I had had little opportunity of meeting in the Hôtel Impecuniosity or in Ninon's bedroom.

Madame d'Albret introduced me to the duchesse de Richelieu, to whom she was in a way related since the duchesse's first husband was a younger brother of the maréchal. One day Madame d'Albret sent a servant to bid me come to her house.

"There, Madame," she said to the duchesse when I arrived, "here's the person I was telling you about, who is so witty and knows so much. Come, Mademoiselle Scarron, say something."

She called me "Mademoiselle" after the old custom of the nobility, for she thought I was a mere bourgeoise.

"Madame," she went on, "now you will see how she can talk."

Seeing me hesitating, she thought she ought to give me some help, as you might prompt a singer by telling her the song you would like to hear.

"Say something about religion," she told me. "You can talk about something else afterwards."

I was more embarrassed than I can say, and cannot even remember how I acquitted myself. I could not have done too badly though, for the duchesse de Richelieu in her turn took to me and introduced me into other circles.

It was through her that I got to know Madame Fouquet, the grass widow of the financial secretary. She was amiable, sad and pious, and I used to go and see her at Saint-Mandé whenever one of our friends could lend me his carriage to go there. I was so fond of her company that Scarron began to tease me about the frequency of my visits, saying there must be something immoral about my liking for the lady. In her house I sometimes met the little marquise de Sévigné, who was a great friend of the financial secretary and his wife. I greatly admired the sprightliness and playful wit of this young widow, whose fire stood out against the ashes of her usual background of bigots. But although I laughed with her, I somewhat mistrusted her character—she prided herself on her birth, and I feared her contempt when I was no longer in fashion all the more because she struck me as extremely volatile. Even her eyes were changeable, brown, green or blue according to the time of day or the light, and since the eyes are the mirror of the soul this seemed to me to be Nature's warning to those who came near her not to put too much reliance upon her friendship.

I had more confidence in that of Madame de Montchevreuil, another pious lady who was Madame Fouquet's neighbor. Although her company was far from being as agreeable as that of Madame de Sévigné, for she was extraordinarily ugly, thin and sallow, and had so little wit she was almost inane, I soon realized she had a sound and almost rustic heart, an equable temperament and above all an affection for me so strong and sincere I could not help being touched by it. By associating with ladies of quality, I had got into the habit of making all the effort myself, without their ever doing anything to try to please me. So I was surprised now to see one of them come all the way to meet me without my having to move an inch. Madame de Montchevreuil became so violently attached to me that she protested she loved me like a sister when we had met only two or three times. And as she was too unsophisticated and too naive mentally to feign what she did not feel, her protestations of friendship, excessive though they were, reflected her true feelings. So I allowed myself to become intimate with her, the more so since she was the only one of all these pious ladies who was about my own age. All the rest were fifteen or twenty years older.

I responded to her friendship with small services which she appreciated all the more because she had few servants of her own, being then almost as poor as I. I remember going to see her one day when she expected company and wanted her room to be clean; she could not clean it herself because she was ill, nor could she get her servants to do what was necessary, for at that time she had none. So I set to work and scrubbed the floor with a will, and I did not think the work beneath me. Though I was unsure about my fate, I was very certain of my worth, and I believed then as now that while one cannot acquire the breeding one does not possess, neither can one lose the breeding one has.

My very pride made me obliging, and I did Madame de Montchevreuil, and on occasion the duchesses d'Albret and de Richelieu, all kinds of services. I wrote their business letters, did their accounts and ran a thousand little errands such as fetching water and finding a carriage, which the introduction of bells has since rendered less inconvenient. At Madame de Montchevreuil's I was always surrounded by children. I taught one to read and another to repeat his catechism and shared with them all everything I knew.

I made such efforts to respond to the lady's feelings for me and show myself worthy of her esteem that she insisted the following summer on taking me with her to the country, where she was to give birth to another child. The estate was her husband's château in the Vexin, where his family had its origins.

The château was in fact quite a small, dilapidated house, and the land itself was equally neglected for lack of money. I spent only a few days there, doing my best to help, and it was then, as I have already mentioned, that I put my uncle de Villette's instruction at Niort fair into practice and sold the calf. As I was entering the house with the fifteen livres from the sale carefully bunched up in my apron, I passed a magnificently dressed young nobleman on his way out. He looked at me curiously and smiled. I blushed to the roots of my hair, thinking he was laughing at my soiled apron, dirty shoes and rustic appearance. He went on his way without saying anything, and I, taking him for some wealthy neighbor, did not even try to find out who he was. I could not know I would subsequently have a hundred opportunities to see those slightly scornful lips wearing that same tender, mocking smile.

When I stop and think about those days, I wonder at my ability to get used to every kind of situation and society. I had been a typical *poitevine* in Poitou, an *Indienne* in America, a Huguenot in Mursay, a Catholic in Paris. I had been a drawing-room coquette, then a virtuous society lady. I had been friends with chambermaids and duchesses and been sought after by atheists and bigots alike. I had been as much at ease with Ninon as with poor Madame de Montchevreuil. I had been maid or mistress according to circumstance and always given general satisfaction. I had become so skilful at adapting myself to my current circle and making them like me, and there was sometimes so little connection between the personalities I assumed one after the other or all at once, that I sometimes wondered who I really was. The need to be liked by everyone, which had been a condition of survival in the deserted state to which I was born, had become second nature. My ideal was to cut a fine figure of no matter what kind and to win general approval. I was capable of enduring anything to make people speak well of me. I imposed many constraints on myself, but I did not mind so long as I was liked and well thought of. I did not care a jot for wealth; I was miles above sordid self-interest; but I did want honor and glory, and the wholehearted pursuit of this goal gave my character its unity and sincerity.

To go back to 1657, where I interrupted my story, my thirst for honors was momentarily assuaged when I least expected it. Queen Christina of Sweden, visiting Paris, wished to meet Monsieur Scarron. He had himself carried to the Louvre on his plinth, and I accompanied him, most embarrassed at having to make my first appearance at the palace as part of such a strange equipage. After having talked at length and laughed a great deal with the poet himself, whom she authorized to call himself her "chevalier" and her "Roland," the Queen addressed a few words to me. She found me graceful and witty and was kind enough to say she was not surprised that Scarron, with the most charming wife in Paris, was the merriest man in the capital despite all his ills. This unexpected tribute spread quickly round the town and filled me with pride.

The duchesse de Richelieu, however, pointed out that a respectable woman would not glory in such praise, when the only other person of her sex in France the eccentric Queen had chosen to single out was a notorious courtesan. It was true that Queen Christina, passing through Lagny, had insisted on meeting Ninon and spending a whole afternoon talking to her in her convent. After which she left for Rome, advising young King Louis to frequent Mademoiselle de Lenclos if he wished to learn good breeding and requesting the Queen Mother not to let a woman of such extraordinary worth waste away in a nunnery. The strange thing was that while the King, from whom I later heard about the Amazon Queen's suggestions, felt no need to follow his cousin Christina's advice, Queen Anne, despite her religious principles, authorized Ninon to return to her house in the rue des Tournelles in May of the same year.

As soon as she was back in her kingdom, the Marais, Mademoiselle de Lenclos wanted to see me, according to her for the pleasure of my conversation. Although her compulsory absence had enabled me to measure the danger of being too close to her, I could not resist doing as she wished, so pleasant, witty and instructive did she seem to me still.

Besides, I was no longer the giddy young thing I had been two years earlier. I was beginning to know very well where I was going and what kind of games were played in society, and I concluded that my calls upon the "goddess" would not do me much harm provided I strengthened my new reputation for virtue by more regular visits to the hospital and a few extra afternoons of penance and embroidery at the duchesse de Richelieu's. One session with Ninon and two with "hideous Hélène," as people called the duchesse, whose face was not very attractive, seemed to me the right mixture, and one guaranteed to save me from suspicion.

And so it turned out, except for one day when Madame de Sévigné, who had reasons of her own for disliking Ninon—she had once stolen her husband—said in the midst of a circle of pious dames, "Well, it may be that Madame Scarron does nothing worse at Mademoiselle de Lenclos's than at La Charité,† but it is certainly less edifying for the world in general." This treacherous remark soon went the rounds, and here and there I met with some faint remonstrances. I answered that I went to see Ninon on the instructions of my husband; as he could no longer visit the rue des Tournelles himself, he sent me as his ambassador. People had the good taste to accept this explanation.

So I went once or twice a week to Ninon's house, where I knew I should find my maréchal, sitting by the hearth so many thwarted lovers had blackened with their fiery sighs. The hours I spent there seemed like minutes. Anyone who has not seen Ninon sitting on a stool and accompanying herself languishingly on the lute singing "Memories of love," or dancing a saraband as gracefully as an Italian actress, knows nothing of beauty. And anyone who has never heard her recite poetry, philosophize gaily about love and friendship or airily recount some new amorous anecdote without ever lapsing into malicious gossip, does not know what wit is. I was soon almost as infatuated with the lovely libertine as I had been with my beautiful Soeur Céleste, though to all appearances there seemed little similarity between the two friendships. I did not, however, let myself be led astray by the ribaldry Mademoiselle de Lenclos indulged in when she started to dogmatize about religion. Sometimes I even showed my disapproval, with some haughtiness.

So Ninon, who was fond of me, did her best to avoid the subject when I was present.

"Let us talk about something else," she would say when Alexandre d'Elbène or someone else was goading her to blaspheme. "Madame Scarron fears God."

Not that this stopped her from occasionally throwing me a challenge I declined to accept: "Do you not think, Françoise, that people who need religion to tell them how to behave are to be pitied? I think it a sure sign of a narrow mind or a depraved heart."

One day when with great difficulty I had on some invented excuse stolen an afternoon of freedom from Madame de Richelieu, who would now scarcely let me out of her sight, I slipped quietly into Ninon's room and was surprised to find her deep in conversation with a gentleman with his back turned toward me. She seemed to be rebuking him for something, and with some vehemence.

"One of these days, my dear, you will have some horrid duel that will leave you very sorry, me not easily consolable and your child without support . . . You never enter the lists except to disturb somebody else's peace of mind. Confess now, a mistress without lovers would hold no attraction for you . . ."

She paused on seeing me and said,

"I don't think you know the marquis?"

While she spoke, I had come face to face with the gentleman, and I do not think I could have been more astonished if I had found myself confronted with the Devil himself. It was the man I had passed in the vestibule at the Montchevreuils', and he was looking at me with the same smile and the same mocking air as when he had seen me dressed like a shepherdess.

"Oh, but indeed we do know one another!" I heard him answer for me. "Nobody who has once met Mademoiselle could ever forget her. She has the finest eyes in the world and a way of wearing her apron that is all her own."

I must have blushed at this speech as I did at my first meeting with Ninon, for the traitor whispered, "I told you to have your blood let!"

Somehow, despite the shock, I managed to say somewhat

curtly, "If Monsieur says so, we must have met before, but I have not even the honor of knowing his name."

"Louis de Mornay," he said with a bow, "marquis de Villarceaux and cousin to Monsieur de Montchevreuil, who I believe is a friend of yours."

Now I was sure my intuition had not deceived me: this really was the Devil. He had the appropriate smile and way of speaking, the too sharp eyes, the too sweet manners and even a red doublet. Above all, the reputation.

All that I had heard about him from Madeleine Croissant, Boisrobert, Scarron himself and others, and to which I thought I had paid little attention, now came back to me with a rush. His love affair with the beautiful Madame de Castelnau, who slept with him under a full-length portrait of her husband, a lieutenant-general, and who at the critical moments would gasp alternately, "G-great hero, will you ever forgive me?" and "How could I b-betray such a b brave man?" His struggles for possession of another mistress with Jérôme de Nouveau, whom he infuriated one day by bringing him two hundred letters from the lady in question, together with some portraits and bracelets made of hair from all over, saying "he who has had the least of her must hand her over to the other." His mad liaison with Ninon, who for his sake had sacrificed her "payers," Paris, her friends and even her long golden hair, which she had cut short just to please him. The violence of his jealousies, the fierceness of his quarrels over gaming, the pranks of his brother the abbé, his own atheistic excesses, his spells in the Bastille, his singular extravagance, the even more singular extent of his wealth—his sumptuous châteaux, his pack of seventy hounds, his horses and carriages . . . And his eyes. He had only two of those, but they shone like ten thousand diamonds.

I did not feel much inclined to pursue a long conversation with a man like this. His mere presence caused me an uneasiness I had never experienced before: it gripped my stomach, heated my cheeks, brought a lump to my throat and made my legs tremble so much I felt I should fall down if I did not find a chair or stool nearby. I had no doubt but that this was the effect produced by the effluvium of his vices and congratulated myself on being so good a Christian that I could smell it from afar and feel such strong aversion. After two or three polite words, and as soon as Ninon had told the marquis who I was, for he persisted in thinking me unmarried, I left the gentleman standing. He was quite put out, for he was in the mood for banter.

I sought refuge with my old chevalier de Méré, who had just entered and who to me, who had just seen the Devil, seemed almost like God.

It was quite a long while before I met the marquis again. Since the end of his affair with Ninon two years earlier he was not often seen in the rue des Tournelles except for brief calls to get news of the son he had had with Ninon, whom she had put out to nurse in the country. He did not frequent the Scarron circle, still less the afternoon causeries of my pious lady friends. I could not help asking his cousin Madame de Montchevreuil about him, and Boisrobert, who lived in the same house.

No one thought fit to say any great harm of him, but neither did anyone tell me anything good. At the most they agreed, like the maréchal d'Albret whom I steered on to the subject, that Villarceaux had not distinguished himself in the wars, having known no other battlefield than Ninon's bed, but that there he had fought ardently enough to seize the citadel and keep it longer than anyone before him. And after all, this feat of arms was as good as another.

As the months went by I forgot him.

Life went on as usual in the rue Neuve-Saint-Louis. Monsieur Scarron wrote long poems and songs in which, though in private he expressed himself completely reassured about my good behavior since I had made friends with the most virtuous women in Paris, he narrated my alleged infidelities. Fortunately he did not name me.

> *Ingrate, I love but you*
> *And you feign love, ingrate!*
> *But while of faith you prate*
> *Your heart is most untrue!*
> *Ingrate, I love but you.*

I protested one day that all these complaints were unfounded.

"I know," he said. "But I do not love you any more than Petrarch loved Laura or Dante Beatrice. They are just the diversions of a scribbler who has to squeeze out sighs and tears every day to keep the pot boiling."

In reality things were not going too well. One evening, after being present at a brilliant supper party, my brother, Charles, who used to come and see us on his occasional visits to Paris, said to me:

"Well, Sister, you've come a long way since the days when you used to go with me begging your bread through the streets of La Rochelle. I am delighted with your present prosperity. What a fine thing marriage is for a woman!"

"I may have changed my status when I got married," I replied, "but I did not change my situation."

Lifting my petticoats a little, I laughingly showed him the holes poverty had worn in my shoes. I confessed that we had recently been obliged to sell most of the silver I had been so proud of, that the roast for our suppers was getting hard to come by, and that as the plates were handed round, Monsieur Scarron and I had to perform prodigies of ingenuity to prevent our guests from noticing that some item or other was missing. If it were not for our friends, I said, we should soon be without a roof over our heads or wood to keep us warm.

Charles did not seem unduly upset. At least he did not see fit to expedite the repayment of his debt, which was long overdue. He repaid me with two or three grimaces and four or five jests, and I fell into his arms laughing; I loved him. He was all the family I had. There was no one else with whom I could talk over the unhappy days of our strange childhood. So when he deposited his luggage for a few days at the Hôtel Impecuniosity, it was a holiday for me. For the sake of our old friendship I willingly forgave him for not keeping his word about money, for drinking our wine rather too fast and for making free with my maids before my very eyes.

Toward the middle of 1658 Boisrobert brought Scarron a note from his landlord, Monsieur de Villarceaux. The marquis, emerging from a short stay in the Bastille, humbly begged the favor of being admitted to our company one evening. Scarron was grateful to Monsieur de Villarceaux for having offered to help him at the failure of the Fronde, when all his friends were deserting him to curry favor with the Cardinal. So he welcomed the marquis's very courteous request. I, remembering the first impression Monsieur de Villarceaux had made upon me, tried to invent the excuse of some urgent visit to the hospital, or perhaps a sermon delivered by the young Bossuet, said to be so gifted that he filled churches to overflowing. My husband would not hear of my being absent.

Since I had no choice, I received Ninon's former lover pleasantly, but every time I drew near him I felt so physically ill that my head swam. I mechanically drew my kerchief more tightly over my bosom, and even made myself ridiculous by unconsciously pulling down my skirt as if to hide my ankles, which were already hidden in any case. As soon as I made this convent-girl gesture, which set me among the fools rather than the prudes, I was so astonished and ashamed I looked around to see if anyone had noticed. All I encountered was the mocking glance of Monsieur de Villarceaux, who took advantage of my confusion to undress me calmly from head to foot in his imagination. But he behaved perfectly the whole time and managed to flatter Monsieur Scarron so skilfully that he was asked to come again as often as he liked.

"Villarceaux is very rich, you see," said my husband as he was being put to bed, "and before long I might write him a little dedication."

Of the two, however, Villarceaux was the first to write. Admittedly, as he did not print what he wrote, it did not take him so long.

One evening I found a note on my dressing table, left by one of my servants who had been prevailed upon by the marquis's crowns, which were certainly more tangible than potable gold.

"I am in despair, Madame," he wrote, "because all declarations of love are alike and yet feelings may differ so. I am convinced my feeling for you is greater than what men commonly call love, but I can tell you of it only in the words men commonly use. I am aware it seems unlikely a man as fickle as I have been, alas, could be made constant by goodness and modesty, even when, as in the present case, those virtues are joined to the greatest beauty. But amazed as I am myself, and as you may be also, I love you. I have loved you since the first day I saw you, and I shall love you until the last moment of my life. But your pride, which I find so captivating, makes me fear I may not be given a hearing. Please think, then, on the way I shall behave toward you, and if it shows you that to continue so long unabated, it must stem from a real passion, accept the evidence and know that if I love you so much when you do not love me, I should quite adore you if you gave me reason to be grateful."

This letter, which I was weak-minded enough to read to the end, struck me as touching but too studied, nor was it consistent with what I had been led to believe about the marquis's character. I did not reply. A few days later the marquis had the audacity to renew his protestations in the very vestibule leading to my husband's room.

"If you are not believed when you speak of your love," I said, "it is not because that love is unwelcome but because you speak of it too well. Great passions are usually more shy. It seems to me you write like a man of much wit who is not at all in love but wishes to be thought so. So I must ask you to stop playing a game which does not amuse me, or else to stop coming to my house."

That kept him quiet for a while, and then one day he did something I could not understand. I had a very pretty amber fan which I had bought once on the advice of the maréchal, and when I laid it down for a moment on the table, the marquis, either carelessly or by deliberate design, picked it up and broke it in two. I was surprised and shocked, and somewhat grieved as well, for I had been fond of it. The next day the wretched fellow sent me a dozen fans just like the one he had broken, perhaps to show me how rich he was and at the same time to force me to accept his presents. I sent a message saying there was no point in breaking one fan and then sending twelve others, and that while he was about it I would as soon have had thirteen. I sent them all back and went without a fan at all. I told this story to all my lady friends and made him laughed at everywhere for his foolish gift. But he was not discouraged.

My scorn only increased his folly, and he started to pester me by having love letters left everywhere—in the pockets of my aprons, in my comfit-boxes, the books I was reading, even my Psalter. Every time I saw his handwriting I felt the same confusion as in his presence; just to touch a piece of paper he had touched made me feel quite faint and ill. Seeing he would not leave me in peace, I endeavored to speak sternly to him again, though I shrank from being alone with him.

"There is no need for you to bribe my servants," I told him. "I do not read your letters, and all that will happen is that I shall be obliged to dismiss all my maids."

The marquis was not used to being rebuffed in this way, and as he was by nature arrogant and aggressive, pride for the moment got the better of pretended love.

"You'd have to be able to pay their wages first," he answered.

This supercilious reminder of a poverty of which I was ashamed made me furious, and I shut my door to him for good and all. But he was the kind of man to climb back through the window.

He went about everywhere flaunting such dreadful despair at my cruelty that some people took it upon themselves to reproach me for it. In those days it was not the custom for a respectable woman to shut the door on an admirer who had not exceeded the limits of deference and good breeding. A declaration of love accompanied by public protestations was not regarded as something requiring secrecy and mystification. D'Albret, Boisrobert and even Ninon spoke in the marquis's favor.

"Come now," said Mademoiselle de Lenclos, "even if—especially if—you grant him nothing, could you not be less cruel and at least stop depriving him of your presence? You did not banish your other admirers in this way."

"Madame," I replied, "I confess it is not only out of concern for convention that I have ceased seeing Monsieur de Villarceaux. It is because I hate him more than anyone else in the world. My feeling is so strong I ought to acknowledge it to my confessor."

"You really loathe my poor marquis's company so much?"

"More than I can say. Sometimes his mere presence makes me almost swoon with horror."

"Swoon, you say? Then I fear it is much more serious than you think. At any rate, I am sure that if I were to tell this to our friend Villarceaux this evening he would jump for joy."

"How could that be?"

"It could be, it could be, I assure you. What a child you are! Be more indifferent or you are lost."

Boisrobert took to hymning his landlord's blighted hopes:

> *What can ail you, Marquis mine?*
> *We who see you peak and pine,*
> *Dull in city, sad at court,*
> *Eyes unseeing, lost in thought,*
> *Absent still where'er you rove,*
> *Must conclude you are in love.*
> *Can it be a certain fair,*
> *Black of eye, with chestnut hair,*
> *On whom your glance is ever bent*
> *With meaning far from innocent?*
>
> *If 'tis she for whom you smart,*
> *Then, my friend, accept my pity,*
> *For the lady of your heart*
> *Is near as proud as she is pretty.*

Fortunately this effusion passed almost unnoticed between Gilles Ménage's "capriccio amoroso alla gentilissima e bellissima signora Francesca d'Aubigni" and La Mesnardière's latest epistle, which assured me that the suns of the West Indies darted forth no more fires than did the "two glorious stars" men worshiped in my eyes.

Thinking over what I had been told, I concluded that Monsieur de Villarceaux was not any more guilty than all the rest, and, having ceased to fear him because I no longer saw him, I allowed him to return to the rue Neuve-Saint-Louis. My only condition was that he should promise to be respectful and obedient. He promised all that was asked of him. But it was no more possible for Louis de Villarceaux to be good than for the Devil to turn monk.

No sooner had he set foot in our vestibule than he began his antics again, throwing himself at my feet to mimic a sinner at communion and saying, "Madame, I am not worthy you should receive me, but say just one word and my heart will be cured." And so forth, all intermingled with tender speeches, sighs and ready floods of tears.

One evening when he was kneeling in front of me and importuning me thus, he seized my hand and I was unable to snatch it away. As soon as he touched me, I was drained of all strength and as if devoid of feeling. I could escape the spell only by fleeing to my room. This time my malaise was so severe I thought I was really ill, and I had myself bled three times, much as I hated that operation. I drank mineral waters and took purges, but all to no avail. In the end I was obliged to admit the astounding fact that against my will I loved the marquis de Villarceaux. I was none too sure what sort of love it was—the mind had nothing to do with it, and even the heart played no great part. I was so unfortunate as to love a man I did not respect. I blushed for my weakness, and still more for my lover.

Although it had been quite different in the case of Monsieur d'Albret, I scarcely thought of Monsieur de Villarceaux at all when I was away from him and could easily have forgotten him if he had not contrived to be always in my way. He soon realized that I knew my uneasiness at last for what it was, and that the bolder he grew the less I could resist him. I sought help from my maids and wanted them always with me, but he had won them over long before, and they took the first opportunity that arose to leave us alone. Although I understood very well what was going on, I could not, as he knew, threaten seriously to dismiss them, because I could not afford to pay them their wages. I was forced to give ground little by little, clinging to the thought that I was holding out in the last citadel. He kept urging me to surrender and delighted in overturning one by one the frail obstacles I tried to interpose between us.

"My husband . . ."

"You don't love him. And he surely doesn't expect you to go hungry all your life when he satisfied his ample appetite long ago."

"Other people . . ."

"I am neither ungrateful nor indiscreet."

"God, who knows everything . . ."

"He won't tell."

It was all the more difficult for me to resist because I was getting no support from anyone else. Madame de Montchevreuil had returned to the country, and in any case she and her husband were almost blindly fond of their cousin. Ninon still had so much affection for this man who had once been the object of her passion that she put his happiness before my peace of mind. Scarron had other things to worry about.

His health was failing. He could no longer write long works and applied his talents to brief epigrams and lessons in versification for provincial ladies. Even his company was going out of fashion. Too many tedious nonentities now came to the rue Neuve-Saint-Louis and spoiled the conversation; the most undistinguished banker was welcome so long as he brought a ham with him. Things got so bad there were days when I refused to appear in the yellow room and shut myself up in my own quarters, as on the occasion when the tiresome comte du Lude, the little marquise de Sévigné's lover, invited himself to supper on the grounds that he had had a grouse and a basket of pears delivered beforehand.

People hurried to Ninon's, hastened to Madame de La Fayette's and were beginning to find their way to the hôtel de Richelieu, while the Hôtel Impecuniosity was turning into an inn where the guests brought their own food, and was gradually sinking into silence and oblivion. My husband was worried about all this far more than about the intrigues of a man none too sane and a woman all too virtuous.

Seeing myself on the point of surrender, I called on my only remaining resource and turned to my Heavenly Father with the hope born of desperation. I haunted the churches; I plunged into prayer. I had never come so close to sin; my reputation had never been so high. The more I despaired of my weakness, the more I was praised for my regular religious observance. Occasionally I found some peace in front of the altar, but Villarceaux was always waiting for me outside.

He laughed at my excessive devotion. Prudes, he said, usually went to church only after the sin had been committed, and it was strange to see me praying by way of precaution. But unworthy as I was, God did help me: I realized that although I did not have too much esteem for Monsieur Scarron, I had a great respect for the sacrament of marriage, and nothing could make me break a contract to which God was one of the parties.

Finally, my pride put the finishing touch to my resolution. I was snatched back from the brink by the fear of spoiling my own image of myself in an unsavory adventure with a man who would only laugh at me afterwards. Monsieur de Villarceaux, seeing my early favors were followed by nothing more, lost his temper and went so far as to remonstrate with me in public.

It was one evening at Ninon's. The company had been talking about Madame de Langey, who had asked the Congress† to allow her to prove publicly that her husband was incapable of consummating their marriage and had left her a virgin as before. Someone asked me if I intended to go, for it was then the fashion, even for the most religious and sensible people, to go and watch the indecent spectacle of a man and a woman jousting with one another in front of a board of priests and doctors just as if they were alone in the privacy of the bedchamber. I replied that I certainly should not go, and that moreover I was thoroughly tired of all the nastiness that was being exchanged about the case in the salons.

"You are right not to go," said Monsieur de Villarceaux to me in front of everyone. "If Monsieur de Langey were successful, and at last found in his breeches the wherewithal to win the case, you might learn something. You might even be sorry for what you've missed."

From this we saw that the flights passion inspired in him were far from insipid. They had all the piquancy of insults.

I am surprised that I should feel the humiliation of those insults more forcibly now than I did at the time Monsieur de Villarceaux inflicted them on me. This is probably the reason why, with the passage of time, a love which was long, variable and in the end very passionate on both sides seems to have left in my heart only painful memories, obliterating all the accompanying joys.

True, when people have ceased to love one another, the fact that they did so once gives no more satisfaction than does the memory of having drunk when one is no longer thirsty. But the deteriorating remembrance of this particular passion seems to me due to a peculiarity of my own nature rather than the inevitable evolution of feelings in general. When I am hurt, all I feel at the time is a kind of superficial prick; the moment when the wound is made is the moment when I feel it least. In early life I sometimes used to doubt whether I had been hurt at all, for in the midst of astounding reverses, unexpected sufferings and sudden misfortunes I easily put on an air of indifference which deceived even myself. As time went by and the memory of what had caused them faded, pains which had been slight at first began to be more severe. The further my emotions were from their source, the deeper and wider they became, like a river running its course through my life, ever more vast and irresistible, until many years later and in a completely different landscape, it filled my thoughts like a boundless sea. I was well aware how pointless such feelings were, out of their proper place in time and space, but they affected my mind so strongly that they eclipsed immediate joys and sorrows. I have never been able to experience together at one and the same time what has happened to me and the feelings to which those events gave rise.

The last few months of my life with Monsieur Scarron were spent in trouble and uncertainty. His illness and our poverty grew worse simultaneously, and both were then approaching their climax.

The twisted limbs of this poor "abridgment of human woe" were now so bent his knees pressed into his ribs. They caused him such pain in his chest I had to put small squares of cloth in between to lessen the bruising. Even opium no longer made him sleep. "If I could do away with myself," he told one of his friends, "I'd have taken poison long ago."

Enfeebled as he was, he still found the strength to have himself carried to the treasury offices to ask for another advance on the pension granted him by Monsieur Fouquet. But the officials there were tired of his ceaseless requests, and they had their servants cudgel our man and threatened his master with the same fate if he dared come begging again.

"My only hope now is the potable gold," he said to me one night with tears in his eyes. I had no expectations at all from that quarter and was terrified.

Poverty even forced me to decline an offer which we thought might turn out useful to me in the future. Mademoiselle de Mancini, known as Marie and said to be the young King's mistress, sent a message asking me to go with her to Brouage, where her uncle the Cardinal required her to retire for a while. I could not accept as I had neither clothes nor coach in which to go to Saintonge and cut a dash.

Instead, Monsieur Scarron and I went to Fontenay-aux-Roses, where my sister-in-law Françoise had a modest country house. The poor invalid thought the change of air might improve his health. I saw it chiefly as a chance to escape the harassments of our landlord, Monsieur Mérault, and his bailiffs, and the different importunities of Monsieur de Villarceaux.

When we returned to Paris it was plain to everyone that Scarron would never finish the third part of his *Roman comique.* The gazettes all gave him out as dead. He agreed, in one of his last epistles, that he would die before long, but that it would be of starvation.

Edible contributions appeared more and more rarely at our table, and if I had not been sometimes able to sup at the house of one of the pious great ladies who now sought my company, I might have run the risk of accompanying my husband into the grave. Quite apart from the pleasure of eating a capon from time to time, I valued the friendship of people of quality all the more because I could see the time coming when I would find myself turned out into the street and dependent on the great for my subsistence. All in all, I felt I would rather owe my bread to friendship than to charity.

So I went everywhere with Madame d'Albret and Madame de Richelieu, and it was in their company that in April 1660, from a balcony in the rue Saint-Antoine, I watched King Louis's entry into Paris on his return from Spain after his marriage. I was pleased to recognize Beuvron in the procession, marching in the rear of the light cavalry; and Villarceaux, riding a fiery steed, stood out as one of the most elegantly clad gentlemen, his fine dark face as usual winning general admiration. But, as was only right, it was the King who struck me as the most magnificent. I wrote that evening, in a letter to a friend, that "the Queen must have gone to bed very pleased with the husband of her choice."

That procession was my last diversion as a married woman. Soon afterwards Monsieur Scarron was dying. In the streets of Paris and the houses of the Marais people were heartless enough to mock at this, just as they had laughed at his marriage. Pamphleteers hastened to bring out two sham prayers and a description of his funeral, which were hawked outside our very windows. The drawing-rooms discussed the poet's salvation in the same way as they had wagered eight years earlier on his ability to beget a child. His death was bringing him back into fashion.

With windows and shutters closed for fear of songs outside, coming and going between the medicine bottles and the commode, I tried to persuade the poor man to confess his sins, but his atheist friends, especially Alexandre d'Elbène and my maréchal d'Albret, came and undid by day what I had done by night. If I got him to agree to see a priest, they would say he must be jesting, that he was not so ill as all that, and that there was no hurry. Finally I flew into a rage with them and was surprised to receive support from Ninon, who had no objection to keeping up appearances at the last gasp. She arrived just as I was admitting a Capuchin friar to Scarron's bedside. Ninon, in her own particular way, exhorted them both to do their duty. As the dying man was still arguing a little with what the priest was saying, she broke in and said to the latter, "Come, Monsieur, do your duty. My friend may argue, but he knows no more about it than you do."

After he had received extreme unction, Monsieur Scarron spoke to me.

"I am not leaving you much in the way of property," he said quite affably, "but try to remain virtuous."

I told him I knew what my mind owed to his, and that such a legacy was not to be scorned.

"My only regret," he said to Segrais, "is that I have nothing to leave my wife. She is most deserving, and I have every reason to be proud of her."

He told me that if I had "taken the plunge" before he died, he would willingly have forgiven me, for our life together, agreeable as it had been sometimes, had not always been a very happy one for a young woman. In short he was much gentler and more restrained toward me on his deathbed than he was in the *Testament burlesque* published after his death but written several years earlier. In it he bequeathed me the right to marry again for fear of worse, since the deprivation I suffered as his wife must have sharpened my appetite.

He died during the night of the 6 to the 7 October 1660, with as much decency, if not as much sanctity, as possible.

In composing his own epitaph he had congratulated himself in advance on the fact that the night of his death would be the first in which he could get to sleep. For similar reasons I was at first glad rather than sorry that he had breathed his last. Now that I could no longer do anything for him, I slept for thirty hours at a stretch; I had not closed my eyes for many nights, sitting up with him to keep him company.

His poor body was buried in Saint-Gervais, at the expense of the parish. I broke with custom and attended his funeral. The very next day the bailiffs put seals on the doors and at the creditors' request made an inventory of everything, including my shifts and petticoats. Monsieur Scarron had left ten thousand francs' worth of property, and twenty-two thousand francs' worth of debts.

At his death I was once again without any family and penniless. But I was twenty-four, and mourning suited me wonderfully.

Eight

My eight years of marriage were soon accounted for. The balance was entirely positive as far as the mind and knowledge of the world were concerned. I had a perfect understanding of Spanish and Italian; I knew enough Latin; I could write pleasing verses; I knew and was known by the most influential people at Court and in financial circles—better still, they liked me. But as regards the heart the balance was nil. I no longer hoped ever to experience the feelings one read about in novels. I saw that men, when they were not driven by passions and sometimes even when they were, were not kind in their friendships. As for finding what I longed for in complete surrender to the love of God, I could not even think of it, for my piety was still nothing but worldly prudence. In the autumn of 1660 I was divided between anxiety at being suddenly without either food or shelter and relief at being able to enjoy a hitherto unknown liberty.

All the furniture in the rue Neuve-Saint-Louis had been seized in the week following Scarron's death, and everything, even including the invalid's chair, had been publicly auctioned at our very door. I had not been able to pay the servants all their wages, but I compensated them as best I could, giving my husband's clothes to Jean Brillot and the gowns which I as a widow could not wear to my own maid. I was informed that if I pleaded my cause properly against our creditors, who included my sister-in-law Françoise, the duc de Tresmes and some of our former friends, I might hope to clear between four and five thousand francs, for Monsieur Scarron had provided for a widow's dower in our marriage contract, and my claim, being the first and the largest, had priority over the others. Apart from this hope held out by the lawyers, I was in the most wretched situation—without hearth or home, without even the wherewithal to pay the baker.

Kind Heart Franquetot, who was generosity itself, offered to take me in, but I pointed out that her house was not large enough, for I did not wish, by living so intimately with her, to give the good ladies of the Marais more to gossip about. Madame d'Albret also did her best to make me promise to go to her, but I refused for fear of seeing the handsome maréchal at too close quarters.

In any case, I did not want to be dependent on anyone; I preferred to go into a convent. In thus following my own inclination, I was also making quite a sensible calculation, for the world considers it less humiliating to live in retirement in some cloister of good repute than in a poor lodging in a distant part of town. The maréchale d'Aumont, Scarron's cousin, had a furnished room in the convent of the Charité des Femmes near the place Royale which she lent to me. She was also so kind as to send me everything I needed, including some habits. I shut myself up in this retreat, at first seeing no one and so distressed at the new position in which I found myself that my sadness was ascribed to my bereavement. I believed I was not destined to be happy and tried to accept my fate with resignation and lay all my tribulations at the foot of the Cross.

I must admit, however, that I derived more consolation from the little mirror on the wall of my cell than from the crucifix that hung nearby. Nothing is more becoming to a woman who is young and beautiful than a mourning veil. Black made my complexion look paler and my eyes look darker. The dark rings under them, from watching by Monsieur Scarron's deathbed, only made my face more interesting and added to my appeal as a widow. This became clear when the first weeks of solitude were over, and I began to have a few visitors.

All my fine lady friends, who were exerting their influence in my favor, came to see me to tell me of their efforts. My godmother, Suzanne de Navailles, who had charge of the young Queen's maids of honor, and Madame de Montauzier were trying to get the Queen Mother to give me a pension. Madame Fouquet was seeking some generous gesture from her husband. Even Madame de Richelieu, though she did not do much, appeared very concerned about my fate.

I had men visitors too. I was only a lady pensioner at La Charité Notre-Dame, so I was not enclosed. Moreover, as many of my admirers were abbés they could come and go as they pleased. The future Cardinal d'Estrées, then of the Academy, was always doing me new services which, though they did not touch my heart, were pleasing to my intellect. He brought me books and engravings and wrote me amusing letters interspersed with religious pictures and quite rare relics, which I gave away at once to the good sisters. A trace of Calvinism gave me a horror of such pagan baubles.

All this, however, did nothing to advance my affairs, and my own pride made things even worse.

The duchesse d'Aumont had told so many people of all her kindnesses to me since I had been widowed that I began to grow tired of it. I would rather have earned my bread with my own hands than endure the humiliation of so public a charity. So one day I sent back in a cart the wood she had just had noisily unloaded for me in the courtyard of the convent. Thereupon the nuns immediately received orders to work out the cost of my board and lodging and present me with the bill for the first three months of my stay. I had not a sou to my name and was about to pack my things when the mother superior came and told me that Monsieur and Madame de Montchevreuil had said they would answer for me until the end of the year. I was so grateful for their generosity that the advantages I obtained for them later, when I was in favor, never seemed to me to match the kindness they did me at a time when they were poor themselves.

Madame de Montchevreuil also invited me to her little château in Vexin for the summer. I was delighted to accept.

We made the journey by coach, in very hot weather, occupying ourselves with tapestry work. Some of Madame de Montchevreuil's young brothers-in-law threaded our needles so that we should not waste our time and made lots of jests so that they should not waste theirs. The journey was very merry, and so was our visit. The château was crowded that summer. In addition to the brothers-in-law there were several lady friends, including a witty young Ursuline nun called Madame de Brinon, as well as cousins of all ages and conditions. Hidden among them like Tom Thumb in a forest was Louis de Villarceaux, whose wife had declined to leave Paris. He stood behind everyone else, spoke little, put himself forward even less, no longer pursued me with importunities and in short behaved with such discretion and discernment that I found him tolerable again.

No country amusements were lacking. Every day there was sport and mirth all over the house and grounds: blindman's buff, more or less innocent, tag, bowls, battledore and shuttlecock. During the day there was hunting in the woods; in the evening there was talking round the fire. The men played the guitar; the girls made eyes. The food and drink were so excellent and so ample I wondered how the poor Montchevreuils could afford to be so lavish. If I had known the answer, I would have fled the place like the plague, and the marquis too, for, as I found out too late, it was he who had drawn up the list of guests, provided everything and set the table for everyone. But meanwhile I saw no further than the tip of my own nose and profited from the general merriment. While observing the discretion proper in a lady recently widowed, I joined in every excursion and partook of every collation.

One day when Monsieur de Villarceaux had to go through the fields to the village of Le Mesnil to settle some business with a farmer, and the young girl cousin who was to have gone with him was indisposed, Marguerite de Montchevreuil, who thought only of her cousin Villarceaux's amusement, told me to accompany him instead. I saw no way of avoiding this ordeal.

On the way the marquis was so distant he was scarcely polite. I was congratulating myself on this coolness when, on the way back, a trivial incident changed the whole course of my life. There had been a storm the previous day and the lanes were still wet from the rain. My shoes, though they did not yet have holes in them, were not altogether new and were far from fit to withstand these conditions, and one of my heels caught in a rut and broke off. I hobbled on as best I could, but as I had refused the arm Monsieur de Villarceaux none too cordially offered me, I could not get far without difficulty.

We had left the meadow and were in sight of the house when on the pretext of mending my shoe enough to let us get on more easily, the marquis had me sit down on a grass bank by some outbuildings, under a row of scanty laurels which Madame de Montchevreuil was trying without success to inure to the harsh local climate. I took off my shoe and gave it to him, quickly hiding my unshod foot under my skirt. Two years earlier this maneuver would have made Monsieur de Villarceaux burst out laughing, but now he did not even seem to notice.

He bent over my shoe, looked at it doubtfully and asked for the other one to compare it with. I handed it over without more ado, and he pretended to measure them against each other, turning them over and over and weighing them. Then he said:

"I am afraid I am no further forward. I am no shoemaker. I shall have to carry you home."

"No need for that," I said. "I can manage on my own."

And with that he threw both my shoes over the hedge.

"Do you mean you would go barefoot through all this mud?"

I was so astounded at what he had done that for the moment all I could think of was my stockings, which were about to be ruined by the mud and the stones, and which I was too poor to replace. To be carried back seemed a lesser evil. But Monsieur de Villarceaux had already gone further. Taking advantage of my hesitation, he showed his hand even more clearly, resting it on my neck and toying with a lock of my hair. Again I thought of taking flight, but we were surrounded on all sides by a sea of mire.

Fear of ridicule or dread of scandal undermined my resolution and deprived me of my last chance of escape. In my mind I could already hear the quips I should be exposed to from everyone if I arrived back at the château in stockinged feet and up to the waist in mud, without any convincing explanation of what I had done with my shoes. Misplaced pride, together with poverty, brought about my downfall. Louis de Villarceaux was already gently removing my neckerchief and laying his head on my bosom.

As to what followed, I cannot claim to have been forced or even hurried into it. Pressing kisses upon my mouth and neck, the marquis carried me as far as a little barn overlooking the bank on which we had been sitting. He laid me down gently on some straw between two rows of rose laurels and orange trees in tubs which the gardeners had put there out of the storm. Having thus removed me both from the mud and from sight, he proceeded with his purpose.

He used neither haste nor violence, as if he were sure I should no longer attempt to escape and as if he did not think it worthwhile entering into any argument. Admittedly I found nothing to say throughout the whole scene except "Please, please!," which might as easily have been taken for an invitation as for a rebuff. I probably did not quite know myself how I wanted him to understand it. He took it as he pleased, and me likewise. Before I knew what was happening or could foresee all the consequences of a mere broken heel, I fell in a barn at Montchevreuil, under a crown of laurels which added nothing to my glory.

People are right when they say it is the first step that counts. I, having stumbled in every sense of the word, had nothing to stop me hurtling to my doom but Monsieur de Villarceaux's sense of decency and the love, sincere in its way, which he felt for me. I myself did not know what I ought thenceforward to allow or refuse. Fortunately all he asked was to come and see me every night in the room I had to myself in a distant recess of the château. There I gave him the welcome he looked for; sometimes I even made him stay.

Thinking it over, I cannot really say that the pleasures of love brought me happiness at first. The repugnance I had felt with Monsieur Scarron was still too strong in my memory. But I cannot pretend, either, that I felt any remorse for my sins. I was overwhelmed, and the absence of plans for the future was a source of complete peace of mind. I had ceased either tormenting or defending myself; I had stopped calculating or being afraid. I left it to someone else to organize my life and made no further attempt to dispose of myself. In short, for a few weeks I lived without thought or awareness, under a spell like Sleeping Beauty.

The naivety of those around us, fortunately, was amazing, though no greater than that shown ten years later, with respect to other love affairs, by the subtlest of courtiers. The world attaches such importance to appearances that most people are deceived if you merely observe a few definite rules. If you are never the first to mention the name of your beloved in conversation, and in private let fall a few sharp jests about him; if you are careful to seem not to know anything about your lover that everyone does not know, while pretending not to know what everyone does know; if you do not seek to speak to or of him in company, but do not particularly seek to avoid him; if, finally, you are known as the devoted friend of his mistresses or his wife, and support your own reputation for virtue by demonstrating a preference for things of the mind—then, seeing all this, fools will think you have nothing to do with the man who enjoys your favors, and even the most perspicacious will be uncertain. As with all other sins, I have found lying both easy and pleasurable, and mystery is not the least piquant spice for love.

I shall not now try to justify that adultery, and the three years of dissimulation with which I concealed it, by saying that while I was capable of calculation and disguise I was not incapable of true emotions and strong feelings. Nor shall I plead the emotional isolation in which I lived then, though sometimes it made me suffer greatly. None of these things can excuse me in other people's eyes when they fail to absolve me in my own, not only for the sin but still less for its repetition.

On my return to Paris, I gave the lie to the belief that every lady loves a lord of the Treasury by rejecting first the propositions of Monsieur de Lorme, chief clerk of the ministry of Finance, who valued me at thirty thousand crowns, and then those of secretary Fouquet, who like his superior was ready to raise the bidding. Nor would I take anything from my lover. The more overwhelmed I was by fate and the consciousness of my sin, the more I desired to support myself. I was resolved to suffer want or servitude rather than belie my own character on so essential a matter.

Then, unworthy as I was of divine solicitude, Providence came to my aid. Monsieur d'Albret had roused all his friends at the Louvre to such effect in my favor that Queen Anne, touched by reports of my distress, agreed to revive in my name the pension she had long ago ceased to pay my unfortunate husband. The grant was two thousand livres paid out of her privy purse, a modest amount but sufficient for anyone who knew how to manage it properly. This piece of good fortune, at the beginning of the winter of 1661, ended the period of my direst poverty.

At the same time Heaven sent me a first sign that I should have to change my ways. When I went to the Val-de-Grâce† to thank the Queen Mother for the pension she had just granted me, one Court lady, instead of praising the Queen's kindness like all the others, said, "The Queen does well to give a pension to the finest eyes in the world and the biggest flirt in the kingdom." When I heard this, her compliment to my eyes could not erase the rest, and I began to hate her so much that every time I met her at Court later I felt ready to swoon away. Unmerited insults are harder to bear than those one has deserved.

This warning, so disagreeably delivered, did not however give me pause. Back in my convent with my pension, I went on seeing Monsieur de Villarceaux.

I do not like to say I loved him, for I have a different idea of what love is, but his society was valuable to me. Life is a terrible adventure, an adventure so lonely that sometimes one is glad to feel one has company part of the way. Even though I found in Louis de Villarceaux neither César d'Albret's nobility of conduct, nor Monsieur de Barillon's distinction of mind, nor the gentleness of feeling of Monsieur de Beuvron, the energy of his spirit and his physical strength made him more necessary to me every day.

And, since when one is confessing one had best do it properly, I admit it pleased me to see my kisses gradually extinguish the rather cruel light which had burned in his eyes and soften the hard outline of his lips. I was delighted to discover, in his arms, a power whose sway I had never before suspected. In short, after a brief moment of abandonment, I enjoyed vanquishing my conqueror.

I have always thrown myself completely into whatever I have done and tried to do it as well as possible. If I had been bad, I believe pride and consistency would have made me carry wickedness to perfection. When I sinned, I staked my pride, or what was left of it, on not being the least skilful of sinners. I could not bear Monsieur de Villarceaux to make comparisons between me and Ninon, too often to my disadvantage. And so gradually, like Rome by Athens, the marquis found himself subjugated by his prize.

At the beginning of our relationship, first at Montchevreuil and then in Paris, he had had the advantage over me, in experience, age and absolute indifference to sin. I at that time was sunk in ignorance, painfully awkward, riddled with aversions and, when reason returned a little, harrowed with fear and remorse. To make up for my former severities, the marquis, although really very attached to me, liked to put pressure upon me in every possible way and was never sure of his power over me except when he had made me yield to his whims.

He even came to see me in the convent, accompanied by his brother the abbé, one of the most profligate of men. Sometimes he would take me to dinner in a private room at the Fox in the Tuileries, where the young King was said to have gone to dally with Mademoiselle de Mancini before either of them was married. On other days, or perhaps nights, he took me through the paths of the park at Boulogne, where ladies with solitary tastes led one another astray; or I accompanied him, masked as was then fortunately the fashion, to the fair at Bezons; or we went boating on the Seine; or again, he might take me to the fair at Saint-Germain, not the most respectable place in the world, with its noisy flutes and bagpipes, the foolish cries of its puppeteers and its crowds of wenches and pickpockets. He said it was delightful to be in turn the cause and the cure of my remorse.

Meanwhile for everyone except the Court lady whom God or the Devil had enlightened about me, I was still the virtuous widow Scarron. I had to be if I was to go on getting my pension.

I had kept up all my connections with the hôtel d'Albret and the hôtel de Richelieu. I was still great friends with Madame de Montchevreuil, and did all kinds of errands for her. I continued visiting the Hôtel-Dieu and the Quinze-Vingt,† where everyone was astonished by my indifference to the stench and my zeal in washing the filthiest bodies. And everywhere I went, I was very modestly dressed, wearing plain coarse muslin at a time when no one else did. I stood out in this simple garb, and was admired for trying not to attract admiration.

In fact I did not dress like this out of mere modesty. Being too poor to equal others in magnificence, I preferred to go to the other extreme: I chose to seem above matters of attire and adornment rather than let people think I was struggling to do the best I could. Moreover, I appeared to better advantage like that than if I had been dressed in washed-out silk, like most young ladies who try to be fashionable without having the means to succeed. My hair was simply dressed also, for nothing is more unbecoming than ringlets and ribbons worn with a gown of cheap muslin or indifferent silk. And, on the pretext that I was a widow, I concealed my bosom even more carefully than before. All this edified people considerably; society does not see into souls.

The sisters of La Charité Notre-Dame were the only ones not to be taken in by the laudable character I played in the hôtels in the Marais. They thought I saw altogether too many people in my cell; they did not like it at all; and they made so many complaints that I finally decided to leave the convent and take a lodging of my own.

I moved into a little house in the rue des Trois-Pavillons, just by the rue Pavée. The hôtel d'Albret was on the corner of the rue Pavée, and the hôtel de Richelieu a little further away on the place Royale. My house was humble but charming. A rose climbed up the yellow stucco to my window; a fountain outside my door recalled night and day the soft murmur of the rivers at Mursay.

To live there alone would have been pleasant for my love but dangerous for my reputation. With my pension, modest though it was, it would have been unseemly not to have a servant. I therefore sought a little maid to keep house for me, but I was in no hurry. On the pretext that it was difficult to find someone pleasant yet at the same time capable of doing all that was necessary, I prolonged my solitude by at first hiring women by the day.

In this way my dear marquis and I were able to spend a few nights made sweet to me by the absence of any constraint or anxiety. It was then I liked Louis de Villarceaux the best. He had at last persuaded me that he had nothing in common with my poor husband, and that if all sins are equally detestable, some are more pleasant than others. I even came to love him enough to think that certain marriages of inclination could be delightful to start with. This idea—a foolish one—came into my head one day when he was talking about his wife's illness and saying that the doctors had given her up. I could not help asking him if he would marry me if she died.

My lover was taken completely by surprise. Then, after a moment of stupor, he began to laugh.

"Françoise, are you dreaming? You are too intelligent not to know how foolish a Mornay would look marrying Monsieur Scarron's widow."

"I may not be of good enough birth to be your wife," thought I to myself, "but I have too noble a heart to remain your mistress long."

For the time being, however, I swallowed the insult in silence, having deserved it for my naivety. Besides, I owed the marquis some gratitude for thus handing me the key with which I should one day escape from the love in which I had imprisoned myself.

Now, though, it was only in himself I could find help against him, so I laid my head on his shoulder and consoled myself for my weakness at the same time as I measured my strength.

The marquis sometimes used to say, "My God, you've become an expert!"

In the morning as we lay in bed listening to the bell of Saint-Eustache, Monsieur de Villarceaux would say, "Hurry up now, Françoise—I don't want you to miss mass." He wished me to be more pious than I really was so that he could always feel himself to be the god I preferred to the real one. Fortunately for me, I have never been divided between two such unequal alternatives. I might have hidden my faith and my pride temporarily under a bushel, but I had only to bring them out again and Monsieur de Villarceaux would cease to exist.

To begin with, knowing that my lover was doomed and believing I should one day have the strength to carry out the sentence made me feel an access of tenderness toward him. Once he wanted me to wear a page's costume which he had brought me, and I did so without demur. Another time he asked me to strip naked so that he could paint me as if emerging from my bath. He filled some idle moments by exercising a small talent for painting, and the brush did homage almost as well as the artist himself to my legs and bosom. When it came to the face the portrait was luckily not so faithful as to be recognized with certainty, and as for the rest, a sheet which knew its business hid what ought to be concealed. This picture must still be in a tower in the château de Villarceaux, where I think the marquis put it; for thirty years I trembled lest it come out.

In April or May of the same year, 1662, I decided to engage the maid I had pretended to be looking for for many weeks. I settled upon a poor girl of fifteen called Nanon Balbien. She lived on the Butte Saint-Roch near one of the robbers' dens known as *cours des miracles,* the resorts of beggars and vagabonds, and her lodging looked out over a dark shop called the Fair Price.

Nanon came from the country round about Brie. The famine which that year had driven so many of the poor from the fields had brought the Balbien family to this "court" in Saint-Roch, where it had met with further disaster. The father had taken a casual job as a mason to support his family and fallen from some scaffolding; he was now a bedridden invalid. The elder brother worked as an odd-job man near the Port-Saint-Bernard, wading up to his waist in icy water all day long to bring in flotsam from the Seine to the longshoremen of the île Louviers. This had given him a continual fever and a hacking cough, and some mornings he was so ill he could find no one to employ him either at the Arsenal or at the Port-de-Grève or at the Port-au-Foin.† Four or five younger brothers covered in vermin were dying of hunger in the family room, while the mother, to keep a roof over their heads, went through the streets hawking wares belonging to the owner of the Fair Price. The family only survived thanks to the "King's corn" which was handed out on certain days from the Louvre.

Nanon, the eldest daughter, had been sent out into the fields as a child and knew nothing about housework, except that she could sew a little. But she seemed strong and goodnatured, and her family was a Godfearing one. Moreover, I saw that if I did not take her away from it, she would die of starvation. She needed me more than I needed her. So I took her on, and that day was for her the beginning of a life which, all things considered, was no less prodigious than my own.

I took Nanon back to the rue des Trois-Pavillons, dressed her properly and began to teach her a trade of which she had so far no inkling; I also taught her the alphabet, about which she was equally ignorant. At first I sometimes did her work for her so that she could get on with her reading. In short, I soon became as fond of her as if she had been my old nurse Marie de Lile when she was still a child.

I had been moved by what I had seen in her parents' house, and I resolved to do what I could to help the common people in their suffering. Although their misery was plainly visible in all the streets of Paris, perhaps even because it was so evident and one gets accustomed to anything, I had never before paid it much attention. Now I allotted one tenth of my meager income to charity and vowed to dispose in this way of everything I might possess in the future over and above what was necessary.

Nanon was too innocent and too confident of my virtue to suspect anything about my dealings with Villarceaux. But as she began to wake up a little, for she was no fool, I thought it wiser not to receive the marquis at home when I had no other visitors. Strange as it may seem, Nanon's respect meant a great deal to me, and I did not want her to have the slightest doubt about my conduct.

So I now saw the marquis alone only at the house of Mademoiselle de Lenclos, where I always went once or twice a week. Ninon sometimes used to lend us her yellow chamber, without inquiring too particularly what we did with it.

In June 1662, Montchevreuil again became the scene of our amours. I was not sorry to see again the setting of my first sin. I never passed by the outbuildings of the château and the laurels without vividly remembering my shame, but the giddiness of youth, the affection I then felt for Monsieur de Villarceaux and my ever-increasing attachment to the Montchevreuils and all their children, who were then small and charming, combined to make the Vexin countryside even more pleasant to me now than when I had seen it for the first time.

I made a striking entrance among my friends there. Out of the tiny pension which was my only income I had managed to buy so many toys for the children that I could find no room for my feet on the floor of the coach; so I lifted them up and laid them on the opposite seat, and I arrived in this position before the steps leading up to the front door. The children greeted me with transports of joy. From beneath my petticoats they drew forth a barking dog, a sedan chair with little bells, a parrot that whistled when you moved its tail, a chapel with a belfry and a procession of nuns, a little carriage with a monkey driver and countless dolls and sweetmeats. I have long had a great and even somewhat ridiculous passion for children, but I think it was then it began, and then that I started to acquire a real art in looking after them and making them love me. I never hesitated to leave my ordinary companions in order to be with children, even nurslings. This surprised some people, but did not displease mothers, who found it convenient that my preference should serve their need.

My days were passed thus in innocent diversions. My nights less so, though Monsieur de Villarceaux did not visit me as regularly as he had done the year before. I had made him aware of the risks we ran, and with a very jealous wife he was no more anxious than I to have our relationship revealed. So at night, alone in my room, I was tormented in turn by fear that he might not come and remorse that he had. The future and the past have always spoiled the present for me, though that present, when the marquis held me in his arms, was, admittedly, not without happiness or pleasure.

Marguerite de Montchevreuil told me how glad she was that my aversion for her husband's cousin had given way to friendship. She knew he was something of a freethinker but had not given up hope that, surrounded by friends like me and relatives like her, he might one day make a surprising conversion. She was convinced that when anyone came upon us talking in an arbor or a wood, we were discussing his salvation.

At Montchevreuil one country excursion succeeded another. First we picked cherries. I can still see Madame de Brinon, the young Ursuline who had broken with her convent, a friend of Madame de Montchevreuil, perched at the top of a ladder and throwing the fruit down into our aprons. After that we picked plums, to make tarts as big as millwheels; every day I was up to the elbows in flour. Then we picked apples, and drank the sweet cider straight from the press in silver goblets stamped with the Mornay arms. When the time came at last to gather the grapes, we had to shut up the house and go back to Paris in the autumn rain.

The summer of 1663 was much less agreeable. It had been said everywhere that Villarceaux had paid for everything at Montchevreuil, and Henri de Montchevreuil refused, out of pride, to accept his cousin's contributions any longer and had no visitors that year. Fortunately the marquis had enough friends not to be inconvenienced. He arranged for me to be invited by Monsieur de Valliquierville, one of his Vexin neighbors, to spend a few weeks in his château, fortunately only a couple of leagues from the marquis's own estate.

Villarceaux had already exploited his neighbor to the hilt in the past and more than once had recourse to his good offices: nine or ten years earlier Charles de Valliquierville had taken in Mademoiselle de Lenclos when the marquis and his "goddess" were enjoying their secret love in the house in Vexin, and the unexpected arrival of the marquise caused Ninon to leave in haste.

Valliquierville had formed a warm friendship, if not more, for Ninon and made it a condition of his assistance that she come with me. The marquis liked this suggestion, which would help to conceal our own dealings. If he came from Villarceaux to Valliquierville every day, people would think it was for Ninon, because of some reawakening of passion. As for me, they would think I was staying with Monsieur de Valliquierville in order to be with my friend Mademoiselle de Lenclos.

"Chaperoning Ninon may not be the best way to acquire a good reputation," the marquis said to me, "but all things considered it is less compromising than having her chaperone you!"

So that was how it was arranged. Ninon was delighted to be with Valliquierville again, for she admired his wit, and she pretended not to notice that she was acting as a cover for us. I do not know if her former lover told her anything. I myself, true to my policy of secrecy, had not spoken to her of what had happened at Montchevreuil two years earlier, and had left her in uncertainty about the nature of my feelings for the marquis.

At Valliquierville she and I slept in the same bed. The château was chill and damp, and my room, facing north, was cold even though it was summer. Ninon, seeing I was uncomfortable, kindly invited me to share her bed, where we kept each other warm as much with our minds as with our bodies. We spent hours talking, discussing love in general and carefully avoiding the particular.

Ninon's friendship made my stay at Valliquierville pleasant, but I was thwarted all the time in the expression of my passion. The marquis and I, not living under the same roof, were reduced to the chances offered by country walks. I have never liked danger, and moreover these circumstances reminded me too much of my first downfall. I soon came to feel that I did not love Monsieur de Villarceaux so well in the broad daylight of the meadows as in the dusky shelter of a bedroom. Whatever the cause of this falling off, to see that I might love him less was a new thing for me. I felt the pain of it before I perceived the advantages.

Another cause of my uneasiness was that I did not care for the company of our host. Charles de Valliquierville was an eccentric gentleman, and one of his singularities was that he would eat nothing that had been alive, and this not from aversion but out of pure fantasy. He ate only whey and plants which grew above ground and wanted us to do the same. Moreover he was a great freethinker who, like Ninon, believed in nothing. One day they shut themselves up in a little room to talk, and finding them there in the dark I ingenuously asked what they were doing.

"We are trying to formulate our beliefs," said Ninon. "We have made some progress. Another time we shall really work at it."

She and Valliquierville vied with each other to make fun of my virtue.

I sadly missed my kind friends the Montchevreuils, and above all the company of their children, with their amusing prattle and their affection for me. One day when Monsieur de Villarceaux found me in a gloomy mood and asked me the reason for it, I admitted it was the absence of the little Montchevreuil girls.

"What a strange thing to suffer from!" he exclaimed. "Well, Françoise, if you like infants so much you'll end up having some of your own. I'll go and swallow two fresh eggs and give you a fine boy first go!"

I could not have been more appalled if a thunderbolt had fallen at my feet. I had often thought about the great danger known as "widows' peril," but at first I was too much in love with the marquis to dwell upon it. I had then become so dependent that, while I knew a woman's sin carries its own condemnation within itself, I had stopped thinking about the consequences of my actions or worrying about what might happen before circumstances forced me to. The marquis's jest, coming at a moment when my feelings for him were cooling, reminded me that I was still on the edge of the abyss.

I recalled Scarron and Rosteau once saying that Monsieur de Villarceaux made such pretty children he should do nothing else. But I knew that an acknowledged child, or even the suspicion of one, would be my ruin; I should lose my pension and all my Marais friendships. I suddenly became much more aware than before of the danger that the marquis might "complete my happiness," or that God might decide to make my sin public. When I thought about it, I was amazed that it had not happened before, and that some kind of barrenness which I could only regard as miraculous had so far come to the aid of my semblance of virtue. This newly reinforced anxiety deprived me of the last enjoyments of this affair.

To see myself being confused all the time with Ninon; succeeding her a few years later on in the same woods for the pleasure of an over-affluent gentleman; having to rely on a courtesan and a libertine to hide a guilty love—everything combined to make me hate my own behavior even more in Vexin than at Montchevreuil. Remembering again the marquis's scorn when I had dared to speak to him of marriage two years before, and thinking of the difficulties I had suffered early in our affair, I felt a great pang in my heart. I was seized once more with doubts as to my lover's good faith, and somehow got the idea that when he left me he went straight to Ninon and told her all I had said and done.

I can bear that God can see my sins, but I cannot endure that anyone else should do so. I resolved that as soon as we were back in Paris I would break off a commerce which now gave me nothing but shame and anxiety.

It was difficult to carry out my resolution coolly, however, for the marquis was at that time overwhelming me with tokens of affection. So I decided to go into retreat for a few weeks with the Ursulines in the rue Saint-Jacques. I let it be known that I did not wish to see anyone while I was there, and the marquis was not excluded from this general ban. I intended this first separation to be the prelude to a more complete rupture, for as I have said, I did not love Monsieur de Villarceaux all that much when he was absent; my heart grew less fond as soon as he disappeared from sight. Using the sisters as a rampart, I sought in solitude the courage I had lacked for nearly three years.

When, after a month of meditation, I left the rue Saint-Jacques, I sent word to Monsieur de Villarceaux to come to see me at once: I was all too well aware of the danger of putting it off.

My handsome dark-haired lover came running, full of hope. I dismissed him on the spot. Such a development was so far from his thoughts that at first he appeared not to understand what I was saying. Even though, to justify my decision, I went so far as to invoke his wife's virtue, he still believed I was joking. In the end

I was obliged to speak plainly and say I did not want to meet him anywhere for a whole year. Afterwards we might perhaps find ourselves together in the same place and behave as good friends. But henceforward the door of my room was barred to him for ever.

He was so amazed, so staggered, so hurt that I felt I would have done better to murder someone than to have dealt him such a blow. He wept, he implored, he threatened; he made a scene, in short, unworthy of a gentleman and very painful for a mistress. But the more my resolution cost me the more I clung to it, for I feared I could never muster the courage to go through all this again. The painful scene lasted so long that in the end I no longer saw his tears; I was dropping with fatigue and had only one idea in my head— I wanted him to leave as soon as possible, no matter how and no matter what became of him. When he saw I was so genuinely adamant, he went away.

For several days I thought I had been the death of him. Although I did not doubt I had acted for my own good in sending him away, I used to wake up in the night bathed in anguish and remorse. Every day I expected to hear of some act of folly. I had made him so desperate I feared he would put an end to his own life, or to mine.

But he lived for thirty years after this supposedly fatal blow, and sixty years afterwards I myself am in moderately good health. While people never love as much as they say, they always love less than they think.

Nine

With my scamp of a marquis I had almost known love, and I considered this "almost" not bad for someone without birth, possessions or expectations. Moreover, my liaison with Villarceaux had delivered me from the naivety of youth, and innocence is not too high a price to pay for such enlightenment. Sin had even taught me to defend my virtue better. Ever since I had been the marquis's mistress I had found it easier to resist the blandishments of all the others besieging me. I let them go as far as it suited me, then dropped them exactly where I chose. Though freer than ever in word and deed, I knew none of my assailants could take the citadel. I saw this as proof that knowledge, albeit of vice, is preferable to ignorance, even when this is a by-product of virtue.

I was not sorry that my life took on a more regular rhythm. In the morning I used to write to my friends, my brother, my dear Villettes and my worthy Céleste. When Nanon had finished her work she would sit by the fire and sew, or read some improving book I had given her. After a quick meal, which we ate together—it would have been ridiculous to make the child have her dinner alone in the kitchen—I would go and spend the afternoon at the house of the duc and duchesse de Richelieu, where great amusement was provided by a very lively young abbé.

The abbé Testu, prior of Saint-Denis de la Chartre, prided himself on being at once a preacher and a poet, writing amorous verses and hymns alternately. He was the most diverting company, with a style full of paradox and epigram, exactly the kind of person who is now described as a court priest. He was fond of boasting of his prowess with the ladies, playing the gallant so enthusiastically that in later years the King could never bring himself to make him a bishop.

On other days I would go to the hôtel d'Albret, where I was always sure to find the maréchale between two glasses and her husband between two ladies. César d'Albret liked to have me as one of the pair of live caryatids whose presence upheld his reputation just as their marble counterparts used to support temples. He took pleasure in bringing me forward in society, encouraging me and teaching me all he knew or thought he knew about people of influence. He looked upon me as his own handiwork, and perhaps up to a point he was right.

It was in these houses that I met three women who were to play an important part in the sequel of my adventures. One after the other they came into my life, brilliant and majestic. I will not say they came into the game I was playing, for at that time I did not know that in them I possessed court cards, and I entered unwittingly into a game against fate in which, once they were played, I alone would emerge victorious.

The first had dark hair and fair skin, with violet eyes and the kind of pointed face usually attributed to the Queen of Spades. Whenever she was in company, you could hear her laugh from one end of the apartment to the other. She would throw her head back and seem about to swoon away with mirthful abandon, but sometimes from her half-shut eyes there shot a cold and acid look that chilled my heart. I suspected that this cryptic spirit contained strong impulses which frightened me as much as they attracted me. Like me she was from Poitou and was fond of introducing a few words of patois into her conversation so that she and I could understand each other without being understood while everyone else was left baffled. She was already partial to codes and secrets.

This laughing beauty was Anne-Marie de la Tremoille, married to the comte de Chalais, with whom she was said to be much in love. Everyone regarded her as made for love and amusement, but beneath her frivolous exterior she had more political brain and masculine spirit than any other woman I have ever known. She longed to be involved in serious matters and must have had plenty of opportunity to indulge this taste later on when she became the princesse des Ursins and governed Spain. But at the time I am speaking of now, she was quite vexed that I rather than she was always taken to receptions to talk about public affairs and private intrigues. She admitted as much when we were both at the height of our power and wrote to each other two or three times a week about European events. As for me, in those days I would have preferred to be in her place; to be thought less capable and left free to do more as I wished.

My second card was not really one of those master cards around which you construct your game, just one of those small trumps you play to enlighten your partner.

Her name was Bonne de Pons. She was twenty years old and a relative of the maréchal's, with a captivating face and no dowry. She had come up from the country with her cousin, Judith de Martel, who like her had just abjured Protestantism so as not to put off eligible Catholic suitors. The duc d'Albret had appointed himself their protector, and having taken them under his roof was trying to marry them off. Mademoiselle de Pons was one of those frail and elegant little beauties who are all show and no substance. As to her character, she was whimsical, natural, full of imagination and always original and amusing. She never opened her lips without making me laugh. Although I could see she exercised this talent at other people's expense, and I myself would not have wanted to utter such witticisms, I could not help admiring this caustic, excitable young woman, seething with hopes and plans under her mop of red hair.

As for the third of these ladies, she was a real Queen of Hearts, with the right nobility of figure and ample bosom, and the appropriate triumph in her face. Her beauty was amazing. She had the bearing of a goddess, a porcelain complexion, the hair of an angel and azure eyes. She knew how to use those orbs too: when she was jesting her glance was sharp enough, but on softer occasions she would dart languishing looks between her long lashes which could not leave their object unmoved.

"Athénaïs," Bonne de Pons said to her one day when we were in the maréchale's room and the goddess was ogling in this way a young nobleman among the company, "Athénaïs, I do think that for a young married woman you look too much at the gentlemen."

"When speaking of Madame," I put in, turning toward the lady in question, "the word 'look' is a slander. She does not look, she caresses people with her eyes and drowns them in her glance."

The blonde divinity smiled. I could see she did not dislike compliments, and I was quite good at making them in those days.

This wondrous creature's name was Françoise de Roche-chouart-Mortemart, but she had been dubbed Athénaïs or Athénaïste by the literary ladies of the Marais in the same way as they had nicknamed me Lyriane. She was twenty-four, and after an unhappy affair with Alexandre de la Tremoille, brother to the little comtesse de Chalais, had just made up her mind to marry the marquis de Montespan, son of one of Monsieur d'Albret's aunts and cousin to Madame de Richelieu. Monsieur, the King's brother, was her protector and had had her appointed maid of honor to the young Queen. She used all her wit, which was considerable, to distract her forlorn mistress.

When she came among us with her courtly air, her torrents of fine lace and floods of strong perfume, she told us, with the skill of an accomplished storyteller, about the unworthiness of the King's mistresses and the unhappiness of the rejected Queen.

"For my part," she said with unfeigned indignation, "if I, like Mademoiselle de La Vallière, had been so unfortunate as to be the King's mistress, I'd run away and hide for the rest of my life."

I thought to myself that it would have been a pity to deprive mortals of the sight of this Venus in majesty. I found her regal, and I did not know how right I was.

All three young women pleased me with their wit, though in each of them it was different. Françoise de Montespan had more learning than the rest, Anne-Marie de Chalais more judgment and

Bonne de Pons more audacity. I tried to win their friendship, or rather their goodwill, for I was not yet on terms of equality with the rest in these great houses. Although the d'Albrets and the Richelieus were very fond of me, they did not fail to make me feel the distance between marquises and duchesses and myself. Thinking it better to be called in than to be driven out, I was very discreet and never took any but the lowest place. I spoke only when asked. I forgot myself in order to be pleasant to ladies better born. And I made myself get used to other people's moods, without hoping to bring them round to mine. In short, the humility of my behavior bore constant witness to the modesty of my position. And people were grateful to me for this.

I had fairly free scope at the hôtel d'Albret because I was sure of the maréchal's protection but had to keep more in the background at the hôtel de Richelieu, for while the elderly duchesse was still very well disposed toward me, it was a different matter with her young husband. The duc was very inconstant in his likes and dislikes, and he soon grew tired of those he saw too often. His friends could tell what place they had in his heart from that which their portraits occupied in his room. At the start of an acquaintance or fancied friendship, he would at once have pictures painted of those he thought he liked and hang them by his bed. But gradually these dear friends would be replaced by others and fall back to the door, then the vestibule, then the attic and finally cease to be seen at all. When I saw myself hung in a stairway, I thought it best to visit less and be wished for more.

During the months that followed I went to the hôtel de Richelieu only by chance and spent most of my time at the Montchevreuil's and Ninon's.

"Tell me, Françoise," Ninon asked me one day as I lay beside her on her great red damask bed, recounting my life story gaily enough, "can one really be happy as a widow?"

"Yes," I answered, "though old ones are no doubt freer than young ones, who have to sacrifice their pleasures to their reputations. But whatever your age," I added, parodying my father, "the great thing about being a widow is that if you can't always do what you want yourself, at least you don't have to do what someone else wants."

In fact, having for so many years been dependent on other people—aunts, guardians, nuns, husband, lover—I was beginning to enjoy my new freedom.

My pension covered my expenses. Though I dressed simply, I used only wax candles, which was not very common in those days. I even had enough money left over for charity, and for putting something away. Nanon loved me like a sister and anticipated my smallest wishes, which were not all that difficult to satisfy since I have never loved comfort or indulged my own whims and fancies.

If I wanted to see my women friends, I could go to their houses whenever it suited me and be sure of a welcome; or they would come to me if I let them know I was not going out. Nor did I have any of the passions which might have troubled my attachment to this semblance of happiness. The gazettes had forgotten me; my love affairs were no longer the subject of drawing-room verses. My life was obscure and peaceful, without sorrow or trouble. I was content and could not understand why existence should be called a vale of tears.

My only worry was my brother, who had been displaced through the reordering of his regiment and found himself without employment. I had arranged for him to go to Mursay and sent the Villettes a small sum for his maintenance out of my own income. But he was even more immoderate in the wilds of Poitou than in Paris. His life consisted of nothing but duels, love affairs and gaming; he went from one unfortunate escapade to another. He was up to his eyes in debt and not only accepted from Monsieur de Villette the money he needed but also helped himself to some which was never given. In short, he fell out with all the people to whom I recommended him.

But although his behavior destroyed my good opinion of him, my affection remained unchanged, and my pain was in proportion to it. Like every other passion, the unwarranted passion I formed for him at the age of eight was never to bring me anything but suffering.

I was thirty. I was back in favor with the duc de Richelieu: my portrait was by his bed again, and this return from the attic to the bedroom was too infrequent to pass without comment. I was also more advanced than ever in the good graces of my maréchal. By a strange coincidence, it was now, when I no longer troubled to conquer that fickle heart, that he began to feel for me something resembling love. He wrote me a few pretty letters on the subject, and one evening, seeing me home, he spoke.

"Monsieur le Maréchal," I said, "your feelings are not very timely."

"I know, I know," he said gravely. "But is it really too late?"

"Yes."

"You love another?"

"No."

"So you do not forbid me to hope?"

"One may always hope. I myself hope to convert you one day. And you can see how likely that is! But I do not think you the sort of man to live on hope."

And indeed, a few weeks later, already tired of waiting, the handsome maréchal began to woo Bonne de Pons, his red-headed young ward. For some reason this caused me a certain vexation. When the maréchal gave the young lady a portrait of himself to wear on her arm, and Mademoiselle de Pons passed it on to me for fear her aunt might find out too much about it, it gave me more pleasure than I would have imagined to take the picture home with me. Monsieur d'Albret had had a miniature of himself set in a wide gold bracelet, and the work was so skilfully done that no one looking at the bracelet on its owner's arm would have suspected it had a hidden spring on one side and a portrait concealed in the thickness of the metal. I kept the portrait for more than fifteen years, until long after the maréchal's death. Even when I had been intimate with the King for some time, I still wore it on my arm, which was a very foolish thing to do. I did not think of getting rid of it until a few years after my second marriage. Sometimes, perhaps, we love a little more than we think.

Sitting on a stool by the maréchal's chair, I would listen to the chatter of the young ladies and gentlemen. It was not as in the days of the Hôtel Impecuniosity: I was no longer the center of conversation, the queen of the salon, the tactless little girl whose laughter rang out, in season and out of season. Others had taken over, but there was much to be gained by holding my tongue and listening. It taught me a great deal about everyone's likes and dislikes, their hopes and idiosyncrasies. The only person who sometimes noticed me watching the ladies was Madame de Montespan, who was not lacking in shrewdness.

"Take your black eyes off me, if you please, Madame Scarron," she would say, laughing. I smiled.

But although I used the distance these people set between themselves and a widow of no particular family in order to get to know my friends better, this analytical approach did not stop me from being strongly attracted by the charms of some of them. Bonne de Pons especially intrigued me. No doubt I realized that no given name had ever been less appropriate, but I was enchanted by the freedom and amazing originality of her conversation. Sensible people always like giddy women and worthless men. Bonne de Pons had not yet made me suffer by her follies, and I thought her my only real friend among all those people.

I had the pleasure, in January 1666, of finding her a husband. It had not been easy, for Monsieur d'Albret, more and more taken with his pretty niece, was in no hurry to set her up in an establishment of her own. Did I hurry matters myself out of spite? After much trouble and worry over the success of the match, I at last drove her one fine snowy day to Heudicourt, near Pontoise, where her husband awaited her. This was Monsieur Sublet de Noyers, marquis d'Heudicourt, grand master of the wolf-hunt to the King. I was exhausted to the point of illness by the care I had taken over this marriage. On the wedding day itself I had given so much time to dressing the bride and arranging her hair with my own hands that I forgot all about myself, and I appeared before the whole Court, who came to the wedding, as ugly and neglected as a servant girl.

I was quickly led to a room where I could get dressed myself, and when I returned, clad in white watered silk taffeta and English point lace, no one recognized me as the person they had just seen. Their praises of my looks did not fall disagreeably upon my ears.

This story often resembles the tale of Cinderella, and indeed I have frequently found myself in her position. I have helped my friends put on dresses and try out hairstyles; I have put a hasty stitch in their skirts and run to fetch them some paint or perfume; then, when they have gone, I have stayed at home by the fire, sewing. When they got back, one would say, "What a pity you weren't at the ball, Françoise!" And another, "Madame, you never see anything, so you cannot imagine how sumptuous the princesse de Monaco's gown was tonight! Impossible to describe it—you'd have to see it!" "I do feel sorry for Madame Scarron, Bonne dear, not knowing what that palace is like." "Athénaïs, did you see the gilt chandeliers? and the silver tables?" "Judith, did you have any of those big chilled peaches? Did you drink any of that champagne?" "And the King, Françoise, the King . . . If only you'd seen him!"

I could hear the echo of the ball and smell the scent of the roast meat, but I had no godmother to give me my reward. My own godmother was dead, and unlamented, for she was more of a witch than a good fairy.

The advantage of going up in the world, even if it is only as a lady's maid, is that in the end you enter circles which, while not being quite the highest, contain a few people who in other surroundings do contemplate the summits. I myself did not see the King or the princes at the hôtel d'Albret or at Monsieur de Richelieu's house, but every day I saw a few people who did see them from close to; and if I did not yet feel the rays of the Sun, there were faces around me which reflected its light.

The first to show that radiance was my friend Bonne d'Heudicourt.

Madame d'Albret had taken her niece to Saint-Germain a few months before her marriage, and wherever Bonne appeared her charms caused a stir. The young King himself had not looked upon her with indifference, and he was said to have hesitated for some time between her and his current mistress, Mademoiselle de La

Vallière. The maréchale saw nothing of all this herself, so easily was she deceived, but her women friends soon told her the young lady should not be left at Court any longer or she would swiftly be lost. At this the maréchale had quickly taken her ward back to Paris, on the pretext that the maréchal was ill. When Mademoiselle de Pons found Monsieur d'Albret in good health and realized why he had been said to be ill, she did not conceal her regret.

"The King isn't only the King, Françoise. He's also the finest gentleman at Court."

"I know he's magnificent," I said. "I saw him from a balcony six years ago, when he entered Paris after his marriage."

"He's more than magnificent," she whimpered. "He's handsome, I tell you."

I put some severity into my reply.

"He may be handsome, Mademoiselle, but he is certainly married. Surely you do not think of being his mistress!"

"You don't understand anything about it, Françoise. Being the King's mistress isn't at all as horrid as being the mistress of an ordinary man," she said, pressing her little fists to her face. "And I've missed it just because of that stupid maréchale, who'd rather throw me into the arms of her husband."

For weeks I heard of nothing but the King and his hates and enthusiasms. The King didn't like scent. The King loved dancing. The King sucked cinnamon drops. The King never wore a wig. The King played the guitar. The King ate *médianoche,* a midnight meal, during Lent; the King doted on violins; hated the Carmelites; loved strawberries; acted in plays; spoke Spanish; liked blondes; liked brunettes; liked redheads; liked duchesses; liked chambermaids. Liked his gardener's daughter.

But it was in vain that my crazy friend, so well informed from her first sojourn there, went back to Court after she was married. The place was taken. It was now Madame de Montespan's turn to enlighten me on the subject.

Not knowing much about where I came from and by what chance someone like Madame Scarron was admitted to the hôtel in the rue Pavée, she treated me at first with more condescension than I liked. But when she learned that I knew her brother the duc de

Vivonne, who had been a habitué of our house in the rue Neuve-Saint-Louis, and when she saw the consideration with which Monsieur d'Albret treated me, she deigned to speak to me more often. And so, little by little, with one epigram leading to another, she took to my wit as I to hers.

She could not hold me in high esteem because of my birth, and this haughtiness prevented me from really liking her. But apart from that, we got on very well, for she had such wit she could not resist anyone able to appreciate it. Thanks to her I was let into the secrets of everyday life in the Tuileries and at Saint-Germain.

"The Queen never goes to bed until the King has come home. Can you believe it? Fickle as he is, he never stays out all night. My job is to amuse Her Majesty till the small hours while we wait for the King to get back. Extremely tedious, I can tell you, for the Queen is not at all witty. And what is more, she's as virtuous as a Carmelite—and a Spanish Carmelite at that! Meanwhile the King is only too pleased to try her virtue by his amours. The truth is he likes practically every woman except his own wife. And me, of course," she added, smiling.

I enjoyed these somewhat free conversations; I gave myself up to the pleasure of these surface friendships; and I did not bother about the rest. In the summer I used to go to Montchevreuil, or to Conflans, the duc de Richelieu's country house on an island in the Seine. In 1667 I went with the duc and duchesse to Richelieu itself, where I passed six well-filled weeks. I was always up by six, while my lady friends lay abed till noon, so before they were dressed I had put the whole house in order, chivvied the footmen, picked the caterpillars off the roses, and got the children downstairs.

I took advantage of the trip to go to Poitou. My brother had fresh troubles there: he had called himself the "baron de Surimeau," and agents instructed by the King to prosecute sham noblemen had summoned him before the administrator of the province. So I went to Mursay to find evidence of the antiquity of our family, then took my proofs to Poitiers, where they were found good enough to have the prosecution called off. For some time I moved between Niort, Mursay and Surimeau, renewing my acquaintance with my Huguenot relations.

When I got back from this journey I received a very extraordinary proposal from my former admirer Cardinal d'Estrées. His sister the princesse de Nemours, who by her marriage had become Queen of Portugal, had sent for me to be her lady-in-waiting and go with her to Lisbon. Maréchal d'Albret at once pointed out all the advantages of this suggestion: it guaranteed my success and prosperity; it gave me a chance to use my talents usefully and to enter public affairs.

"You cannot spend your whole life serving your lady friends," he said. "You must think of getting some position. Apart from a brilliant marriage, which you are too sensible to hope for, you will never have a better offer. To tell you the truth, it strikes me as beyond all expectation."

I hesitated for a moment. The advantages which the maréchal pointed out to me with such force were by no means negligible. I felt within me, more and more strongly, a reserve of unused strengths, as some joyful impulse would seize me at the most unexpected moment, bear me along for a while, then fall away for want of object. Moreover, there was nothing to keep me in France, nothing in the world which belonged to me, neither husband, child nor home. My reason told me to link my fate to that of the Queen of Portugal. My friends urged me to accept.

A strange thing about life is that it does not offer any more good opportunities which should not be missed than it does false ones which should be avoided: the greatness of a person's fate depends more on what is refused than on what is accepted. The difficulty, of course, is to distinguish with certainty between true luck and false strokes of fortune. I have always thought that in cases of uncertainty one does not go too far wrong following one's own inclination; then at least, if one does make a mistake, not everything is lost.

While my mind inclined toward Portugal, my heart kept me in Paris. As a sort of desperate wager, I refused Cardinal d'Estrée's proposal. People could not understand my decision, and I was unable to explain myself.

All that was sure was that I felt relieved as soon as I had conveyed my answer to the young Queen. My unreasonableness appalled maréchal d'Albret. I told him, jesting, that I had thought him in too much of a hurry to put three hundred leagues between us, and that this consideration alone had made me decide to stay.

I went on with my peaceful existence, or rather with what is regarded as such in this world: a mixture of hopes and fears, inconstant affections, a multitude of desires, occasionally a fleeting joy, usually a good deal of boredom.

"To be sure, you are sweet, lively, obliging, and everyone likes you," the duc d'Albret said to me one evening, "but pleasing everyone is not an occupation, Françoise, and it does not give you a situation, unless you go in for a life of gallantry. And I suppose that is not your intention?"

"Not yet, Monsieur le Maréchal," I replied, laughing. "I do not seek to please out of self-interest—indeed I agree it is not to my advantage, except perhaps that it is always useful to avoid making enemies. Let us say I try to please in order to suit my own inclination, my own weakness if you prefer, for pleasing the humblest porter gives me as much happiness as pleasing the noblest duchesse. Will you believe it, I spend a good deal of time charming Nanon, my own servant maid. I dine with her, I chat with her, I alter dresses for her, choose books for her to read . . . Partly because I love her, of course, but much more because she loves me. And there you have it, Monsieur le Maréchal: I have too great a need to be loved and praised. It is my only weakness!"

"I am the last person to reproach you for it, Madame, especially if you think you might need my friendship as much as that of others."

"*Mon maréchal,*" I said, using a jesting and familiar form of address, "my own dear maréchal, I love you so well that you are the only person I do not try to charm. I esteem you so much that even if you were to hate me, you would not destroy my affection for you."

"Stop joking, Françoise, and listen. I shall not always be here to back you up. I shall soon be fifty, and before I leave this world I would be glad to see my handiwork risen to high rank, or at least settled in some position. You have reached an age when it is time to make a decision."

The maréchal was right. I was bored. I was still beautiful, but only the looking-glass got any good of it. I was lively and active, but you cannot polish the brass more than once a day. I had a fair amount of wit, but I no longer felt inclined to waste it on salon conversation. In my long gowns of brown muslin I moved like a phantom through the tumult of other people's lives, and I was beginning to think that freedom was not an end in itself.

On 18 July 1668 my slow ascent toward success, begun unwittingly and alone in about my fourteenth year, was for the first time manifested in public: I was presented at Court. It seemed to me then that I had made some progress since the prison at Niort. I was thirty-two, and for the first time I danced at a ball given by my prince.

The King had just emerged victorious from his first war. The peace of Aix-la-Chapelle gave him eleven strongholds in Flanders and a large stretch of territory. Not content with military conquests, he had at last taken into his bed the Queen's too magnificent lady-in-waiting, my worthy maréchal's cousin, Françoise-Athénaïs de Montespan. He thought fit to celebrate the combined political and amorous victory by an entertainment designed to surpass in brilliance "The Pleasures of the Enchanted Island," a fête organized five years earlier in honor of the shy La Vallière.

The party took place at Versailles. Although the King still lived in the Tuileries or at Saint-Germain, he was beginning to grow very attached to his little hunting lodge at Versailles, to which he added new improvements every day.

So it was at Versailles that the King celebrated his new mistress and his supremacy over the kings of Europe. Only three hundred ladies were asked to attend, and I owed the privilege of my invitation to the wit ascribed to me by the splendid Athénaïs.

The "Great Royal Entertainment" was worthy of the most lavish fairy tale. First came a pleasant comedy by Molière, performed in a leafy bower set amid rich tapestries and lit up bright as day by thirty-two crystal chandeliers. Between the acts the wondrous strains of a symphony by Lully, played on unseen instruments, seemed to issue from the skies. After the play the ladies, accompanied by the King's twenty-four violins and dozens of oboes, moved to the banquet, which was in another bower, roofed over by a painted, gilded dome.

Hundreds of white wax candles burned in candelabras set on tall silver pedestal tables. The cornices were decked with garlands, alternating with porcelain vases and crystal balls. In the middle of the room stood the "rock of Parnassus," from which flowed four turbulent rivers; held aloft on pilasters in the bower's four corners, marble conches poured forth pools of water. It was hard to know which to admire most, the amazing hues of the rare flowers on the silver tables, or, all around them, the colors of the ladies' gowns, like tints on an artist's palette. Or to say whether the pearls around the duchesses' necks were more beautiful than the drops splashing from the waterfalls; or to decide which was more intoxicating, the Alsatian wine in the glasses or the scents of musk and marjoram drifting up from the ladies' lace.

I sat at the duchesse de Montausier's table. Bonne d'Heudicourt was beside me, and we spoke together very freely. I was as delighted as she with the entertainment, and yet felt a certain dim uneasiness, which I put down to the thought of how unhappy those who were not bidden to the feast must be.

"A magnificent *Te Deum,* isn't it?" said the marquise d'Heudicourt.

"The *Te Deum* of a king," I answered, "is often the *De Profundis* of a people."

I was thinking of the sorrow of my poor Nanon Balbien, whose youngest brother, who had joined the army, had just died in Flanders for the King's greater glory. I was thinking, too, of the marquis de Montespan: the duchesse d'Albret, his cousin, had told me all about his unhappiness and humiliation. He was reduced to extremes, wearing mourning for his wife and raising the lintels in his house supposedly to make room for his horns. The great have but short funeral orations for those whose happiness they trample underfoot. "My husband, my dog and my parrot amuse the mob," said the marquise, while the King applauded the insipid rhapsodies which Molière and Benserade were still performing to justify his misdeeds: "To share with Jupiter is no dishonor . . ."

But the pleasures of conversation soon chased away these bitter thoughts. And perhaps I was mistaken about the cause of my sadness, due less, no doubt, to compassion for others than to the thought that this magnificence had no sequel for me, and that when dawn broke, my coach would turn back into a pumpkin.

When supper was over, the King went to the room which had been built for the ball. It was of marble and porphyry, garlanded with flowers. Masked figures bore aloft torches, and everywhere the lights vied in beauty with the glitter of the water, and the sound of fountains mingled with the strains of violins. The "three queens," as Marie-Thérèse, Mademoiselle de La Vallière and Madame de Montespan were called, danced a little; only the marquise danced well.

"Are you not shocked by the effrontery of this seraglio?" Mademoiselle de Scudéry whispered to me.

"Yes indeed," I answered. "But if I remember my Plutarch, Alexander had more than one wife. Heroes are like that."

"Alexander was not a Christian king," snapped the author of *Le Grand Cyrus*.

At this point the Christian king performed his figure in a dance, and I saw him from less far away than before. While fortune had caused him to be born a great king, nature had given him the looks for it. He was indeed handsome, with that reserved masculine beauty which keeps others at a distance as much as it attracts them. He had ash-blond hair; large, brown, rather gentle eyes; a grave smile; superb presence; a general air of grandeur which added to his height, which was no more than average. His majestic bearing extended even to the dance, in which he excelled every other gentleman at Court. He smiled as he danced, and for some reason, although he was only two or three years younger than I, I saw in that smile of pleasure a childlike look which touched me. The next moment, passing among his courtiers and allotting praise or blame with a word, he was no longer a child at play but a great king in action. "Kings must be respected," I had been taught when young. "They can do anything they please."

The guests left the ballroom by paths deliberately left dark, then emerged from behind a group of trees in front of the château, radiant as a palace of the sun. Antique statues shone in the windows; dazzling urns stood on the balustrades of every terrace. Fireworks gushed forth from the fountains, pools and flowerbeds. All the ornamental waters were playing, and like them the flames seemed to spring out of the earth. The two elements were so closely intermingled they could not be told apart. Last of all, rockets fired from the Tour de la Pompe marked the sky with the double L of the King's monogram multiplied a hundred times, each one shining with a light that was bright and clear.

Day, jealous of so favored a night, was already beginning to break. In the rose-colored glow of a dawn as magical as in a romance, the first coaches drove back along the road to Paris. In gilded carts drawn by black horses, ladies in crumpled gowns and faded roses, tossed about together like rag dolls, were already deep in dreamless sleep.

My own eyes had been too badly scorched by the sun to close so soon. In the duchesse de Richelieu's carriage, which was taking me back to the capital, I was experiencing strange regrets and singular longings. In the place Royale I sadly gave back the gown the duchesse had lent me, ignominiously put on my "rags" again and returned slowly to the oblivion of my little lodging.

When the curious bitterness I had felt on leaving the ball had abated a little, I realized that the company of the great was not good for me. I shut myself up more closely than before in my house in the rue des Trois-Pavillons with my good, simple Nanon.

At the beginning of 1669 I decided I must have a spiritual director. This does not mean I was resolved to think seriously about my salvation, for had it not been for society, which would have blamed me, I would still have spent every Sunday without going to mass. But I did think that following the directions of a priest would be a salutary occupation for a mind that was restless and unusually inclined to reverie. Besides, in the circles I now frequented, it was considered good form to have a spiritual director. A lady of quality owed it to herself to have a director and a coachman. I could not afford the coachman, but the director would cost only a little restraint. I thought, too, that such a person might give me useful advice about my charities, and perhaps also about the education and care of a little boy called Toscan, whom my brother had just had with a married woman, and of whom he had made me a present. Charles often gave me presents of this sort in the years that followed; they were the only gifts I ever did receive from him.

Madame de Coulanges recommended the abbé Gobelin, a former officer who had found his vocation after he was forty and then taken orders. Though he had obtained a doctorate at the Sorbonne, he still had all the roughness of a soldier. His language belonged to the camp, not the drawing-room, and he had no illusions about human nature. He was as poor and thin as a church mouse, and he carried to inordinate lengths a belief that piety should exclude all pleasure.

While everyone else exclaimed at the plainness of my dress, when I went to confession at the convent of the Filles-Bleues he found me too well turned out.

"But Monsieur," I said, "I wear only simple stuff."

"That's as may be, honored lady," he answered, "but somehow when you kneel down I see at my feet quantities of stuff so pleasing I am sure it must be too good."

He thought me too fond of my own wit and disapproved of the desire to please which inspired my every action. One of the first exercises he set me was to try to bore everyone in conversation. Wishing to obey, I resolved not to talk at all—I who the day before had spoken with such charm and vivacity. I tried so hard I positively hurt my tongue and repented of my obedience.

No doubt about it, I did not feel at all pious. Saint John said God loved him before he loved God, and my life, too, has been a miracle of divine love as constantly renewed as it is completely undeserved. At the time of which I speak, that love, though it encompassed me always, did not yet touch my mind, and if I followed all the spiritual exercises prescribed by my director it was only in the hope that I might, like the Stoics of old, attain complete self-mastery.

And indeed I had an adventure about that time which was worthy of those one reads of in Plutarch. In the courtyard of the hôtel d'Albret I often passed a kind of mason or architect who worked there. I used to greet him very civilly, for such courtesies toward humble people are in my style. But this politeness, to which he was not at all accustomed, caused this man, whose name was Barbé, to become interested in me, and one day he sent a message asking me to go and speak to him. He then told me he had had a kind of vision about me and knew that before long I should enjoy the greatest honors a woman may possess. My success would be unexampled, my rise in the world amazing. I thanked him very kindly for his prophecy and did not believe it. When I was back again in the drawing-room, my lady friends wanted to know what great secret the mason had revealed to me. I answered, jesting:

"If you only knew, Mesdames, you would pay court to me here and now! But do not put it off any longer—my success has begun."

"It would not be a bad thing for our little circle," said Madame de Coulanges, "for it is said that our friend's star is on the wane." She was speaking of Madame de Montespan. "Apparently she is very ill—thin and sallow and so changed altogether as to be unrecognizable. They say it's fatal."

"Very well then," said Madame de La Fayette, who was then with Madame, the King's sister-in-law, and close to everything, "Bonne d'Heudicourt will succeed her. She is so free with her favors they call her 'the great she-wolf' at Saint-Germain." This was a pun on a word for a wanton and the fact that Bonne's husband was master of the King's wolf-hunt. I was very grieved that people should speak so of one of my dearest friends, but I knew Bonne had no common sense and followed her own whims without any thought of restraint. When she came to Paris I would speak to her of reason, and she would speak to me of pleasure, and we had no common ground.

She had a little girl aged one or two, whose name was Louise and who later became Madame de Montgon. Bonne took no more trouble about this child than if she had been someone else's daughter; she said she was a nuisance. The poor little creature was left to the mercies of the coarsest servant maids, so I had her with me from time to time to console her and give her a modicum of education.

But my energy was not sufficiently employed playing with little Louise now and then, and every day the uselessness of my life weighed on me more heavily. In that year 1669 my soul was like the layers of skirts being worn by fashionable ladies: on top was the only one that was visible, the "modest" skirt; underneath that, suspected perhaps by some friends or lovers, the "naughty" layer; and last of all the "secret" one. I alone knew its color and what it was made of. The material was strong, for the warp was bitterness and the weft desire for greatness.

Ten

In the summer of that same year, 1669, Bonne d'Heudicourt, who now rarely left Saint-Germain, came to Paris for a few days and left her daughter with me. When she came to fetch her she said:

"What a pity you don't see Athénaïs any more. Her beauty is the admiration of all the ambassadors. No one has ever managed to combine audacity and triumph so well, or mingled splendor with so much effrontery. So, as you may imagine, the King's passion increases every day!"

"She is no longer ill, then?" I asked.

"No. To tell the truth, she never was." Bonne lowered her voice to a whisper. "I tell you this because I know you can keep a secret—she only had one of those illnesses that gets better in nine months."

"You mean—"

Madame d'Heudicourt looked furtively at the doors and tapestries.

"You may speak," I told her. "I have never hidden lovers in my cupboards—nor in the chimney either," I added, in answer to another mute inquiry.

"Only a few of us know about it," she went on, "but three months ago the marquise had a child which is not her husband's. Her anxiety at finding herself pregnant sent her into a kind of decline which completely spoiled her looks. That is all over now, fortunately, but she still lives in fear lest the marquis learn of the child's existence and take it away, for he is legally its father. The King is afraid of that too. Between ourselves, their double adultery is a sin they may have cause to regret. At best the child will have to be kept shut up, for neither of them can acknowledge it. It will never be seen in the world; its birth must remain unknown and its life obscure. Its mother and father have decided it must be so; they had no choice. But if I tell you this, my dear, it is because I have permission to do so . . ."

Madame d'Heudicourt got up and went over to the mirror. She shook some of her red curls over her brow, put on a more skeptical smile and a more mysterious glance, then assumed a general expression of gravity: all these tricks to convince me, or perhaps herself, that she was about to impart something of great moment.

"I have been entrusted with a most important mission," she breathed.

She popped a sweetmeat into her mouth to give herself strength to carry it out.

"Our friend would like you to take care of the child." She gasped, as if the effort of completing her task had been almost too much for her.

Although her attitudinizing had made me suspect something really out of the way, I could not help showing my surprise.

"I?" I exclaimed. "Why me?"

"Our fair friend, on my advice, thinks you are the best person for so delicate a task. I have told her how good you are with children and how fond you are of my little Louise. She herself already knows your virtue and your wit, and the whole place Royale is aware of your perfect discretion when entrusted with a secret. The infant is out at nurse outside Paris. Up till now Mademoiselle Desoeillets, the marquise's chief maid, has been in charge of it, but this will not do. The connection between Mademoiselle

Desoeillets and our friend is too public; Monsieur de Montespan has spies everywhere and nothing would be easier than to trace the maid back to the mistress. Nor is Mademoiselle Desoeillets a suitable nurse for a child of the King's, even if it is a bastard: she is not well born—worse, she is the daughter of an actress—nor is she virtuous. At this very moment she is pregnant herself, and no one knows the father . . .

"In short, it suits the parents that you should take charge of this inconvenient infant. It is always worthwhile to serve the King, no matter what the employment. Moreover you will be doing a kind deed—I know you're not the sort of person to underrate the worth of giving a Christian education to the fruits of sin. Think of all this, I beg; do not hesitate to be useful both to God and to yourself; and send me your answer before the end of the week. They are anxious at Saint-Germain to hear that you accept."

Madame d'Heudicourt left me deep in thought. I had been offered a very strange honor. Ladies more pious than I might have shrunk from becoming accomplices to a guilty passion and been reluctant to hide its outcome. Those more proud might have been sorry to give up their freedom for a task so far below a lady of quality. At first this was my own feeling, but I pondered further.

While to be the mistress of a King is no less wrong than to be the mistress of the lowest of his flunkies, to be his servant is not quite so base as to be the servant of someone else. Kings enhance whatever they touch; gentlemen respect even their close-stools. Moreover, if I scorned this offer I risked incurring the favorite's displeasure, and I might lose my pension, which since the Queen Mother's death had come from the King's treasury. It is not wise to deny one's services to those upon whom one is dependent, especially when one can adduce no good reason. I could scarcely refuse in the name of virtue: kings do not like commoners preaching at them; they have confessors for that.

My reason showed me clearly where my interest lay. And my inclination pointed in the same direction.

I loved children and they loved me. I never minded swaddling them, or washing, feeding, teaching or amusing them. In fact, I thought myself so good at all these things that I enjoyed being praised for my talents. And then I had been so bored for the last few months that it would be a welcome change to see again the "Queen of Hearts" whose influence was increasing every day; to observe the Court from a closer standpoint; perhaps, one day, to speak to the King. What Bonne de Pons had told me about Madame Colbert† clinched my decision. She said the minister's wife supervised the education of the bastards the King had had with Mademoiselle de La Vallière. I considered this lady sufficiently rich and well thought of to serve as a guide: there could be no dishonor in accepting what she had not refused.

As I drove toward Saint-Germain, where Madame de Montespan was to give me instructions, I thought with amusement of my maréchal's anger if he ever heard of my new employment.

"What, Madame? Refuse to be lady-in-waiting to a queen, and then become nurse to one of my niece's bastards! You must have taken leave of your senses!"

Fortunately, as the King wished to be served without defying public opinion, Monsieur d'Albret learned nothing of my new office, and no one suspected that my life had changed.

Yet it immediately began to follow a different course. The first thing I did was to move, in October, to more spacious quarters in the rue des Tournelles. This brought me close both to salvation and to perdition: the abbé Gobelin, my spiritual director, lived a little further up the same street, and my old friend Mademoiselle de Lenclos lived a little further down it.

Every day I went out into the suburbs to see the child, a little girl, and the nurse with whom Mademoiselle Desoeillets had placed her. Louise-Françoise was a charming little creature for her age. She had a lively eye and something very promising in her look. Although such young children can be very tedious, and we do not usually like them until they are capable of learning, I at once became attached to this babe and soon loved her as if she had been my own. Indeed, the nurse's behavior showed she thought I really was her mother.

I soon had cause to multiply both my affection and my duties by two. On 31 March 1670, as secretly as before, Madame de Montespan gave birth to a second bastard, a boy this time. Louis-Auguste, as he was called, later duc du Maine, and from the first my little darling, my beloved little prince, the joy and sorrow of my heart, was born in the château at Saint-Germain. The event was shrouded in the deepest mystery.

As soon as the marquise's pains began I was summoned to the château in haste. It was at night, and as arranged, I put on a mask, took a hackney carriage and went and waited by one of the park gates. Two hours later a very short man enveloped in a black cloak and carrying a large, loosely wrapped bundle came creeping like a conspirator through the trees. This was Monsieur de Lauzun, then the King's favorite, who had been asked to help Madame de Montespan in this matter. He tossed the bundle into my lap with a great sigh of relief, pausing only to whisper that he'd thought he would die of fright carrying his burden through the room where the Queen was asleep. "But the child promises to be clever," he said. "He knows what's what already. In the Queen's bedroom he was as silent as the grave."

The cab started off at once, and I saw that no one had taken the time even to swaddle the infant: he was naked except for a loose cloth wrapped around him. I wound this more tightly about the little body, and to protect the child from the chill night air held him under my cloak, close to my bosom. He was only a few minutes old, and I do not think anyone but myself had even bothered to look at him. I was soon glad to notice that the warmth of my body was reviving him, and he made little animal movements. He was so close to my heart he entered into it quite easily. That night I learned what it feels like to be a mother.

With the two children, my task began to present great difficulties. So that no link might be established between the infants, the nurses lived at a considerable distance from one another, and the royal children had not only to be kept hidden but also frequently moved about. I was always renting different houses in and out of Paris and moving all my staff from one district to another. Every time the furnishings had to be rehung, and I would climb up the ladder myself, since it was impossible to employ a strange workman or maid, and the nurses could not lend a hand for fear of tiring themselves and spoiling their milk. All night long I would go to and fro between the various hiding-places of Françoise and Louis-Auguste, hurrying from one nurse to another in disguise and carrying linen or food under my arm. When one of the children was ill, I would spend whole nights outside Paris, staying up to let the nurse get some rest.

In the morning I would let myself into my own house through a back door, dress, then go out through the front door to call at the hôtel d'Albret or the hôtel de Richelieu, so that my ordinary acquaintances should not know I had a secret. Though I was ill with fatigue, I had to look as if I had slept well. As I was still shy and blushed easily, I was afraid I would go red if anyone mentioned anything to do with my secret. So I decided to follow Ninon's advice ten years earlier and had myself bled, but it did little good.

No one knew the part I was playing except Bonne d'Heudicourt, the abbé Gobelin and Monsieur de Louvois. The King had appointed the young minister to watch over Madame de Montespan's children in the same way as he had charged Monsieur Colbert with the care of those of Mademoiselle de La Vallière. I do not know how this arrangement came about, but I do know that the two ministers entered into their tasks with such earnestness that Monsieur de Louvois and Madame de Montespan for a long while considered their fortunes to be linked, and the marquise, with reason, regarded Monsieur Colbert, together with his sons and daughters and brothers, as her sworn enemies. They were great friends to me, later; but we have not yet reached that part of my story.

In 1670 I thought Madame de Montespan was fond of me, and I was learning to know her. Every month I went to the Tuileries, Saint-Germain or Versailles, wherever she was at the time, to give her news of her children; sometimes I even took them to see her, at night, in Madame d'Heudicourt's apartment. To tell the truth, she cared as little about them as she did about the son and daughter she had had a few years earlier with Monsieur de Montespan. But she very much enjoyed chatting with me.

Through Madame d'Heudicourt, who lived in the closest intimacy with her and the King, I knew what suffering the new favorite inflicted upon poor La Vallière and even upon the Queen, who had once been so taken with her. Mademoiselle de La Vallière, though still the King's acknowledged mistress, was treated like a drudge by Madame de Montespan, who made use of her, praised her and protested that she never felt properly dressed if the other did not put the finishing touch to her toilette. Mademoiselle de La Vallière, for her part, behaved like a lady's maid whose future depended on pleasing her mistress. It was heartrending, for anyone who had a heart, which at any court is fortunately rare. The favorite was constantly making jests about the Queen; she sometimes went too far and was rebuked by the King, infatuated as he was.

But I could see that Madame de Montespan's character was not all bad. Far from being a born libertine, she was naturally inclined to virtue. She had, moreover, been excellently brought up by a very pious mother who had sown seeds of religion in her heart which remained there for ever. It was pride alone, and boundless ambition, which caused her downfall.

One day she told me that her idea at the beginning had been to rule the King through the power of her wit alone. She prided herself on controlling the King's passion as well as her own, thinking she would always be able to make him desire what she had resolved not to grant. The outcome was a more natural one. But although she lived with the King in an effrontery of sin hitherto unexampled, she was often haunted with remorse—for example, she observed the fasts so strictly she had her bread weighed. One day when I remarked upon such scruples, she answered:

"Because I commit one wrong, Madame, do I have to commit all?"

On the whole, I thought her to be pitied rather than blamed, and as far as I personally was concerned, she deserved nothing but praise. She was always amiable, lively, ready to give credit where it was due; and she assured me that if I served her well she would prove her gratitude.

It was quite different with the King. He had agreed with reluctance to my being his children's governess and had only given way after much insistence on the part of his mistress. Judging by what he had heard about me (I did not know then that I owed this fine reputation to my friend Bonne d'Heudicourt), he thought I was interested only in the sublime and feared me as a typical *précieuse*. At this period he saw neither his children nor me, but I knew through Madame de Montespan that he always referred to me as "the wit." He suspected I affected the manners of the hôtel de Rambouillet,† of which the hôtels d'Albret and de Richelieu were imitations, and at Court people laughed at these groups of idle folk with nothing better to do than pass judgment on fine feeling and fine writing.

One day when I had gone to spend a few hours at Versailles with Madame de Montespan, I went for a walk with her and Madame d'Heudicourt, who told the King that Madame de Montespan and I had spoken of such exalted matters that we had soon left her behind. The King was angry at the thought that his mistress might get more pleasure out of talking to me than from being with him, and by a refinement of passion he made her promise not to speak a word to me at night after he had left her room. I soon noticed that all my questions were answered by a curt yes or no.

"I see," I said. "It's a game. I shall take advantage of it and get some sleep."

But as I stood up to leave, Madame de Montespan stopped me, delighted that I had guessed the mystery, and the conversation became more lively.

We spent whole nights talking when I went to see Madame de Montespan in her various palaces. I was so sure of her liking for me that I cared little for the King's dislike. She had such power over him that he always did as she wanted.

But in February 1671 my modest hopes seemed all at once to collapse. At Court people dislike any scandal they do not invent themselves. The marquise d'Heudicourt, whom I then took to be my best friend, was suddenly found guilty of giving two of her lovers a detailed account of private life at Saint-Germain. She had been so much in the secret of the King's amours that she was said to have lent him her own bed during the Flanders campaign when

Madame de Montespan became his mistress; and she had told the secret to all and sundry in long letters which were now travelling all over France. They had even reached the comte de Bussy-Rabutin, whom the King feared like the plague since his *Histoire amoureuse des Gaules,*† and who now lived in exile in the provinces.

The style of these letters was as dangerous as their content. With her usual effrontery, Bonne had sketched little portraits of the King and his favorite which though skilfully executed were by no means pleasant for their subjects to contemplate. The existence of the children was not concealed, and many details were supplied about their lives. Since I had been put in charge of their education on Madame d'Heudicourt's advice, and we were known to be close friends, and since I might be suspected of having betrayed the secret just as she had, I thought my downfall inevitable. Fortunately, Madame d'Heudicourt had treated me as badly as everyone else in her letters; she had even given a long account of my alleged relations with the maréchal d'Albret, heaping every imaginable misdeed upon us both and depicting me as the most abandoned of women. I could not believe in such wickedness and ingratitude until I saw the letters with my own eyes. Her venom saved me, for because of it the King knew I was not in the plot.

I did not plead with the favorite to save Madame d'Heudicourt from the King's wrath: I should only have been destroyed myself. Besides, I did not find it so bad that this viper-tongued siren be winged a little and brought to her senses by a really public disgrace. And so she departed, in extreme despair, guilty of every treason and bereft of all her friends. When she got into her coach to go back to her husband at Heudicourt, she was a broken woman. But she had the consolation of knowing it was mostly her own fault.

The King wished to demonstrate at once the limits of his displeasure, and to show Monsieur d'Albret he was not included in his niece's disgrace, he appointed him governor general of Guienne the same spring. As for me, whom he knew to have been close to the exiled Bonne d'Heudicourt, he asked Madame de Montespan to tell me that he wished to meet me.

This first meeting took place in the favorite's apartment, where

I awaited him instead of running away as I had been used to doing at the time of his customary visit. My heart thumped a little, and I trembled at the thought of having to offer a few paltry apologies for having been friendly with Madame d'Heudicourt. Instead of which, he did not say a word about her but was easy and affable, perfectly amiable yet perfectly regal. He was dressed like a king, in gold upon gold sprinkled with diamonds. He spoke like a king, nobly and succinctly. He even jested like a king, for while he deigned to amuse us with a story, he told it with so majestic a turn of phrase I was confused as well as charmed. He asked me a few questions about myself; inquired after his children, whom he did not know; and finally, very simply and as if he meant it, told me that Madame de Montespan was very attached to me and that he himself was grateful for all I was doing for him. I was very nervous in his presence and much moved by these words after my recent fears, and could answer only very indifferently; but this at least had the advantage of overcoming his prejudice against my wit.

Madame de Montespan wrote to me afterwards that the King had found me simple and sweet, and was amazed I had "so much fire in my eyes." To make her laugh I replied that "I burned but was not consumed." This was the device I then used to seal my letters.

A little while later, to emphasize still more the fact that Madame d'Heudicourt's follies had not lowered me in his esteem, he invited me on the spur of the moment to drive with him. It was the beginning of September, and Madame de Vivonne had taken me to Versailles to see Madame de Montespan, who was her sister-in-law. I had dined with "the ladies," as Mademoiselle de La Vallière and her rival were then called, and just as I was about to withdraw, the King sent for them to go for a drive around the gardens. I had the honor to be included, which surprised me as much as it did the courtiers. Fortunately I was quite well dressed that day, in a gown of blue plush which covered the bosom but was cut deep around the shoulders, with some rather pretty lace about my arms and ribbons of French point in my hair. I had given up my muslin dresses for my visits to the favorite; I would have cut a very strange figure in them at Court.

The King did not speak to me, but the mere fact that he had invited me to drive in his calash made all heads turn. Monsieur de Lauzun, whom I had not seen since the night he made me a present of a newborn babe, spoke to me a great deal, and Monsieur de Turenne was pleased to renew a little friendship we had established a long while ago. All this entertained me vastly, but Mademoiselle de La Vallière, sitting at the back of the carriage with red eyes and wan cheeks, was such a picture of desolation it was enough to put one off all notions of royal favor.

Two months later, after the death of the duchesse de Montauzier, the King appointed the duchesse de Richelieu to her post solely on the recommendation I had made to Madame de Montespan. I congratulated myself on my new power. On the King's orders, Monsieur de Louvois arranged to get my brother back into the army, and gave him first one company of a hundred men in the Picardy regiment, and then in August 1671 another in the light horse. All these acts of generosity touched me more than I could say. I thought the King as magnanimous as he was magnificent. This only made me regret the more that I did not see him again for many long months; at least, they seemed long to me.

I spent those months in watching and prayer, because of the continual anxiety the two children caused me.

Little Françoise, who was approaching three, was in very poor health. Colics succeeded fevers, and convulsions abscesses. By the end of 1671 she had become so pale and thin that she had lost all her beauty, though she still kept the gentle, affectionate ways which made her so charming, and she never uttered a complaint or shed a tear however severe her sufferings. When she was ill she would come and sit on my lap, and for whole nights I would sing to her, mingling the songs of my childhood which I sing so badly with the saucy Creole ditties of Zabeth Dieu. The child would listen in silence, sucking her thumb, her great pale eyes fixed on my face.

Louis-Auguste was a beautiful infant, fat, fair and curly-haired, but I thought it strange that he could not yet walk. He was straight and well made, but whenever I set him down on his feet I was surprised to see he could not stand. Madame de Montespan did not take my fears seriously.

"You'll see," she used to say, "my son is lazy and my daughter's a sleepyhead who likes being nursed."

I tried to distract myself from my allegedly needless apprehensions in the company of my friends. My usual circle was scattered. Monsieur and Madame d'Albret had gone to Bordeaux, and the duchesse de Richelieu, now supervisor of the Queen's maids of honor, never left Saint-Germain. I wrote every week to my maréchal, and was very disconsolate if he was slow to answer. Fortunately I still had Mademoiselle de Lenclos to amuse me, as well as Madame de Montchevreuil, Monsieur de Barillon and Mesdames de Coulanges and de Sévigné and their circle.

Ninon did not lose her looks as she grew older, but she did become constant. And her constancy had chosen an undeserving fop as its object. The affair brought Ninon nothing but bitterness, for the young man was fickle, indecisive and devoid of wit.

"He's got a soul of pap and a pumpkin heart, both fried in snow," she said, asking whether she ought not to console herself by taking up religion. "As you know, I have sold my body dear enough in my day. Well, I think I'll get an even better price for my soul—the Jesuits and the Jansenists are outbidding each other!"

With her I enjoyed all the pleasures of unconstrained friendship. Monsieur de Barillon gave me those of a former passion turned into a feeling which was mild and moderate. He no longer dashed himself against the wall as he had fifteen years before; age had made his despair modest rather than turbulent, though to tell the truth he was still very affectionate. I have always thought the slight inclination of a man of wit preferable to the wild passion of a young fool. Monsieur de Barillon, like the maréchal d'Albret, felt for me the kind of inclination which is neither irksome nor affected, which does not lead to tragedy and which does not exclude the subtle and cruel badinage which for distinguished minds is the very salt of friendship. So long and so charming a love should have its reward, and I showed him my gratitude when the occasion arose.

But most of the time left over from the children I spent with Madame de Coulanges and Madame de Sévigné. They had gathered around them a very agreeable little circle. It comprised ladies of wit like Madame de La Fayette; authors who were gentlemen of quality and so had neither the attitudes nor the faults of men of letters, such as Monsieur de Guilleragues and Monsieur de La Rochefoucauld, author of the *Maximes;* lastly there were a few relics of the hôtel de Richelieu, including my abbé Testu. I often went to sup with them, and we talked endlessly about the latest excitements at Court.

Little Lauzun, a great favorite of the King's and almost his cousin, had committed so many acts of forwardness that in the end the King, and still more Madame de Montespan, tired of him, and on 25 November 1671 he was arrested and taken by Monsieur d'Artagnan to the fortress at Pignerol. The fall of a great personage makes as many ripples in society as a stone falling into a pool, and two months later people were still feeling the repercussions of this event when someone else took the center of the stage. This time, to my astonishment, it was the marquis de Villarceaux, whom I had thought to be sobered down once and for all.

But he had seen fit, when talking to the King about a position for his son, to tell him that some people had whispered to his young niece, Mademoiselle de Grancey, that His Majesty had some designs on her. He added that if this were the case, he begged the King to make use of him, for the matter would be handled better by him than by anyone else and he would guarantee success. The King only laughed.

"Villarceaux," he said, "we are too old, you and I, to meddle with girls of fifteen."

This escapade did nothing to enhance the small esteem in which I held this former admirer, whom I had loved but never respected, but it did bring the thought of him back to me, and I trembled lest Madame de Montespan, who knew very well what such suggestions portended, learn something about my earlier commerce with the marquis and suppose me in league with him now.

In the spring of 1672 little Louise-Françoise's health grew suddenly worse. A few weeks before she had had an abscess in her ear. It had disfigured her face somewhat and caused me great anguish, but she was thought to be cured. But one day I was horrified, when I went to see her and her nurse, to find her unable to see. The next day she could not speak, and then she fell into a condition of great weakness, accompanied by convulsions. I never left her bedside. The doctors connected her present state with the abscess in the ear and said it was now developing inwards, in the brain, and there was little hope of saving her.

I hastened to Saint-Germain to inform Madame de Montespan of what I considered to be her daughter's condition. The King was with her when I arrived. I blurted out my account without pausing for breath, so afflicted by the child's sufferings that I could scarcely speak of them. The King kindly told me to rest a little before going on. I had not slept for several nights, and fatigue was beginning to deprive me of both speech and judgment. I was so stunned by what had happened that I even implored them to send one of the Court physicians to save the child. "That is not possible, Madame," the King said simply, and Madame de Montespan explained with emphasis why outsiders might not be allowed near the children.

I went back to the patient, who had fallen into such a torpor the nurse doubted whether she were still alive. When I put a mirror to her lips it did not mist, but her pulse was still beating. I waited for morning. The child had been given an emetic, but there had been no result from it all day. Then suddenly, during the night, when I no longer expected it, the medicine worked: the child opened her eyes, stroked my cheek, and said she would like a cap of French point to wear. This filled me with enormous hope. I gave her some broth, which she liked, and the medicine produced its full effect and made her feel better. The fever had abated, she could see quite clearly and asked for her doll. In the morning she ate some bread and milk. This improvement had lasted for several days when I went again to Saint-Germain.

Madame de Montespan sent for the King, who came at once to hear the news. He listened with delight but seemed very downcast, and when he left the room the favorite told me that by a strange coincidence little Madame, his five-year-old daughter by the Queen, had also just shown all the signs of a serious illness.

There was said to be no hope, and the King, who was very fond of the child, had not slept for several nights and sent every half-hour to know how the princess was.

I went back to Paris very glad that my darling's condition was better than that of the Queen's daughter, but I did not rejoice for long. Five days later the convulsions and other incidents recurred with such violence that the doctors at once declared that Françoise could not survive. I never left her room, but tried to keep her dry lips moist, held her hand and spoke to her from time to time, as much to ease my own suffering as to lessen hers.

Although I knew death was an enviable fate for an innocent, and that eternal happiness awaited her in the other world, I prayed to God to save her for me. I tried to make a strange bargain: I offered God my own success in exchange for the child's life; not my present success, which was nothing, but those dreams of fortune which I still nourished in my heart and which were now beginning to have a semblance of foundation. I offered up all the promises the old stonemason had made me, all my hopes; I even agreed in my mind that God should bring me back to the want and shame of La Rochelle, so long as the child might live.

But God would not agree to the bargain. The child lay dying for two days and then expired in my arms at dawn on the third day, February 23.

By a strange irony the child's death marked a new stage in my rise to fame. When I went to Court to relate the sad outcome of her illness, I could not hold back my tears. Madame de Montespan, then six months pregnant, could find nothing better to say to me than, "Do not distress yourself, Madame—we will provide you with others." I could feel the drops coursing down my cheeks, and I hid my face in my hands. When I looked up again, I could see that the King too was weeping.

"This lady knows how to love," he said quietly to Madame de Montespan, and left the room without addressing me further.

Six days later "la petite Madame," his other daughter, died, and Shrovetide ended with us all in a state of profound melancholy. I did not know, however, how much my own affliction had been noticed by one who, though a bad husband, was a tender father.

That spring all the talk in Paris was of the war we were going to have against the Dutch. All the young noblemen pawed the ground with impatience, and I was glad for the sake of my brother, for I thought he might have the chance to win some distinction. There is no other way for a gentleman who has nothing but his sword to make his fortune, and it was said that the forthcoming campaign would bring great conquests.

On 25 April 1672 Monsieur de Louvois brought me instructions to leave at once for Genitoy, near Lagny, taking little Louis-Auguste with me. The King was to spend three days there when he left Saint-Germain to join his armies. So I installed myself there in the little château belonging to the King's major-domo in ordinary. Early on the morning of the twenty-seventh, a calash with closed curtains, drawn by six horses, pulled up in front of the house, and as Madame de Montespan stepped down, the King offered her his hand. They seemed closer than ever. The King spent the whole day at Genitoy and decided that Madame de Montespan should stay there with me for two or three months until the child was born. It was the King's habit, when he went to join his army and did not take the ladies with him, to organize his harem before he left. This time he decreed that Saint-Germain should be the residence of the Queen, that Mademoiselle de La Vallière should stay with the Carmelites at Chaillot, while he shut Madame de Montespan up at Genitoy under my supervision.

This last amorous escapade before the two armies met gave the King the opportunity to see his son for the first time. He seemed pleased with the child, and found him handsome, which indeed he was. The father paid no attention to the weakness of the boy's legs, which were hidden by his dress: the child still looked so much like a big baby doll that if you did not think about it, you took him for younger than he was and so noticed nothing amiss. He was always clinging round my neck or sitting on my lap, and he played up very well, with no sign of shyness, to the greatest monarch in Europe. I spent a very pleasant day in the company of the prince and his mistress. I was wearing for the first time a new gold-embroidered gown which I owed to the generosity of the marquise and which seemed not to displease the King. Admittedly the favorite's repeated pregnancies did not show her to advantage, and even when she was not expecting a child she let herself put on weight terribly. Her face was still beautiful, but she was losing her figure. That day I saw in the King's eye certain looks the meaning of which was very plain to an experienced coquette. I was amused, but did nothing to encourage a feeling for which I had no use.

The marquise and I grew closer than ever before during the three months we spent together at Lagny. We lived like two sisters —or rather two cousins, one rich and brilliant, the other poor and obscure.

It was a continual delight to hear Madame de Montespan talk. She made the most serious matters agreeable and ennobled the most ordinary. She had read a good deal and knew almost as much Greek and Latin as her sister the abbess of Fontevrault. She was a good judge of literature and paid pensions to many poets. On top of all that, she had an incomparable talent for mimicry and could fill a roomful of people with mirth. When she was in good form she could depict ministers, princes and flunkies with such devastating satire and such amusing comparisons that those who passed by her windows when she was there with the King used to say she was "playing the executioner."

I myself am incapable of imitating anyone, but the marquise's skill at observing and reproducing everything with a couple of grimaces made me die of laughter. I soon noticed, however, that she was not so good as I was at seeing within people's minds. I vaguely sensed things about others which I could not always express, but which always enabled me to act upon them. While I, naturally reserved, could penetrate inside other people, she, who was all outside, saw only their external aspects. Another difference between us was that I liked to be liked, and this made me more careful in my judgments, while she thought herself above such things and did not attempt moderation. She spared no one, not even the King, and sometimes loosed her shafts against him even in his presence.

"I'll tell you one thing," she said one day after dinner as we sat on the large tiles on the edge of a fountain with little Louis-Auguste between us, "the King is incapable of delicacy. What do you think of the idea of making me share the duchesse de La Vallière's apartment? I complained about it the other day and he was quite embarrassed. 'I know,' he said, 'I didn't realize.' 'You may not have realized,' I told him, 'but I certainly did.' The fact is, he is not really in love with me—he just thinks he owes it to the world at large to be loved by the best-born and most beautiful woman in the kingdom. True, at that rate I need fear no rivals but one or two princesses. The rest do not exist."

As she said this she played with a red top which the child had dropped. She made it whirl around so fast on the white rim of the fountain that it was soon only a crimson stain on the smooth stone. Suddenly I felt myself transported as if by magic to more than fifteen years before, and I saw again the tablecloth in the rue Neuve-Saint-Louis and the red wine stain spreading over it, that day when I learned the irrevocable truth about the amours of the maréchal d'Albret. Now as then, I felt as if a dagger had been plunged into my heart, and for some unknown reason I was overwhelmed with deathly sadness.

"What's that face for?" said Madame de Montespan, who never let an expression escape her. "Stop it—it makes you quite ugly. Especially those pinched nostrils!"

She tried to imitate me.

"Quite ridiculous! What's the matter?"

"Nothing, Madame. I am just a little tired."

"No, that's not it. I know what it is. You are religious, and while you don't mind bringing up my children you don't want to hear about my amours. You don't want to be made an accomplice in something all the Paris preachers attack from the pulpit. Very well—take their part! But make haste, for the King will get rid of them all, he'll drive out my enemies, he'll repudiate the Queen, he'll love me as much as that, do you hear? I don't care a rap for the opinions of all the pious ladies in France! Take that nasty face away—it gets on my nerves!"

I took this as an excuse to escape, snatching up Louis-Auguste as I went. While we had been talking with such vehemence, he had crawled to the edge of the fountain and was about to fall in. As I ran toward the house I could scarcely see for tears, and the child, amazed, buried his head in my neck as if to console me for a sorrow he could not understand. Fortunately his mother had not understood either: her talent was for faces only, and she knew nothing of hearts.

For the rest of our stay at Lagny she avoided all further mention of her relations with the King. But she amused both herself and me describing the goings-on of his ministers.

Lying across her bed, for the weight of the child she was carrying tired her, she spent whole days reading, writing or talking to me, sometimes overwhelming me with praise and flattery, sometimes peppering me with shafts of malice. In reality she was a very troubled person, uncertain as to her future. The downfall of others was her favorite subject: if she was not speculating about the likely end of Monsieur Colbert, she was meditating upon the decline of Monsieur de Lauzun or Mademoiselle de Mancini. The latter, now the wife of constable Colonna, was the talk of every drawing-room.

"I believe Monsieur Scarron once wrote something for her?"

"Yes, a few epistles."

I suddenly remembered the suggestion the Cardinal's niece had made twelve years earlier, that I should go with her to Brouage. My poverty, which I regretted so much at the time, had saved me from linking my fate to one who was heading for destruction. Thus we lament over an opportunity missed, when in fact it often turns out to be another opportunity saved.

"Poor woman!" said Madame de Montespan. "She has gone into an abbey near Fontainebleau in the hope that the King will recall her to Court. She has written him two or three very piteous letters, and, would you believe it, he was on the point of giving in."

As she spoke she twined her pearl and ruby necklaces round the chubby arms of Louis-Auguste, who crowed delightedly. The fair-haired child and his blonde mother looked like a living portrait of Venus and Cupid. A rather fat Venus, and a crippled Cupid.

"But," she went on, "I scolded him in no uncertain manner, and he has just sent her a very curt order to leave the kingdom at once. When you think what she was, and see what she is . . . When you think of the passion he once felt for her, and see how harshly he treats her now, just at the whim of another . . . Almost a queen yesterday, and today a lost soul in a vagabond body."

Her great blue eyes clouded.

"I don't know if she who is victorious should rejoice or tremble . . . And look at Monsieur de Lauzun. Someone said the other day in the Queen's room that this first of courtiers now looks like the last of hermits, there in his cell with his long beard. And Monsieur Fouquet, who used to be so powerful and proud? And Madame d'Heudicourt, who came near to being mistress of the King and of the kingdom—now she has to invite her tenants to dinner in order to have any company at all. That's the Court for you —everything today, tomorrow nothing."

"Kings are like other men," I said. "They lack constancy . . . But I believe all the people you mention committed great errors."

"Not all of them . . . Mademoiselle de Mancini committed only one, and that was to obey orders and surrender without a fight. That is not my way—I never give in. I know how to keep our gentleman. Softness will not do—I ill-use him, mock him, lecture him, make him cry . . . But," she added sadly, "he may get tired of that too."

When she reached this point in her reflections, I would intervene with some allusion to religion: a seed sown in that harrowed soul might one day bring forth fruit.

I was never on such a friendly footing with her that I could speak without reserve; I doubt if anyone was. But I did preach to her in the most general terms, without specific allusion to her sin, of the need to detach oneself from human passions.

"Leave all," I said, "and you will find all."

She understood me, was ready to meditate with me upon some topic out of François de Sales† and liked to contemplate the four last things—between composing an epigram and writing a letter to the King. The drawback of preaching in general and not in particular is that in general the sermon is well received but in particular nothing is changed. After Madame de Montespan had meditated and even prayed, she shut her book of hours and went back to her amours.

On 20 June 1672 she gave birth to a second son, who was named Louis-César and who later became comte de Vexin. Now that there was a Caesar and an Augustus, all Louis needed was an Alexander to make the family of heroes complete. Alexander finally arrived in the person of the comte de Toulouse.

Little Louis-César was weak from birth. He had a pretty face, but his body was deformed, with one shoulder higher than the other and a back that was not altogether flat. Madame de Montespan affected to be indifferent to these defects.

"His figure doesn't matter," she said. "We intend him for the Church."

But the infirmities of her children troubled her more than she would admit. By a strange chance, while the bastards of Mademoiselle de La Vallière were radiant with a beauty they did not get from their mother, all Madame de Montespan's children by the King had some visible defect. Little Louise-Françoise had had blood that was poor and tainted; the duc du Maine had weak legs; the comte de Vexin had humped shoulders; Mademoiselle de Nantes limped; Mademoiselle de Tours had a squint; Mademoiselle de Blois spoke so slowly and confusedly it was painful to listen to her; only the comte de Toulouse, the last, born at a time when the rupture between the parents was already complete, seemed to obtain God's forgiveness and escape the general anathema. Later on, thinking about this family so full of charm and wit but so unlucky physically, I could not help remembering the story of Mélusine which I used to be told as a child. All the children this beautiful fairy bore the comte de Poitiers, strong and valiant though they were, had some obvious defect: a large tooth, different colored eyes, six fingers on one hand, a hairy face, a club foot . . . According to the legend this was because a child's diabolical origins could never be completely hidden. I leave others to judge whether this applied to the children of the pearl of the Mortemarts.

The very evident physical shortcomings of her latest-born persuaded the favorite to take an interest in the less visible defects of little Louis-Auguste. My repeated requests were heard at last, and various learned physicians were consulted. They said that the child's legs were too thin and that one was longer than the other; but they suggested few remedies and left us little hope.

I resolved to do all I could myself to strengthen the child and teach him to walk. I told Madame de Montespan it was necessary for him always to be with me if I was to do all his condition required, adding that in view of little César's weakness it was desirable he too should be under close supervision. I insisted that I wished to live in the same house as the two children. And so that the secret about them should continue to be kept, I even agreed not to see my friends and to leave all my acquaintance ignorant of where I lived.

The King having agreed to this plan, I found myself in August 1672 in a large and beautiful house surrounded by an extensive garden. It was situated just on the far side of the Vaugirard gate, beyond the Carmelites, in a deserted suburb which had all the charms of the country. I took Nanon Balbien with me and was provided with other domestics. To counter the danger of some outsider coming upon a nurse or hearing a child cry, I also took the little d'Heudicourt girl with me. Her mother, afflicted by her own disgrace, made no difficulty: she hoped by this arrangement to revive the friendship between us, which she did, and to win the King over, which she did not. To make up the numbers I added my nephew Toscan to the rest.

I had disappeared from the capital as suddenly as if some magician had whisked me away on a cloud, and this produced much gossip at Ninon's and at the hôtel de Coulanges, and caused much ink to flow between Paris and Bordeaux. But I was too busy with the children, the eldest of whom was only four, to bother about the suspicions and cares of Marais society.

I spent all my time looking after, teaching and amusing my charges; handing round infusions, administering worm powders, soothing toothaches, bathing, purging, teaching the older ones to read and the younger ones to use a spoon. I also tried to strengthen my special pet's legs with massage and ointments. All this gave me plenty of exercise.

I was visibly losing weight. My duties were the more numerous because Nanon only looked after Louise d'Heudicourt and did not help me at all with the other three. Her small-town religion still lacked magnanimity, and she declared she would not so much as touch a child of sin. She was not in the secret about the royal children and thought they were the offspring of one of my lady friends. But, with a boldness derived from ten years in my service and my fondness for her, she made it quite clear that she disapproved of my taking charge of them. As for the nurses, they had come to their own conclusions on the subject, based on my attentions to Louis-Auguste and César and the luxury of the children's clothes. One day when I jokingly asked one of them who she thought their father was, she said, "He must be a magistrate at least," that being the highest rank she could imagine.

I was rewarded for all the pains I took by my children's affection and the improvement in their health.

The little d'Heudicourt girl was as pretty as a picture and had the most winning ways. Whenever a visitor came I would pass her off as the sister or cousin of the other children, in order to justify their presence. She was so eager to be helpful that she would sometimes ask, "Who am I today, Mamma?" Little César, though still at an age when a child is only an animal, was always smiling at me. Louis-Auguste and Toscan, who called me either "nana" or "madame," spent all their time hanging round my neck. Not that this happy retreat was without excitements.

One day a chimney caught fire and spread to a beam in the children's quarters. Fortunately it smouldered for a long while, and we had time to muster our forces and avoid a conflagration. I sent word by coach to Madame de Montespan so that she might send help or tell me what to do to prevent our secret getting out. All the answer she gave my messenger was: "Very good. Tell Madame Scarron that fire is a sign of good luck for children."

Another day when I came back from a walk with the two elder children and little Louis-César, I found Monsieur Colbert awaiting me and anxious to unravel the mystery. To preserve the secrecy which honor enjoined on me, I tossed the baby into the dress of a passing maid, who quietly carried him off like a bundle of dirty linen.

But my greatest agitation came from an even more unexpected visit. It happened one nightfall at the beginning of autumn. I was sitting by the fire in the children's room telling them one of Perrault's fairy tales.† Louis-Auguste was sitting on my lap, little Louise d'Heudicourt sat on the arm of my chair holding my hand, and as I spoke I absently rocked the baby's cradle with my foot: he was teething, and fretful. The children of queens have special "rockers" to lull and look after them; not so the bastards of kings.

Suddenly, without being announced, a gentleman in hunting costume came into the room; I could not see his face in the dusk. I tried to stand up and conceal the children from sight, but was too encumbered, and before I had managed to struggle upright I recognized the voice coming out of the darkness:

"Don't be afraid, Madame, and do not disturb the children. I would gladly hear the rest of the story."

I do not think Moses was more surprised by the voice that came to him out of the burning bush. I had difficulty finding my voice, and I really do not know how I finished the story. Perhaps I altered it and made Prince Charming marry the wicked fairy. But the children did not complain, and nor did the King, for it was he.

He told me he had wanted to see for himself how I was settled in the new house, and whether I had everything I needed. I thanked him profusely for the services Monsieur de Louvois rendered me and for the way he provided for the children's requirements.

I would have sent for lights, but the King did not wish it. So we stayed chatting in the firelight. The two little princes had fallen asleep, and Louise d'Heudicourt, perhaps sensing something extraordinary, was as still as if my story had changed her into a statue of salt. The King said he had been hunting on the plain of Châtillon when he had the idea of galloping to the village of Vaugirard. He had left his small train of followers at the garden gate. He inquired at length after the children's health, then asked me kindly if this life was not too lonely for me.

"Sire," I said, "I gave you my word that no one should learn your secret, and I would suffer anything to keep my trust."

We spoke for a while about this and that, then he took his leave, preventing me from getting up to see him out or to curtsy.

"You make such a charming picture with the three children," he said, "I should hate to disturb the arrangement."

I was so overcome by this visit that for more than an hour after the King's departure I sat on in the darkness, thinking. I might have been there yet if little Louise had not broken her respectful silence to pluck at my sleeve and say she was hungry.

I did not have time, however, to become more intoxicated with the honor the King had done me, for a fortnight later Madame de Montespan ordered me to take Louis-Auguste to Antwerp. The remedies of the Paris faculty of medicine having failed, she wanted me to show the child to a much-praised healer. So I left Nanon in charge of the rest of my little family and made the journey as the marquise de Surgères, a lady of Poitou, passing the little boy off as my son. The old doctor, who was consulted by people from all over Europe, made use of very violent remedies which caused the poor child great pain. By traction and the use of various instruments and unguents he did achieve some result, but I am not sure the cure was not worse than the disease: he lengthened my little prince's bad leg until it was much longer than the other, and he did not make it any stronger. As I brought the child back over the uncomfortable winter roads, he cried out at every jolt; he was as irritable as a wild beast and was still unable to walk. I pitied him greatly, but could do nothing to comfort him. It is terrible to watch the suffering of someone you love.

At Vaugirard I resumed my hermit-like existence. I saw no other living soul except Monsieur de Louvois and wrote to no one but my brother. Every day was alike in that magnificent but hidden house, but I had too much to do to be bored. I would have been perfectly happy had it not been for the illness of my little prince. I had books, trees and children, and I have never needed more to make me praise God for His creation and warble songs of joy.

I do not know whether the King had felt something of the peace that reigned at Vaugirard and the peace that filled my soul, but he began to hunt more often on the plain of Châtillon and came to see me three or four times during the months which followed my return from Antwerp.

He played with his children, spoke of ordinary matters like the weather, hunting and his building projects, then left me with a word, as suddenly as he had arrived. His parting word at first was just a phrase like "I'll see" or "perhaps," in answer to some request of mine, but later it was often something with a double meaning. One day when my darling had a quartan fever and I was gently stroking his brow, the King's farewell was "How pleasant to be loved by you," uttered very brusquely, almost like an insult. Another day he asked me which was my favorite play, and when I answered that it was Racine's *Bérénice* he just said gravely, "So I ought to be jealous of Titus," and slipped away.

All this gave me much to think about. I had a certain experience in such matters and would have thought I was dealing with a timid admirer if the speaker had not been the King of France, a king, moreover, who was very much in love with a mistress radiant with youth and beauty. His position and what I thought to be his feelings for Madame de Montespan blinded me as to his intentions, and I put the strangeness of his visits down to eccentricity of character or clumsiness in turning compliments.

When I realized that Madame de Montespan knew nothing about the King's visits to Vaugirard, I grew more worried. But I thought I owed the King secrecy about this as about everything else. "How likely is it," I asked myself to quiet my scruples, "that the most important man in the kingdom should pick out Monsieur Scarron's thirty-six-year-old widow?" I explained my imaginings as the result of isolation and bade myself think no more of the matter lest I become like one of those lonely old coquettes who think every man of importance is in love with her.

On 20 March 1673 the King showed his satisfaction with my services in a more decent, but still very obliging way. Presented with the list of pensions, he saw that I had been set down for the same two thousand livres for twelve years, so he crossed out "livres" and inserted "crowns," thus multiplying my income by three. Then he told Monsieur de Louvois to tell me he wanted me to accompany Madame de Montespan that spring when she went with him to the wars. The favorite was pregnant again, and he wanted me to take the child at birth, as usual.

But this pregnancy was not quite so secret as the previous ones. There even began to be rumors that the King and the favorite had several children already, and that the hidden princes were going to be legitimized. I was no lawyer, but I did not see how this was possible, for in such cases the mother has to be named at least, and here this could not be done without giving the marquis de Montespan the theoretical rights of paternity. But the ministers, who knew more of such things than I, regarded the matter as certain, and Monsieur de Louvois gave me permission to see some of my friends again before I left Paris for the citadel of Tournai, where the King and his mistress awaited me.

One evening I went to the hôtel de Coulanges and found myself among people I had not seen for a year. The abbé Testu thought I had dropped out of the sky and nearly died of shock. But no one asked any questions. Madame de Sévigné shrewdly remarked that my dress showed I had been spending my time with people of quality. Everyone thought I was beautiful, amiable, magnificently turned out and looking very well.

On 1 May, I set out for the army with the ladies. This time the King wanted to have everyone where he could see them, so the Queen, Mademoiselle de La Vallière, Madame de Montespan and their suites piled into the coaches and we all jolted along the roads of Flanders. I felt very sorry for Madame de Montespan, who rode in the King's carriage, for she was near her time and suffered greatly from the discomforts of the journey. The dust thrown up around the coaches by the bodyguards and equerries got into everything inside; but in the royal carriage, which had all the windows down because the King liked fresh air, there was no question of even drawing a curtain. Many a time the favorite thought she would choke, but to be ill in the King's presence was an unforgivable sin. At night we usually slept in wretched inns, and sometimes even on straw. Sometimes, too, after twelve hours on the road, there was nothing to eat but thin soup or one egg for two.

The reason why the luggage and provisions failed to keep up was that the King always travelled extremely fast, in stages. This also meant that ordinary needs were disregarded. Sometimes we dined without getting out of the coaches, and the ladies suffered so much from having to defer the relief of nature that they almost swooned. Madame de Montespan's condition made this hardship worse for her than for anyone else, but she dared not admit it except to me. As for the King, if he felt the call of nature he did not scruple to alight. The great of this world are so constituted that they think only of themselves and do not even imagine that others have desires and pains. So the King's mistresses had a great deal of discomfort.

At Tournai I saw the King every day until he and his troops entered Holland, but I never saw him alone. Madame de Montespan was not in the best of humor after the fatigue of the journey, and she bullied the King in front of everybody. She made no bones about taking him up on everything he said or did, and sometimes even went so far as to criticize him for the lowness of his birth. She recognized only two families in France—that of the La Rochefoucaulds and her own. She allowed that the King's family was distinguished but questioned its age and was fond of reminding him of her own family's motto: "Before the sea was in the world, Rochechouart its waves unfurled." Not a day went by that she did not make him feel she was lowering herself by consenting to be the mistress of a Bourbon. Her elder sister, Madame de Thianges, who was even more obsessed than she about her birth, went even further and maintained that the beauty of her person and the delicacy of her physique derived naturally from the difference set by rank between her and common mortals, among whom she included the King. He, though as the journey had shown he could be harsh enough, was bemused by these arguments, listened to them patiently and even humbly and ended by shyly soliciting the honor of kissing a hand that was denied him. I soon grew tired of being a third in scenes where the King and his favorite took turns at being either hateful or ridiculous. I found the citadel of Tournai wearisome; nor did I much care for the mission I had been charged with vis-à-vis Mademoiselle de La Vallière.

It was commonly said that this tender, virtuous and abandoned lady had at last decided to quit the scene where for a long while she had no longer had any part to play; but that she meant to make a sensational exit and take the veil with the Carmelites in the course of the following year. Madame de Montespan considered this somewhat exaggerated, and saw it as a kind of sermon addressed to herself. She dreaded the scandal and the rumors to which it would give rise, and would have preferred her rival to withdraw merely as a pensioner to the Filles de Chaillot. The King, for his part, was easily reconciled to Mademoiselle de La Vallière's decision, but he hated the Carmelites and would rather she had chosen any other order. He went about saying that the austerities of the Carmelite nuns were repulsive, but that their pretence of piety did not stop them from being mischievous, meddling, intriguing and even given to poisoning.

The King and Madame de Montespan charged me with persuading Mademoiselle de La Vallière of the advantages of a less ostentatious withdrawal from the world, and the charms of a more moderate and comfortable retreat. They thought my reputation for virtue would make their scapegoat listen to me.

The duchesse de La Vallière was at her toilet, dejectedly combing her long fair curls. She was magnificently dressed in brocade and gold, for right to the end she was always clad like a princess and never appeared unfresh or neglected. Despite my reluctance I set out my arguments, or rather those of my sponsors, with the glibness of an ambassador. I said one should beware of certain impulses which might be mistaken for a religious vocation; that being a nun had its drawbacks too; that for someone who had lived in the world as she had, enclosure and silence could be torture; and that she would certainly miss her friends, her brother and her children, who were still so young . . .

Suddenly she interrupted me, looking straight at me, and said in a faint voice:

"Madame, I have already told myself all you are saying now. I know very well I shall have sorrow and regrets where I am going.

But I know too that they will be as nothing when I remember all those two have made me suffer." She meant the King and his mistress.

Seeing I could not dissuade her from becoming a nun, I advocated an order less strict than the Carmelites, describing all the latter's austerities and painting a very gloomy picture of their life. As a crowning argument I said:

"Just see the gold in which you are still dressed! Do you think you could abandon all that from one day to the next for shifts which will chafe your skin and robes of sackcloth?"

She gave me a gentle smile.

"Madame, let me tell you something which I beg you not to repeat. For years I have worn a hair shirt under these garments of gold, and for years I have taken the mattress off my bed every night and slept on the wood. I put it back in the morning so that my maids suspect nothing—I do not wish to seem eccentric. So you may imagine whether it would be difficult for me to get used to the hard life you describe."

I did not know what to say. I gazed at the splendid brocade and the jewels decking that young and fragile body but could not stop thinking of the shirt of hair beneath. For days afterwards I had a bitter taste in my mouth which made Tournai unbearable.

On 1 June, with the full knowledge of the whole Court, Madame de Montespan gave birth to a little girl who was at once named Louise-Françoise. Three weeks later I left the citadel with a new burden, delighted to have an excuse to return to the peace of Vaugirard and the affectionate ways of my darling.

When I got back, Monsieur de Louvois spoke to me more openly than before of the legitimation of the children. To please the King, Monsieur de Harlay, then the procurator general, had taken a first step by managing to legitimate the chevalier de Longueville, natural son born of the double adultery of the duc de Longueville and the maréchale de La Ferté. Contrary to all previous practice, the mother had not been named. This constituted a precedent, and it was thought that my little princes would emerge into the light of day before the end of the year. Like Minerva, they would be born of Jupiter, motherless.

I now took up again with my usual acquaintance and supped every evening with Madame de Coulanges, Mademoiselle de Lenclos or Monsieur de Barillon. At midnight I would be driven home to my magnificent house at Vaugirard, the envy of all my friends. I greatly enjoyed those talkative, mirthful autumn evenings. Moreover I was in excellent health and even looking younger, for nothing puts off aging like being in favor. Lastly, it grew plainer every day that my career would not always be as unsuccessful as it had been hitherto.

"What I like about talking to you," the marquise de Sévigné used to say, "is that, with a Christian moral here and a political moral there, one finds one has been led much further than one expected." It is true that in those days it gave me pleasure, for my own benefit and that of others, to draw some instruction from the scenes and intrigues I witnessed at Court, and it often took the form of the maxims which Monsieur de La Rochefoucauld had made fashionable in our little circle. But, to use Madame de Sévigné's terms, such morals were more often political than Christian.

To tell the truth, the abbé Gobelin was none too pleased with his penitent. When I read the New Testament or the *Imitation of Christ,* † the tears flooded all too easily to my eyes; I was more moved by such books than by any of the passions I experienced in my life. But I had not the strength to carry religion any further, to detach myself from a world which then seemed to me so seductive. I consoled myself by thinking that apart from that little weakness I committed no sins that I knew of. My whole life was devoted to the service of others; I possessed no wealth and no desire to acquire any; I was a faithful friend; I gave regularly to charity; my behavior was completely irreproachable.

This quiet virtue impressed even the great ones of this world. One day when I was visiting Madame de Montespan at Saint-Germain, I found myself among a group of ladies and gentlemen. The King was also of the company, and some of the wilder youths took it into their heads to overturn the ladies' chairs in order to admire their petticoats. Madame de Montespan having warmly applauded this idea, the King himself joined in. He boldly overturned

Mademoiselle de La Vallière, who hurt her arm as she fell; Madame de Saint-Geran, who flapped her feet very elegantly; Madame de Thianges, who declared herself enchanted to be able to show a perfect leg; Madame d'Uzès, the comtesse de Soissons, the maréchale de La Mothe, and even an old ruined baronne who revealed a moth-eaten underskirt which called forth many a spiteful remark from the favorite. All these ladies thought to curry favor by wearing sickly smiles.

I was a little apart from all this, for I always thought it more seemly to acknowledge the inferiority of my birth by keeping at a distance. So the King came to me last. As he approached, I looked him straight in the eye, without any special severity but without indulgence either. He looked straight back, with an air of challenge. I was already resigning myself to displaying some rather pretty lace when, having got hold of my chair, he suddenly let go of it and said in a low voice, "With this one I just dare not."

There was a silence, broken by a courtier who saw fit to remark: "Your Majesty is right. If I had to choose between pinching Madame Scarron's bottom and that of the Queen, I would not hesitate—I'd be much less afraid of tackling the Queen."

Madame de Montespan burst out laughing, but the King replied curtly, "I think you forget yourself, Monsieur," and he who had made his entrance like a page made his exit like a king.

I was not sure whether the special treatment he had afforded me was a mark of favor or of disgrace, and soon afterwards I had another occasion to ponder. One day as Madame de Montespan was talking to me about my brother, who had been made governor of Elbourg and who was now promised the governorship of Belfort, the King turned to me and said:

"I am not sure, Madame, how Monsieur your brother understands his duties. I hear he is busier with his own interests than with mine. It is said he is more concerned with pillaging the people he rules over than with fortifying the strongholds I put in his charge, and that he tries to extract benefits from the inhabitants over and above his emoluments. I must tell you, Madame, that I am very dissatisfied with him. He behaves in a way I would never permit in anyone else."

You may imagine what I felt on hearing these words. Monsieur de Louvois had already told me my brother did not always act like a man of honor, and for months my letters to him, urging him not to be cruel to the vanquished Huguenots and not to risk his reputation in shady business affairs, had pleaded in vain. But this public rebuke from the King renewed and increased my shame.

Once I had overcome my surprise, however, I began to think about the singular manner in which the reproach had been delivered. And once more it seemed to me that there was a double meaning in the last sentence. Why was he prepared to endure from my brother what he would suffer from no one else? This was food for thought, and I concluded that the King had a very attractive way of framing his reprimands. But I shrank from carrying my speculations too far and merely decided that despite appearances I had not fallen into disfavor.

On 20 December 1673 the Parlement recorded letters of legitimation for Louis-Auguste, Louis-César and Louise-Françoise, who assumed the titles of duc du Maine, comte de Vexin and Mademoiselle de Nantes. The King thus made public "the affection which nature made him feel for his children, and other reasons which greatly increased his natural sentiments."

At the end of the same month Monsieur de Louvois instructed me to leave Vaugirard and take the three royal children to Saint-Germain. The King wanted to have them with him at Court now and wished me to be with them. I was given an apartment in the château.

The orders of a King brook no argument. From what I had seen of the Court I could guess that I should have no freedom there and because of my birth and fortune would not even be able to cut a good figure. But I had to obey, and I tried to be indifferent about the kind of life to which I was destined.

But I had some very strange dreams, far removed, in their glimpses of hope, from the keen regret I expected to feel on leaving Vaugirard. One night at the end of 1673 I dreamed I was flying up to the church roofs and could see all the world at my feet. Another time I dreamed that Madame de Montespan and I were both going up the grand staircase at Versailles, and she shrank and became very small while I grew and became quite huge. Unthinkingly I told my dream to the favorite herself, and she was furiously angry. She went in for all kinds of divination, and saw all too clearly what the dream portended.

I am not superstitious, and believe not in dreams but in merit, patience, restraint and the strength which accumulates in a passionate nature when it is curbed and confined.

Thus, in the royal gardens, we see fountains shooting skyward. Their waters, long held back in narrow channels, were there gathering the strength which now bears them aloft. The fountain itself seems sudden and wonderful; but the force behind it has travelled league upon league, secretly, underground.

Eleven

Madame de Montespan's state apartment in the old château at Saint-Germain resembled its mistress: it was extravagant, and more like a fairy grotto than an ordinary reception room.

Two great rockeries rose up in the middle of it, and perfumed streams cascaded down from them into huge pools. Tuberoses and jasmines that were changed every day seemed to grow out of the stone, from which there spurted a fountain ten feet high. Dozens of birds made of gilded wood sang among silver branches; stuffed wild animals emerged on the hour from caves hollowed out of the rock and told the time by each uttering its own particular cry. The whole construction was surmounted by an Orpheus for ever plucking the same string of his lyre, while all around the room mirrors multiplied to infinity the magic grotto and its automata. This clock-work spectacle, wonderful though it was at first glance, became rather tedious after a time, though my little princes, like their father, never seemed to tire of it. "It's fox and parrot," my little duc du Maine used to say when he meant it was two o'clock in the afternoon.

The other rooms of the favorite's apartment were equally amusing, for children. Amid the gilt panelling Madame de Montespan raised pigs and goats; little black pages decked in pearls and emeralds tamed monkeys, tied ribbons round the necks of lambs and tried to teach all kinds of red and green birds to sing. White mice in tiny gold cages waited for the marquise to harness them six at a time to a filigree coach and make them draw it along in front of the King. She herself liked playing with them, and would let them nibble her beautiful hands. The King, who was not always so well treated as the mice, used to show his mistress to his ministers and expostulate about the Mortemart family's sense of humor. From this menagerie, between one childish prank and another, the marquise ruled very effectively—not the kingdom, for there was never any question of that, but at least the faces and favors of its master. At the first hint of one of her whims, palaces, coaches and jewels sprang up beneath her feet. Everything happened through or for her; nothing without her.

And so there was not a lady of quality at Court who did not cherish the ambition of becoming the King's mistress. Most of them would say quite openly that to succeed in being loved by one's prince was no offense against one's husband or father, or even against God. Worse still, the families themselves, and even certain husbands, were proud if their ladies' efforts were crowned with success. Etiquette then required ladies who passed through the King's chamber when he was not there to curtsy to his bed; and this was more than a symbol. How could a man not sin when he was surrounded with so many devils trying to tempt him?

The Lucifer in chief took some precautions, however, to prevent any young female demon from stealing her place. Having heard, in that year of 1674, that the King was making free with Mademoiselle de Théobon, Mademoiselle de La Mothe and others among the Queen's maids of honor, the imperious favorite professed to be scandalized because, she said, these young ladies were turning the Court into a place of ill repute. And through her devoted ally the duchesse de Richelieu she aroused the scruples of the Queen. The latter, who was both a genuine saint and a perfect innocent, asked the King to dismiss the young women in question. This was done, and the wife thus ensured the mistress's undivided sway.

Perhaps it is not quite accurate to say the beautiful Athénaïs reigned unchallenged over the King's desires. He was not the most constant of lovers, and his mistress, who was often either ill or pregnant, did have to share him; but it was usually only with her own servants or attendants, so the royal favors were kept, so to speak, in the family.

One such case was the relationship between the King and Mademoiselle Desoeillets, lady's maid to the favorite. When this young woman and I were talking one day in an antechamber, she gave me to understand that the King had had dealings with her on various occasions. She even seemed to boast of having had children with him, and I found out later that this was true. She was neither young nor beautiful, but the King was often alone with her when her mistress was busy or unwell. La Desoeillets told me the King had problems and would often sit by the fire for hours, deep in thought and sighing.

I, like the King, had my troubles and my melancholy moods, which I tried to soothe by taking long solitary walks in the park and the forest. Court life filled me with weariness and disgust. I could not get used to its follies, still less to the profound boredom it inspired in me.

No one at Court had anything to do except the King, his ministers and his generals. The days were spent in empty words, gambling and intrigues. When they were not losing pots of money at faro and other card games, the ladies passed all day and all night eating sweets and jams, getting drunk on strong liquors, or even, for want of something to do, taking medicine. I met some who were addicts of purges and bloodletting. Their bodies thus provided for, they occupied their minds with astrology, the interpretation of handwriting, palm reading, love philters and all the different forms of divination and magic. What space was then left in their little heads was filled up with gossip about the royal family. A single look or smile on the part of the King supplied conversation for a week. As you may imagine, a month was not enough to do it justice if he uttered a witticism.

Having lived for years in the most brilliant Paris society, I was afflicted by the impossibility of finding any intellectual nourishment in this company. The only person who reminded me a little of my former life was the duchesse de Richelieu, whom I glimpsed from time to time when, having got away for a moment from the Queen, her dogs, her jesters and her Spanish chambermaids, she came down to the "ladies' apartment," as that shared by Madame de Montespan and Mademoiselle de La Vallière was called. But the Court gradually spoiled even that small pleasure. The duchesse was not so partial to me now: she liked to have dependents, and did not care for them to change their condition without permission. That one who had formerly been her humble protégée should have come to Court without her help struck her as the blackest ingratitude. She preferred Madame Scarron in muslin to Madame Scarron in gold.

Nor did the place itself have any charms to distract me. I hated the château of Saint-Germain. The situation and the surroundings were beautiful enough, but I disliked the buildings. The architecture is unpleasing, the brickwork undistinguished, the courtyard of the old château extremely ugly and the inside of both palaces indescribably uncomfortable.

The brilliant entertainments which were always being given to amuse the courtiers, the balls, the operas, the fireworks, the plays —all these could not disguise what was repulsive about the place once the lights were out. To get into the main courtyard you had to make your way through booths and stalls where certain servants sold for their own advantage the leftovers from the King's table. In order to reach the magnificent state apartments of the monarch and the rest of the royal family, you had to elbow your way through the crowd of poor courtiers and ordinary people swarming round these rickety sheds, braving the smells of burned fat and trampling over chicken bones, scraps of game birds and hunks of bread.

Once that was done, you had the pleasure of climbing up some dark and stinking staircase where dogs and gentlemen relieved themselves. You then crossed landings covered with garbage and entered vestibules scented with the heavy perfume of closets and privies. The King and Monsieur, his eldest brother, were accustomed to dirty houses from their childhood and thought all this quite natural. And if the sovereign could put up with it, everyone else had to put up with it too.

Thereafter, if you were lucky enough to escape the cutpurses and pickpockets who circulated freely in the reception rooms and did not lose the pearls from your necklace or the fringes and lace from your dress on the way, you might hope to withdraw at last into a private apartment, which was usually no more than a single room, airless, unheated and without a view.

I myself had two tiny rooms on the second floor of the King's wing, to the left of the grand staircase and opposite the apartment of Monsieur Le Nôtre, architect of the gardens. This story had been divided horizontally to provide rooms overhead for the chambermaids, and my own room was not as much as six feet high. As I am rather tall, I had only to wear an especially full mob-cap or have my hair dressed high in the style then fashionable to be always scraping against the ceiling.

And it was for these outstanding advantages that all the nobility of France committed such follies. Dukes and marquises with sumptuous mansions in Paris and huge châteaux in the provinces left everything behind to cram themselves ten at a time into one dark entresol room; and they professed themselves delighted with the privilege.

Fortunately I had the education of my little princes to keep me from sinking into the general brutishness. Teaching and looking after the children gave me so much to do I had no need of apothecaries or soothsayers.

The air of Saint-Germain and the dissolute life that was lived there did not suit my charges any more than it suited me. They did not get enough sleep because their mother kept them up till midnight on the stage where they had their parts to play. They were fed at their mother's table with spicy foods, rich sauces and champagne. So it took only a few months for these delicate infants to fall into a dreadfully weak state. Quartan and tertian fevers, vomiting, colic, abscesses—all these attacked the frail bodies one after the other and brought them to the brink of death. They were handed over to the doctors, and the cure was worse than the disease, for Madame de Montespan was not averse either to experiments or to

quacks. The most cruel treatments were followed by the most bar-
barous medicines. To flatten the comte de Vexin's back, she had
them apply thirteen cauteries along his spine; I thought the poor
child's screams would drive me mad. Half the number of surgeons
and physicians who now surrounded the wretched children would
have been enough to kill them. I was wasting away with sorrow and
lack of sleep. I divided myself between the three of them, serving
them like a chambermaid because the girls themselves were worn
out. But I had the pain of seeing that all my efforts were useless:
the orders, counterorders and whims of their parents undid any
progress in a moment. The poor children were being killed before
my eyes, and I could do nothing to prevent it.

At first I had made up my mind not to get too involved in what
I was doing and to leave the supervision of the children to their
mother. I told myself it was foolish to love so ardently children who
were not my own, whom I would never be able to influence and
who in the long run would only give me mortal pain without giving
any pleasure to those they did belong to. I knew it was a nurse's
duty to love her charges with skill but not with passion.

But soon my affection for the children, my belief that to abandon them would be an offense against God and my natural inability
to hide what I feel combined to make me enter in spite of myself
into angry arguments with Madame de Montespan.

For six months I had not made the slightest remonstrance or
reproach. But when we were at Versailles in July and my little duc
fell into a state of extreme prostration followed by violent convulsions because his mother, just for a whim, let him stay out in the
sun without a cap for a whole day, I could stand it no longer.

"Madame," the poor child said to me, burning with fever, "I
am going to die and I am glad of it. God cannot have meant me
for this world, since it has not pleased Him that I should be able
to walk like everyone else. I am so small I shall go straight to
Heaven. I am glad."

I was appalled, and as I left the room, I passed Madame de
Montespan going in. Without thinking I suddenly told her all I had
on my mind, and she flew into such a rage I thought I was irrevoca-
bly lost. But I was in no condition to care.

I went to the chapel to cry my heart out. I realized with pain that I loved my "darling" as much as I had loved little Françoise, and the dread of having once again to sit by the deathbed of an innocent child drove me almost out of my mind. But as my great love for the duc du Maine forbade me to go as well as to stay, there was no remedy for my torture and no foreseeable end to my suffering. That evening they sent Monsieur de Louvois to make me see reason. It seemed to me he understood my arguments, which I put forward perfectly openly, and in the end it was agreed that I should spend a little more time trying to resign myself to the situation.

Madame de Montespan and I were reconciled, and she even, to win me over, agreed to found a low mass to the memory of Françoise at the church of Saint-Sulpice. But every time one of the children was ill the old disagreements recurred.

"Your sensibility needs a strong bridle," my confessor said when he found me in tears. He always acted as mediator.

"I have more trouble making peace between you two than between all the countries in Europe," the King used to say, laughing.

When the marquise's fancy turned toward other subjects than the education of her children, I could enjoy with her the old moments of freedom and friendship. Then we would compare at length the virtues of our favorite authors. We would read Madame de La Fayette's† latest book together and lament together over the woes of the "princesse de Montpensier." With her sister the abbess of Fontevrault, we vied in lampooning the Jansenists and the Jesuits. In these conversations the marquise was always the most brilliant embodiment of the famous Mortemart wit, which was to a certain extent reflected by all those about her—her brother, her sisters, her children and even her servants. This wit consisted in original thoughts inimitably expressed and unforeseen even by those who uttered them. But the wit of the d'Aubignés, though less inclined toward denigration, is not to be despised either, and in calm moments Madame de Montespan's gestures of affection showed me she could not altogether do without it.

This strange mixture of friendship and hatred, esteem and contempt, sugar and bile, which was to be our fate for fifteen years, made it very difficult for us to live together. Sometimes I would have preferred a little continual unhappiness to the shallow and fleeting joys whose passing left me brokenhearted.

For unfortunately these relapses were as frequent as they were unpredictable. I could not always make out why "la belle madame" suddenly spat her venom at me and without warning stuck me with darts to amuse her audience. Moreover, I did not feel I had the right to reply, and nearly choked in the attempt to bite back my retorts. Worst of all was when, a few months after I came to Court, she started to treat me like a servant.

She was pregnant again and near her time. For such occasions she had invented the fashion of hanging panels which concealed the waist. She might as well have written what she wished to hide in large letters across her forehead. The wits at Court used to say, "Madame de Montespan has put on her hanging panels; she must be pregnant." But only the King and I knew that with the hanging panels she put on her most disagreeable mood and that the sack dresses covered not only her curves but also a heart full of rancor.

Whether it was because of the hanging panels or for some other reason, she suddenly began to make my life more of a burden than ever. She started by dismissing quite gratuitously Mademoiselle de La Harteloire, a niece of Monsieur Scarron's who had been in the direst poverty and whom I had placed with the marquise as lady's maid while I took her elder sister to be my companion. She then did her best to harm my cousin Philippe de Villette, and on the pretext that he was a Huguenot she prevented the minister from advancing his army career. These disservices were performed without a word of explanation and for no other purpose than to vex me.

Then she exacted services which I thought I was under no obligation to render. One day I had to dress her hair; another, to put wood on the fire; to hook up the buttons on her dress; get up at two in the morning to read to her; pin up a hem; make her an egg nog. She had plenty of maids to do this sort of thing for her, but she said no one served her as I did. And believe me the word "serve" came out of her mouth as round and fat as a cherry, and not before she had had time to savor it to the full.

I am obliging by nature, and had done Madame de Montchevreuil much greater services a hundred times, and errands much more degrading. But I could see what the marquise was after: my position at Court was so precarious that a few months of this treatment would reduce me to the rank of a Desoeillets, if not worse.

I remembered a rather profound remark my dear little prince had made a few weeks earlier. As we were driving from Saint-Germain to Versailles, he ordered the coachman to gallop, and I said laughingly that at that rate our carriage would overturn.

"That cannot be," the little fellow of five replied haughtily. "God does not allow the carriages of princes to overturn."

I said, jesting, that he was very proud of his rank and that the King his father was more natural and not so touchy as he. He was suddenly very serious.

"That is because the King my father is sure of his position," he said, "whereas I, as you know, have reason to be uncertain of mine. So I have to be more haughty than most people and must be very particular about the respect I am shown."

I was in a situation very like that of my darling, and it was all the more necessary for me to see my position was respected because at first sight it was indistinguishable from that of the marquise's attendants. So I responded to insults by making it plain I took orders about the children from the King alone, thus showing I was ready to obey the father but not the mother.

This did not discourage the marquise in the least. One day when the duchesse de Richelieu was with her, together with some other ladies I had known quite well in the past—Madame de Vivonne, Madame de Fiesque and Madame de Saint-Geran—she asked me to fetch her a fan, a comb and a handkerchief, one after the other. And each time, when one of her maids started up to do the errand, she said, "No, no—Madame Scarron will be glad to bring it for me." My friends were much embarrassed on my account, but I obeyed with a smile, inwardly determined to put an end to this scene in my own fashion. When she asked me finally to bring her the pot of rouge she used for her face, which was always pale and puffy when she was pregnant, I did as I was asked with an appearance of willingness, but suddenly dropped the pot in the middle of the room. The jar broke into a thousand pieces, and all the cream was wasted.

"How clumsy you are!" she exclaimed in a fury. "It will take several days to get more of that cream prepared!"

"Yes," I replied, "I fear I am very clumsy. But that is because I was not brought here to fetch cosmetics or hem gowns. That is not my job, and I ask your pardon if I am not very good at it."

Madame de Vivonne, who liked to see her sister-in-law put in her place, laughed up her sleeve. I could see my insolence might cost me dear, but I had had enough and could not help giving way to my feelings. "La belle madame," who had to admit to a pasty face for three days, learned her lesson and was in no hurry to have it repeated.

I think the real reason Madame de Montespan, after having sung my praises for so long, suddenly started to ill-use me in public, was that she was in a way jealous. Not that she could ever imagine me as a rival or think of me as a possible mistress for the King, but she was starting to be irritated by his friendship for me. She did not see that the cause of this friendship was the spitefulness and caprice she heaped upon him.

She liked to keep him waiting when he came to see her; and my duties concerning the children brought me often to the ante-chamber where he was left cooling his heels. Now the King liked women, and in those days readily admitted that nothing in the world affected him so much as the pleasures of love. Whatever the favorite might think, I too was a woman, and, if the gallants of the Marais were to be believed, not the most repulsive of specimens. Admittedly I was six years older than Madame de Montespan, but as I had not borne nine children, I had a better figure and a fresher complexion at thirty-eight than she had at thirty-two. With wit, good temper and natural obligingness it might be that I possessed, apart from birth, all that was necessary to imperil the most staggering of successes in the most envied of positions.

However that might be, the King enjoyed talking to me. At first, as I have said, it was in the antechamber; then it was in the children's room, where he would stay for quite a long while; then anywhere would do for him to chat with me, even the room of his "belle madame."

To begin with, the conversation was about the royal children. He was very fond of them, dandled them on his knee and made up nicknames for them. The duc du Maine was his "darling," as he was mine; Mademoiselle de Nantes, then as pretty as a picture, was his "dolly" or his "bow-wow"; and little Marie-Anne, who was born that summer and legitimized two years later as Mademoiselle de Tours, was "chubby-cheeks." He took a great interest in the children's education, all the more so because of the neglect he had suffered in his own early days.

He liked to tell me about his childhood: how he and his brother were left to the tender mercies of the servants of their mother's, the Queen's, maids; how, when he was five, he was nearly drowned in a pool at Saint-Germain through the negligence of those supposed to be looking after him; how Monsieur his brother and he, so as not to die of hunger, had to steal scraps of the omelettes the servant girls made for themselves and hide away and eat them in some corner. He was obliged to wear his nightshirts and dressing gowns for so long that in the end they did not reach down to his knees. He had only a manservant to teach him history, and no other playmate besides a maidservant's little girl, whom he called "Queen Marie" and whose every whim he obeyed, drawing her about in his little cart, bowing low to her and presenting her with gooseberries and strawberries picked at great danger to his doublets.

He would grow quite animated as he talked of these things, losing for a moment his natural air of severity and abandoning his habit of impenetrable silence. In private like this, with a twinkle in his eye and a smile on his lips, he was quite different from what he was in public. But I noticed that if the door chanced to open, or when he himself left the room, he composed his attitude and changed his expression as if to make his entrance on a stage. In front of his courtiers he acted the part of a king; with me he soon came to act the part of a man, allowing himself to indulge in the pleasures of unconstrained friendship.

While I played with the comte de Vexin or taught the duc du Maine to read, he would play some charming piece to us on his guitar. He was passionately fond of music, played the guitar better than a master and could arrange anything for it. He liked to adapt the operas of Lully and sing the airs to his own accompaniment. As these works were always encomiums upon him, I sometimes had to smile as I listened to him naively singing his own praises.

Gradually he came to confide in me about the trouble Madame de Montespan caused him and began to consult me as to her moods, seeing I was the person who knew her best. I did not like to complain to him about what his mistress had been making me suffer these past months. Apart from our quarrels over the children, which amused him, he thought we were still the best of friends.

He was sad because the marquise had not liked the château of Clagny, which he had recently bought for her. She said it was too small. "Hardly enough for an opera singer!" she had exclaimed, and ordered it to be demolished.

"It's my fault," he said to me. "She certainly ought to have been given something better. I do not know how to make amends."

He also worried a great deal about how to get the marquise to accept presents which she pretended not to want. In the greatest secrecy he would order necklaces of magnificent pearls, diamond clasps, drop earrings made of rubies, buttons and bracelets set with every kind of precious stone. He took my advice about the designs, and fretted lest the marquise, with a sudden loss of interest, refuse them. I did not share this fear, for I remembered her saying a few weeks earlier, "At Court one should take all that's going; that way you'll get everything in the end." And I had a good enough idea of the millions her whims cost the Treasury to doubt whether her austerity in the matter of royal presents would last very long.

Finally the King took me into his closest confidence and spoke to me at more and more length about his mistress; he saw her faults quite clearly, but still loved her with extraordinary passion. "She is so touching when she cries," he would say. "True," I would answer, not daring to add that her weeping was always well timed. "Don't you think her eyes are incomparably brilliant? Isn't her smile charming? Have you ever seen such lovely fair coloring?"

I agreed with everything; it is useless to try to teach a blind man to see. My docility meant that our conversations went on and on indefinitely, and the marquise grew alarmed at these long tête-à-têtes, not knowing she was their subject and I was having to make myself praise her to the skies.

"Your conversations with the King are curiously long," she said to me one day. "What are you teaching him? Latin or geometry?"

Thereupon she suddenly took it into her head to marry me off. Her choice alighted on a duc, Monsieur de Villars-Branca, who had been widowed for the second or third time. He was related to the Villars-Orondate who had paid court to me in the early days of my marriage to Scarron, but unlike my former admirer, who was astonishingly handsome, Villars-Branca was ugly and nicknamed "the hunchback." On top of this he was uncouth, said to be a bad husband and very poor. When I urged all these objections the marquise exclaimed:

"But you'll be a duchesse! You'll have the right to sit on a stool in the Queen's presence!"

"I'm quite happy standing!" I answered, laughing.

"That's right, make witty remarks, you poor fool! I'll give you a dowry, and then you'll have a strongbox as well as a stool and a coronet! Isn't that an unhoped-for piece of good luck for a widow Scarron?"

"I don't believe in unhoped-for pieces of good luck, Madame. And I have enough trouble living a single life without seeking more in a state that makes three-quarters of the human race miserable. I have had experience of marriage, and believe me I know all about it. I am quite resolved never to marry again, and if by some strange chance I should change my mind, it will certainly not be in favor of someone who revolts me."

"Oh . . . You want a prince of the blood, perhaps?"

The marquise was beside herself with rage at my refusal, and perhaps in a way she had cause. Admittedly this marriage was designed to get me out of the way, but she was not deliberately doing me a bad turn. In the eyes of someone as obsessed with birth and titles as she was, for a woman without rank to marry a duc, whatever he was like, was to be rated a success. But she did not realize I was devoid of this kind of ambition, and the idea of sharing my bed with the "hunchback" did not appeal to me at all.

The favorite saw my refusal merely as proof that I was on even better terms with the King than she had thought, and as a sign that this dangerous inclination must be nipped in the bud as soon as possible. She gave her wrath free rein, bitterly reproached the King for his excessive friendliness to a proud wretch who served her badly, explained my refusal to marry as it suited her best, made fun of me, said I was an eccentric of whom one should be careful and in short did all she could to lower me in the King's esteem. She was so intelligent and had so much influence over him that she could always make him do as she wished. On this occasion she used all her skill, and after stupefying him with reproaches and insinuations begged him with all her customary blandishments to show his love for her by being disagreeable to me.

This he did, and for several weeks he abstained from speaking to me in private, while in public he treated me with studied coldness. But one day in the marquise's room, exasperated that she should keep nagging him about me after he had done as she wished, he exclaimed:

"Madame, if Madame Scarron displeases you so much, why do you not dismiss her? You are the mistress. You have only to say the word and she will leave at once. You know all I want is to please you. And I've heard enough about Madame Scarron!" This was duly reported to me, and my so-called friends complimented me on my fall from grace.

I was in the depths of despair. I wept night after night and was consumed with unreasonable alarms. A hundred times I was on the point of telling Monsieur de Louvois that I was going to retire, but a hundred times I was stopped from doing so by a vague apprehension which I did not yet dare to name. Though I died a thousand deaths, I could not make up my mind to leave the scene of my suffering. I think I was beginning to understand something of what Mademoiselle de La Vallière had gone through. The abbé Gobelin, the only person to whom I confessed my anguish, could find nothing better to suggest than that I too should take the veil. But I told him abruptly that I was not at all suited to the contemplative life.

Then suddenly, when I least expected it, the storm of rages and insults abated. Madame de Montespan, reassured by the King's behavior and not really anxious to lose an amusing companion, began to be affectionate toward me again. She spoke to me kindly and got the King to give me a hundred thousand francs. This was the first present they had given me in five years, and it did not fail to surprise me, coming after so much hatred and disdain. A fortnight later she obtained the renewal of a lease for a farmer-general† for whom I had presented a recommendation worth money to me if it was successful. A month after that she arranged for me to get a monopoly on the manufacture of forges and furnaces. All of a sudden I found myself in easy circumstances where the day before I had nothing, and publicly privileged when two days earlier I had been decried everywhere. These ups and downs made me dizzy, and I was more determined than ever not to remain in so disagreeable a position. Now that I was reconciled with the marquise, I intended to leave Court the following December.

It was then that the King, who had used me so badly, made it up with me too.

He approached by small steps at first, a smile here, a word there. Then by giant strides, with tender looks, slight gestures and conversations of an hour or more again. Certain condescensions made my return to favor public: two or three times he asked me to dine with him and his mistress or to go out with him for a drive.

In private he revealed his feelings by significant gestures. Once when he was handing me a doll which one of the children had just broken, he held on to my hand. I disengaged it so quickly and deftly that both of us might doubt whether we had remained in contact any longer than necessary, and I could pretend to be ignorant of an attempt which he pretended not to have made. A week later I was talking to him as I embroidered and had rested my hand and my canvas on a little table at my side. He, as he spoke, again tried to take my hand, which I saw, as if it were quite separate from me and had a will of its own, move swiftly across the red damask tablecloth to my knee, where he did not dare pursue it. All he got out of his clumsy venture was my needle, which I had left in my sewing, stuck painfully into his palm. My heart pounded for a few minutes; in my mind's eye I could see my hand withdrawing across the red cloth and the drop of blood on his hand, and I thought the humiliation I had almost unthinkingly inflicted on him might cause a quarrel. But he had sufficient self-mastery to take up the thread of the conversation as if nothing had happened, and I was more affable than ever in order to efface the strange effect this scene had had upon us both. A fortnight later he made a third attempt, for if he was shy he was stubborn too. And, as in the songs, it was the third time that the ramparts fell. I let him hold my hand but still pretended not to notice, while he for his part did nothing but clasp it very lightly. We behaved as if nothing were more natural for a king and the governess of his bastards than to paddle hands while blithely chatting about this and that.

For me the situation was plain. By her rash and excessive attacks upon me, followed by a sudden return of affection, Madame de Montespan had abruptly turned into desire an inclination which I myself would have preferred to convert into friendship. Even then, so long as the matter did not go beyond words and looks I felt fairly safe. But when it came to actions I was lost. Though I knew myself to be cleverer than most at making an admirer languish and despair without actually putting him off altogether, I was also aware that firmness is needed when he becomes too daring, and that a well-placed box on the ear is sometimes the only way to resolve the situation. Now this method might be followed with every man but him who was then wooing me, for to defend one's virtue like that against the assaults of a king was too close to lèse-majesté. There was no more to be said; with the approach works so far advanced, flight or surrender were the only alternatives.

I chose flight, without hesitation though not without regret. I knew this great and magnificent king was the only man I could have loved without demeaning myself in my own eyes, and that, while not yielding easily, I would have found it delightful to give myself up into the peace and safety of his power. And when the nascent impulses of my heart, inspired by so worthy an object, were so strongly backed up by thoughts of glory and almost by reason too, it took a certain amount of heroism to flee the field.

I could see all too clearly the difficulties involved in the other course of action. First among them was the sway of Madame de Montespan, so powerful that it left room for chance desires or friendships but not for a love of the kind I dreamed of; then there was the danger of being reduced to a subordinate and humiliating role like that of Mademoiselle Desoeillets; lastly there was the Queen, and my horror of a sin which already in the past had cost me sleep and imperilled my soul. With all these things in mind, I suddenly announced to the King and his mistress my intention of leaving Court in December. I said I was tired and ill, and that after looking after the children as I had done for five years, I needed a rest.

"We'll see," was all the King said.

Three days later he again showed me how satisfied he was with my services. Having summoned the little duc du Maine to his apartment and asked him all kinds of questions about his life, he told the child that his answers showed him to be very sensible.

"That should not surprise you, Sire," said my little prince. "I have been brought up by Reason personified."

"Well," said the King, "you go and tell Reason that this evening you will bring her a hundred thousand francs for your sweetmeats."

It is difficult to leave people who treat you so well, but I now had two hundred thousand francs in presents and several thousand livres derived from two or three business ventures, and could buy the house and land that would deliver me both from the unbearable slavery to which Madame de Montespan sometimes reduced me and from the temptation to which I was exposed by the King.

"But Madame, you can't leave me," said my darling. "I want to marry you when I grow up."

"I shan't really be leaving you," I answered to console him. "You shall come and see me at my house if your mamma lets you. I shall have cows and geese, and a big park for you to walk in."

"If you desert me, Madame, I shall never walk anywhere. You were going to keep teaching me, and next year you were going to take me to Barèges to take the waters and strengthen my legs. But now you don't care about that any more, and I shall never be able to walk."

I put my arms around him and we wept together.

In order to break the chains which still kept me at Court, I made myself concentrate on looking for a house and got the abbé Gobelin to help in the search. The poor fellow could make nothing of my changes of mood. In my letters I had described my quarrels with Madame de Montespan over the children, then gone on to unspecified troubles of another kind and finally referred to sudden feelings of joy which I also left unexplained. He always counselled remedies which were unsuitable because my soul was in no fit state to receive them. He would suggest I go to communion more often, or would send me little books in which to note down my religious reflections. "Too many communions would make me look ridiculous," I answered, "and as for pious thoughts, my mind produces none." I did admit, to please him, that I was leading a life which "did little honor to my confessor."

So the worthy abbé applied himself with more success to my earthly establishment than to my eternal salvation. With his help I found, ten leagues from Versailles and four from Chartres, the lovely and noble estate of Maintenon, which brought in an annual income of eleven thousand francs. In mid-October I started negotiating the purchase for 250,000 francs, all I possessed. I congratulated myself on the fact that I should be able to leave the Court in January, and thought I was strong enough to arrange things satisfactorily in that short time.

For several weeks I had taken great care not to expose myself to any more private conversations with the King, and he for his part seemed to seek my company less. This did not help me with Madame de Montespan, though: she was in a bad humor and at the end of October I had some more very violent scenes with her. She picked quarrels, obstinately put forward the most ridiculous arguments and began thwarting me again over the management of the children.

We were back at Saint-Germain. I had spent the night in alternate agitation and prostration, and at dawn, with my blood burning and my head aching, I decided to seek fresh air in the park. I slipped on a gown of black velvet decorated with gold braid, put a short fur cape over my shoulders, took my muff and went out. It must have been about six in the morning.

A grey day was breaking over the magnificent long terrace which Monsieur Le Nôtre had finished the previous year. I leaned for a moment on the terrace wall and watched the mists rising from the Seine. Not wanting to be seen from the château, for people would think it strange for me to be out in the park at this hour, I decided to go down to the river. As I was passing the new château, built by King Henri IV, I saw a gentleman enveloped in a long grey cape jump out of one of the ground-floor windows, walk across the flower beds and make off rapidly in the direction of the old château. I paid no attention, for this was the time of day when all kinds of gallants used to head back as fast as they could to their wives' apartments. I went on down the steps leading from the new château to the landing stage. When I had descended the main steps, I passed the caves hollowed out of the retaining wall of the second terrace, and felt an inclination to stop there.

There were four of these grottoes, and during the day they attracted passers-by to admire their various clockwork mechanisms. In the first, all kinds of fabulous characters came and bowed to the King and the Dauphin. In the second, a shepherdess sang, accompanying herself on different instruments. In the third, Perseus smote a sea monster with his sword and freed Andromeda, while Tritons stood around and blew loudly into their conches. The last showed Vulcan and Venus watching a dragon flapping its wings and belching forth torrents of water. Behind the fourth grotto was another cave, smaller and more natural. It was damp and mossy, and so cold even in summer that it was said anyone who spent an hour there would freeze.

It was there I decided to halt for a moment. The place was not visible from the terraces, and I was glad to be alone to think. The coolness was also pleasant against my fevered brow.

I sat on the edge of the fountain and gazed at length at the reflection of my face in the water. I was vain enough to think it was beautiful, but I knew that before long the tortured life I led at Court would put black circles around the fiery eyes beloved of the King, and trace wrinkles on my as yet smooth brow. I smiled sadly at my reflection, and at the last brightness of my departing youth.

The water was dark and deep like the rivers at Mursay. For some reason I suddenly thought of my brother Constant's death. Whenever I was sad, drowning always seemed a good death. A tear fell into the water and disturbed my image, and I thought I saw a ghost leaning over my shoulder.

> *In this murky cave*
> *We see elements fight,*
> *The rock with the wave*
> *The dark with the light*

whispered a grave voice behind me.

The gentleman in the grey cape was standing on the threshold of my cavern. I looked at him calmly and, strangely enough, without real surprise. I neither stood up nor curtsied; it did not seem appropriate. I went on sitting on the edge of the pool, beside my reflection; he came over to me.

> *Your face in the beck*
> *I tremble to see,*
> *Lest sighing I wreck*
> *Both your image and me*

he said slowly.

I smiled as I recognized the lines by old Tristan l'Hermite, Scarron's friend, who used to come and see us sometimes in the rue Neuve-Saint-Louis. He was coarse and dirty, but his *Promenoir de deux amants* (Two Lovers Walking) was almost like Racine, and probably was never quoted more aptly than that morning in the little cave at Saint-Germain.

The King sat down beside me on the stone ledge and leaned over the water.

"Smiling suits you," he said to my reflection.

"The dawn suits you," I answered, not looking at him except through the mirror of the water.

"I did not think you a reciter of verses," I went on, to break the spell which was gradually falling over us.

"I know thousands. I can recite whole plays by heart. Have you not heard that I act sometimes?"

And indeed the black water sent back the image of an actor of thirty-five, magnificent in his wig and the great grey mantle hiding his gold coat. His usual role was that of a wealthy prince or a conquering hero.

"I did not know you were such an early riser," he went on pensively.

Fearing he might misunderstand, I began to explain, but he interrupted.

"I was not asking for an explanation, Madame . . . Have you heard that one cannot stay in here more than an hour without being frozen to death? Shall we try it, or shall we go and talk somewhere else?"

"I like this pool," I said.

"It is stagnant."

"No. Calm."

There was a long pause. I ought to have got up and gone away. But whether it was the numbing cold, my weariness after a sleepless night or my certainty that I would be leaving the Court in a couple of months, I could not take my eyes off our two reflections. A black lady, a grey man.

"Madame de Montespan is like a torrent," he said. "You make me think of a pool."

"Sire," I answered, "that is a comparison worthy of the *pré-cieux,* and you hate the *précieux."*

He laughed, and his laughter stirred the surface of the water. I shivered.

"You're cold, Madame."

He took off his cape and wrapped it around me. When he had done so he left his hands resting on my shoulders. At that moment I knew I was lost, and that I had probably wanted to be. One last time I looked away toward the fountain before foundering altogether. Then I shut my eyes, perhaps in the way children do, thinking it makes them invisible.

I did not open them again for a long while, when I heard the King murmur:

"It is dreadfully cold in here. I don't think we can stand it any longer, Madame."

I saw I had lost the big grey cloak he had put around me, yet I had not felt the biting chill.

Suddenly a terrible din came from the cave of Venus: the dragon was spouting forth jets of water through every shrieking vent and flapping its wings like an army of bats; to the sound of bells and trumpets, Venus and Vulcan began to circle around their pool. For a moment I thought hell was about to yawn at my feet, but it was only the gardeners setting the machinery in motion for the new day.

In an hour the first valet, the first physician and the first surgeon would enter the King's bedroom. At a quarter past eight the lord chamberlain would be summoned, and with him the "great entries," the only people who had the right to see the King in his dressing gown and short wig. At half past eight came the second entries and gentlemen who had the privilege of talking to the monarch on his commode; and they would crowd around the bed while the barber put the last touch to the royal toilet. And then at nine o'clock this man, who had not slept in his bed all night, would be considered "up."

On the little terrace by the grottoes, the King, after a last affectionate gesture, said:

"I think you should walk on as far as the lawn."

This prudence delighted me. I made a deep curtsy and was about to leave him when he stopped me.

"Will you not be walking near the Val† tomorrow morning at about five?"

"Sire, the comte de Vexin is to be bled then, and . . ."

"His nurse will see to that, Madame," he replied somewhat curtly. "It may be that I myself shall have occasion to be at the château du Val tomorrow."

"Sire, if it is Your Majesty's order, I shall be there."

"I give you no orders, Madame. I only ask."

"In that case, Sire . . ."

"In that case, you will not go?"

"If Your Majesty permits, I shall stay with the comte. He is very frightened of bloodletting, and I am the only person . . ."

"Your embarrassment does you no more service than your impertinence," he said severely.

His tone was so harsh I almost thought I had dreamed his tenderness in the cave. My pride suddenly flooded back.

"I admit, Sire, that I am not as docile as Mademoiselle Desoeillets."

"But . . ." This time he smiled quite openly. "I do not think I was confusing you with her."

He took my hand and kissed it.

"To begin with," he said mischievously, "she is not so virtuous as to mortify the flesh by sinning in uncomfortable places . . . Au revoir, Madame. I must not impose on you."

He walked rapidly away along a path, leaving me dazed at what was happening to me.

At one moment I would be transported with pride, for to be singled out by a King is no small matter; at another I would be overwhelmed with shame. I could not find words harsh enough to describe my weakness, nor could I decide on a line of conduct that would give me peace of mind.

Only the flight I had resolved upon three months earlier could deliver me from the doubts and fears gnawing at my soul. But as soon as I thought about this plan, so recently quite settled in my mind, I saw all the difficulties involved. I was more uncertain than ever whether the King would let me go, and even less sure whether I had the strength to tear myself away.

I did try to convince myself that I could gradually persuade this man, whose friendship was now all too dear to me, to accept a purely spiritual relationship; then scorn for my sin and shame at my fall overwhelmed me again and toppled those castles in Spain. But scarcely had I begun to sink into humiliation and remorse than I remembered the King's words, the delicate and charming manner in which he had declared himself, and other pleasant things which then ensued, and all this filled me with strange and soothing languors. Bliss alternated with horror, Hell with Heaven.

The next day I wrote to the abbé Gobelin and told him of my extreme agitation. I said nothing about its cause; there are things which must be concealed from other people, and to keep them between God and oneself calls for a good deal of steadiness. The poor abbé, realizing the violence of my feelings, at once offered to come and see me at Saint-Germain, which he normally did not do more than a couple of times a year. Just as promptly, I begged him to do nothing of the sort, saying I had not a moment to myself and could not even find time for confession. The truth was I felt I could not look him in the face. Not knowing what to do or advise, he suggested at random that I should devote myself to prolonged spiritual exercises and adopt a more austere style of dress. But this advice met with no more success than the rest. As I had told him, I had no leisure for meditation, and I could not add to the oddity of my dress, having already at his request given up wearing colors. For the last two months I had worn no red, pink or green, limiting myself to black and white and vague tints like russet, plum, tan, midnight blue and grey. But for good measure and on the pretext that these were metals rather than colors, I did wear gowns embroidered with gold and silver. I did not want to dress like an old woman, and if I must alienate the King, I did not want to do it by making myself unattractive to him.

After a few days of anxiety I set my mind at rest by asking God to break my chains Himself if my freedom could be of use to Him. Today, now that I am a slightly better Christian than I was then, it seems to me very convenient to leave God to decide by tacit permission questions we do not want to resolve for ourselves.

I had a few more opportunities to transgress in the course of that winter, and I did not altogether escape them. A lingering scruple made me try to avoid temptation, but I did not succeed in avoiding sin.

There was one afternoon, for example, when Madame de Montespan had gone to the château de Clagny to give orders about the building in progress there. I was standing in the embrasure of a window in her apartment, looking out sadly at the courtiers coming and going between the old and new châteaux, when a hand was placed on my arm. I did not need to turn round to know who had taken this liberty. Only one man at Court could dare.

"Dreaming, Madame?"

"I never dream, Sire. I was star-gazing," I said, smiling.

"You wrong yourself, Madame," he replied. "Everyone knows you are too sensible for that."

No one can know what the King was like if they did not know him as he was then, at an age when everything smiled on him, when France was prosperous at home and victorious abroad, when the greatest monarch in the world was surrounded by happiness and magnificence. One had to get used to looking at him gradually, and even then it took a long time to be able to do it without breaking down. In his presence it was best to shut one's eyes and submit one's will.

But I did hint one day that while I could not master the inclination which drew me toward him, I knew how much I offended God by entering into this sort of relationship.

"Why?" he said with surprise. "Are you not a widow?"

I was not bold enough to answer that though I was widowed, he was not. To kings, as to God, one may offer prayers, perhaps even suggestions, but not rebukes.

But he could guess what struggles were going on within me, for one evening when he would have liked me to be on the crest of happiness I could not conceal my tears. He was vexed and wanted to know why I was crying. So I had to confess the shame I felt, though in order not to displease him I added that my shame was in proportion to the affection I felt for him. I was all the more afflicted by my shame, I said, because I knew how he despised prudes, and my greatest possible sorrow would be to displease him.

"No, I do not like prudes," he said, lifting my hair aside and drying my tears, "but I do not hate good women. I have not had occasion to get tired of them in these parts!"

These soothing words did not leave me entirely comforted because I had not been completely truthful. My agitation derived not so much from the shame of betraying my principles as from that of ranking poorly on an over-long list of royal escapades. It is always easier to come to terms with public morals than with private pride.

Other fears, even more shocking and unworthy, also came and tormented me. Not knowing, through lack of experience, whether what the marquis de Villarceaux had taught me was what a husband usually teaches a wife or what a libertine expects from a courtesan, I did not know whether my behavior in our encounters might not be giving the King a different impression of me from what he had had before. Not seeing how I could combine great virtue with great complaisance, I was unable to decide upon what was the best policy, or whether it was wiser to satisfy my lover or disappoint him.

In December the children were terribly ill again. The little duc had an abscess on his leg which made us fear for his life.

The physicians, all dressed in black, with long capes and tall hats, sat around him in conference, presided over by Monsieur Daquin, the most foolish Hippocrates in the world, whom by a whim Madame de Montespan had had appointed the King's chief doctor.

"Acute diseases which act swiftly end on the odd critical days, that is to say, those made up of two odd numbers: the fifth, seventh, ninth, eleventh and fourteenth," he told me sagely, condescending to abandon for a moment the Latin he spoke so imperfectly. "Therefore, as it is now the fifteenth of the month, nothing may be hoped for before the fifth of next month. If however the fever by some strange chance should abate on an even day, this would only be because nature, thwarted and weary, was expelling some of the superabundant humor that is irritating it; but this would not mean the patient was cured. For my part, I would not pronounce him better against all the established rules."

Seeing my little boy left in the care of this pedant, I began to fear God might give a very cruel answer to the request I had addressed to Him just after my downfall: how could He break the chains which bound me better than by taking away the duc du Maine?

In January I signed the contract for the purchase of Maintenon. I could not leave my little sufferers unattended for more than two days, but in that time I was delighted to find I had acquired a large château very much like Mursay, with towers and steep slate roofs, adjoining a large village. The river Eure flowed through its wide moats, and it had meadows, a fine park and a pretty and unspoiled view.

I returned to Saint-Germain all the more reluctantly because I again had to endure the moods of Madame de Montespan, which were now more uncertain than ever. She treated me with violence both of speech and of behavior, with never a vestige of reason or even any consistency in her unreason. I dared not complain to the King, and put up with it all in silence, waiting with growing impatience for the time when I could take my dear boy to Barèges and the marquise could vent her wrath on her maids.

I had no scruples as far as she was concerned about my new connection with the King. It seemed to me that even if she had known about it she would not have cared. Only friendship frightened her; for the rest, she considered herself in a very strong position, and saw no real danger except in women who were very young, very amorous or very well-born.

Meanwhile nothing emerged in public of what was passing between the King and me in private. In the presence of his mistress the King may even have treated me with more reserve than in the weeks preceding our morning encounter. I even came to wonder if anything had really happened. On reflection, I guessed that for him nothing really had occurred. He was so used to the passing relationships he had with dozens of the ladies of his Court that he saw nothing in these brief and light encounters but what Ninon professed to find in her "caprices": a hint of desire, a trace of pleasure and, at the worst, a tear of remorse. There was only one woman he truly loved, and that was Françoise de Rochechouart-Mortemart, marquise de Montespan.

But that year he had the audacity, for the first time, to take my side against her.

One day in February when he was playing cards with some courtiers in his mistress's apartment and I was amusing the children with a little doll's house which Madame de Thianges had just given them, "la belle madame" suddenly flew into a rage with me. Her fury, though not unprecedented, soon reached an intensity hitherto unexampled. A few days earlier she had discovered a new affair between the King and a charming young lady who was one of Madame's maids of honor, and because the young woman in question was not within her reach, she avenged herself for her anxieties upon all her own entourage.

The prelude made use of an air I was beginning to know.

"Madame Scarron," said the marquise, clapping her hands, "go and fetch me a glass of water."

A lackey came running.

"No," she said. "I want it from Madame Scarron's own hands."

I brought the glass of water and satisfied two or three other whims of the same kind, but already she was changing her tune. My marriage to Monsieur Scarron provided material for a more novel sort of scene.

"Tell me, Madame Scarron—your husband was a very ridiculous character, wasn't he?"

"Madame," I answered gently, "he was a sick man. I do not know whether cripples are more to be mocked or to be pitied. No doubt it depends upon who it is that is looking at them."

I knew it was foolish to oppose her in this kind of mood and that for every riposte she would launch a hundred new shafts. But I am impulsive by nature and I could not always control myself. The whole company had fallen silent to follow a contest of which no one, I least of all, doubted the outcome. In the eyes of all those fine gentlemen I could see the same bloodlust as the Romans must have shown when defenceless Christians were thrown to the wild beasts.

"Did you know, Marsillac, that when she was young, Madame Scarron dragged so many hearts at her chariot wheels that people wrote about it? Was it not for you, Madame, that Gilles Boileau, the brother of our satirist, composed the little quatrain which so wittily adorned your husband's forehead?"

"I see, Madame, that you make yourself my biographer. But I must put you right. In the matter of which you speak I have nothing to reproach myself with. And even if I had, I am sure you would agree that only she who is without sin should throw the first stone."

Everyone held his breath. The tigress had flinched at this insult, but she only resumed the hunt more hungrily. In the onslaught which followed I resigned myself to silence.

"I believe Monsieur Scarron was penniless, and people used to bring their own food when they came to supper? And would you believe it, my dear Langlée, Madame Scarron's furniture was sold outside her very door to pay off her debts? When I took poor Madame Scarron into my service, she was living in the direst poverty with only one maid. So nowadays I never tire of admiring her golden gowns. But it does seem to me she has retained a certain bourgeois taste in dress from that long period of destitution—don't you agree, Langlée? You ought to give her the benefit of your advice. She is very clever and will be able to dress like a courtier one day."

Everything was brought up: the Hôtel Impecuniosity, the foolish things Scarron had written against the Queen Mother during the Fronde, the frustration to which my husband had condemned me, and even indecent anagrams, which she thought witty, on Scarron's name. Marsillac, the son of my old friend La Rochefoucauld, Langlée and all their usual crew split their sides laughing.

It was the first time the King had been present at such a scene, and the "belle madame" surpassed herself in his honor. He did not say anything; he did not look at me; he just played his cards as if unaffected by what was going on.

Then suddenly the storm, which I had done nothing to prolong, passed away as swiftly as it had come. Someone mentioned the name of Dangeau, and the favorite gladly seized upon it. She hated Dangeau because he had been a go-between in the King's affair with Mademoiselle de La Vallière.

When I saw she was launched in this new direction, I allowed myself a few minutes to pull myself together and then, when my heart was no longer pounding and my palms no longer showed the mark of my fingernails, I turned to the King and said quietly:

"I do not think Madame de Montespan needs me any more this evening. Have I Your Majesty's permission to withdraw?"

The King smiled, made a gesture of acquiescence and then, just as I was about to leave the room, said slowly and clearly:

"I am infinitely grateful for all you are doing for me, Madame de Maintenon."

As soon as I was outside the door I had to lean against the wall, for my head was spinning with happiness, surprise and gratitude. He had called me Madame de Maintenon!

Never had a woman who had suffered humiliation been given so brilliant a revenge in so few words. At a stroke he had obliterated poor Scarron, done away with the wretched past which still clung to me and forbidden any remembrance of a life which the Court judged unseemly. In one phrase he had disavowed his mistress's malice, recalled that I served not her but him and rewarded my discretion even under insult by elevating me to striking eminence. Madame de Maintenon, Madame de Maintenon—already every corridor and landing and salon in the château repeated it. Dozens of pens were plunged into inkwells and sped over the paper to convey to Paris, the provinces and abroad the King's pronouncement and what could be concluded, imagined or deduced from it. The old marquise de Sévigné in her hôtel Carnavalet sealed a packet she was sending me with the question, "Tell me, my dear, is it true . . . ?"

"It is true," I told all who asked me, "it is true the King called me Madame de Maintenon and that I shall do him greater services than that of bearing the name of the property he has given me."

The sensation the news created was enormous, and the favorite's resentment was in proportion. As she was not easily vanquished, and as her mood was all the sourer because of the pints of vinegar she was drinking in order to lose weight, she treated me to a few more stormy scenes in the days that followed. This was to show me that though I might have changed my name I had not changed my job. But I no longer felt such pinpricks. I had but one regret: that I could not openly throw myself at the King's feet to show my gratitude. To have to stifle that impulse was all the more distressing because up till then I had never wanted to kneel to anyone.

But everything had to be hidden, including both the extremity of my joy and the depth of feeling for him with which my heart overflowed. The more the fact that I was in favor was revealed, then reinforced, then demonstrated and finally brought right out into the open, the more my behavior had to prevent anyone from so much as suspecting the reason for this situation. Through a mixture of pride and a sort of piety which I myself did not understand, I did not wish my weaknesses to be revealed either to the world at large or to my confessor. Call it hypocrisy if you like, but at least that kind of hypocrisy does show one knows what good is and that one is not entirely lost to virtue.

So in the King's presence I increased the reserve and respectfulness which were natural to me. If he did not speak to me, I did not let myself look at him, even furtively. On everything to do with him I showed a complete coldness relieved only by the deference due to his position. For every other man I flaunted an indifference which was easy to display because I really felt it. To all this I added a modesty and a steadiness which were not feigned and a leaning toward spiritual matters which was already not far from the surface.

It was not difficult for me to play a part, for I had had a long training in constraint and dissembling: the need to hide one after the other the shame of my birth, my father's crimes, my husband's impotence, an unrequited passion for Monsieur d'Albret, a guilty relationship with Monsieur de Villarceaux, the secret responsibility for children hidden from everyone and a thousand other intrigues which from the age of sixteen I had either witnessed or been drawn into against my will.

Fortunately the King was as impenetrably secretive as I. There was no need, with him, to fear the indiscretions and excesses of such as Villarceaux. Nothing was easier for him than to dissimulate and be silent. In affairs of state he sometimes carried this talent to the point of duplicity, yet he never lied and prided himself on keeping his word.

In these as in other matters of which I shall speak later, our natures were much alike. We both thought that while lying is wrong, it is permissible and sometimes even desirable to choose mystery, to make use of the uncertainty which with skill may be thrown over the most self-evident facts without a single untruth being pronounced. I could not have answered a direct question except with candor, but the thing is to ensure the question is never asked, that it never even occurs to anyone.

I marvel at myself for having managed to do this for so long. It involves a continual tension to maintain it in an enclosed world where two thousand people are crammed together as in a hospital, sharing the same wardrobes and the same beds; where for want of proper corridors for moving from one public room to another, everyone goes in and out of everyone else's private room at all hours of the day and night. It meant shrouding in invisibility a most extraordinary relationship when every intimate moment was normally observed by an audience of lackeys and pages, and never giving ground for suspicion where gossip was the mainstay of all conversation.

Fortunately deceit has its compensations. Apart from the complicity it creates between the two lovers concerned, there is, as I had already discovered in the days of Monsieur de Villarceaux, a particular pleasure in the thought of deceiving, in the thought that you alone know yourself, that you are putting on a performance by which the rest of society is taken in and in which the trouble you have taken to mount the play is counterbalanced by all the delights of contempt for its audience.

Moreover, to set a strong will in control of one's passions, to hold down one's soul with a cover of steel, only reinforces the power that is being bottled up. Or, in the case of love, the pleasure.

Twelve

The spring of 1675 was freezing; it had not been so cold in France for more than a century. I have an extraordinarily vivid memory of that Ash Wednesday, when violent gusts of wind rattled the slates of the chapel roof at Versailles, while the rain beat at the windows like waves against the portholes of a ship. The tempest outside was nothing compared to the storm which raged within.

Rolling out over curled wigs, lace caps and crowns alike, the voice of Father Bourdaloue† swelled and thundered, and at the truths with which the prelate assailed them the courtiers bowed their heads.

The day before, Father Mascaron's† sermon had been considered out of place. At Court courage is useless unless it goes with a certain amount of tact. Mascaron had chosen to speak of war, but he had gone too far, saying that a hero was a thief who did deeds at the head of an army which robbers did on their own. He had condemned conquest and the campaigns then in prospect so vehemently and at the same time so clumsily that the King had been more vexed than distressed.

"I am quite willing to apply a share of a sermon to myself," he said aloud as he left, "but I do not care for someone else to apply it for me."

It took more skill than that to preach at Versailles or Saint-Germain, yet it was as if the prelates were in collusion, for Bourdaloue, who was usually moderate when necessary, filled the chapel with stinging phrases of unusual violence, which his catarrhal voice made even more rough and rasping.

He pressed the challenge even further than Father Mascaron by taking purity as his subject, and while he spoke in general of mankind and its debauchery, he also made allusions which everyone knew referred to the King. When he spoke of the occasion of sin, "the reef which wrecks your firmness and constancy," everyone saw this was aimed at the marquise, covered with gold and jewels, sitting in the front row opposite the King and Queen.

The storm raged around the Court for a good quarter of an hour. Those present hardly dared look at one another; they held their breath, and over their missals they darted a few furtive glances at the King, completely impenetrable before his prie-dieu, and the favorite, haughtier than ever and from time to time curling her lip. As soon as mass was over everyone crowded round the King hoping for a reaction even more marked than that of the day before, and in proportion to the affront. But he made his departure calmly and thoughtfully, and said nothing.

His silence did not surprise me as much as it did the rest of the Court. It seemed to me that despite appearances Bourdaloue had not given such dire offense as Mascaron. As I was beginning to see, the King, though he would not be criticized or advised by a prelate as a monarch, did not set himself above the judgment of the Church in what concerned his behavior as a man. And in this connection he could not but know that this dual adultery, insolently flaunted in the face of all Europe, caused so great a scandal that he would sooner or later have to put an end to it.

But any preacher who openly advanced such arguments needed a good deal of temerity, and I began to respect the priests' courage whereas I had hitherto admired only their talent. Admittedly I had not had much reason to be impressed by the ecclesiastics I had met so far; it might even be said I had retained my faith in spite of them. Apart from the abbé Gobelin, who was a decent man, I had known only little sham abbés, frivolous and licentious, interested only in trivialities and the latest song. With such specimens one was lucky if they were not lovers of young footmen into the bargain, like Boisrobert, or out and out transvestites like the abbé de Choisy. Had I not seen the latter writing his *History of the Church* while wearing a brocade negligée and caps of Alençon point? And had I not watched him taking the collection at Saint-Médard in a gown of pink taffeta cut low in front, with matching ribbons and ruby hairpins, diamond earrings and more than a dozen beauty spots? All his bishop used to say was, "If only every woman went into society as modestly dressed as the abbé!" So you may imagine how novel it was for me to hear men like Bossuet, Bourdaloue and Massillon every day.

Madame de Montespan did not appreciate the sermons that Lent as much as I did, nor did she take them as calmly as the King. She became more and more badtempered, as she did whenever she felt her position threatened.

The day after the famous sermon, as we were crossing the bridge at Saint-Germain, her carriage ran over the body of a poor man. Madame de Richelieu, a few other ladies who were there and I myself were shocked and distressed, as one usually is on such occasions. Only Madame de Montespan was unmoved, and she even rebuked us for our weakness.

"If you were as kindhearted and compassionate as you claim, you would feel the same whether such a thing happened in front of you or a long way away," she said.

Madame de Richelieu looked at me in astonishment; I shrugged my shoulders; and the poor wretch who lay there disembowelled received no further attention or funeral oration from "la belle madame."

A few days after that, the comte de Froulai having been killed in the wars, his mother and his young wife came to Court to try to obtain the reversion of his office, which was their only means of support. They were counting on the help of the favorite, thinking she must be touched by their distress; but they only supplied the marquise with another opportunity to show her ill-humor. The young countess, shrouded in her black veils, approached the "incomparable" in her antechamber, but as soon as she began to tell her troubles Madame de Montespan, without even looking at her, thrust her aside so roughly that she would have fallen had not Madame de Sévigné chanced to be there to catch her.

Madame de Montespan, with me still following, swept on into the corridor, where she came upon Madame de Froulai the elder, who, knowing nothing of her daughter-in-law's rebuff, begged the marquise to intercede in her favor to prevent the bread being taken from her grandchildren's mouths. But the "marvel" passed on without a word. The poor old lady, taken aback, fell on her knees and dragged herself along the corridor at the marquise's feet, sobbing and begging for pity. The sorrow of the bereaved mother, her ravaged face and white hair, her black robes—everything combined to rend the onlooker's heart; but the marquise just walked on without stopping and without even doing anything to raise the elderly comtesse from the floor. The courtiers themselves were indignant at this behavior, and I could hear murmurs from the other end of the corridor.

When we reached the staircase and Madame de Montespan had slightly slackened her pace, I took my courage in both hands and stammered a few words on behalf of the two unhappy women.

"Enough!" said the favorite, stopping short. "Enough, wretch! Not another word on the subject! I hate all this weeping and wailing! I shall have the office given to Monsieur de Cavoye straight away. You see the result of your softheartedness!"

"*I* am not pious," she fumed as she started up the staircase. "*I* am not kind," she said on one stair; "*I* am capricious," she hissed on the next. "*I* am profligate; *I* am extravagant; *I* am lewd"—and so this strange *mea culpa* continued right to the top of the stairs.

I was silent, drew back into my shell and waited for the rainbow which with her always appeared after the rain.

But Cavoye got the office, and the Froulais were ruined.

Lent was coming to an end, and already the usual games and laughter were returning to the magnificent apartment of twenty rooms which the favorite occupied in the château de Versailles. The Queen herself was not so amply accommodated there, and she and her household had to make do with a modest suite of ten rooms. Admittedly the lawful wife was not half so beautiful or so regal as the mistress. When I first saw the Queen close to, early in April 1675, I realized that comparison could only be to her disadvantage.

Though I had lived at Court for more than a year I had not yet had occasion to approach the Queen or become known to her. The King had presented Madame du Montespan's children to his wife when he acknowledged them, but I had not been present at that touching family ceremony. So it was not until spring 1675, when I was asked to take the duc du Maine to see her, that I was introduced to the Queen and could form my own opinion of her whose place I should one day occupy.

While Madame de Montespan's apartment was redolent of rose and jasmine, in that of the Queen the odor of garlic vied with the smell of chocolate. Typically Spanish. And the rest gave no reason to revise this first impression. Heavy draperies obscured all the windows, and in a half-darkness full of monks and jesters, surrounded by Castilian maids, hid a fat little woman with fair hair and bad teeth, a shy look and a foolish laugh. As we entered she paused for a moment in a game of omber which she was in the process of losing; she had never been able to learn the rules of any game, and was said to be cheated by all her household without realizing it. She whispered to the footman who was carrying the child to come forward, and she had a light brought nearer so that she could see the little boy's face. She gazed at him for a long while without saying anything. Even though the candles were shining in his eyes, my beloved prince gazed straight back at her without blinking.

"What a pretty child," she lisped at last, patting him on the cheek with her chubby little hand.

"He's fair, isn't he?" she added, looking at me inquiringly.

I did not know what to say. I could not see how this statement of the obvious could be expressed as a question. So I nodded very civilly, bestowing on her my most charming smile.

"His eyes . . . they're blue, aren't they?"

That was no subject for discussion either. I nodded again.

"His cheeks . . . very pink, no?"

This too was obvious and provided no subject for conversation. I was beginning to wonder what she would find to say when she got to my darling's feet, when Louis-Auguste himself came to the rescue with the little complimentary speech I had taught him for the occasion. The Queen looked touched, though she was unable to appreciate all the nuances I had seen fit to include in this address.

"Sweet, isn't he?" she murmured to me shyly when he had finished.

"He is indeed very good," I said, "and full of respect for Your Majesty already. To make him worthy of the kindness with which Your Majesty may generously honor him is the dearest wish of all those who look after him."

"Yes," she said, "I think he is sweet. *No parece a su madre,*" she added with sudden assurance, turning to one of the Spanish maids. *"Se parece al Rey. Tiene una cara muy agradable.* How fortunate he is not like ze marquese . . . *Como odio a esta diabla! Te lo digo, esa puta* will be ze death of me! *Tu lo veras, de verdad! Recuerdalo!"*†

She kissed my darling on the brow, slipped some biscuits and cakes into his hand, gave him a last smile and thanked me for the pleasure of seeing him again.

She was already picking up her cards. In a corner of the room the Dauphin, then about twelve years old, was stumbling through some Latin verses under the rod of Monsieur de Montauzier, his tutor, who was buttoned up in black from head to foot and always looked as severe as a duenna. With one last glance at this gloomy picture, I dropped a deep curtsy and left the room. The brief interview had left me with an image of a woman who was perhaps timorous rather than really silly, and apparently mild and patient. But those admirable qualities, even more than her intellectual shortcomings, made her incapable of creating a suitable impression on the French Court.

Yet the Queen's fragile sovereignty was in less danger than the sway of the favorite, as the days which followed were to show.

On 12 April, in memory of poor Biam Coco, I was teaching the catechism and alphabet to Angola, a little Moorish page whom my cousin de Villette had brought back from abroad for the marquise, and to whom she, together with Monsieur de Barillon, my eternal lover, had stood godparent, when I thought I could hear the muffled sound of a harpsichord coming from the other end of the favorite's apartment.

Listening, I realized someone was playing, and playing very well, the tune from *La Descente de Mars*. I was surprised, for I had thought I was alone with the boy in the empty apartment. Most of the Court was with Monsieur at Saint-Cloud that day; the King was out hunting with Marsillac and Mademoiselle de Ludres; and I knew the marquise was at Clagny, where her château was nearing completion. I was wondering that one of her women should have had the impertinence to touch her favorite instrument in her absence, when the player, after a few bars at random, began to play a melancholy air and to sing the words. It was a woman's voice, and the song, asking "Shall I always shed tears at each returning spring?," told of a lover who went back to the wars every year when winter was over. I recognized the lines which the marquise had written for the King three years before at Lagny; and I recognized the beautiful voice which was singing them.

Suddenly the voice broke, the music ceased, and I thought I could hear great sobs through the silence. I at once sent my little Moor away and went to the music room. I opened the door and pretended to be surprised.

"I beg your pardon, Madame—I thought you were at Clagny and that one of your maids . . ."

She turned toward me, her lovely face bathed in tears. With her fair hair hanging loose over a dressing gown of silver moiré, she looked like a madonna at the foot of the Cross. But today, for once, she also had something of the crucified about her. She threw herself into my arms.

"Oh, Françoise, I am lost!" she cried. She was weeping so bitterly I could not understand what she was saying. I tried to soothe her as one does a child, wiping her eyes and stroking her hair. I was so unused to the spontaneous impulse of trust and humility which had brought her close to me that I was quite overcome.

"I am lost," she repeated, when she was a little calmer. "Yesterday Lécuyer refused to give me absolution, and the curé of Versailles backed him up. The King consulted Monsieur Bossuet, and Monsieur Bossuet said I was a great sinner and the Church could not give me absolution until I repented of the life I lead and make the King lead. Then the King saw fit to ask the opinion of the wretched Montauzier, and that Lenten-faced gravedigger was even worse than the others. I am lost!"

"Come, come," I said. "You've known for a long time that the priests don't sing your praises."

She began to weep again.

"Yes, but this is the first time they have all refused to give me absolution. Imagine what a scandal there will be if I can't make my Easter duty."

"I did not know you were so easily frightened," I could not help saying. "What is one more scandal to you?"

She looked at me, shocked.

"You don't care for me either. Nobody loves me," she sobbed.

I gave her a hug.

"Don't be foolish, now! After all, you have asked for it. And you are too clever not to know you could not pursue your chosen path without a few difficulties now and then."

"Yes, but this time there is a plot against me. I did not expect that. Do you know what they are up to, all these Bourdaloues and Mascarons and Bossuets?"

All of a sudden she was her usual proud self again. She shut the harpsichord with a bang and stood in front of me.

"The first thing they have to do is frighten the King. He's a coward, he's afraid of the Devil, and they've given him to understand that the next time it will be he who is refused absolution. They hope this will make him dismiss me. And do you know what for? Why, to replace me with little de Ludres, that infant, that rag, that nothing he makes sheep's eyes at. And do you know why all these fine preachers want her to take my place?"

Indeed I did not see why the bishops should conspire to put Isabelle de Ludres into the King's bed, and I expected to learn something new from the lips of my inspired interlocutor.

"Well," she went on with flashing eyes, pronouncing each word quite clearly, "it's because Mademoiselle de Ludres is a canoness."

I was astounded, and could not help bursting out laughing.

"Oh no," I cried, choking with mirth, "I cannot believe the Church would consider the sin less because it was committed by a canoness! Oh no! I suppose adultery is sanctified if it is committed with an abbé? In that case, Madame, all you have to do is enter into a relationship before Easter with Monsieur the archbishop of Paris, who is said to be susceptible to feminine charms, and you will be able to take communion . . . But what are you doing?"

"La belle madame," furious with my jesting, was plucking angrily at the strings of a lute, no doubt as a substitute for pinching me.

"Very well, laugh! I know what I know. I see what their game is . . . But that doesn't help me," she said, suddenly breaking down and with her lovely eyes once more brimming with tears. "He will dismiss me just the same. He does not like being bothered. He will dismiss me, I tell you. And it will kill me."

I consoled her as best I could and tried to speak to her as a true and Christian friend. I pointed out that she would still be the mother of legitimized children, a position which could not be taken away from her; that the King had boundless admiration for her wit and that if she chose to return to the paths of righteousness not only would his friendship not be lessened, but his esteem and respect would actually increase; and that it was better to retire voluntarily than to be forced to do so sooner or later because of age or the caprice of a younger rival. I said she would be living at Clagny, adjoining the grounds of Versailles, so that she could be at Court whenever she wanted to without giving rise to gossip. If she could avoid reverting to her old ways, her authority and prestige would be greater than ever: she would be mother, friend, adviser—a unique position. And surely nothing could be more satisfactory than to see her own policy and interests coincide with Christianity, and to see the counsel of her friends accord with that of Monsieur Bossuet.

It looked as if she was listening. To set her mind completely at rest I told her I would not desert her but would go and keep her company at Clagny until she began to be accustomed to her new way of life. After that I should go to Maintenon, but she and I, and her children, would often meet, and we should enjoy talking about the Court without having to endure its pains. While I was painting this idyllic picture of two great ladies living a life of retirement on their country estates and chatting by the fire while their offspring played around them, I could not help thinking that my inveterate desire to please and persuade was leading me into some exaggeration. For how likely was it that I could live in peace at Clagny with a woman whose moods had been unbearable to me for months, and why should I promise to share her banishment when it was not I the King was dismissing!

This perfectionism, this desire to be loved and recognized as a devoted friend often made me add some touching feature to a scene I was describing. Intoxicated with the notion of my own good deeds, I failed to foresee the undesirable consequences of my words; for once a thing was said in the heat of the moment, stubbornness and pride prevented me from ever going back on it.

So, moved by Madame de Montespan's tears and bemused by the fine figure I might cut in these arrangements, I said so many pleasant things that I calmed her; but when I got back to my own apartment, I myself was smitten with fears and regrets.

Before I had time to order my thoughts or recover my balance, the King sent for me to go and see him by appointment in his study.

There are moments in life one would hate to have to live again. I sometimes think the torture of the damned is just going over and over such moments in their minds for ever. Hell is nothing but our memories. The whole time between my going to Court and the day when I at last understood the King's true nature, deciphered his feelings and at the same time saw what God expected me to do, is for me one of those miniature hells.

It seems to me my life throughout that period was ceaselessly beset with events which were unforeseen, momentous and disturbing. I was going up in the world fast, but though my progress was swift, my mind was confused, my heart pounding and my soul clouded.

It was in this state of uneasiness that I knocked that evening at the door of the King's study.

This room, also known as the cabinet of the Council of ministers, was a real holy of holies and I had never been inside it before. It was regarded as a singular piece of news that the King had asked to see me and that at his request and to the knowledge of everyone I was having a private interview with him. Two months after "Madame de Maintenon" had created such a stir, I had no doubt that this new mark of favor would spread throughout the Court within the hour, and within the week throughout the kingdom.

The room I entered, followed by envious whispers, was small and hung with crimson velvet, and at that time had only two windows. The King was sitting at the great Council table. He looked preoccupied, and did not get up when I came in, thus omitting a courtesy to which I had grown accustomed. I could see his eyes were red, and he was holding some papers in his hand which he passed to me without saying a word. It was a letter. "Read it," he said gravely. I tried to refuse as best I could, but he insisted.

"Madame, please read that letter."

So I began to glance through it, though I could not altogether conquer the repugnance one naturally feels at looking at a letter addressed to someone else.

It was from Monsieur Bossuet. "My words have made Madame de Montespan shed many tears," wrote the bishop, "and certainly, Sire, there is no juster subject for weeping than to feel one has given to a creature the heart which God desires for Himself. But, Sire, it is necessary; otherwise there is no hope of salvation."

The whole letter was written in the same vein, noble yet humane, for Bossuet let it appear that he knew how deep the King's love was for his mistress. "May God put the finishing touch to His work," he said, "so that all the tears, the trouble and the effort you make to conquer yourself may not be in vain."

This reference to the King's weeping, and the red eyes I saw before me, caused me some impatience, which I could not altogether hide from one who was sensitive to other people's reactions.

"Am I to believe you do not altogether approve of what Monsieur Bossuet writes?" he asked.

I was glad he mistook the reason for my irritation; it was bad enough having to admit my jealousy to myself without having to reveal it to someone else.

"It is not for me to approve or disapprove of the words of the Church," said I.

He pressed me to say more, for though Madame de Montespan had told him all I had said that afternoon he wanted to hear my views on the whole matter from my own lips. I said a Christian could not avoid the duty of obedience, and that Madame de Montespan would certainly submit to it. I could see he had no doubt about it either, and that his own mind was made up; but it gave him pleasure to talk about his mistress to someone he regarded as her truest friend.

So for almost an hour he sang her praises to me.

"She is so goodhearted," he said. "Haven't you seen those lovely eyes fill with tears when anyone tells of a good deed?"

In short, he said enough to convince me that the picture of "The Man Born Blind" which Poussin had painted to go over one of the doors of the study was a portrait of the King himself.

"She is so fond of me," he went on, "that I really do not know how she will bear the separation. Please, Madame, go with her in her retirement, never leave her, surround her with your most diligent care. I ask you to do this for love of her . . . or for love of me."

This last word was so well said that it struck me as redeeming all the rest; so for love of him I promised to take Madame de Montespan to Maintenon the day after Easter. I would then go with her to Clagny, and join her there for ever three months later, after taking the little duc to the waters at Barèges.

From what the King had said I could no longer doubt that I

would be included in the favorite's disgrace, if disgrace it was, and that her fate and mine would again be joined together. I had not flattered myself that I exercised any influence over the King, but to see he contemplated my absence so lightly after having so often assured me of his friendship caused me to turn seriously to God once more. For three days I drank my fill of François de Sales and St. Augustine, and after that I felt stronger if not happier. My reason applauded the turn things were taking, even if my heart still wished that the King would keep his mistress and that they would go to the Devil together and take me with them.

On the fourteenth Madame de Montespan made her Easter communion, and all the Court was edified by a separation which cost the two lovers so much. We left the following day.

It was very pretty at Maintenon and Madame de Montespan was charmed with the place. I would have been so myself had it not been for her ceaseless agitation, to which I did not think I should offer any resistance. She countermanded whims as fast as they came into her head, wrote from morning till night and then tore everything up before she went to bed. She prowled about at night, and steeped herself all day in vinegar and anxiety.

"Mademoiselle de Ludres has red patches all over her body," she said one day as we were walking by the river, "because she was poisoned as a child. The King should be told."

"He'll see for himself," I answered, "and draw his own conclusions."

While I did not believe there was a conspiracy between the churchmen and the canoness, I did believe Mademoiselle de Ludres was in favor. At Versailles, on the mere belief that the King loved her, princesses and duchesses already rose when she entered the room, which they had never done before except for the Queen and the marquise. So the latter's suspicions seemed to have some foundation, and I sometimes wondered how much of the King's renunciation was due to religion and how much to what was all too human. This caused me some vexation, but as I had never thought I possessed a major share of the King's affection, I saw no need to grieve over having lost it. The end of our relationship would at least set my mind at rest about my salvation.

Next Madame de Montespan shut herself up in our house at Vaugirard. Every evening she had long conversations with Monsieur Bossuet, who used to shroud himself in a grey cloak and slink out through the ramparts to come and bring her the good word. I think he had some hopes of converting her as he had Mademoiselle de La Vallière; he considered her ripe for the cloister. I personally was very doubtful about this and thought the great preacher was probably being led up the garden throughout. While the marquise talked to the bishop, I chatted endlessly with my dear Nanon; I had been reunited with her with mutual transports of joy after being away from the house for more than a year.

She was as fond of me as ever, and I did all I could to maintain her affection. I noticed with amusement that during our separation she had taken to dressing her hair and herself as I had done a few years earlier. She now wore brown muslin and imitated my manners and way of speaking. This struck me as touching, and it lent this child of the people a petit-bourgeois air which suited her very well. She had become much more refined both physically and morally, and no one would have suspected in this elegant young woman the ruddy, ignorant little peasant I had adopted in an alley in Saint-Roch.

At the end of the month I went with Madame de Montespan to her house at Clagny, where the work had made enormous progress. The favorite's plans were so grandiose that when I watched her inspecting the site it made me think of Dido building Carthage. It was a queen's palace they were building; but, as the King had told me, he wanted to spare no effort that might mitigate her exile. She already had a semicircular courtyard and an orangery paved with marble; a long gallery with frescoes illustrating the story of Aeneas; a wood made up of orange trees in tubs, with tuberoses, jasmine and carnations to hide the palings screening the tubs; and a model farm furnished with the most loving turtle doves, the plumpest pigs, the most prolific cows, the curliest sheep and the silliest goslings. According to Court gossip, the building had already swallowed up nearly three million livres—about a quarter of what it cost to maintain the navy; but admittedly there never was a ship so gallantly rigged as the marquise that spring, decked out in her gold and silver veils and with her tall white headdress streaming in the wind.

I said as much, to please her, but evidently she had just made up her mind that we were to part in anger. She treated me very badly during the two days we spent together in her château and gave me good reason to dread the life in store for me there in the autumn. She was especially difficult about Nanon; she thought her not sufficiently well born to be my attendant and was afraid I might inflict her company upon her in the future.

"I don't know why you cumber yourself with such trash," she said. "I always have roomfuls of them at St. Joseph's"—a convent where she provided board for poor girls—"but I wouldn't have them in my house for all the money in the world. I suppose it's another fine consequence of your Christian charity, but you might spare me its inconveniences!"

I left her to her own cold heart, and I managed without too much difficulty to tear myself away from the little comte de Vexin, Mademoiselle de Nantes and Mademoiselle de Tours because I was going to have the duc du Maine to myself for three months.

When I called in at Versailles to collect the boy, the King, who was to leave for the army a few days later, pretended to want to give me some instructions about his son. In fact it seemed to me he wanted chiefly to have news of his mistress. The only tidings he had otherwise were from Monsieur Bossuet, who told him every day of the marquise's progress in piety in order to edify the King himself. I did not feel I ought to destroy so fragile a construction, so I spoke to the King in the same vein as the bishop. He looked grieved but was not angry with me.

He said he would look forward to my letters on the journey, and when I pointed out that I should not like to be the first to write, he assured me he would write himself. He added, smiling, that he was afraid, otherwise, I would quite forget him in the company of the only man on earth who could touch my heart—meaning my little prince. He also promised to grant a request I had made a few months earlier, and to allow my friend Bonne d'Heudicourt to return to Court. Finally, he held on to my hand for a long time, to show me that while he willingly sacrificed me to his mistress's happiness, he still felt something more for me than mere indifference.

At least, that is what I thought, and what made me happy for the whole of my journey.

I left Paris on 28 April and did not reach Barèges until 20 June, after some agreeable enough adventures on the way.

We had set off in two coaches with a large following: three servants for the duc du Maine and two, including Nanon, for me. There was also a doctor, a tutor and a chaplain, and the whole crew were Parisians who thought Etampes was the end of the world.

The duc du Maine was a delightful companion, with his fresh ideas and winning ways. He needed constant care, with continual attacks of fever or pains in the legs or pelvis; but my affection for him made all these attentions a pleasure. To save his strength we travelled only three hours in the morning and three hours in the afternoon, and beds and meals were ready waiting for us at every stage.

The governors of the provinces we went through gave great entertainments in our honor, and in the villages the little children ran after our coaches with cries of joy. Sometimes I would invite one or two of them into the inn where we slept, so as to amuse the young prince with their company. I was very glad to see these poor little peasants were fatter and better clad than on my previous journeys. Thanks to the good government of the King and Monsieur Colbert the people were not so wretched; on Sunday the girls put on some finery, and certain laborers even displayed well-filled bellies. Only the universal lack of education still gave me pain: none of these people knew their letters or their catechism. I should have liked to save the brightest of them from this dreadful ignorance, and if it had been left to me, would have stowed our trunks full of tattered little ragamuffins with a gleam of intelligence in their eyes.

In Poitou we were almost stifled with caresses. In Guienne, which two months before had been in revolt against the authority of the King, we met with even more splendid receptions. Everywhere the duc du Maine was treated as the King's son; the Dauphin could not have been more honored. At Blaye the old duc de Saint-Simon was a magnificent host, before the jurats or aldermen of Bordeaux arranged for us to embark in a large boat. We sailed along happily, rowed by forty oarsmen; when we were in sight of the town, a number of other ships set forth to greet us, some full of violins and others of trumpets. Then the guns of Château-Trompette, together with those of all the ships in the harbor, joined in the music which followed us. A vast crowd waited to welcome us at the water's edge with cries of "Vive le Roi!" The jurats made long speeches. Fortunately the maréchal d'Albret, governor of Guienne, who had gone on ahead of us, refrained from answering. He just picked up our prince and carried him to the waiting carriages, into which we climbed together with about a hundred other people. It took us more than an hour to drive from the harbor to the house where we were staying, so huge was the crowd and so eager their demonstrations of joy.

I cannot say how happy I was to see Monsieur d'Albret again after four long years of separation. I found him somewhat older: his eyebrows were white under his dark wig and his face was thinner; but mentally he was the same as ever. He presented the same extraordinary mixture of the wisdom which comes from experience and the most extreme freethinking; and at the same time he was charming, agreeable from every point of view and head and shoulders above everyone else in whatever company he found himself. Bordeaux society doted upon him, and it was said no other governor had ever given such elegant entertainments.

We walked together for a long while in the grounds of his house. I realized he still felt the same toward me, and I myself had not changed much toward him. We still wooed each other very well in words and enjoyed the rather melancholy enchantments of an unfulfilled love. We spent a long while sitting in a little green bower overlooking the river. Night was falling. It was the end of May, and mild.

"Do you not regret," he asked, "what we have not done together?"

"No," I answered, blushing a little, "because my feeling for you could not have been increased. To tell the truth, I do not know anyone for whom I feel more, or anyone who means so much to me."

"Well," he said, "as far as I am concerned, I must admit I sometimes hanker after that little Madame Scarron whom I followed to her room one evening to console her for the harsh behavior of her husband; and I often tell myself I am the greatest fool that ever lived . . . But I am glad others have been cleverer than I. It is said you enjoy the highest favor . . ."

I could not help laughing.

"You couldn't be jealous, by any chance? Whatever you may hear about the favor I enjoy, I am far from ruling France."

"Maybe . . . Maybe . . . But if I wanted to curry favor with you, Françoise, I'd tell you that if I had to choose between you and my niece de Montespan I would not hesitate."

I smiled, and we began to talk very agreeably about the past. He thanked me for having had his other niece, Madame d'Heudicourt, recalled to Saint-Germain.

"But you will find her changed," he said. "She has become horrible to look at in her exile. You are the only one who grows in grace and beauty with the years."

"Time does not harm your looks either."

"It may not harm my looks, but it kills me. It is likely you and I will not meet again in this world."

"In this world, *mon maréchal?* Do you by any chance expect to meet me in another world, and are you taking steps to do so?"

"I see you are very sure of going to Heaven, my dear lady. But perhaps it is you who are taking steps to join me! I can just see myself frying away with you, between a couple of devils with cloven hoofs!"

I was put out by this insult even though it was delivered in a light and friendly manner.

"What do you mean, Monsieur?"

He took my hand, laughing, and went on in the same jesting tone.

"Nothing that need make you angry, Françoise! But you take

offense rather quickly on this subject, and that might make me suspicious . . . To tell you the truth, I am not really afraid of Hell, and I think I'd prefer Hell to nothingness, which is certainly what I am bound for. But I hope I am wrong—I hope so more than you can imagine. Even the everlasting fire would be pleasant to me, because I should still have the happiness of feeling something . . ."

"You really are absurd!"

"Madame, I am the same as ever. But may I carry absurdity so far as to ask one last favor? You can hardly refuse a dying man . . ."

"I did not think you so timid as to be frightened by the gout! For apart from that you seem to be very well."

"No, my dear," he said, suddenly pensive. "I am tortured by the stone, and there is something wrong with my heart."

"Too much love," said I.

"Not any more. I am on very good terms with my wife now . . . No, as I said, I am dying. Will you not grant this last favor?"

"Let's see what it is . . ."

Night had fallen now. Ships with their lights on skimmed along the river, shedding faint gleams on the bower in which we sat.

"All I ask is for you to lay your head on my shoulder," he said gently, "and leave it there a while. Don't object, I beg. I shan't touch you, I shan't say anything, you needn't be afraid of any word or movement. I am too old for that sort of thing . . . and you are too advanced in royal favor. All I ask is one last mark of friendship. You won't refuse it?"

"You're mad," I said. "The air of Bordeaux doesn't agree with you."

But he pressed me so eagerly that, half out of pity and half out of affection, I ended up doing what he asked. We remained for some time in that strange attitude, and I found it more pleasurable than I would have thought. The lapping of the water could be heard from below; between the branches of the little arbor I could see the stars. This reminded me of my last evening with my father on the beach at Marie-Galante. It was as if I had been asleep for the thirty years in between.

If anyone had found us there like that it would have been the end of both my reputation and my success, but I had not the strength to break the spell. My feelings struck me as decidedly strange: as to the King, I still wanted to throw myself at his feet; but as to the maréchal, I was ready to throw myself into his arms. I wondered where this instability came from.

The next day the maréchal did me the honors of his capital, not sparing me one palace or church. When we passed a funeral near the cathedral, I noticed that he uncovered his head when the crucifix went by.

"But yesterday you gave me to understand you and God were still at daggers drawn," I laughed.

"Oh," he answered gravely, "we bow to each other but we're not on speaking terms."

Seeing he was so determined in his impiety, I tried to find out from his wife if he was as ill as he had said. I arranged to see her at her toilet the next morning, before the wines of Bordeaux had made too many inroads on her judgment.

"He is not ill," she said. "He's bored, that's all."

I was relieved to hear this, but vexed that he should have lied in order to get round me. But such deceptions were so much in his style that I could not be really angry with him. I knew what he was like, and had only myself to blame if I loved him all the same.

Before leaving Bordeaux I wrote the King a ten-page letter telling him in detail all the maréchal had done to make the prince's visit an agreeable one. As agreed, we had been keeping up a regular correspondence.

His first letter had reached me a week after I left Versailles; it was short but very nice, and to me all the more marvelous because this was the first time I had had anything in the King's own handwriting actually in my hands. I was so elated that I wore the piece of paper on my person for three days and put it under my pillow at night. To give myself an excuse to keep looking at it, I pretended to be studying the formation of the letters: an Italian named Primi had made this kind of calligraphy fashionable at Court, but it was new to me. All I could see was that the King joined all his words together, and it occurred to me that if he accorded other people as little space in his life as he left them in his letters, they would all die of asphyxiation. Why did I not abide by that shrewd analysis! But after a few days I told myself I was being foolish, for the King probably dictated his letters to Rose, his secretary. So I stopped idolizing the form and adored the content.

The King soon supplied material for my adoration by writing to me three or four times a week. I wrote lengthy answers, and his letters grew longer too. I could see he liked telling me about the war or about his building projects, and on my side I did not confine myself to accounts of the prince's health and progress. I sensed that he would like to have exact information about the state of his people and the government of his provinces, and I sent him minute reports on these subjects. But if I thus turned politician, I was a merry one, and to amuse him I described all the members of our party, the doctor's ailments, Nanon's apprehensions, La Couture's naiveties and the chaplain's stomach aches.

He was so delighted with my letters that he was soon telling everyone about the long missives I sent him, and finally started to read out great extracts from them to his ministers and officials at his *coucher* or ceremonial retirement to bed at night. This caused surprise, and the abbé Gobelin, alarmed, wrote to say he thought the King's friendship toward me was more ardent than was desirable. But no one dared draw any conclusions, for at the same time the King recalled Madame de Montespan to Court and revived their adulterous relationship in great style right under the nose of Monsieur Bossuet.

"Do not say anything, Monsieur!" the King had exclaimed when the bishop was about to remonstrate. "Do not say anything! I have given my orders, and I mean them to be carried out."

Despite all that, the growing length of his letters and the increasing warmth of the civilities they contained made me think the abbé Gobelin had good reason to believe I had made progress in the Master's regard. The sequence was just the opposite of what it had been with Monsieur Scarron: the conquest of my husband had begun with my letters and been concluded by my person; now

I was finishing off from a distance, with my pen, what I had started in a much more immediate manner.

I was much less amply supplied with news of Madame de Montespan, who did not write once during the whole of my journey. She was furious with me for accounting to the King directly about his son's health, thus showing that I had shut myself up in the Pyrenees because of the father and not out of love for the mother.

Her silence did not trouble me unduly, especially as her letters always showed as much disregard for spelling as for morals, and I had great trouble deciphering them. I learned from people at Court of her reconciliation with the King. It did not surprise me, and though in certain private letters I expressed my disapproval, I was glad that her return allowed me to escape from Clagny.

At first I was told that the love between the King and his mistress was greater than ever, and that the favorite made so bold, on two occasions, as to let herself be seen with her head resting on his shoulder in the informality of her apartment. But a few days later Madame de Coulanges wrote that suspicion and dislike had already followed the first reconciliation. People spoke openly of the favor enjoyed by Madame de Louvigny, and whispered of that bestowed on Madame de Soubise. By September, all was tears, sulks and vexations. Madame de Richelieu informed me that the favorite had been refused confession at Fontainebleau. Even though the Queen's chief lady-in-waiting herself had asked the priest, assuring him that despite appearances the marquise had reformed, he had declined, saying that to hear this lady's confession was too great a matter for him.

The hot baths at Barèges and Bagnères had done the duc du Maine some good, and the King sent orders for us to return in October. Our homeward journey was as slow as our outward one had been.

I spent ten days at Niort and Mursay. At every visit I found a few new faces in the Villette family, and this time I was delighted with a little girl of two called Marguerite-Marie. She had the sweetest little face and charming manners; she already spoke extremely well; and it was hard to resist the temptation to keep kissing the lips which uttered such pretty sayings and the eyes which held such loving looks. She was always with me, and I promised to take an interest in her later if she grew to be more than five or six years old. This was doubtful, as the Villettes lost most of their infants at an early age. But they did have a couple of boys aged eight and ten, and I tried to persuade Philippe to guarantee their future and his own salvation by being converted. It was his attachment to Protestantism which made his advancement in the army slower than he deserved; he was subjected to innumerable attempts at persecution which he complained of and which had long grieved me. But I could not make him see reason. He gloried in his obstinacy, which he said he had inherited direct from our grandfather, Agrippa d'Aubigné.

We had a few quite lively arguments on the subject, while his wife, Marie-Anne, who grew frightened as soon as we raised our voices, wept silently into her apron. That was about all she was fit for—to weep and do as she was told. The idea that one might fight for something or someone never entered her head. But after a few stinging remarks on both sides, Philippe and I were reconciled, and we parted as affectionately as if we had been brother and sister.

On 20 November I at last reached Saint-Germain again, expecting to cut a better figure there now than when I had gone away. I thought I deserved general admiration: as a governess I had succeeded where all the doctors had failed, and my little prince could walk if someone held his hand; as a woman I had considerably increased my influence over the King's heart and mind, without endangering my reputation.

The triumph of the governess was indeed complete. The King had never had a more pleasant surprise than the one I gave him. I had not told him about his son's latest progress, nor did he expect the duc du Maine until the following day. When he suddenly saw the boy walk into the room with me just leading him by the hand, the King was transported with joy. I supped that evening at Madame de Richelieu's, with Monsieur de Louvois. Some people kissed my hand, others kissed my gown—the whole apartment was filled with a chorus of praise.

As a woman, however, I soon perceived my victory was less dazzling. Noticing I did not mention Madame de Montespan's return, the King took the first opportunity of speaking of it himself. He used the most general but the most unmistakable terms.

"I know that I am doing wrong," he said calmly. "And sometimes I am ashamed. You have seen I have done all I could to prevent myself sinning against God and giving in to my passions. But they are stronger than reason. I cannot resist, and I do not even want to."

After that there was little to say and still less to hope.

To tell the truth, his mistress, though she no longer had much power over his heart, still held sway over his mind and senses. He still liked to go to her apartment, where one was sure of being very well entertained, certainly better than in the Spanish entourage of the Queen. He also retained an inclination for her physical charms, enough anyway for her to present him with two more children during the period I am speaking of—Mademoiselle de Blois in 1677, and the comte de Toulouse in 1678.

Nevertheless, when the King spoke of yielding to his passions he meant all of them, and made no pretence of confining himself to his passion for "la belle madame." When I got back from Barèges I found Madame de Soubise as much in favor as I had been led to expect.

Madame de Montespan had just found out about this affair through Madame de Soubise's habit of wearing a certain pair of emerald earrings on the days when her husband went to Paris. Madame de Montespan had kept an eye on the King and had him followed, and it turned out that the earrings were indeed the signal habitually used for their rendezvous. Since this discovery the marquise's wrath had not abated, and the stream of insults she directed at Madame de Soubise made public a relationship which otherwise would never have been suspected. Fortunately for the King, Monsieur de Soubise was more accommodating than Monsieur de Montespan, and went on studiously ignoring everything. This was how he in due course exchanged his little house for the magnificent hôtel de Guise.

I did not think, though, that the marquise had anything to fear from her rival's stratagems. Madame de Soubise was tall and had marvelous red hair and an ample bosom, but her beauty was merely statuesque. Though she was pleasingly proportioned, in my opinion she could not hope to win a man's heart from Madame de Montespan with all her piquant charms. Moreover, Madame de Soubise's mind was set on nothing but business, which made her conversation dull and lifeless, and the King, though his fancy was sometimes caught by the attractions of a pretty figure, was never fixed for long except by those of a lively mind.

So several other ladies filled the monarch's idle moments when Monsieur de Soubise did not have the good sense to go to Paris. At Saint-Germain either Chamarande or Bontemps would lead them at night up a little staircase to the door of a study which provided a back way into the King's apartments. This door was usually locked, but on certain evenings the King would leave the key on the outside—a secret familiar to all, though everyone pretended not to know it.

I myself might not have agreed to be among the ladies who thus went in by the back entrance, but when I went into the King's apartment by the front door and in full view of everyone, ostensibly to talk about the royal children, I was really acting no differently. For at the same time as the King had told me he was temporarily abandoning his good resolutions, he had given me to understand that I was the object of one of the passions he did not wish to resist. For six months his letters had made me hope we might be friends, and I had flattered myself that I might bring him to substitute milder feelings for a relationship which had caused me much remorse; but now I saw I must abandon this dream for good and all.

I offered no more resistance to temptation than I had in the past and did not even have the strength to think of quitting the Court. Every time he spoke to me coldly, reestablishing a regal distance between himself and me at the very moment when I had thought I could do with him as I pleased, my feelings for him were redoubled. I did not regard the guilty love he forced upon me as a mark of affection, but rather as a denial of the principles on which my life was founded; yet I enjoyed feeling his power over me and found pleasure in seeing that power increased by the humiliation he inflicted on me by leading me into sin. The pious sometimes introduce peculiar refinements into pleasures libertines have come to regard as dull.

I justified my conduct to myself by saying that if I wished to make the King break off his connections with other women, I had to make him see me as accommodating and willing. For certain it was that if he did not find his pleasure with me he would go and seek it elsewhere.

Thus, through pure unreason and impure reasons, I settled into sin, and sought to base my life upon a situation which was false.

This was made all the more difficult by the fact that the King's attraction for my charms was as intermittent as his friendship, and he made no attempt to change my situation. In theory if not always in fact, I was still Madame de Montespan's subordinate. I had none of the things which may give one an independent position at Court. I had no apartment of my own, only a garret at Saint-Germain, a bed in the children's room at Versailles, and at Fontainebleau, Chambord and the rest, whatever corner I could find among the wardrobes and the antechambers. I had no right to live at Court but that derived from my position as governess to the royal bastards, which was not official or even properly recognized as mine. Lastly, I had no adequate or regular pension, and so no reliable income, for Maintenon as yet brought in nothing and was costing me a fortune in repairs.

Thus everything combined to make me dependent upon a woman who could have had me dismissed with the utmost ease if she had known, and been apprehensive about, my relationship with her lover. So to throw dust in her eyes I was more tactful, obliging and flattering than ever, though as her unsuccessful rival and often ill-used attendant my real feelings for her could only be hostility and dislike.

Every year during the summer, whether I liked it or not, I had to take her to Maintenon, assure her she was mistress of it and endure all her whims in my own house. I even had to conceal her there for months when she had her last two children, one of whom was actually born at Maintenon. One had to keep praising her looks and her clothes, reassuring her about her attractiveness and putting the finishing touch to her curls and her lace. I supervised her charities and the making of tapestry hangings for Clagny. I lavished exotic and useless presents on her which my cousin de Villette brought back from his travels—monkeys, pineapples and parrots. I entertained her with the latest gossip at Court or the most recent publication in Paris. I smiled at her, I embraced her—and all the time I longed to strangle her.

How far was she taken in by these stratagems? She gave me large sums of money to have my château altered to suit her taste, thus forcing upon me a menagerie and countless other extravagances which I afterwards had to get rid of. She passed on to me skirts which were unattractive, pictures she had tired of, tedious books, which she would accompany with compliments on my wit and elegance. Then, after a fond embrace, she would suddenly criticize me bitterly for my manners or the way I was bringing up her children, and not say another word to me for a fortnight.

But these female twists and turns were not the worst of it. I hated it most when she made me preach to her. Sometimes she would come to me tormented by scruples of conscience and overwhelmed by the enormity of her sins. In the absence of any confessor willing to hear her, she fell back on me, expecting me to dispense some of the edifying speeches I had once uttered at Lagny or Vaugirard—as if I were still fit to expound the Gospel to her. I did as she wished, but the words scorched my lips as I spoke them. Lying and pretence might have become second nature to me, but I was breathless with dread at having to mingle them with religion. I thought I would lose my reason; as for my soul, I considered that already lost.

So I cannot say that was the best period in my life. It included five or six years so shameful that I should like to think them part of someone else's life. I was prostituting myself for my career, and people praised me for my virtue. I paid for my charities with money taken from a woman I was deceiving, and people lauded my generosity. I was helping a king to damnation, and everyone commended my piety.

At the best, during those years, I remained a faithful relative and friend.

I gathered around me the remnants of the Scarron family and saved all of it that could still be saved. My brother, whom I spent all my time recommending to ministers, was able thanks to me to leave the frontier fortresses and became governor of Cognac. As a reward for my trouble he made me a present of a little girl he had had with a woman from Paris and a little boy named Charles who was born in 1676 in Belfort. I had little Charlot live with me at Maintenon and brought him up there until he was of age. My cousins—de Villette, Fontmort, Sainte-Hermine and Caumont d'Adde—received constant help from me in their lawsuits and business affairs; the fact that they were Huguenots did not prevent them making use of my credit.

I had had Bonne d'Heudicourt recalled to Saint-Germain, her past wrongs forgiven, and arranged for her to enjoy countless little everyday favors—a place in the favorite's carriage, a winning ticket in the King's lottery, a smile from the monarch himself. I obtained dowries for the little Montchevreuil girls, and in the years that followed I had my good Henri made tutor to the duc du Maine and my devoted Marguerite mistress of the Dauphine's maids of honor.

When handing out all these favors I did not forget Mademoiselle de Lenclos, who had recourse to my services in a number of dubious enterprises. I tried to lure her to Court, but she nimbly backed out, saying she was too old to get used to new surroundings. Afterwards I was glad she had refused: it was better, by way of a former friend, to produce the prudish Madame de Montchevreuil than the elderly but still rakish Ninon. Mademoiselle de Scudéry, who lived in respectable but not very nourishing poverty, received a pension. I saw that d'Elbène, who had been my first husband's close friend, had a decent end. I made Monsieur de Beuvron's sister a lady-in-waiting, Basville administrator of a province and Guilleragues an ambassador.

In addition to this loyalty to my friends I had, even in those days when my heart was consumed with hypocrisy and ambition, kept my sympathy for the lowly and humiliated, for the poor and for children. Though I cannot claim to have loved them more than wealthy churchwomen usually do, I think I sometimes did love them to better purpose. I remember talking one day to some of the peasant women of Avon whom I was helping through my charities to have bread to eat and a roof over their heads, and they said that what they would most like to do would be to have a really good meal for once in their lives. I had seven or eight of them come to the château at Fontainebleau one evening and had them served a supper fit for a princesse on plates made of silver. Their happiness gave me enormous pleasure. A few worthy souls who heard of this folly criticized me for it, but I considered I knew more about poverty than they did.

When I had fed my protégés' bodies, I tried to strengthen their minds, arranging for the youngest and brightest to go to school or receive some training in a workshop. I cannot tell you how many poor children or orphans I took in and educated at my own expense during those years. My room at Versailles, as at Maintenon, always contained four or five children of all kinds, six or seven howling dogs and an indescribable commotion of laughter, chairs over-turned, yells and barks, in the midst of which I wrote my letters, said my prayers and kept the accounts of my estate. So, when I think of it, it is not surprising that I always had a migraine. But by way of compensation I acquired unusual skill at educating both peasants and princes.

Unlike most teachers, and in contrast to the method I saw applied to Monseigneur le Dauphin, the Heudicourt children and the sons of the burghers of Fontainebleau alike, I made it a rule that in education there are no rules. One must never be in a hurry to draw conclusions. One must start by observing at length the nature and abilities of every child, and act accordingly with each individual. Education is a long act of patience, where what does not come sooner may come later. There is no such thing as a bad disposition if you know how to manage and you start managing soon enough. At the worst you sometimes sow what others reap. Even as regards knowledge itself it seems to me pointless to be in a hurry. Children do not like being forced, and it often does great harm to try to make prodigies of them before their time. Between Monsieur de Montauzier's rod and Bossuet's interminable lessons every day, the Dauphin had learned a thousand Latin verses by heart by the time he was six years old. But he vowed that when he was his own master he would never open a book. And he kept his word.

So I did not attempt to belabor my little duc with Greek verbs, but instead tried to develop gradually his power of reasoning, and to impart to him by example rather than constraint a love of reading. I also aimed at inculcating a strong desire to be respected, which would remain with him always and be much more useful than all the professors' Latin.

In educating my charges I would have nothing of the severity advocated by Madame de Montespan. A sad education is a poor one. Recreation, laughter and relaxation are necessary. I always arranged for lessons to be interrupted by errands, games of cards or dice, visits to the zoo or to the kitchen garden. Every lesson could be turned into a game, and just as later I wrote my "conversations" and "proverbs" for Saint-Cyr so that vocabulary and morals might be taught with pleasure, so for the duc du Maine and his sisters I invented little parlor games, puzzles which taught them grammar and arithmetic without their realizing it. Even these games were not invariable, but were adapted to suit each child's temperament and tastes.

I held only two principles to be absolute and universally applicable: that gentleness should be the rule in bringing up children, and that there should be reason in everything.

One should speak as reasonably to a child of seven as to a man of twenty. Obedience can be made easy if you give a reason for everything you forbid or require, especially if you never make an unnecessary fuss or create unnecessary fears but present what is true and what is false quite straightforwardly. One should never promise anything without keeping one's word, whether it be a matter of reward or of punishment. And rigor should never be used until all the possibilities of reason have been exhausted.

While one should be firm as to ends, one should always be very mild as to means; that being so, it is best not to see every fault. To think no mistake should go unpunished is foolish: one should act according to the mistake itself, to the child one is dealing with, and to the circumstances. Some children are so wilful and passionate that once they are angry you may whip them ten times running and still not get them to do what they are told; they are temporarily immune to reason and punishment is useless. One should give them time to calm down, and one should calm down oneself. But so that they do not think you are giving in and their stubbornness has won, it is best to contrive to get them separated from you for a while and say you are putting the matter off to another time, thus making it more ominous.

My little duc, though by nature the sweetest child in the world, was always the prey of his ailments and of the violent remedies applied to them, and this sometimes gave rise to rages and impatience which everyone, including his mother, blamed me for tolerating. They would put him in a boiling hot bath, and then when he was rude or ill-tempered they wanted me to scold him. I confess I had not the heart. And in any case all that treatment so heated his blood that nothing I said or did would have had any effect. So I arranged to be called away on some pretext, so that he should not think I was condoning his moods and short temper. But when next day, having chosen my moment, I found him quieter, I chided him for his behavior the previous day and together, quite calmly, we tried to find suitable ways to correct it. But if ever I had to punish him, I did so in such a way as to make myself feared once and for all, for it cost me so much to be severe with him that I did not want it to happen again.

These methods, derived quite naturally from practice, succeeded remarkably well with my "darling." Having accustomed him to reason from earliest infancy, I could do anything with him by means of moderation, good example and rational argument. And since, on top of all that, he had inherited great discernment from the King and a talent for satire from the Mortemarts, he was always saying clever things which made everyone regard him as a prodigy, in advance of his years.

I remember he was sitting by the window of his room at

Versailles one day when he saw the gloomy Montauzier go by in the courtyard. Montauzier, tutor to his half-brother the Dauphin, was holding a stick with which he was hitting some dogs to make them run and jump.

"So, Monsieur de Montauzier," said my seven-year-old prince, "I see you never spare the rod."

This thrust at the way Montauzier tried to train both his pets and his pupil delighted everyone who happened to be there in the Cour des Princes.†

Another time we were having *médianoche* with the King, Madame de Montespan and the gentlemen favorites of the moment in a gondola on the Grand Canal at Versailles. Suddenly the duc, who had had some wine and was bubbling over with mirth as he sat on my knee, pointed to the King and said aloud, "He's not my papa."

"Hush!" I said, for the King had forbidden his natural children to refer to him in this way.

My little one started to laugh and said, more loudly:

"I know I mustn't say he's my papa . . ."

The King was frowning.

". . . But," said Monsieur du Maine, rolling about with delight, "if he's not my papa, no one can deny he's the King my father! And I can't be forbidden to love the King my father!"

The King forgave this little joke, which as well as being quite clever showed the boy's affection and respect.

I was also very successful with little Mademoiselle de Tours, who had the same sweet and affable character as her father and was eager to learn whatever anyone tried to teach her. She adored Monsieur du Maine, and was dearly loved by him—much more than the older sister, Mademoiselle de Nantes, who though she had inherited her mother's lovely face and a fair amount of wit, had an odd character which I was never able to like. As for little César, he gave me scarcely any satisfaction, though it was not his fault. While I was at Barèges, he had fallen into a decline which lasted until his death. He was always in a fever and had a violent cough which racked him day and night, making him so weak that he could not even bear the light and had to live in funereal darkness. From the age of three and a half, when this illness began, until he died at the age of eleven, all I could teach him was to read a little, and my skill in education was reduced to occasionally distracting him from his suffering with a toy or a sweet.

Because of César's state of health the King destined him for the Church from infancy, but the more great benefices were heaped on him, including Saint-Denis and Saint-Germain-des-Prés, of which he was abbot, the more weak and sickly he became. In the end he expired like one of those little candles whose flame is so faint that when you have blown it out you wonder if it was ever alight.

I was not asked to look after the marquise's last two children, Mademoiselle de Blois and Monsieur de Toulouse, because at the time they were born, the King wanted me to take more care of my health; he also had other plans for me. Madame de Montespan herself was relieved of most of her duties at about that period, so was able to devote all her time to the two children. In the end, by a strange reversal, she owed her position at Court solely to the fact that she was governess to Mademoiselle de Blois.

But in 1676 she was still well enough loved to allow herself many scandals and extravagances. She wanted three ships to trade for her in the Levant: they were built and equipped at the country's expense. She wanted some bears, which were to be allowed to roam about freely in the gardens and apartments: she got her bears and in one night they ruined all the woodwork in the rooms at Versailles where they were quartered. She wanted cards to be played for higher stakes at Court. Every day, at faro, basset and hocca† she would stake more than a million. One Christmas Day she lost 700,000 crowns, then bet 1,500,000 livres on three cards and won. Three months later she lost 400,000 pistoles in one hour. In short, she turned the Court into a gambling den. The King, who did not like to find fault with her, paid.

But in the spring of 1676 came a new threat to her sovereignty.

The King, preoccupied by the approaching Church jubilee and thinking that he and his mistress ought to set an example of repentance, decided once again that they must separate; and he probably really meant it. Madame de Montespan retired to her hôtel at Vaugirard, went to church, fasted, prayed, wept for her sins and to finish off her purification went to take the waters at Bourbon-l'Archambault. The King for his part did all a good Christian should. But when the jubilee was over, the question was whether Madame de Montespan should come back to Court.

"Why not?" said her friends and relations, even the most virtuous among them. Monsieur Bossuet, after having hesitated for a long while and gone so far as to tell the King that one "could not be sure of a rebel stronghold so long as the instigator of the revolt still had credit there," ended by thinking she should return. But there was still a difficulty: could Madame de Montespan appear before the King without preparation? To avoid any inconvenience arising from surprise, they ought to see each other privately before meeting in public. So it was agreed that the King should visit the marquise, but to avoid any occasion for gossip a number of respectable dames were to be present at the interview, and the King was to see Madame de Montespan only in their company.

The King duly came, but gradually he drew Madame de Montespan into a window embrasure. There they whispered together for some time, wept and said what people usually say in such circumstances. Then they bowed low to the venerable matrons and went into another room. The result, as I have said, was first Mademoiselle de Blois and then Monsieur de Toulouse. It seems to me one can still see, in the character, face and whole person of Madame la duchesse d'Orléans, as Mademoiselle de Blois later became, traces of that struggle between love and the jubilee.

After this reconciliation the two lovers seemed more attached than ever, and for a few days they could not take their eyes off one another. So sure was I that their love would revive, I thought it would be wise to get ready to retire to Maintenon at once if I wanted to avoid being led captive behind the triumphal chariot. But the magic did not last, because of lassitude on the one side and, on the other, more jealousy, caprice and bad temper than ever. The King did enough to annoy the Queen, the priests and everybody else, but he could never do enough to please the marquise. And in her agitation of mind, and because of all the intrigues she carried on at once, she began to get muddled and make mistakes.

Thus, as a counterpart to Madame de Soubise, about whom she was quite unnecessarily apprehensive, she brought Mademoiselle de Ludres, who up till then had been forgotten, back into favor. This was a great error, for while the Court had been wrong two years earlier in thinking the King in love with the canoness when she was really just a screen for other affairs, this time, thanks to Madame de Montespan herself, the King was genuinely smitten. The affair lasted from the autumn of 1676 until the end of 1677.

It drove the favorite mad, and her family with her. Madame de Thianges collided with poor Ludres every time she passed her in a doorway. The two sisters hatched a plan to get the King back to the Mortemart family by throwing one of the favorite's nieces into his arms. They chose Madame de Nevers, then her young sister Mademoiselle de Thianges, later duchess of Sforza, who was then twenty years old and very pretty. They dressed her up, trained her and set her before the King at every opportunity. They also put me forward, just in case. Although Madame de Montespan still frowned on the King's friendship toward me, my age, which she regarded as canonical, and my birth, which was so low as to be nonexistent, made her think his feeling for me could only be intellectual. Ordinarily even this would have been enough to alarm her, but in 1677 she thought Mademoiselle de Thianges and I would make an interesting pair, the girl to provide the pleasures of love and I to provide those of the mind. In any case, she regarded me as belonging to her own household in the same way, if not in the same rank, as Mademoiselle de Thianges. The plot met with some success. Although the favorite may not have managed to eliminate Mademoiselle de Ludres, who destroyed herself through her own indiscretions, the King did look very affectionately on his mistress's niece and, at the same time, displayed a renewed attachment to me.

The marquise, furious at having thus shut up the wolf in the fold at the very moment when the canoness was disappearing into a convent, then hit upon Angélique de Fontanges. She was another of Madame's maids of honor. She was eighteen, with definitely red hair, grey eyes and a pale complexion, and she was quite angelically beautiful from head to foot. But she was madly romantic, and stupid, which made the marquise think she would be able to do as she liked with her.

Again the favorite's scheme was a success: the King swiftly married off Mademoiselle de Thianges to an Italian nobleman, and despite my prayers refused to let me go with him that year to the front. But he fell so much in love with Mademoiselle de Fontanges, to whom the marquise used to lend her make-up and jewels, omitting nothing which might make the girl more attractive in her lover's eyes, that he no longer looked at his acknowledged mistress, who after nine pregnancies was growing stouter every day. By then her thigh was thicker than my waist, and with legs like that, even if you do have wit and a pretty face, you cannot afford to play the dangerous games she indulged in but should assume with good grace the role of dignity and friendship. But she had apparently decided to destroy herself utterly, and had not yet completed the process.

One day I was watching her play chess with her friend Marsillac. She was extraordinary. She prepared so many ploys at once, and so confusedly, that she always ended up ruining her own chances. Marsillac, who was not very bright and had not a tenth of the wit of his father, Monsieur de La Rochefoucauld, was incapable of winning and in fact did not do so: she lost by her own efforts. "Oh, I'm never lucky any more!" she said suddenly, and deliberately overturned the table. I saw her play the following day with her sister the abbess of Fontevrault, and the day after that with my little duc, who played like a dream, and each time it was the same—she purposely did as badly as she could. Her whole behavior seemed to reflect a strange dichotomy in her soul.

Fortunately for her the King was, as he himself liked to say, "a creature of habit," and if she was losing him as surely as she lost her king at chess, at least she was losing him more slowly.

My life in the midst of these storms and uncertainties was neither easy nor peaceful. It would have been enough to drive a more sensitive person crazy, but for a long while I had lived at Court in accordance with Plutarch's harsh but true maxim, which says you should treat everyone as if they will one day be your enemies.

Some days the chief sultana would worship me and take my advice. Together we would read *La Princesse de Clèves*, which Madame de La Fayette and her elderly lover had just amused themselves by writing. We each had our favorite, the poet Racine and the satirist Despréaux, appointed official historians to the King. We kissed one another and joined together in insulting Madame de Soubise or Mademoiselle de Fontanges. Then on other days she despised and abused me, and once even raised her hand against me.

Once again it was about the management of the children. She had come into their room just as they were having their tea.

"Why are they having jam and stewed fruit?" she demanded. "I thought I told you they weren't to have anything but dry bread at this time of the day."

"Madame," I answered, "they have such bad teeth for their age that they would rather eat nothing at all than dry bread. So I thought —"

"I don't ask you to think, Madame—I ask you to obey! With all your bourgeois notions about butter and jam you are ruining their health. If they eat stewed fruit at this hour, they won't eat any supper."

"As to that, Madame, they eat too much supper as it is. It would be better for them not to stuff themselves with meat with you at midnight but to eat more at other meals during the day."

"Is the governess of my children by any chance trying to tell me what to do?"

"If it is humiliating to be their governess," I retorted, pretending she was referring to their being illegitimate, "what is it to be their mother?"

She raised her arm as if to slap my face. At that moment, by chance, the King entered the room and seeing us at loggerheads asked what was the matter. I said coolly, "If Your Majesty will go into the next room I shall have the honor of telling him."

He went, I followed and Madame de Montespan was left alone and thunderstruck.

When I found myself alone with the King I told him everything. For the first time I gave him a vivid description of Madame de Montespan's cantankerousness and severity and explained my fears for the future. I was still hoping to change my position so as to be able to remain at Court without being subject to the favorite. Most of what I told the King was not new to him, yet he seemed not to understand my own wishes and only tried to calm me down once more. Then in the end he asked if the marquise had asked my advice before putting the duc du Maine in the hands of an English doctor called Talbot, whom she praised to the skies but who inflicted such strange remedies on the child that I was in the greatest anxiety on his account.

"No, Sire," I said, "Madame de Montespan did not consult me. And I venture to say it is a pity she does not consult more with herself before subjecting her children to such peculiar methods of treatment."

"You do not approve?"

"No, Sire, and I can see that Your Majesty does not approve either. The prince, who could not walk very well before, is now so weak again that he has lost the use of his legs. And the only result of all the miraculous applications of snake venom and toad's slime has been to reopen the abscess on his thigh. A fine piece of work! To say nothing of the pints of wine poor little Vexin has to swallow as medicine."

"Do not be angry, Madame. It doesn't suit you and it makes you unfair. The marquise was acting for the best."

"Perhaps, Sire. But her first concern is to surprise people. She must always do that—cause astonishment and never do anything that anyone else does. Bears among the panelling, a rockery in an apartment, a dress made of diamonds, dromedaries to carry her luggage, three million wagered on three cards, mice harnessed to a coach and children treated with snake poison. Very wonderful! As worthy of going down to posterity as the exploits of Alexander!"

"I agree," he said, laughing, "that she has more imagination than reason. But she does not mean to do wrong, and as you are the more sensible of the two, make it up with her once again. Do it for love of me."

I made a low curtsy and said simply: "You are my king and master."

And once again I did as he asked.

I judged his friendship toward me too uncertain still to risk displeasing him in any way. But he gave me a number of signs of his attachment.

In 1676 he spoke of me to several people as his *"première amie,"* the chief among his women friends. The same year, when they were singing extracts from operas in Madame de Montespan's apartment, he asked me in front of everyone which was my favorite opera. When I said it was Lully's *Atys,* which had been performed at Court three months before, he answered with a quotation from the first act: "Happy Atys!," spoken in such a meaning tone that everyone noticed and commented upon it. The same year he sent Monsieur Le Nôtre to alter the gardens at Maintenon. But above all he did one thing which was so tactful and sensitive that I was moved to the depths of my heart.

On 3 September 1676 maréchal d'Albret had died suddenly in Bordeaux. He had not lied to me about his health, and as he predicted we did not see each other again after my visit with the little duc. His death was an irreparable loss for me, and I was terribly grieved. An hour before he died he had written to me in a way which showed his esteem and affection. His departure left me alone in the world, and inconsolable. At the beginning of October I withdrew to Maintenon for three weeks, quite ill with sorrow, and when I arrived, I was amazed to find a portrait of the maréchal in the gallery. The King had sent it without telling me and ordered it to be hung there ready so that it should be a surprise. I was overcome with gratitude.

Later on it occurred to me that although I had said nothing to the King about my feelings for Monsieur d'Albret, he had probably thought himself enlightened on the subject by the malicious letter Madame d'Heudicourt had written about me five years before. That was why, though he knew from rumor that my marriage to Monsieur Scarron had never been consummated, he never asked himself or me about what happened to me between 24 October 1660 and that other October morning when he made me his mistress. He apparently still thought his predecessor was the maréchal, and on reflection I thought he would dislike that less than the idea of having followed on after Monsieur de Villarceaux. So all our lives we lived with that misunderstanding, which, though it lied as far as fact was concerned, corresponded pretty well to the truth of feeling.

On "apartment" days at Versailles—those three evenings a week when the whole Court foregathered to be entertained in the suite of seven magnificent rooms known as the *Grand Appartement*—it was noticeable now that if during the gaming the marquise let fall some disagreeable remark aimed at the King, he did not answer but just smiled at me. For some months now, while he ostentatiously left the Queen to play at one table and himself sat at that of his mistress, he insisted that I be there too, sitting facing him on a stool.

In the spring he fell ill and had to stay in bed for a few days. He sent for me and I spent my afternoons in his room, sitting in a chair by his bed and chatting familiarly with him—an honor neither Madame de Montespan nor the pretty canoness enjoyed.

"You introduce me to a new world, Madame," he said one day with a very tender look. "The world of tranquil friendship."

But I could measure my progress chiefly by the change in our subjects of conversation. The King was not bashful by nature and did not mind weeping in public or putting his arms round his mistress for all to see; he had concentrated all the modesty he was capable of on his position as a king. In this he was as shy and delicate as the most secretive and passionate of lovers, and he said nothing about it except to a very few people, and then briefly and with the utmost circumspection. At that level one is too solitary to be able to confide in anyone.

So I was more than flattered when the King abandoned at last the subject of his children, his mistress and his building projects and began to talk to me about his feelings as a king, the maxims he tried to follow as a ruler and the pleasures he derived from his position, though he did not as yet let me into any political secrets. He confined himself to expounding the principles of government and the main outlines of the ethical rules he set for himself as a monarch; but what he said about these things was so great, so just, and the confidence he reposed in me was so new that I was more delighted and intoxicated with him than ever.

"You know," he said one day when we were talking about those who sometimes criticized his decisions, "I do not say that some of these men are not more talented than I. But they have never ruled, or ruled France. And I do not mind telling you that the higher the position, the more things there are which cannot be seen or understood except from that position alone. So I cannot take account of criticism from people, however intelligent they may be, who are unable to see as I can all the factors on which a decision has to be based.

"But do not think I do not realize that my good intentions are not always successful. Only small minds, which are often mistaken, think they never make mistakes, and those who deserve to succeed usually think it right to acknowledge their errors. But I am the only man in France who can know for certain whether I have erred, and the only one who can really criticize my own actions as a ruler."

He devoted more than eight hours of every day to affairs of state.

"A king rules through work," he used to say to me. "It would be ingratitude toward God and tyranny toward man to try to rule without effort. Even gradual familiarity with detail teaches a thousand things which may be useful in taking general decisions . . . The vocation of a king is not free of trouble, fatigue and anxiety; it is, above all, great, noble and delightful to someone who feels himself worthy to meet all his obligations."

As he taught me that love of glory involves the same fine sensibilities as the most tender passions, he naturally came at last to speak to me of the feelings of a monarch toward his mistresses.

"Although he may give away his heart," he said, "a king must remain absolute master of his mind. I have always separated the affections of the lover from the decisions of the king, or at least made sure that the beauty which serves my pleasure is never free to speak to me of my official business or those who serve it."

I could not help asking, respectfully but with a laugh, whether he was saying this by way of warning to me.

"No," he said, smiling. "You are not like the others. Before

I knew you, I always thought women could not keep secrets, but you are teaching me that certain ladies have the wit to know what should be hidden and are not given to intrigue. Yet I do not think I shall change my policy because of you. Happy though I am to be able to talk to you, I think I should lose credit with the public if I broke my rule for you, and that would mean I went down in your estimation too. And so just to preserve your friendship I shall observe the same precautions with you as with the others."

The art of conversation consists not in speaking a great deal but in seeming to listen to the other person with pleasure, in entering into what he says and in skilfully setting it off to advantage. I listened to the King with genuine and passionate interest. I sympathized with his arguments and applauded his ideas, and took every opportunity to slip in a piece of skilful flattery, for which he was always grateful. This was all the easier because the maxims he set before himself often resembled mine: like him, though on a different scale, I too was familiar with the demands of pride and fame, with concern for reputation, love of action, the necessity of work and the imperatives of secrecy.

And so our conversations, which gradually changed from pure monologue to a semblance of dialogue, became increasingly tinged with complicity and confidence, which often made them very merry. Between our more serious thoughts we liked to laugh together. Provided the tone was light and the criticism moderate, I even managed to say things which no courtier would have dared to utter to the King. One "apartment" day when I had the honor of strolling with him while everyone else was playing cards, I stopped when I saw no one could overhear us and said:

"Sire, you are very fond of your musketeers. What would you do if someone came to Your Majesty and said that one of them had taken the wife of a man who was still alive and was living with her? I am sure that he would leave the barracks that very evening, however late it was."

The King saw the joke and laughed, saying I was right.

But, as I have said, this warm and growing friendship had its ups and downs, being at the mercy of circumstances and partings. In the summer of 1677 I had to spend a number of months at

Barèges and Bagnères for the sake of my little duc's health, and I suffered cruelly from the neglect of those who were far away. Letters were rarer than they had been two years ago; apparently conversation was now preferred to correspondence. I was very anxious this time to bring my exile to an end. My poor director, mistaking the cause of my anxiety and impatience, counselled me to withdraw from Court when I returned; the unfortunate abbé had a genius for unseasonable advice. I answered that when I had been unsuccessful at Court I had been advised not to leave it, and now that I was successful I did not see how I could tear myself away from someone who kept me there with friendship and affection.

"These chains are more difficult for me to break," I wrote, "than if I were retained by force."

My worthy Gobelin understood my drift, and confined himself henceforward to managing my charities, doing my errands in the Paris shops and conveying my letters to my friends.

When I got back to Versailles I was ill for a few days with the American fevers which attacked me from time to time. The King came to see how I was.

"Sire," I said cheerfully, "I think I shall live to be a hundred."

"Madame," he replied gravely, "that would be the best thing that could happen to me."

If I thought I had reached the height of royal favor, I had plenty of time to change my tune in the days that followed, for either as a result of some rebuke from the marquise or as a mere precaution, he began to cold-shoulder me again. But now I knew how to get back into favor: I got the little princes to write touching letters innocently asking for what I myself wanted, and above all I flattered, shamelessly but not without wit, both "la belle madame" and "the center of all things." Neither resisted for long.

I had a cool head, and beak and claws enough not to give in without a fight. Angelic natures rarely manage to rise up the social scale. Although I was now falling into the low ways practiced by the world in general, one belief set limits to my wrongdoing, and that was the certainty that however high one wants to climb and whatever methods one uses, one can always be sparing in the use of them. And so I did wrong only when necessary, harming as few people as possible and as briefly as possible. I practiced my morality with the utmost discretion and was temperate even in sin. It was not piety which held me back on that slippery slope, but the ordinary respectable ideal of moderation. The rule of God and the rule of Reason were still one and the same to me.

No doubt the same was true of Mademoiselle de Fontanges, and she probably trembled lest one or the other interrupt her swift and dazzling rise to fame. Since the marquise had brought her forward to distract the King's attention from her niece and myself, and the King had looked kindly on the prettily disordered tresses of the redhaired Angélique, the little seventeen-year-old had rapidly gone through all the stages leading from obscurity to splendor. She and Madame de Montespan seemed to be treated as equal in rank. When they went to mass at Saint-Germain, they both sat where the King could see them, Madame de Montespan with her children in the gallery to the left and Mademoiselle de Fontanges to the right. At Versailles Madame de Montespan was on the Gospel side and Mademoiselle de Fontanges in the tiers on the side of the Epistle. Thus, one balancing the other, they would pray with their rosaries or their missals in their hands, raising their eyes to Heaven like saints in ecstasy. Court is the finest theater in the world.

In private, however, I knew this apparent equilibrium, in itself so humiliating for the marquise, had already been upset, and that the King now only went to see Madame de Montespan for a few moments after mass, and then scarcely spared her a glance.

"Better to see each other a little and in peace than often and with trouble," said the marquise bitterly.

From now on, everything was for Madame's maid of honor— smiles, favors, jewels and pensions.

At first the speed of her elevation surprised me and made me almost as uneasy as the marquise herself. But I soon perceived that with her lack of wit, her capriciousness and her uneven temper, Mademoiselle de Fontanges was no rival to me, while on the other hand her physical beauty and charms must make her a threat to Madame de Montespan. As always, she had only herself to blame, with her foolishness and all her intermingled plots, but as always it was me she attacked, since her other rival was beyond her reach. Now, in 1679, she had a flash of her former insight, and was seized with the same doubts as in 1674 regarding the nature of my relationship with the King.

"You're trying to become the King's mistress!" she said to me one day at her toilet. "It's as plain as a pikestaff!"

"Madame, I assure you I am not trying to do any such thing," I replied truthfully, saying inwardly that I did not need to seek for what I already had. Then I added gently, to appease her wrath, "You pay too much attention to your prejudices."

"Oh, I know your tricks," she answered, "and my misfortune comes from paying too little attention to my prejudices. I have been good to you, and you are destroying me."

She reminded me of all she had done for me, her presents and those of the King.

"Madame," I said, "I know what I owe you, and that after God you are the cause of my present good fortune. The modesty of behavior which I always practice should prove to you that I do not forget who I am or my debt to you."

"Your modesty, my dear lady," she retorted, "is only the mantle of your pride."

Another day, when she had pursued her conclusions further and while I was playing crambo with the King's "chubby-cheeks," sweet little Mademoiselle de Tours, the marquise exclaimed:

"Go on, pretend to be devoted to me! I know very well you're the King's mistress!"

So as not to tell a lie I said coolly: "He has three, then?"

"Of course," she cried. "Me in theory, that girl in fact, and you in feeling!"

When she tried, the "incomparable" could reason well enough.

But this fit of lucidity did not make my position easier. It became more difficult still when the marquise, after once more trying in vain to marry me off, this time to Monsieur de Saint-Aignan,† told me that since I was the King's mistress, our interests were the same, and asked me to go and lecture Mademoiselle de

Fontanges. She wanted someone to tell the poor creature of the sin she was falling into. Despite my protests I could not avoid this strange mission, but I knew that Angélique de Fontanges was stupid and venal and quite unlike Louise de La Vallière, and it might be much more difficult to send her to the Carmelites.

"But Madame," Mademoiselle de Fontanges said haughtily, "you talk about casting off a passion as if it were a matter of casting off a shift."

"It is true such shifts cling to the skin," I answered, without expecting to be heard, "but one may always choose to be flayed alive."

When Madame de Montespan was quite sure I had failed in my errand, she said no more, but surrounded herself with fortune-tellers and astrologers more numerous than ever, shut herself up in mysterious discussions with Mademoiselle Desoeillets and in short shrouded herself in a cloud of what seemed to me very evil-smelling smoke.

As for me, once the first apprehension was past, I expected less and less that Mademoiselle de Fontange's success would last. The King had really never been attached to anything except her form, and he was growing increasingly ashamed of her whenever she opened her lips in public. One may grow so accustomed to beauty that it goes unnoticed, but one never gets used to foolishness which inclines toward what is false and exaggerated, especially when one lives among people of such wit and character as Madame de Montespan, who detected everyone's least extravagance and pointed it out to the whole world in the inimitable Mortemart manner.

When Angélique de Fontanges had squandered eleven millions in a year, an instance of greed never yet paralleled at Court, the King evidently began to tire of her. And death soon delivered the marquise from a rival whom she herself had created but whom she feared above all the rest.

Mademoiselle de Fontanges, who was pregnant, wanted to leave Fontainebleau on the same day as the King, whom she sensed to be slipping between her fingers. But she was on the point of giving birth, and through her own folly was injured on the journey and lost the child. According to Monsieur Fagon, a friend of mine and the duc du Maine's chief doctor, the delivery went wrong. The stomach was poisoned, one lung filled with water and a series of hemorrhages left her in a decline. At Court, where she had few friends and was very little missed, they said she had been "wounded on active service."

At Saint-Germain, at the beginning of her illness, the King went every evening from the old to the new château to see her. "How is the invalid today?" someone like Madame de Thianges or Madame de Saint-Geran would ask ironically; they belonged to Madame de Montespan's coterie, had shared her fears and now rejoiced with her at this reversal of fate. Gradually the King wearied of visiting a woman who had lost her looks completely and had never had more intelligence than a brute beast. In the summer of 1680 he made her a duchesse and came to see her less.

The grief of this desertion made poor Fontanges's illness worse: her little body was racked with fever; she could not breathe. Courtiers who not long ago had praised her to the skies and crowded her antechamber now did not go near her. Suddenly no one mentioned her name; it was as if she were already dead. Even her women, seeing her end was near, hastened to place themselves under the protection of her rival, bowing and scraping to Desoeillets, Cateau and the other Mortemart followers whom a couple of months earlier they had snubbed whenever they met them.

"Madame," Nanon said to me one evening, "are we going to let that poor girl die like a dog?"

I shared her feelings, and as I no longer had to humor Madame de Montespan, who did not in the least try to humor me, I made so bold as to go and see Mademoiselle de Fontanges.

I found a dying child in the bed of a courtesan. There were pearls and plumes everywhere, but under the counterpane embroidered with the arms of Venus I could see the thin body of a little girl, to which death restored a semblance of innocence. The grey of her eyes seemed to have spread to her face. Her whole bloodless body was already the color of the dust to which it was returning. Only her long red hair, lying scattered around her face, seemed endowed with life—the parasitic life of a poisonous flower growing on carrion.

When I arrived she was delirious, watched over only by an old half-crippled maid whose rheumatism had probably prevented her from going with the others to offer her services to the lady in the old château. In her fever the little duchesse naturally reverted to the lilting accent of her native Auvergne, becoming once again the child she had never quite ceased to be—cruel like all children, but like them innocent of the crimes she had committed, and almost pure when on the point of appearing before God. I took her hand and spoke to her gently, doubting whether she would recognize me.

She had a momentary return of consciousness.

"Won't the King come and see me, Madame?" she asked brokenly.

I was strongly tempted to say it was God's visit she should be hoping for, but she was clearly so little prepared for death that I held my tongue for fear of making her condition even worse. She had said she could not divest herself of a passion, and now she had to say farewell to life. Such farewells are always difficult, and I felt her weakness deserved some indulgence. So I assured her the King would come, vowing inwardly that I would persuade him to make this last visit and try to get him to speak to her himself of the need to prepare herself for the great change. She had been taken from nothing and made a duchesse, and now she was going back to nothing again. The second transition might well be more difficult than the first, and a king was not too much to prepare her for it.

I remained for a long while at her bedside, as she lamented softly in her childish patois and slipped back into unconsciousness. I reflected that she was not yet twenty years old and might have been my daughter. This little brainless bird, whom at this moment I profoundly pitied, had meddled in a struggle where the combatants were built on a completely different scale from herself, and in it she had lost first her heart and then her life. The marquise de Montespan, King Louis XIV and Madame de Maintenon—they were all strong pieces of machinery with hearts as solid as rock, and when this little featherbrain was destroyed, they could go back to their old games, to the three-sided combat which they had been engaged in for so long that they knew all the rules, gambits and tricks.

"In a nutshell," Madame de Thianges said to me one evening as we were chatting in her sister's room, "once Mademoiselle de Fontanges is dead, we shall be face to face with the problem as before."

But it is not true that life provides such returns to the past. A few months later Mademoiselle de Fontanges died in the convent at Port-Royal to which the King had had her transferred. But we never went back to the strange equilibrium or disequilibrium we knew between 1675 and 1679, in which I suffered because of the marquise, who suffered because of the King, who was lucky enough to suffer scarcely at all. The world had tottered in the meanwhile, and Hell had momentarily yawned at our feet.

Thirteen

Y_{ou} cannot approach the brink of the abyss without suspecting what lies beyond or be on the edge of a precipice and remain entirely ignorant. Yet in those days I thought happiness was within my grasp, and in the contemplation of such delight I was blind to everything else.

Mademoiselle de Fontanges's period of favor had vanished like a dream, only serving to emphasize by contrast the depth and constancy of the King's feelings toward me. As Cateau, one of Madame de Montespan's attendants, said one day—like most of the favorite's maids she was friendly to me—"The King gave himself to Mademoiselle de Fontanges through weakness; he returned to Madame de Montespan through habit; but he is drawn to you by inclination."

That inclination seemed to grow stronger every day, in the eyes of the world and in my own. A few days before Mademoiselle de Fontanges went into the decline which was eventually to carry her off, the King had surprised everyone by appointing me second mistress of the robes to the Dauphine. Princesse Victoire of Bavaria, then eighteen, was to marry the Dauphin the following spring, and her household was already being formed. This occasion provided me with something I had given up hoping for after so many years, namely a situation which freed me from the authority of Madame de Montespan.

My new post was not only more than honorable, it also gave me an excuse for remaining at Court, a regular income and a right to my own apartment. To avoid fuss I kept the same little room at Saint-Germain, but the King had an apartment of several rooms prepared for me both at Fontainebleau and at Versailles. Both were situated so that he could easily see me.

He did not fail to take advantage of this arrangement. Every forenoon before dinner he spent a good hour with me, and every evening I was alone with him in his room between eight and ten o'clock. Monsieur de Chamarande conducted me there and back in full view of all the world. I do not know which courtier's tongue was the first to make a slip, but it was not long before I was referred to in all the anterooms as "Madame de Maintenant"—Madame Now.

But people did not yet know what to make of our relationship. The reserve we showed in public threw even the subtlest observers off the scent, and the difference in age between Mademoiselle de Fontanges and myself, together with the position still held by Madame de Montespan, made people doubt that there could be any question of love between us. As I was acknowledged to be very clever, the rumor spread that the King was seeing me in connection with his official history. He was known to be somewhat dissatisfied with his accredited historians, Racine and Despréaux, and when they read him passages from their efforts, he sometimes muttered, with a mixture of irritation and scorn, "News sheets! No better than news sheets!" And so, seeing the sobriety of my attire and the seriousness and respect with which the King treated me in company, everyone was sure that once the door was closed upon us every evening we did nothing but rewrite plans of campaign and then sand the pages.

Only Madame de Montespan was no longer deceived. When she saw that I was escaping her clutches and that the friendship with which the King had honored me for years in secret was now manifested in broad daylight and amazing the Court, she was beside herself with rage, and immediately mounted a plot to destroy me. Her cabal included first of all Marsillac, the King's favorite, who after having for a while backed Angélique de Fontanges had returned full of repentance to the marquise. Nor did she have any difficulty in enrolling Monsieur de Louvois, for the two were linked by long habit and many services rendered. All these people and their hangers-on tried to persuade the King I had lived an immoral life in my youth, looked for defects in my birth and person, in short sought any means of doing me harm.

But the plot failed. The King listened patiently to the recital of my transgressions, then ended the whole thing with a word. One day when Madame de Montespan was regaling him at length with my past misdeeds, he said wearily:

"Is it likely, Madame, you would have chosen a courtesan to be governess to your children? Please, let us seek no further for truths that would hurt you more than Madame de Maintenon."

That very evening Marsillac began to curry favor with me, and Monsieur de Louvois hastened to distance himself from the favorite. He even refused to let his daughter marry young Mortemart, the marquise's nephew, who made do with one of the Colbert girls. The rivalry between the two servitors and their tribes was such that one among them could always be found to snap up what one of the others discarded.

But I, now admitted to the precincts of happiness and glory, was indifferent to all these intrigues. Now that I was near the goal I had set myself my last scruples vanished. By some strange process my conscience, replete with honors and marks of affection, left me in peace.

I loved the greatest king in Christendom, the "King of Nijmegen," who had just imposed his peace on Europe, won Valenciennes, Cambrai, Freiburg and Franche-Comté and subjugated Lorraine; a monarch whose law ran as far as Sweden and Brandenburg, and who ruled the world more through admiration than through might. I loved him with a shy love full of respect and fear, in which the sense of my dependence mingled with dazzled gratitude. I loved him with the veneration and awe owed to the gods. And I loved him unreservedly because I thought he loved me.

I did however foresee a time when the kindness with which he surrounded me would come to an end; when a younger woman would oust me from his bed and a cleverer one from his heart. A king who desires someone does not sigh for long, and at the same time as I thought myself so happy, Mademoiselle Doré, one of Madame's young women, was the object of the sovereign's glances at Fontainebleau, while Mademoiselle de Piennes, who was as beautiful as the day, received his warmest attentions at Versailles.

Like all those who had preceded me in the royal favor, I took care not to show any jealousy. I even went so far as to facilitate the meetings between the King and Mademoiselle de Piennes, who was guarded by an aunt more strict than any duenna. I used to invite the girl to a collation in my apartment, and while I kept the aunt busy in one room, the King, having come in as if by chance, would keep the niece busy in another. This splendid arrangement was not premeditated between us, for the King would not have stooped to ask me for that kind of service and I would not have sunk so far as to provide it openly. But I considered my best chance with the King was to be always obliging and good-humored, so I shut my eyes to what I was not supposed to see and put off until tomorrow the fear of my rivals, the redemption of my shortcomings and the salvation of my soul.

I gave myself up entirely to entertainment and amusement, all the Court pleasures which my distinguished position in the Dauphine's suite allowed me to enjoy more freely than I had been able to in the past. Peace after six years of relentless war made all these pleasures more delightful still, and it turned the King's château into fairy castles.

Balls were followed by plays, operas by parades. The Court was always moving from one place to another: it was at Saint-Cloud in March, Saint-Germain in April, Versailles in June, Chambord in August, Fontainebleau in September. And every time it was a marvelous sight to see the King emerge with his bodyguards, his horses and carriages, his courtiers, his servants and a whole multitude seething around him. It was like a queen bee and her swarm setting off for the fields.

Everywhere we went, abundance vied with magnificence.

"The people like spectacles," the King used to say to me. "Display wins their hearts and minds better than rewards and benefits."

Every night the flowers in the gardens were changed: you went to sleep surrounded by tuberoses and woke to the scent of jasmine or wallflowers. Every day something in our surroundings was altered; it was as if the fairies were at work. Where there had been a pond the day before, one found a wood, and in place of a forest there was a hill, a reservoir or a summerhouse of porcelain. The great Magician amused himself by bending Nature to his purpose, and Nature, like everyone else, hastened to obey. Trianon was enlarged, Marly was built, the forest of Compiègne was transplanted to Versailles, rivers were diverted to feed the tiled fountains and their Tritons of bronze.

On "apartment" days I strolled from the billiard room to the salon where cards were played, from the refreshment room to the music room, smiling at one person, chatting with another, here admiring a minuet, there a pyramid of fruit from the Indies. I was always alone and simply dressed; my manners were almost ostentatiously modest and unassuming.

When the King went through the rooms, everyone crowded around him, the gentlemen jostling one another to see and be seen by him, the ladies treading on one another's toes in their efforts to get to the front and hear from his own lips some trifle which would enchant them for the whole year. "Pink suits you divinely, cousin." "Delighted to see you, Madame." "Have you been to see my gardens, Mademoiselle?" I did not mind being pushed against the wall—there was more air there anyway—and I always stood back to make room for everyone, even those who were not of the nobility. The more I affected humility in this way, while knowing I came first with the King and knowing that the others knew it too, the more blissful were the pleasures of pride which I derived from my self-effacement.

The repercussions of royal favor were all around me. Princes whispered sugared words in my ear, pretending to let me into their secrets. Great ladies who had long wearied me by bringing into their conversation the names of people I was too humbly born to know now exclaimed at my wit; sure at last of my position, I calmly said I did not know what they were talking about. Ministers paid court to me as earnestly as others paid court to them. I laughed inwardly at all this subservience. Although he rarely looked at me and never spoke to me in public, I knew that the Master, besieged by a brilliant crowd at the other end of the apartment, was thinking only of me, and that he was scarcely less impatient than I to leave the press of the public rooms for the privacy of his own chamber. I wanted no other witness to my elevation.

I was in that state of intoxication where pride in one's own power is mingled with the sweetness of being admired and the wonder of being loved.

The fumes of glory must have clouded my mind very thoroughly for me not to have noticed sooner how low both Court and Paris society had sunk in the last few years. The great were driven by idleness and boredom to seek diversion in some strange activities. The need to keep up a ruinous style of living forced them to engage in very dubious dealings. In short, no Court in the world was so abandoned to every kind of vice.

The craze for gambling, which the King had never discouraged, was at its height. A man would stake his life on one card. Even in the King's own apartments the players behaved like madmen, yelling, thumping on the table, blaspheming in a way that made your hair stand on end.

The immoderate use of liquor also helped to pass the time for young people with an insatiable desire for pleasure. Duchesses of fifteen liked to meet to stupefy themselves on wine and liqueurs with their lackeys: "Bacchus doth our charms display, / The sofa is not far away," they sang. Princes spent all night in Paris taverns and drove back to Versailles, tipsy, at daybreak. The greatest of great ladies got so drunk they forgot themselves in the middle of the public rooms and overflowed both above and below.

But these refined amusements were as nothing beside some of the diversions of love. The easy virtue of Court ladies had long made young men scorn their charms, and the Italian vice was more in fashion than ever. The King's own brother set the example: he was never seen anywhere without being titivated and made up to the nines, all speckled with beauty spots and jangling with jewelry, and casting amorous glances at one of the "minions" who made up his customary entourage. This fraternity included the nephews of the great Condé; the sons of Monsieur de Ruvigny, deputy-general of the Huguenots; Monsieur de Louvois's cousin; Monsieur Colbert's son; and members of the La Rochefoucauld and the Turenne families. They had set themselves such strict rules they called themselves the true monks of modern times. Their monasteries were a few châteaux in the Ile-de-France where they admitted novices after weird ceremonies which included oaths and mortification. They said their order would soon be as great as that of St. Francis, and they even managed to enroll the young comte de Vermandois, the son of the King and Mademoiselle de La Vallière, then aged about thirteen or fourteen.

In these circumstances it was not surprising that the ladies also, not encountering too many gallants of the opposite sex, began to love their own. The duchesse de Duras proclaimed to all and sundry that she would gladly give her entire fortune, down to her shift, to sleep with the King's daughter, the lovely princesse de Conti, who was just fifteen. Fortunately the young princesse soon showed she preferred the King's guards and her own footmen to other ladies; and this form of debauchery seemed so innocent in comparison with the alternative that she had to be absolved of guilt.

Some princes showed more imagination. A gang of them went to a place of ill fame, treated in the Italian manner the courtesans they thought the prettiest, then took one of them by force and tied her arms and legs to the bedpost and applied a rocket in a place it would be unseemly to name. They then set it off, despite the cries of their unhappy victim. After that they careered through the streets all night, breaking countless lanterns, tearing down and burning crucifixes and setting fire to a bridge. This exploit seemed unsurpassable, yet a few days later the chevalier Colbert set out to improve upon it. He and the duc de La Ferté and the chevalier d'Argenson sent for a street vendor who turned out to be an attractive lad and whom they attempted to deal with as a girl. When he resisted, they administered two good sword-thrusts through the body, from which he was unmanly enough to die. They got away with a reprimand.

When the life of ordinary people is so cheap, it is not surprising if soothsayers and poisoners, who know how to kill the great discreetly, find their skills appropriately prized. They were applied to, alternately or together, for the secrets both of love and of death.

A funny story was told of how Madame de Brizy, whose lover did not require her affection, was told by one of these magicians that an infallible remedy for her problem was for her to take off her clothes so that he could say mass over her stomach. She consented to this, but a fortnight later came back to say her lover was as cool toward her as before. The sorcerer said a greater sacrifice was called for, and if he lay with her at the time of evening service her lover would be filled with uncontrollable passion. The lady went through all these ceremonies with the utmost piety, but apparently her lover's devil was stronger than that of the sorcerer, for it turned out she had said her mass in vain.

But this was child's play in comparison with most examples. To do away with a rival, gain an inheritance sooner, dispose of a jealous husband or win a lawsuit or a minister's favor, people went to some corrupt priest and arranged for a black mass, which included an infant's throat being cut over the chalice. Some procuresses in Paris made a living out of the trade in newborn babies. Such procedures were often followed by poison: what the Devil had been unable to do, arsenic or mercuric chloride could achieve more surely.

At the beginning of 1679 a special court, the Chambre Ardente,† was set up at the Arsenal to examine the cases of several fortune-tellers and artists in poison. At first those who appeared before this tribunal were only small fry: unfrocked priests, lackeys, merchants' clerks, prostitutes, petty alchemists and Sibyls from the city outskirts. But, more surprisingly, they were followed by certain magistrates' wives and other well-to-do bourgeois women. Then the revelations made by all these wretched creatures mounted up step by step to the Court, where, it was said, love powders or inheritance powders were supplied to people of quality. Among their customers they named the pretty comtesse de Soissons, the young duchesse de Bouillon, Madame de Montespan's sister-in-law Madame de Vivonne, Madame de Polignac, Madame de Gramont, the maréchal de Luxembourg and some lesser names. All these people had been blithely murdering one another for years with the aid of toads and alembics and by the light of black candles.

Once the first stupor was over, both the Court and the capital were in an uproar. Everyone tried to find out the latest news, going to one another's houses, talking of nothing else. Every day it was discovered that another of the criminals had fled: Monsieur de Cessac to England, Madame de Soissons to Holland, Madame de Polignac to the Auvergne. Never had there been such a scandal in a Christian court.

I myself, not once having even had my fortune told, might have been untroubled by all this. But what it revealed about hidden aspects of society appalled me.

I made myself go over all I had heard in recent years in connection with debauchery and misbehavior of all kinds, and I concluded that irreligion, which had been spreading like gangrene, might be the cause of it. For shallow minds it might be an easy step from Descartes's philosophy to the powders of Madame Voisin.†

I did not, however, pursue these thoughts any further, either because the spate of entertainments following the arrival of the Dauphine in France left me no time, or because I was too happy to care.

Autumn that year at Fontainebleau was irresistibly delightful. A languorous sun caressed the rosy walls of the château. The forest, steeped in mild showers, gave off a musky perfume that was intoxicating. As I sat by the tall window looking out over the Golden Gate, I occupied hands with some tapestry work and my mind with daydreams. My apartment was on the second floor then, above the one I lived in after 1686, and looked on to the garden through a handsome arcade which had been glassed in for use as a loggia. The hothouse warmth prevailing there at noon lulled my body deliciously and caused my thoughts to stray. I kept musing on a line by my grandfather: "No rose so perfect as the rose of autumn." Perhaps I applied it to the season; perhaps to myself.

In the room behind me I could hear the King rustling his papers. For several days I had been unable to get any conversation out of him; it seemed he had nothing to say to me. When I got tired of making all the effort, I gave up as cheerfully as possible, left him to his silence and turned to my tapestry. I did not know whether he was vexed with me for some reason or merely preoccupied with affairs of state. And as I would not have allowed myself to question him, and he was not naturally communicative, there we were, side by side, dumb.

Suddenly I started.

"Did you know, Madame," said the grave voice which always touched me, "that Mademoiselle Desoeillets was in the habit of frequenting the soothsayers?"

I was immediately thrown back into the turmoil of the Affair of the Poisons.

"Mademoiselle Desoeillets and I have never been great friends," I said without thinking. Then, remembering that the lady, as well as being one of Madame de Montespan's attendants, had been the King's mistress and borne him children, I added: "I do not mean I did not think her worthy. What I do mean is that she did not tell me everything she did."

There was a long pause. My heart beat fast. I stole a look at the King to try to guess what he was driving at, but his face was impenetrable. I recognized the heap of papers in front of him as the daily accounts of the Chambre Ardente which Monsieur de La Reynie, Chief of the Paris Police, sent to him every day through Monsieur de Louvois.

"Did you know," he went on quietly, "that Cateau used to go and see Madame Voisin, who was burned in the place de Grève† six months ago?"

I was taken aback.

"Yes," he continued, before I had time to recover, "Madame de Montespan's women are all respectable young ladies who spend

279

their nights visiting sorcerers and their days concocting and delivering powders. Would you be surprised"—here he tore up a couple of pages—"if I told you that Madame de Montespan herself was a party to certain strange ceremonies in the apartment of Madame de Thianges? That sham priests used to read the Gospel over her and pass herbs, powders and pigeons' hearts under the chalice so that she might win her present position? Would you swear she was not capable of these things?"

I was overwhelmed with surprise and embarrassment.

"It is true," I answered, "that Madame de Montespan has always liked to surround herself with astrologers, but if we wanted to seek out everyone who has consulted fortune-tellers, it would take us the rest of the century."

"We are not talking about astrologers, Madame!" He was almost shouting now. "We are talking about blasphemers and poisoners! Your Madame de Montespan even tried to have the duchesse de Fontanges poisoned, and she apparently wouldn't have been sorry to get rid of me too!"

I found his "your Madame de Montespan" rather hard to accept, and almost said that even if she was "mine" it was someone else who had given her seven children. But the King was so upset by this business that I held my tongue. I was amazed myself at what I had just learned.

"It cannot be," was all I said.

"Perhaps it cannot be, Madame. But it is said."

I made myself sew a few stitches.

"Sire," I said, "one cannot rely on what is alleged by professional poisoners who think to prolong their own lives by denouncing some eminent person who then has to be arrested and tried . . . People are very ingenious when reduced to such extremities."

"That is what Monsieur Colbert says in a memorandum on the subject," the King went on more calmly. "But yesterday Monsieur de Louvois gave me the minutes of a similar trial which took place thirteen years ago, and the marquise is already named there. She was not my mistress then and those who named her had nothing to gain by it. What do you say to that?"

I threaded a needle.

"I don't know, Sire . . . But on reflection I cannot believe a woman as intelligent as Madame de Montespan would have tried to stop up the source of all the favors she herself enjoyed."

"I agree," he said after a moment's thought. "But even if she did not do all she is accused of, she has been trying to cast spells on me for years. Do you think it was pleasant, every time I took a glass of wine in her apartment, to think I might at the same time be swallowing powdered toad, cantharides, fingernails, priest's semen or mandrake sap?"

In other circumstances this list would have made me burst out laughing, but I did not feel mirth would be very much appreciated now.

Moreover, all I had just heard accorded so well with my recent thoughts on the state of society that I was not inclined to mock. In fact, I felt it my duty to speak out, and as I did so a kind of veil was rent asunder. I saw clearly it was God Himself who had wished me to be where I was: I had not demeaned myself in vain by becoming the King's mistress, for Providence wanted to use me to reform the monarch and remedy the scandal of his Court. I had betrayed religious principles only in order to serve religion better. This revelation gave me a peace and strength which I had often felt the lack of since I had come to Court. Now I could see my way ahead. I followed it at once.

"The truth is," I told the King, "nothing is sacred in this country now, not even Your Majesty's person. I say nothing of God, for evidently that is a mere trifle . . . Sire, the example of virtue can come only from above. Now that Your Majesty has brought lasting peace to Europe, it would be easy for you to restore respectable people to their proper position in France. In a few months our country could again be the first in Christendom. Would it not be a noble plan, to add righteousness to might?"

The King listened in silence, tapping his fingers absently on the documents. Then, still without a word, he went and opened the window of the loggia, thus putting us in one of the howling drafts he was so fond of. Then, looking me straight in the eye, he said gravely:

"I've never been told so plainly, Madame, that I have set my subjects a bad example . . . It is only too true. I am more horrified than I can say to see the consequences . . ."

Not long afterwards the King decided that Madame de Montespan, the mother of legitimized royal children, must not be suspect, and the legal proceedings involving her were all suspended. To put a stop to rumor the marquise was even made mistress of the Queen's household, and the King for the sake of appearances went on going to see her for a moment every day after mass or supper. But there was no longer anything between them. He told me that even during those brief visits he was always afraid she might poison him. It got to the point where he suspected her perfumes, and one day when she was about to get into his coach, he publicly criticized her for their strength, saying they gave him a headache. The marquise replied sharply, and the argument became so heated the King would no longer have her in the carriage. In the space of a few moments the downfall of the splendid Athénaïs was complete, though its causes were concealed in the interests of seemliness and the King's authority.

Afterwards I made bold to return to the subject of morality and the need for reform. Whenever the courtiers' extravagances gave me an opportunity, I painted a black but true picture of the state of morality in his kingdom. He listened patiently when I asked him to punish wrongdoers and debauchees; but he still hesitated.

"Would you have me start with my brother?" he asked me one day. And on another occasion: "Do you think one can change people's souls?"

"No, Sire," I answered. "But one can change appearances."

I thought my duty would be done if I restored the dignity of France and saved the soul of its King. As for the King himself, he was no longer under any illusion about how much reform was needed; his only concern was to avoid scandal.

Society then was like the place de l'hôtel de Vendôme, which was being built in Paris in those days. The King imposed a pattern on the facades of the buildings but left private citizens to construct as they pleased behind them. So one is overwhelmed with admiration when contemplating the severity and harmony of the windows and pediments, but overcome with disgust on crossing the thresholds. Once you leave behind the majestic symmetry of the outer shell, all you find is dark corners, courtyards with no view, corridors leading nowhere and airless rooms.

The King imposed on his courtiers the same order as he imposed on the stones of Paris: he recognized the limits of authority and resigned himself to the fact that the reverse side of the medal of his reign would depict folly and darkness. Our age was not ruled by reason. But I think it a good thing that, through the will of the King alone, reason did rule appearances. After all, nothing more distinguishes man from beast than that hankering after respectability which is called hypocrisy.

So, on my advice, the King confined himself in the 1680s to prettifying the face of his age. He dismissed from Court the most notorious homosexuals, forbade soothsayers, regulated the sale of poisons and prohibited the game of hocca on pain of death. The most scandalous ladies were told to mend their ways. He chose as bishops priests who had the strange foible of believing in God and made everyone observe the main Church festivals. Ordinary Sundays soon became what Easter used to be.

He himself set an example of reformation by shutting himself up with his family and living as a good husband and father. I encouraged him as best I could in this. My exhortations were not superfluous, for it was not a very fascinating family.

The young Dauphin, Louis, gave no promise and would have had no opportunity to keep it anyway. His lack of intelligence was compounded by too much education, and he presented an unvarying spectacle of foolishness mingled with boredom, except when he was reading the Deaths and Marriages in the *Gazette de France.* He was so timid he dared not breathe without his father's permission. The Dauphine, whom Monsieur de Meaux and I went to meet at the frontier, combined extraordinary ugliness with equally unusual shyness. She preferred the obscurity of her private rooms to the amusements of the Court and the company of her passionately loved Italian maid, Bessola, to that of princes. She was always ill, and subject to the vapors.

As for Monsieur, the King's brother, a fat little character perched on stilts, I have already shown what he was like. Madame, his wife, looked like a Switzer in disguise beside him. She was only at home among her dogs, drinking German beer and eating German cabbage, always dressed in hunting costume and swearing like a trooper. She was quite intelligent, but as she had unwittingly fallen in love with her brother-in-law and with her appearance could have no hopes in that direction, her wit tended to be caustic and harsh. The King's cousin, Mademoiselle de Montpensier, a worn-out old hack, still treated the Court to the sorry spectacle of her love affair with Monsieur de Lauzun, and thought of nothing but how to get her little lover out of prison in the fortress at Pignerol. As for the Queen, she did not change much. Under her fair curls her wrinkled face looked like that of an elderly child. After twenty years in France she knew no more about the Court or the country than when she first came, having confined her activity to making chocolate, breeding little monkeys and arranging marriages for her dwarfs.

I did succeed, however, in giving her back the King. This was no easy matter, for they had never got on well and he found it increasingly difficult to conceal his irritation at her stupidity. But I thought it in my own interests that he should bestow his favors upon her again. He often told me he was tired of gallantry, and it is true he had been sickened by the Affair of the Poisons, in which three of his mistresses were implicated. But I knew he was too young still, and too ardent, to be satisfied with me alone. And if I was to share, it was best to share with the Queen: she would be a convenient distraction but not a rival.

It struck me as a piquant situation, too, and one which allowed me to measure the extent of my influence. I still did not know how attached to me the King was and thought this compulsory reconciliation, made entirely on my advice and in order to please me, would be a useful test. I still think today that to return a lover to a detested wife demonstrates the acme of a mistress's power. Moreover, it would make an edifying spectacle, score a few points for virtue and divert suspicion from myself.

It turned out as I had wished. The King showed the Queen unaccustomed attentions and went to see her more often. The morning after he had slept with her as his wife, she would clap her hands in bed and say, "The King has never treated me so well as since he started listening to Madame de Maintenon" or "God raised up Madame de Maintenon to give me back the King's heart." And so she came to be very fond of me. As she had never stopped revering the King and fearing him like a God, she always liked me to go with her when he sent for her, so as not to appear alone in his presence. I used to accompany her as far as the King's door, and then had to take the liberty of giving her a shove, for she would be quaking from head to foot.

While the King was in the bosom of his family, trying in vain to initiate the Dauphin into affairs of state and the Dauphine into polite manners, I devoted myself to my friends. I had plenty of time, for the Dauphine, prejudiced against me by Madame, who was jealous of my liaison, and by the duchesse de Richelieu, who was jealous of my success, declined to let me perform the duties of my office. But what would the incense of praise be worth without the fumes of envy?

With Nanon on one side and the peaceable Madame de Montchevreuil on the other, I would sit and read, or sew, or manage my estate, or write letters. After building a hospital and an almshouse at Maintenon, I set up a cloth factory there to give work to the local poor. I also spent some time organizing my brother's affairs. Charles, after rejecting all the sound matches I had put his way, had just secretly married a girl of fifteen without either birth or dowry. She was also spoiled, unsteady and uncouth, and spoke like a huckster in the market—a real Paris wench. I wasted a good deal of leisure on that little goose, either in letters or in visits, endeavoring to teach her French and housekeeping. In vain: she had to have gowns covered with gold and silver, nor could she bear her French point to be less fine than the King's. She helped my brother fritter away a year's income in three months. On top of that she had a vapid look which I could not remove and which made it impossible to produce her in company, where she was always making ludicrous remarks. I finally resigned myself to leaving both of them to their governorship in Cognac.

The education of the duc du Maine provided greater satisfaction. When he reached the age of ten, he passed into the hands of Monsieur de Montchevreuil, whom the King on my advice had appointed his tutor; and so my dear boy had not been removed either from my influence or from my heart. When he was at Court, he spent hours at my side. We spoke with the greatest freedom of everything. I always sought to set the King before him as a model, in order to make him feel the respect, esteem and affection he owed his father and master. I told him I should die of grief if he disappointed the King's hopes and my love. I really believed that, given the mediocrity of the King's family, my little prince was the only one who could console his father for what was lacking in the others; and that the monarch must find the prince his true son in everything. He was already mine, and when he left me to go and have treatment for his leg in the Pyrenees, I was more concerned to know from his letters whether he had had strawberries or a bacon omelette than to find out whether the Empire would tolerate a certain policy or the Dauphine allow me to be present at her supper. I transferred to the most charming of princes and the prince of charmers the affection thwarted by the recent death of the little comte de Vexin and that of the sweet little eight-year-old Mademoiselle de Tours.

The truth of the matter is I could not do without the company of children. The older I got, the more I doted on them. As I no longer had my own little group of the King's legitimized children to look after, I tried to while away my boredom with a charitable project then being prepared by Madame de Brinon. This was the Ursuline nun, a cousin of the Montchevreuils, whom I had known in our hermitages in the Vexin in the days of Monsieur de Villarceaux. Now she had gathered about her in a little house in Rueil a group of poor peasants' and laborers' children to whom she was trying to give some education. I provided her with the means to bring the number of her protégés up to forty and persuaded the King to give her the château of Noisy for them. Whenever I was at liberty, I hurried to Rueil or Noisy bearing linen and meat pies, to delouse the children's heads or teach them their catechism. Occasionally I would bring one of the little girls back to Versailles or

Fontainebleau to brighten her up and show her the world. When the King came to see me, he was amused to find some little Fanchette or Manette always sitting at my feet, spinning or learning to write.

But for me it was not enough. I was insatiable for pink cheeks and dimpled hands; I wanted children who would be entirely my own, for whom I would be accountable only to God; I wanted children of quality, children of my own blood. So my thoughts turned to the children of my cousin de Villette.

For a long time I had been pressing Philippe to provide them an education in keeping with their birth, but as they were Huguenots, this was difficult. The King had forbidden teachers of what was referred to as "the so-called reformed religion" to have resident pupils. The Calvinist Academy in Sedan, where my father had studied in his youth, had just been closed, and that at Saumur was about to be shut. Philippe would not send his children to a Catholic school, and as he was a sea captain by profession, he trailed his two sons around with him all over the seven seas. Since they had seen fighting since the age of eight or nine, this life had left them with a good deal of pluck but no learning, and their ignorance was painful to see. I thought it my duty to remedy it. I was also very fond of their little sister Marguerite-Marie, pretty as an angel but cunning as the devil, and thought I might make more out of her than her mother was doing in the farmyard at Mursay. I was furious with my cousins because their stubborn Calvinism prevented me from helping them as my position allowed, which would have been a way of showing gratitude to their mother and grandmother, the beloved aunt de Villette who had brought me up.

For the King would no longer have Huguenots at his Court. He had shown hostility toward their heresy in his youth. It was said that one day when the Huguenots came to him in a body with some petition, he told their deputy-general, Monsieur de Ruvigny: "The King my grandfather loved you; the King my father feared you; I neither love nor fear you." He believed that uniformity of attitudes was best for a country, and religious differences a blemish. The Protestants agreed, and there was no example of religious freedom in any of the Calvinist countries of Europe.

Nevertheless the King, who had a strong sense of justice, felt himself bound to observe the terms the Huguenots had obtained from his predecessors by the edicts of Nantes and Alès.† But he was resolved not to grant them anything more, and to restrict the interpretation of these terms as narrowly as was decently possible: he said that all that was not expressly allowed by the edicts was to be regarded as forbidden. This being so, since the beginning of his reign many Protestant churches had been knocked down and schools had been closed; Calvinists were forbidden to take in apprentices; Huguenots of both sexes were prohibited from delivering babies; members of the sect were excluded from both the police and the financial administration. The King had other projects in mind, too, and once peace had returned, he hoped for a great campaign to bring about the conversion of the Huguenots. It was plain that if the King were spared, there would not be a single Huguenot in France in twenty years' time. Already they were being converted by the thousand.

My family alone stood out. It seemed to me they were doing so to make me look ridiculous. I was prepared to make allowances for those who were in error; I had been so myself for a time. But I did not think there was any excuse for persevering in error. I was quite willing to be tolerant in order to gain an advantage; but there had to be an advantage.

My desire not to displease the King combined with my longing for children and the legitimate desire to do a good deed: so I resolved to convert the younger generation of the Villettes, the Sainte-Hermines and the Caumont d'Addes.

A declaration of 1669 fixed the age of reason at fourteen for boys and twelve for girls; after that their parents could not prevent them from being converted. The eldest Villette boy, known as Mursay, had already fallen into my toils because of this. He was fourteen when his parents sent him to Paris on business, and I took the opportunity of meeting him. He was no scholar, and more anxious to get on in the world than to be loyal to his father, so he put up little resistance and abjured within three weeks. The King sent him to the Academy at his own expense, to begin the proper kind of study.

This experience encouraged me to try to win over the others.

I asked my lady cousins in Niort and my old companion Philippe to send me for two or three months those of their children who were old enough to enjoy a visit to Paris and the Court; I promised not to bring pressure to bear on them about religion. They all agreed willingly to send their boys and girls to me that winter. All except Philippe. He was angry about Mursay's conversion and did not answer my letter. When he went to sea again, he took his second son with him.

This rudeness made me determined to have his daughter Marguerite at all costs, even though she was only seven. In this I obtained the collaboration of my cousin Aimée, now Madame de Fontmort and a Catholic, and very eager to sacrifice her brother's feelings to her new religion. This was an opportunity not to be missed, for like my father she changed her beliefs so often that Philippe used to say God Himself probably did not know what her religion was.

So Madame de Fontmort, at present a Catholic, wrote to Niort to ask her niece to stay for one or two days. As soon as the child arrived, she packed her into a coach and brought her to join the Sainte-Hermine children and Mademoiselle de Caumont in Paris. Little Marguerite de Villette had no luggage, not even so much as a shift, and she wept a great deal for her parents.

I had her stay with me at Saint-Germain. She still cried a little as she told me how her father, before he went to sea, had told her that if she went to Court without him and changed her religion, he would never see her again. But I took her to see the apartments of the Queen, who made a great fuss of her for my sake. Then she attended Christmas mass in the chapel of the château, and she thought the service so beautiful she agreed at once to become a Catholic—provided she could listen to the motets of Lalande every day and that she would never be whipped. This was all the argument brought to bear on her, and the beginning and end of her abjuration. The easy victory with Marguerite made up to me for the resistance I encountered with the Sainte-Hermine children and the de Caumont girl. These children I sent back to their parents at the agreed time, without regret and sure that they would one day repent of their obstinacy.

Marguerite's conversion made her wholly my own: the King could not object to my keeping her, and her parents could not get her back because heretics were not allowed to reclaim any children of theirs who were converted. But as soon as my cousin Philippe was on dry land again, I was subjected to many harsh words. He demanded his daughter back with the utmost fierceness. I asked him if he thought that having committed violence to get her, I was likely to be foolish enough to give her back. As time went by he calmed down and agreed I was only doing to his children what my aunt had done to me when despite my mother's wishes she turned me into a Huguenot for my own good. Then I allowed him to come and embrace his son and daughter at Saint-Germain, and we agreed to bring the children up together without any more quarrelling.

Marguerite filled me with pride, and as my affection always follows my esteem, I became extremely fond of her. I had been right in thinking she had an extraordinary mind. In order to turn her into a prodigy I had her taught Spanish, dancing and various musical instruments. We had all our meals together, and because of my gift for education this meant she soon developed a pretty talent for conversation. From the very first day, when she still shed tears if her parents were mentioned, I had told her she would come to love me; and soon, sure enough, she loved me as if I were her mother.

When I think about it, I see I have made up a curious family for myself in the course of my life: I regard the duc du Maine as my true son, and Marguerite de Villette, afterwards the comtesse de Caylus, as my true daughter; I had a son-in-law in the person of the comte d'Ayen, though instead of marrying my so-called daughter he was the husband of Françoise, my brother's daughter; lastly, I considered the duchesse de Bourgogne as my granddaughter in spirit, though she was not the daughter of either of my "children" and was not even related to me by blood. Of all this reason can make no sense, but the heart understands.

The three or four years between the downfall of Madame de Montespan and the death of the Queen remain in my memory as years of gladness. I hesitate to use the word happiness.

The King loved me, and he proved it more gallantly every day. And it had become less difficult for me to return his affection since I had rid my conscience of its last scruples. When I found out God's purpose for me and that He had only wished me to be a sinner in order that I might save the soul of the King, my mind was set at rest. And with that peace I acquired sweet and gentle ways, and a languorousness and dissipation of which I should never have thought myself capable.

At Versailles, where the Court settled for good in 1682, the King gave me a new apartment on the first floor. It consisted of two antechambers, a bedroom and a large study and was on the same floor as the King's own apartments, opening like them on the marble staircase. The King had only to go through his own guard-room and a vestibule we had in common to be with me. The Queen herself was not nearer "the Sun" than I.

I used to receive my friends lying on the counterpane of a bed nine feet high, hung with gold and green damask. Its four corners were decorated with tufts of white plumes, and the crimson curtains were edged with heavy gold fringes.

"Who would have thought," Bonne d'Heudicourt said to me one day as she looked at this regal four-poster, "that there could be so short a path from the rue des Trois-Pavillons to the bed of queens?" This was just her subtle way of not referring to the bed of kings; she did not know how prophetic her words were.

On 31 July 1683 Queen Marie-Thérèse died at the age of forty-three. We were dumbfounded. She had not been ill. She had only had a swollen arm for the last few days. But then Daquin had got her into his clutches.

Not all the rogues Madame de Montespan had had appointed to posts they were unfit for had vanished at the same time as she. Daquin, chief physician and a most notorious pedant, had remained. And it was he who decided, against the advice of Monsieur Fagon, whom I supported, to bleed the Queen. The whole medical faculty must know that bleeding does not drain abscesses but makes them turn inward; not Daquin. In three days he brought the Queen to her grave. All the poor woman said as she died was: "I have had only one happy day since I have been Queen." And since she was Queen, that was the only sensible thing she had ever said.

The death of this unhappy creature filled me with grief: she had been fond of me, and I needed for her to go on living. I wept.

Madame de Montespan wept a good deal too and acted as if she did not know what to do. Perhaps she feared falling back into the power of her husband, for by the Queen's death she lost her Court post, and she was not at all sure the King would provide her with another. Never was a wife more sincerely mourned by her husband's mistresses.

But I did not have much time for grief. Just as the Queen was breathing her last and I was on my way back to my apartment, Marsillac, now Monsieur de Rochefoucauld, took my arm and urged me to go to the King, saying, as a zealous courtier, "Now is not the time to leave him—he needs you."

I found the King in tears but did not know what to deduce from that as he wept easily. When I made to praise the virtues of the late Queen, he interrupted me, saying:

"I know more about it than you do. In her God gave me what was needed: she never said me nay."

I accepted the lesson for what it was worth, and dried my eyes.

To tell the truth, the King was more upset than afflicted by his loss. But as, to begin with, perturbation produces the same effects as affliction, and in the great everything appears to be great, the Court started by suffering in sympathy with what looked like a genuine grief. I myself was not taken in. I had to stay at Versailles while the Court accompanied the King first to Saint-Cloud and then to Fontainebleau (since the royal family always left any house where there had been a death). And when I arrived at Fontainebleau wearing deep mourning and what I thought to be the appropriate expression, the King, whose affliction was already a thing of the past, could not help teasing me about it.

I learned from the ladies who had been in his coach on the journey that he had been extremely merry all the way, and they had been expected to laugh continually and eat with appetite. This was the Monday; the Queen had died on Friday. By Tuesday an "apartment" was being held, and when the King asked the Dauphine to dance and she declined because of her bereavement, he ordered her to obey, saying, "Daughter, we are not like ordinary people. We belong entirely to the public."

But while I cast off my grief swiftly to please the King, I could not dispose so easily of my fear. The courtiers, encouraged by the King's good humor, talked of nothing else but remarriage. The Dauphine's entourage compared the respective chances of various German princesses; a Tuscan princesse was also mentioned; but the general opinion backed the Infanta of Portugal. The King still saw me at the usual times, but the fact that he never referred to these fine schemes only added to my apprehensions.

I avoided my friends, could not sleep and had fits of breathlessness. I kept going into the forest for air, accompanied by Madame de Montchevreuil. Sometimes, when my fears got too oppressive, I went there at night. If the King did remarry, no doubt there would be a young and probably charming new Queen who would wield the influence lent by a consecrated relationship. I could lay claim now only to friendship, which could not hold out against a conjugal passion, and at the slightest wish of a pretty princesse I might be disgraced and dismissed. I calculated this process would take less than a year.

If on the other hand the King did not remarry and did not take new mistresses either, the Court could only explain the mystery by perceiving at last, and all too completely, the real nature of our relationship. It would no longer be possible to keep up appearances; people would say I was scheming to prevent a marriage beneficial to the Crown; I should have all the ministers against me, together with the King's family and the Church as well. One day when he was weary of being reproached by the rest, and the too bright light of the candelabra showed how many years had passed over my face, he would send me away humiliated and dishonored.

When I had turned all these things over in my mind and looked at them from every point of view, I decided it was better to leave sooner than to be driven out later, and I resolved to speak to the King.

It was an evening at the end of August, in my apartment. He had just returned from hunting and was about to go over some accounts which had not been brought up to date because of Monsieur Colbert's sudden death. He had got into the habit of bringing some urgent work with him; he said he worked better when I was there and was surprised I never objected to his preferring affairs of state to idle conversation.

The evening was hot and airless, and I felt vaporish and lost for words. I took up a book and then put it down again, got up to rearrange some flowers, moved a stool, tore up some letters I had just written and opened and shut the window. In short, I prowled about like Madame de Montespan's bears in the salon of Mercury. Finally the King looked up from his papers and studied me attentively.

"Well, Françoise," he said gently, "can't you keep still today?"

I curtsied, fell at his knees, and said without lifting my head:

"Sire, I humbly pray Your Majesty to permit me to retire to Maintenon."

He took my face in his hands and raised it so that he could look into my eyes.

"What is the matter?" he said. "Are you ill? Has something upset you? I'll gladly agree to your going home for two or three days. But . . ."

"Sire, Your Majesty misunderstands. I want to leave Court for good and go and live at Maintenon."

He looked completely taken aback.

"Do you know what you're saying, Madame?"

I looked away.

"Yes, Sire," I answered. "Everyone says Your Majesty is going to marry again, and if you took my advice I would say the same. France needs a queen and you need a wife. Neither Your Majesty's age nor your nature fit you to be a widower. And the princesse of Portugal . . ."

"Please do not trouble yourself about the princesse of Portugal. Such matters do not concern you," he replied curtly. "But," he went on more gently, "why should you go away, even if I did marry again? Did you not get on very well with the late Queen?"

"Yes, Sire, but despite her great spiritual qualities the Queen had neither the grace nor the wit to hold or amuse Your Majesty.

It would obviously be quite a different matter with a young and charming princess like the princesse of Portugal. She would be able to provide the delights of a perfect marriage. I should be of no further use. And the new Queen might take objection to our friendship . . ."

"If I did decide to remarry, Madame, I would answer for the Queen's goodwill toward you."

"The Queen might accept me, Sire, if you insisted. But I should not want your friendship in such circumstances. I did not take you away from the late Queen—I gave you back to her, rather. But if I tried to retain your friendship now, it would be different: I should be guilty before God of preventing Your Majesty from giving yourself up entirely to your new marriage, and thus of letting you take part in a sacrament while thinking you might not keep the promise it involves."

The King had listened to me patiently, but toward the end he showed a certain irritation.

"You grieve me, Madame," he said. "I thought you were a better friend than that."

"It is more than friendship I feel toward Your Majesty. That is what gives me the strength to go away."

"Come now, Françoise, won't you tell me what it is you want?"

"All I want is to go to Maintenon, Sire . . . by the Chartres road."

"Please, Madame! I am not in the mood for that kind of pulpit witticism."

And he picked up the portfolio containing his papers and left the room without a farewell. I thought I was lost.

But he came again the next day, and every day after that. He spoke only of indifferent matters; not a word about the conversation which had provoked his anger. So I returned to the subject myself. I could see he understood my scruples, but his own pleasure spoke louder, and it definitely did not suit him that I should leave the Court. But as rumors about his remarriage were growing, I could not conceal my tears. He was touched but nonetheless resolved to sacrifice me to his own amusement. I begged him on my knees to let me go.

"You put your own passing pleasure before the peace of my whole life," I said one day, weeping.

"And you, Madame," he replied brusquely, "prefer your pride to my happiness."

Such scenes reduced me to tatters, and Nanon and my friend Montchevreuil had difficulty afterwards putting me together again. They changed my shift, they bathed my temples, they made me drink orange-flower water and eau de Sainte-Reine. In short they prepared me to reenter the fray.

One day early in September, when the King had taken me out walking with him and we were away from most of the Court, he said:

"I want you to know you have persuaded me. The matter is settled: I shall marry again."

We were walking by the goldfish pond, where there is such a fine view of the Court of Fountains. My eyes filled with tears as I looked at this charming prospect for what I thought was the last time.

"You have nothing to say?" he asked, looking into my face.

I could only shake my head.

"You don't even ask who it is?"

"Oh yes," I managed to gasp. In anyone else I would have taken all this as a sort of jest, but even at his most gallant the King never seemed to trifle.

"Well," he said gravely. "I am going to marry Françoise d'Aubigné."

I was shattered by what looked like the most cruel mockery.

"What is the matter, Madame? Are you ill?"

"It is nothing, Sire. A fit of the vapors . . . Please excuse me, I haven't the strength to walk any further. Madame d'Heudicourt will see me back to my apartment."

Alarmed by this incident, about which the whole Court was agog, for nothing goes unnoticed when one is on the front of the stage, the King came to my bedside, and I saw with amazement that he had not been making fun of me. I was so overcome I thought I should swoon again.

In the manner of one accustomed to command and not have

his reasons called in question, he told me he was marrying me because he could see no other way of keeping me. The future of the dynasty was sufficiently assured by his son and the two grandsons the Dauphine had just produced for him one after the other. To have more children now by a second marriage would only breed discord in his family and insurrection in the country. Finally, neither God nor conscience could be offended by his marrying me.

"But what about the world, Sire? The greatest king on earth, marrying Monsieur Scarron's widow!"

"You talk like Monsieur de Louvois," he said. "And I shall answer you as I answered him. As for what the world will say, it is I who make and unmake nobility. Anyone who is distinguished by me is sufficiently well-born."

And thereupon he launched into a vehement speech maintaining that this was the most sensible marriage he could make, "for it is very sensible, when one is forty-four years old, to marry for love. I gave up the idea of such a marriage when I was twenty and not my own master, and that may well be why I fell into sin. At my present time of life I think it wise to look to my salvation—I am marrying you so that you can save me. But perhaps that consideration means nothing to you . . ."

I had never seen him set forth an argument so enthusiastically: he was like a child explaining sagely to his governess how sensible it was to let him do as he liked. Moreover, he was so sure of me that he had told his minister and his confessor of his decision before informing me. Admittedly, if there could have been any opposition in the matter, it was not likely to come from me.

So, thirty-two days after the death of the Queen, I agreed to become the wife of the King of France. Or rather I was told that was what was going to happen, and I did not object.

Very few others were let in on our secret. On the King's side there were only Monsieur de Louvois, Père de La Chaise, the archbishop of Paris, and Bontemps, the King's head valet. I told no one but Nanon, Marguerite and Henri de Montchevreuil, the abbé Gobelin and Madame de Brinon. Neither the King's family nor my own knew anything; we were old enough to act without their permission.

The King hesitated for a while as to whether to make the marriage known. I could see he had apprehensions about it, but he offered to do so if I wished. I said he should not do something so much above me: he was already doing me too much honor in marrying me, and it was best from every point of view to keep the marriage secret. He readily agreed.

I had had to seem married to Monsieur Scarron when I was not. Now, when I should really be married, I should have to seem a widow. It was clearly my fate never to be married in the usual way.

This time, however, I saw no cause for complaint. I was rapt in dream and transported with bliss; my feet scarcely touched the ground. The King did not feel like this at all. He found our marriage so natural I did not like to point out how extraordinary it was. All that was missing to make my joy complete was to be able to tell Monsieur de Villarceaux.

"Françoise, are you dreaming?" he had said. "A Villarceaux marry Madame Scarron!"

This shaft had stuck so deep in my heart that a proposal from a king could scarcely draw it out.

As Fontainebleau did not lend itself to a secret ceremony, the King decided the wedding should take place on the first night after our return to Versailles, where it was easy to reach the chapel from his apartment. So it was during the night of Saturday the ninth to Sunday the tenth of October 1683, in the old chapel at Versailles, that the archbishop of Paris, in the presence of Père de La Chaise, married King Louis XIV to Françoise d'Aubigné.

I myself was scarcely present at all. In the darkness of the chapel, lit only by the two great torches on the altar, I could not see the man to whom I was giving my hand. The worthy Monsieur de Montchevreuil, who acted as my witness, said something to me, but I did not know what. I did not hear the King answering the archbishop's questions; I did not hear myself consent to my own elevation. I only began to come to my senses during the Agnus Dei, when I thought I was so glorified in this world that I was in danger of being cast down and humiliated in the next. I relapsed into my lethargy again until the Last Gospel, when I suddenly realized I could rise no higher.

Then I began to look out for trouble.

Fourteen

In the early days of my marriage my ordinary life went on unchanged.

I still went to every entertainment: balls in the King's apartments, plays in those of Monsieur, lotteries in those of Monseigneur, and music everywhere. The Court was large and lively in those days. There were journeys too: military excursions to the countries which the King had recently united under his Crown, country rides from one château to another in the Ile-de-France. Courtiers like to change the setting of their boredom, but since we live not in places but in our own hearts, they soon get tired of their same old selves within new walls and have to pack up and move on again.

As for me, wherever I went I had eyes for nothing but the King, and as my new husband had the same ways as my old lover, I met with continuity everywhere. Every day he bestowed five hours of his time upon me. They were very punctually regulated: one hour in the morning before mass and four hours in the evening, after hunting and before his supper. It is not quite accurate to say he bestowed those hours on me, for he spent more of them on business than on talking to me. Thus his occupations often kept me from pursuing my own, and I had as little freedom in my own room as if I were a mere visitor. I must make no noise for fear of disturbing him; I had to drop my work and listen whenever he wanted to speak to me; I was relegated to the darkest corner so as to leave the best place and the brightest light to his portfolio, his papers and his secretary. But one must take the rough with the smooth.

When I was seen to be so well established, and apparently for a long time to come, my anteroom was invaded all day long by petitioners, ministers and members of the royal family themselves. I politely got rid of as many of them as possible, but I could not turn everyone away for fear of being thought infatuated by my own unaccustomed grandeur. So to avoid having more enemies than royal favor made inevitable, I finally let my apartment become a stepping stone for the highest at Court and the humblest in Paris.

But it was a very small apartment. As I had never had Madame de Montespan's grand ideas on the subject, I had contented myself with four rooms at Fontainebleau and at Versailles. Even then, half the space went to menservants, guards and the rest of the domestics, and I had to spend my days squeezed into a bedroom and a little sitting-room, without complaining that I was not even mistress of those few square feet—like a shopkeeper who lives in the shop, which once open in the morning is never empty until the evening.

By the time I had been married two or three years, my life had taken on a form that was to remain unchanged throughout the thirty-two years the Great King and I were husband and wife.

I woke at six o'clock and said my prayers in bed. Almost before I had time to swallow a cup of bouillon and start dressing, people began to arrive. First, Fagon or Maréchal to take my pulse or dose me if it was a day for taking medicine. Then came Bontemps or Blouin, the King's head valet, to see how I was and take the news to his master. I tried to fit in my most urgent letters between half past seven and eight, but I seldom finished before it was time for the first audiences. These might be officials wanting to be helped to a post; monks and nuns seeking money for charity; widows come to tell me their woes; merchants come to present their bills; an artist commissioned to paint my portrait; or other people on trifling affairs. Sometimes, toward the end of the reign, the visitors would include ambassadors and secretaries of state. Always, at every period, there were some of my friends, such as the duc du Maine, who would come to kiss me goodmorning when I got up and stay with me until the King arrived. For none of my visitors left until someone superior came to displace them. When the King came, they all had to go.

The King stayed with me until it was time for mass, which was usually ten o'clock. It could have been an hour of pleasant conversation except that I was still only half-dressed. More often than not I had not had time to finish my toilet and was still in my nightcap and nightgown. And I hate talking to people in my nightcap. My room was like a church where the worshipers are so devout they do not notice the altar has not been decorated yet.

When the King had gone, I concentrated on dressing. Nanon brushed my hair, which was still very beautiful. De Lile, my majordomo, and Manseau, my steward, came to receive my orders for the day. After which the King dropped in again for a moment on his way back from mass.

Then his daughters would make their appearance, or, later, the duchesse de Bourgogne, all accompanied by their attendants, ladies-in-waiting and close friends. They would stay there prattling while my dinner was brought in, and I talked to them as I ate. Often there was so dense a circle of ladies around me I could not ask for a drink.

Just as they were leaving at last to have their own dinners and I was about to have a game of backgammon with Bonne or go out for a breath of air, Monseigneur would arrive. He never ate dinner. He was the hardest man in the world to talk to. I think he must have counted his words and resolved not to go beyond a certain number. But since he was my guest, I had to make some conversation. In another lady's apartment I would have hid behind a chair and said nothing, but within those four walls of mine I had to do all I could to entertain him.

When the Dauphin left, the King, just risen from the table, returned with all the princesses. In that confined space the heat was terrible. The King left after about half an hour, but all the rest stayed, and they came nearer now that the King was gone. I had to listen to the jests of one of them, the teasing of another and the anecdote of a third, while all the time I was worrying about affairs of state, dreading bad news, wondering about what advice to give. While they were roaring with laughter, I thought how in the outside world a thousand people were dying and thousands more suffering. I thought about wars and famines, and the senseless chatter which passed for wit with them became intolerable.

When the King returned from hunting, he came to see me again. The door was shut and no one else could enter. I was alone with him. I had to accept his caresses if he was in the mood, or console him for his troubles if he had any. Then he worked, going through dispatches, writing, dictating; and then a minister would come. If they wanted me to make a third in the discussion, they called me. If they did not want me, I went and sat further off, but I was not free to devote myself to my own affairs or amusement. I used to take up a piece of tapestry or a book and wait until they remembered I was there.

While the King went on working, I would have my supper, but I never ate it in comfort more than once every couple of months. If I had left the King with a minister and he was sad or worried, I had no appetite. If he was alone, he would ask me to be quick, for he hated being on his own. Or else he would want to show me something. One way or another I was always in a hurry. In order to save a few minutes I had them bring my dessert at the same time as the meat, and the table was removed as soon as I had finished.

By then it was late. I had been up since six in the morning and had not had a moment's respite all day. I would have attacks of fatigue, fits of yawning; finally I was so tired I could scarcely bear it. The King noticed in the end, and sometimes said, "You're weary, aren't you? Go to bed."

My women would come and undress me, always in front of the King and often in front of his ministers, and all the time they were taking off my clothes, I could feel the King still wanted to talk to me and was waiting impatiently for them to go. Or else he had some minister with him and was afraid the servants might hear what he was saying. This made him nervous, and I was nervous in sympathy. What could I do? I hurried, I was always hurrying, I hurried so much I felt ill.

I was in bed. I sent my women away. The King came and sat at my bedside to chat a little.

I was in bed, but I am not an angel and would have liked to relieve nature in various ways. But there was no one there to ask for anything and getting up or moving about was out of the question. So I listened to the King, shivering, sniffing or holding back my cough until I was blue in the face.

If the King had thought I needed anything, he would no doubt have allowed it to be brought; but it did not occur to him I might be suffering. The great are so used to seeing everything done for them that they no longer notice suffering.

A quarter of an hour before his own supper, the King went into my dressing-room and rang a bell which sounded in my sitting-room. Then Monseigneur, the princes and the princesses, who had been awaiting this signal, filed one by one out of the sitting-room and through my bedroom, going past me in procession and leaving by the far door that led to the apartment of the King, who followed them out.

It was now a quarter past ten, they were all about to sit down to supper, and I was alone. I quickly did all I needed to do, said a short prayer and went to sleep behind my four curtains, often after having wept, for if I had any troubles this was the only time I had all day to spare for them.

"Heavens, what a lucky woman!" the duchesse de Chaulnes used to say. "She is with the King from morn till night!" She did not remember that kings and princes are men like the others, only perhaps slightly more tyrannical than the rest.

In short, my marriage introduced me to a state of being which had no happy medium. On the one hand there was an excess of grandeur and favors, on the other an excess of sorrows and inconveniences. It was a life which left you alternately elated and utterly cast down.

———————

Meanwhile my public position seemed not to have changed. For the world at large I was still only the Dauphine's second mistress of the wardrobe, and the King was keen that this appearance should be kept up.

At first he had not wanted to declare our marriage for fear of what people might say. Later the public uncertainty on the subject gave our marriage the piquancy which secrecy had lent our earlier relationship, and he began to keep doubt alive by means of confidences that were deliberately misleading. One day he said aloud after dinner to some of his courtiers, "Haven't you heard I'm having a new livery made? That's a sure sign I'm going to marry again." But another day he said at supper that the Council had decided unanimously, in connection with the lawsuit of the comtesse de Granpré, that second marriages were always unhappy. When one privy councillor said quietly, "Sire, that applies only to private individuals," the King replied firmly that second marriages had great disadvantages for all kinds of people without exception. Then, in a further attempt to throw the curious off the scent and cause universal confusion, he revived the notion of a Portuguese marriage, entering into several negotiations in this direction and amusing himself by hinting it was I who was urging him to it. Finally he carried the play-acting to an extreme by offering me the post of matron of honor to the Dauphine before the whole Court. As we had agreed beforehand, I refused it on some pretext of modesty. I was praised for my humility.

In fact I thought all these tricks very childish and would have preferred the situation to be acknowledged, since it was not one which could not be avowed; but I could see these mystifications amused the King, and that was so rare I could not help taking pleasure in anything he found diverting. So I enjoyed the secrecy because he did.

I was thus in a very singular position: first in the King's intimacy, coach and conversation, but among the last, after the princesses and the duchesses, in matters of ceremony and entertainment. In public an ordinary person, out of sight a queen.

Even the King's own family did not know what to think. One reported remark by Madame, the King's sister-in-law, pleased me greatly, which did not often happen with her. She had told one of her intimates she did not think I could be married to the King "because if they were husband and wife, they would not be so much in love. Unless," she added, with a flash of insight, "unless secrecy adds a spice that is not found in a public marriage."

As for Monsieur, he learned the truth only by the most unlikely chance and did not dare pass it on to anyone; this surprised me in such an inveterate chatterbox. What happened was that several years after our marriage the King, suffering from a quartan fever, wanted me with him in his room. He had just taken medicine while I was there when Monsieur, anxious about his brother's health, came in unannounced, before I had a chance to escape.

The King was lying half-naked on his bed with his breeches down. I blushed at the thought of what Monsieur would think on finding us in a situation which would have been very unseemly if we were not married. But the King got out of it superbly. In his most lofty tones he merely said: "Seeing me here like this with Madame, brother, you will easily guess what she is to me." That was all. Monsieur and I went on talking as unselfconsciously as we could, he overwhelmed by the revelation and I disturbed about the confession. Meanwhile the King went majestically into his dressing-room to attend to the effects of his medicine.

My own family was no wiser than the King's. The little Villette girl alone had some inkling, because one day when she had done something very stupid and made me lose my temper, I had blurted out: "And to think, as niece to a queen, you could cut a fine figure here!"

At that Marguerite's eyes had opened wide. They never quite closed again. But she must have held her tongue because Philippe, her father, knew nothing. Every time he came to Paris, he asked whether the King had some new affair. He repeated names which were being mentioned in the provinces, usually those of the Dauphine's maids of honor, and insisted on knowing what I thought about it.

My brother was another matter. He was bored living in Poitou and kept on saying how much he wanted to come to Court and be in contact with me. So I was obliged to tell him that the reason I could not agree to this was very splendid, and he ought to be proud rather than angry because of it. I had hoped that by speaking ambiguously I should be only half-understood; but he understood all too well. While he assured me he was gladly sacrificing himself to "the beauty of the cause," he behaved all the more outrageously. He came to Paris without coming to see me and hobnobbed with the duc de Lauzun, just freed from prison in Pignerol, or with some other semi-exile; with them he played for high stakes, got into debt and then guffawed: "Don't worry, my friends, my brother-in-law will pay!"

His "brother-in-law" did pay. But it was not long before Charles found that a well-lined purse was not enough, and his sister's marriage to the King ought to bring him titles and honors too. He asked me to get him made a maréchal, but I answered that even if I could have him made a lord high constable, I would not do so, because I would not ask unreasonable favors of the man to whom I owed everything.

To keep him quiet the King made him governor of Aigues-Mortes and then of the Berry, and then provided him with a considerable income out of tax farming.

Charles only marked up more gambling debts, boasting to all and sundry that he had had his field-marshal's baton in cash.

I thought to put an end to his claims by getting him made a knight of the order of the Holy Ghost, although he did not possess the necessary titles of nobility, and Hozier, the royal genealogist, hinted that he even doubted whether the d'Aubignés really belonged to the true aristocracy. Even so I did not hesitate to expose the King to criticism and myself to ridicule in the hope of satisfying a brother as insatiable in his demands as he was reckless in his utterances. But Charles was not grateful and presented me with new requirements backed up by still more extravagant behavior.

"I am beginning to get tired of the foolishness of Monsieur your brother, Madame," the King said to me one day as I drove with him in his carriage.

"Sire," I replied, "it is not for me to teach Your Majesty that God sometimes makes our brothers the cross we have to bear."

He could not help laughing, for he had good reason to deplore the vices of Monsieur, his own brother.

"True, Madame," he answered, looking at me tenderly. "So we shall both bear our crosses patiently."

Marriage had not changed the King's feelings for me. As his sister-in-law had so justly observed, his love had even been increased by having to demonstrate its strength before God and not men.

At Fontainebleau he brought me down to his own floor by giving me an apartment on the same level as his own in the pavilion of the Golden Gate. At Versailles he had my room enlarged and furnished more luxuriously. At Marly he put me in a very large room on the first floor, beside his daughters the princesse de Conti and Mademoiselle de Nantes and his brother Monsieur. This was admitting, by means of topography, that I was now one of the family. But it also meant I was continually surrounded by builders and decorators. The King did not think the signs of greatness could be seen as inconveniences.

Before other people he always showed me great respect and even something more. He had been much less punctilious and gallant with the Queen. If he caught sight of me while walking with his courtiers, he would raise his hat and come over to me however far off I was. When we toured the gardens, he would walk beside my chair and bend down to speak and listen to me; and he always had something to say or point out to me. This, and his habit of always trying to catch my eye and seek my approbation, was a new phenomenon which plunged the Court into astonishment.

I think he really did love me. He used to send me little notes two or three times a day about this and that, and in public he could not let a quarter of an hour pass without coming to whisper something to me in private, even if he had spent the whole day with me. He said he could not be without me for more than an hour, and when we were alone together, he proved his attachment in such a way that I cannot doubt the truth of his dying words: "Madame, I have never loved anyone as I have loved you."

Even so, he loved me only as much as he was capable of loving. He never once, until he died, asked me if he made me happy. He just went his own way, a uniquely self-regarding man who saw everyone else in terms of their relationship to himself.

Whatever the state of my health, even if I was ill and had a fever, I had to be formally dressed, bedecked and corseted, travel to Flanders or even further, be cheerful, eat, move to another house, seem not to mind cold or dust—and all at exactly the day and hour he had decided, without disturbing any of his arrangements by so much as a minute. He often made me walk when one would not make a servant-maid do so; sometimes sweat was pouring off me with fever, and I did not know if I was going to die en route. All that mattered to him was to find me there, dressed up and ready by the time he was in the habit of coming to see me.

On his arrival there would be a new commotion. He could not bear warm rooms, even in winter, so when he came in to find all the windows shut, he would profess surprise and proceed to have them all opened wide, even if the night air was chill and my teeth were chattering with fever. Nor, if there was to be music in my apartment after supper, did it matter if I had a fever or a headache: I still had to have my ears assaulted by trumpets and my eyes by a hundred candles.

But this disregard for my physical health was not what shocked me the most. I had seen very early on how he had treated Madame de Montespan in this respect, and other ladies he had loved, and I had never flattered myself it would be any different with me. But I was less guarded in my hopes for tenderness of feeling and gentle words; so I was all the more disappointed.

I already thought I was timid in his presence, but the terrible way he would often lash out at me, even in front of his ministers, made me tremble from head to foot. For example, if in the early days I was unfortunate enough to intercede on behalf of some worthy person for a post or try to do something for a relative, the King would promptly give the appointment to somebody else. Even if the minister ventured to say, "But Sire, Madame de Maintenon wanted . . .," there, before the minister, his secretary, my own "familiar ladies" and anyone else who happened to be in the room, my husband would retort loudly, "I know that. That is why I act otherwise. I will not have her meddling." Sometimes these attacks were so sudden and cruel I could not help weeping. But even that did not affect him; in fact I could see it made him even more pleased with himself.

But the next day Bontemps would bring me a note in which his master, and mine, assured me of his love in the most gallant of terms.

"Madame," he might write, "I did not want to let this morning go by without telling you a truth so dear to me I never tire of repeating it. I love you always and respect you more than I can express. No matter how great your friendship for me, mine for you is greater because I am yours with all my heart. Louis."

This pretty compliment was not some sort of apology for the scene of the previous day, for he did not even suspect he had hurt me, and anyway he did not care. It was just the straightforward expression of one half of him, one face of Janus, and for that, whether I liked it or not, I had to put up with the other half.

"Smiles in the morning, tears before bedtime," I would say to Nanon when she found me fondly contemplating one of these little notes. But how can you hate a man who tells you he loves you?—especially when he is a king. Pride is satisfied even if the heart is not, and you think you still love when really you only want to appear beloved.

But I am anticipating my later feelings. In the first years of my marriage I still felt too much gratitude and admiration for the King to want to admit I suffered from his tyranny. I also saw myself as responsible for his salvation; and I have always felt great affection for those I have to answer for.

As I myself approached the heights, I understood the King's isolation better. At that level you never meet with a single ingenuous look, hear a single truthful word, or are the object of a single disinterested feeling.

Unlike all the other courtiers, therefore, I soon made it a rule never to ask the King for anything, either for myself or for my friends; I resolved never to bother him about private matters, but, when the occasion arose, always to tell him the truth about public affairs rather than offer the compliments which were usual and which he liked to hear. I differed from the other favorites in thinking one truly loved a king only when one had the courage to displease him.

In one of my little secret books I have found a prayer which

I composed at that time and used to say every morning when I woke up; I think it shows the nature of my love for my husband.

"O god, who holds the hearts of kings in your hands, open that of the King that I may make the good which you desire enter in. Help me to please, console and encourage him, and to make him sad when it is necessary for your glory. May I hide from him none of those things which he ought to learn through me and which no one else would dare to tell him. May I be saved with him; may I love him in you and for you; and may he love me in the same way. Grant that we may walk together in all your ways without reproach, until the day of your coming."

To give an entirely sincere and complete account of my feelings toward the King at that period, I must add that, as I see from the prayer I have just quoted and from letters which have been returned to me, I used to write the word "god" with a small letter and the word "King" with a capital. I would not swear this exactly reflected the hierarchy of my respect; but it probably does indicate which of the two I felt more at home with.

So it was a great reverence, together with a great pity, which lay behind the strange love I bore the King.

However it may have been, I was obliged to love him, and to get all my pleasure from our relationship, for in the position I had then reached I did not have many other people to love. It was not hard to see that most of those who sought me out did so only in order to reach someone else, and with some ulterior motive. Every day I wondered afresh at the elaborateness of their manners and the baseness of their flattery. Under the splendor of their dress and the gold of their compliments I could see quite clearly treachery of every kind, boundless ambition, dreadful envy, reprehensible conduct—a frenzied crowd seeking only to destroy one another. The desire to rise, the fear of falling, the determination to push oneself forward, the dread of displeasing—all these produced a state of mind which anywhere else would have been regarded as monstrous.

I did not think I had nourished any illusions about this strange world since I had come to Court; but when people began to suspect something about my marriage, it was as if I had suddenly gone backstage. What had seemed a fairy palace turned out to be only a painted cloth.

In the midst of it all I did not know what disgusted me most: the plots of parents against their children or the intrigues of husband against wife, brother against sister; the flattery with which all these worthy creatures ceaselessly assailed me; or the slanders they spread about me equally unanimously. Often, after being praised all day, I would find a little pamphlet on a table or under a chair cushion in the evening, left there as if by the ebbing away of the crowd. Some nameless great lady did not want me to remain ignorant of what disparaging princes and Dutch printers had to say about me.

Sometimes there were songs.

> The King at Marly we discover,
> A husband now and not a lover.
> 'Tis the old soldier's common lot,
> When he can wield the sword no more,
> To seek again his country plot
> And marry with his former whore.

Sometimes there were big books. I well remember one of the *Loves of Madame de Maintenon* in which the author claimed to tell all about my life, but though according to him he had enjoyed the closest intimacy with me, he did not even know my name and kept calling me "Guillemette." I also remember a work called *The Ghost of Scarron Appears to Madame de Maintenon and Reproaches Her for Her Love Affair with Louis the Great.* Its first revelations were mere trifles, such as my low birth and the allegation that I had been Madame de Montespan's servant. Then, after having procured Mademoiselle de Fontanges for the King, I was supposed to have poisoned her. Lastly, for this was after the founding of Saint-Cyr, I was said to have selected the most agreeable little girls there for the King; this was the means by which I had made myself necessary to him. "The link which exists between the French and Ottoman Courts shows that the King is adopting the vicious habits of the Turks," the charming pamphlet went on. "One has only to look at the school at Saint-Cyr, a veritable seraglio disguised as a religious establishment. It is you, Madame, who are the scandalous instrument in countless practices which supply the monarch with criminal pleasures."

This accusation was to be so often repeated later I became almost indifferent to it; but the first time I actually set eyes on it, I shed bitter tears. I lacked the wisdom of Monsieur Scarron, who always threw such productions on the fire without reading them through. I could never refrain from drinking the hemlock down to the dregs, and every time I was revolted by the injustice of the charges and furious at my inability to defend myself.

The Italian players put me on the stage, and both Paris and Versailles flocked to applaud *The False Prude* or *The Female Intriguer Unmasked.* Occasionally I received insulting notes omitting nothing but their author's signature, and the King added to my torment by showing me letters exchanged between people who were close to him. For the King had set up an arrangement whereby the Post made copies for him of any letters referring to him or to affairs of state. By this means I learned that according to Madame I was a witch or an old tart; this great princesse I had thought to love saw me as "a hypocrite who by some unknown magic manages to combine piety and pleasure."

As for the princes de Conti, who had gone off to Germany to help the Emperor against the Turks, they wrote such jests and such filth about me to their friends Liancourt, Alincourt and La Roche-Guyon that the letter fell from my hands. That particular offense, however, did not go unpunished: I was in too good company. Alincourt gibed at God and the Contis made fun of the King: "A stage king when it comes to showing off, a chess king when it comes to fighting," they wrote. The King would willingly have overlooked the outrage to his wife and to God, but he would not tolerate criticism of his own rule. He banished the lot of them.

I hid all my bitterness beneath an air of gaiety. Court is a place where joys are visible but false, and sorrows hidden but real.

The necessity of being on guard against everyone and of defending my heart against the most natural feelings threw me still more into the company of children. I found in them a naturalness which enchanted me and a freedom from constraint which even spread to me, circumspect and reserved as I could feel myself becoming through living in proximity with the great.

As Marguerite de Villette was getting on for twelve and I was starting to be asked for her hand in marriage, and as my nephew Charlot had left Maintenon to go and be an officer in the army, I seized upon my brother's daughter, then aged two and a half and like me called Françoise d'Aubigné. I was resolved to make her my heiress. My brother, Charles, more interested in haunting the gambling dens of Paris than in living with his wife and daughter in Cognac, gladly handed her over. Nanon became her nurse, and I set about teaching her social usages in hopes of the fine match she might make in ten or eleven years' time, if in the meanwhile the King did not tire of my company and send me to end my days in a convent.

Every time my new husband left me free, I would spend long afternoons in the little "convent" at Noisy. The simple life they led there, the merry laughter of the children, the pleasure of Madame de Brinon's company and the charms of the untouched countryside all took me back to the happy days at Mursay and Montchevreuil. I felt a thousand miles away from the stifling Court. I loved children, and here I had forty of them. But as I could never satisfy my hunger for them, I kept increasing their number. I took in poor girls and waifs sent to me from all over France, until even Noisy was too small to hold them all properly and my purse was strained too. I began to want to do something on a grander scale.

Madame de Brinon and I were really wasting our talents with these little peasant girls. Once they had been taught to read, count, sew and spin, there was nothing more to be done but send them out to earn a living. No possibility there for one of the masterpieces in the art of education which may be produced with pupils well-born and with distinguished minds. Teaching the common people was a task I thought more necessary than did the great ones of this world, but practically speaking it was arid and unsatisfactory.

Another kind of poor pupil seemed to me more worthy of attention. At that time, all over France, there were numbers of penniless noblemen who survived only on borrowing and charity. Many among them were younger sons without either land or live-stock, who eked out a miserable life in shacks with scarcely a roof over them. Then there were the widows of officers who had died in the service of the King, left without a sou to bring up their children. Others had been ruined by their hopeless attempts to rival richer men's palaces and fountains. I pitied these impoverished nobles, especially as I remembered how I had long shared the fate of the most unfortunate among them; there was nothing I did not know about their struggles between hunger and pride. Here was material for carrying the work of education further, perhaps a way of producing brilliant minds, but above all a means of regenerating the nation by providing its élite with the maxims of virtue and the principles of learning. The idea of giving the poorest of the aristoc-racy the same education as that received by the richest of the bourgeoisie, thus restoring the nobility to a position which was being undermined every day in the realm of politics, was a project so splendid that in my view it surpassed the pleasure of relieving poverty.

I confided my thoughts to Madame de Brinon, who immedi-ately approved of the plan. We weighed the pros and cons of admitting both boys and girls to the new establishment. At Rueil we had looked after many little boys, and at Noisy we still had a few. But I thought it would be best to think only of girls.

"The education of girls is entirely neglected," I said to Ma-dame de Brinon. "People say they don't need learning, that it's enough if they know how to do what their husbands tell them without arguing . . . And yet isn't it the women who either run houses and families well or ruin them? Who see to the details of domestic affairs, who bring up the children? In reality women's occupations are scarcely less important to society than men's. And it is the ignorance of the daughters of the nobility that has caused the aristocracy's ruin."

In the course of 1684, when I had worked out my plan, I spoke of it to the King. I then had a hundred and eighty girls at Noisy, including, during recent months, a growing number of young ladies. I ventured to remind the King of the pitiable state to which most of the aristocratic families in France were reduced by the expenses their heads had incurred in his service, and of the fact that their children needed help if they were not to fall into degradation.

"What Your Majesty has just done for the sons of the nobility by founding companies of cadets where the boys are educated without any cost to their families, Your Majesty ought to do for the girls as well. In a way," I said, "they are even more in need of help than their brothers, because of the dangers to which poverty may expose them."

I pointed out how much good might be done with well brought up girls sent out among all the families in France. The King listened to what I had to say, but himself said nothing at first. Three hours later his only comment was:

"The establishment you suggest would be very costly, Madame. I also find it very strange. No Queen of France has ever done anything like it."

I was mortified at having poured out my treasures of eloquence for nothing.

But one afternoon when I had given up all hope, the King came to Noisy unexpectedly and almost alone. The portress, not knowing what to do when she heard the attendants knock and call out "The King! The King!," kept the door closed and said firmly that she would go and tell the head. The King had to wait some time until Madame de Brinon arrived, but instead of being annoyed he praised the portress's reliability.

After such a good beginning everything was bound to please him. He visited the classrooms, watched the children doing their lessons and admired their modest behavior in chapel, where no matter how great the temptation not one of them turned to look at him. In fact he was so pleased with all he saw that he was in a hurry to do something larger and more substantial.

"But on condition, Madame, that it is not a convent. I am tired of seeing such establishments spring up everywhere, stuffed with wealth for the benefit of perfectly useless inmates."

It was soon decided that our school would have two hundred and fifty daughters of the nobility who were either orphaned or poor, admitted at the age of six or seven and then brought up at the King's expense until they were twenty. The teachers were not to be nuns, apart from their head, Madame de Brinon, who was already an Ursuline. They were not to be taught like pupils in a convent school but prepared for their future duties in life.

They would learn to read and write correctly and have lessons in rhetoric and poetry like their brothers. They would know enough arithmetic to be able to keep their own accounts and be given the rudiments of economics: agriculture, the buying and selling of wheat, how to plan and manage farms—they would be taught all those things so that they would not be like those young women who see no difference between country life and that of the savages in Canada. They would have lessons in Greek and Roman history and the history of France and her neighbors, which would set before them eminent examples of courage and disinterestedness. Music with the best masters would give them access to innocent amusement, and painting would not be neglected, for ladies' efforts can never attain true beauty without some knowledge of the rules of drawing. They would learn dressmaking, sweep their own classrooms and acquire a training in child management through a system by which the older pupils taught the younger ones and helped them to dress, wash and do their hair. With this first-hand knowledge of the nature and mentality of children, they would make excellent mothers as well as accomplished housekeepers.

Lastly, they would be good Christians, having been properly instructed in the duties of religion. Convents often do no more than make the children learn God's commandments by heart, without explaining what they entail: the pupils know "Thou shalt have no other gods before me," and they worship the Virgin Mary; they recite "Thou shalt not steal," yet maintain it is no sin to rob the King and the state. Piety is reduced to external practices like confession, communion and long sessions in church, while apart from these observances such schools may forget God altogether and be hotbeds of anger, hatred, revenge, lies, avarice and perjury.

I wanted everything to be quite different in the King's school, and for it to set so persuasive an example that there would soon be dozens like it all over France.

The King commissioned Monsieur Mansart to draw up plans, and the site the architect chose was in Saint-Cyr, a hamlet on the edge of the park at Versailles. The house was completed in fifteen months.

While the timbers were going up, Nanon and I designed uniforms for the teachers and pupils; I planned the lay-out of classrooms and dormitories and drew up timetables. I delighted in this work, and it widened the horizons of my prison. The King, pleased to see I had found some distraction, was good enough to take an interest. He had Nanon try on the teachers' uniform for him, and suggested a change in the cap. He went over the constitution, and issued a warrant giving me the lifelong right to an apartment specially built for me there, together with maintenance for myself and my household at the expense of the school itself if ever I should take up residence. This was an ingenious way of providing me with a refuge in case he should die before I did; the King was then very ill with a fistula.

At the end of July 1686 the whole community at Noisy was transferred to Saint-Cyr in the King's coaches, escorted by Switzers of the royal household. The children cried out in admiration at the dormitories: the white beds and the curtains had green, yellow, red or blue silk ribbons according to the color assigned to their classes; every little girl had her own chest and dressing-table. The four classrooms were decorated each in the color of its pupils' uniform, right down to the ribbons from which the maps were suspended on the walls. Some of the walls had frescoes on them: a forest for the Green class, the sea for the Blues and fields of wheat for the Yellows, with children dotted abut the landscape. The garden and woods were charming; the King himself named the paths. The three courtyards had orange trees in them, and everywhere there were bowers and arbors with swings. The little girls, who had never seen such comfort and plenty at home or at their convent schools, clapped their hands with delight.

From the very first day their time was divided up as we had planned it with the King. The children got up at six, and spent until nine o'clock going to mass and having breakfast. Then came two hours of reading, writing and recitation, with dinner at eleven. After dinner they had an hour's recreation, then some were taught singing and the others embroidery until they all came together again for two hours of spelling, grammar and arithmetic. After light refreshments they went to vespers, then learned their catechism, had supper at six, followed by a good two hours' more of recreation and went to bed at nine.

From then on, for thirty years, the school at Saint-Cyr was my main occupation whenever the King and the Court left me any free time. When I was at Versailles, I used to go and spend the morning at Saint-Cyr at least every other day, arriving at six. If I could, I stopped all day, until five in the evening. I helped to dress the little Reds, still all crumpled with sleep. Then I went about the class-rooms to see the teachers at work; I myself might give the older girls a grammar lesson or a catechism class. I would show some how to do a tapestry stitch, others how to play piquet. I would end up in the infirmary, cheering up and waiting on those who were ill and helping those who were getting better to do their hair. I preferred these duties to all the amusements of Versailles.

In September 1686 the King, still unwell, came to visit. He passed the three hundred ladies and young ladies in review, heard mass and visited the classrooms. When he came out again into the gardens, walking with difficulty, the little girls burst into an anthem which Madame de Brinon had just written to a piece of music by Lully:

Grand Dieu, sauvez le Roi,
Grand Dieu, vengez le Roi,
Vive le Roi . . .†

The King listened in silence, but when he had got back into his coach his usual composure deserted him and he could not conceal his emotion. He took my hand, kissed it and said in a voice charged with feeling:

"Thank you, Madame, for all the pleasure you have given me."

Wild with joy that he should share my own happiness, and at the same time racked with anxiety about his illness, I could not help returning his kiss. This was very daring, and he was surprised. He gave me a quizzical look, shook his head, smiled and kept my hand in his all the way back to Versailles. Saint-Cyr was our child, and brought us together at its cradle.

A few years later the pupils performed some plays which Monsieur Racine wrote at my request to teach them to appreciate fine language, and this left the King entirely convinced of the success of the enterprise. The whole Court wanted to come and see *Esther*. Politicians identified me as the heroine, the King as Ahasuerus, Madame de Montespan as the proud Vashti and Louvois as Haman. But poets saw only a complete and perfect harmony between the music, the poetry, the singing and the characters. The children's acting was faultless, and my niece Marguerite de Villette, whom I had just married to the comte de Caylus, was a triumph in all she did, but especially in the role of Esther.

My own role as her governess was now over, and it was a pleasure to see my work crowned with such success. Never was a countenance so intelligent, touching and eloquent as hers at sixteen. Never was there such freshness, grace, wit, gaiety and charm. In short she was the most captivating creature in the world. I was so fond of her I could not do without her, and I was delighted now to see her outdo the most famous actresses.

King James Stuart of England and his Queen, who had just arrived in France in exile, were at Saint-Germain, and they too wanted to see the play. All the princes of the blood and the ministers were there. People fought to get in, for I could provide only two hundred seats for each performance. The King came every day, and as soon as he arrived, he would go and stand by the entrance and use his stick as a barrier until all the people who had been invited had gone in. Then the illustrious majordomo to this illustrious theater ordered the door to be closed.

Esther was a triumph, first for Saint-Cyr and then for the d'Aubigné family, both through the heroine, supposed to represent me, and through the actress who impersonated her.

I met with more difficulty when I tried to interest the King in my projects for reforming the nation's morals. He did not object to my opening more schools for the children of the poor, though he did not contribute one sou to the costs. I alone supported the few small classes I set up at Avon on the edge of the park at Fontainebleau for a hundred or so little peasant girls and at Saint-Cyr for sixty more poor children. I often went there myself to give them lessons in the catechism and the rudiments of arithmetic. I would sit on the stone floor under the church porch with the bigger children in a circle around me and the little ones curled up on my skirt. I paid the master or mistress in these schools of mine, and I also used to give something to the pupils, as well as their food, for otherwise their parents, not wanting to lose by their children's education, would have kept them away and sent them into the fields. But the results were not in proportion to my efforts: the soup went fast, but the lessons made little progress.

"What do we mean by God?" I would ask Lisette after an hour's eloquence and explanation.

"Yeth," she would answer, in an affected little voice which no doubt she thought more refined and so likely to please a Court lady.

"What do you mean, 'yes'? Haven't you heard what I've been saying for the last hour?"

"Yeth."

I could feel myself beginning to get irritated.

"But what do you mean by 'yes'? 'Yes' and what else?"

"Yeth, Madame."

And so it went on until I gave her a tip and made myself say a silent prayer to soothe my vexation. I would not let my boys and girls be punished if they did not learn well, for people of that class have not much gift for it and it is unfair to expect as much of them as of others.

When I got home, I used to change my clothes, for more than once I had brought fleas back with me from my schools, and the King did not like it. At first the children were indeed dirty, half-naked, unappetizing, but later on I gave them all clothes every winter and they were better dressed. In all this, as at Saint-Cyr itself, I believed I was serving both God and France. But the King did not seem very concerned about succoring his subjects.

One day I asked him at least to increase his gifts to charity.

"No, Madame, I shall not," he answered. "If I did, I should only be taking the money away from my people. I myself should still have all that is necessary and pleasant, should I not? And I see no point in ruining the poor with new taxes and then coming to their aid with charity paid for by themselves. There is no virtue in charities made by me."

This was not a bad argument, except that he might have considered doing without what was superfluous, and this was exactly what he ruled out. As for me, reduced to my own resources and trying to help a growing number of unfortunates, I sometimes had to do without necessities. I told my steward not to buy me any more food and made do with the occasional pigeon or meat pie which the King sent me from his table. I lived on his leftovers to save money and refused to entertain other people to meals. My brother said my apartment was like the house of God: people prayed a lot there but did not eat or drink.

I became horribly miserly, but out of the ninety thousand francs a year I received from Maintenon and the King I managed to set aside between sixty and seventy thousand per annum for my charities. I founded a number of houses of charity to care for the sick, visited the poor at home, looked through their clothes and supplied them with what was lacking, brought them bread, meat, salt, blankets, linen and clothing for infants; to those who did not need any of these things I gave money. Sometimes I would go for a drive and come home without my cap, scarf or cloak because I had given them to some poor ladies.

I do not wish to dwell further on the subject. My good works were already done too much "to the sound of trumpets" for my taste; my only regret was that I had been unable to persuade the King that virtue can only be taught to well-filled stomachs. He had more important things to think about.

Whether the subject was education or charity, I soon got used to uttering general maxims which produced no practical results. It has been supposed that because the King worked in my room, I must have played an important part in affairs of state. But this was true only of the last ten years of the reign, and even then my influence was less than it was said to be. At the time I am now speaking of, when the King was at the height of his glory and power, he did not seek my advice. True, he concealed nothing from me, but he did not provide me with an overall picture, and I was often far from well informed. He did not like ladies to talk about public affairs, and did not admit zeal or affection as an excuse. He had reminded me of this often enough, and I took care not to interfere.

This was made easier by the fact that I partly agreed with him. God had placed him where he was. He had placed me only nearby.

If by any chance the King wanted me to take part in a discussion he was having with one of his ministers, I always began by pleading my incapacity and went on to point out that one does not start dabbling in politics at the age of forty and more. If the King insisted on my giving an opinion, I did so briefly and in the most general terms. I did not say whether three-quarters of Genoa ought to be burned down or only half; or whether we ought to fight for Cardinal de Furstemberg's candidacy to the electorship of Cologne or support a contender from Bavaria; whatever the problem, I advocated peace, moderation and justice, which would please God and ease the lot of the people.

The King appreciated the modesty of this attitude and the good sense of what I said. One day he said, jestingly:

"Kings are addressed as Your Majesty and Popes as Your Holiness. You ought to be called Your Soundness!"

And after that, whenever he wanted my opinion, he would smile and say, "And what does Your Soundness think?"

For all this demonstration of respect, however, he never changed his mind. His decision was usually taken before he consulted me, and the most he looked for from me was approbation.

So, it was that in the early years of our marriage my advice was never followed in any matter of importance.

I hated war both for religious reasons and because I am timorous by nature, and I sang the praises of peace a hundred times a year. Nevertheless, five years after we were married, the King blithely broke the truce of Ratisbon† and with the Palatinate affair plunged into a war in which he soon had all Europe against him. When I reminded him that he had given his word, he replied curtly:

"You know nothing about it, Madame. Treaties are like compliments—they mean much less than they seem to mean. Anyhow, it is time these princelings were punished for playing at being great monarchs!"

I often deplored the luxury and expense of the King's palaces. Every day I was aghast at how Marly, which was first intended to be quite small, was taking on the dimensions of another Versailles. I could not understand why everything was always being changed, so that no sooner was the plaster dry on some building than it would be torn down and the whole thing started again. I do not exaggerate. To take a comparatively minor example, in the antechamber to the King's bedroom at Versailles the chimney made a complete tour of the four walls, not by magic but because the plans were always being changed. First of all the fireplace was in the east wall; two years later it was in the south; next it moved to the west; and it ended up in the north. I think they would have tried the ceiling too if they could. It all ended in 1700 when the whole room was done away with and incorporated into what had been the King's bedroom to make a salon. The old Council Room then became the bedroom, and the new Council Room was fitted out next to that. And so on.

Thirty-six thousand workmen were employed on the reconstruction of Versailles and its environs. It made me furious to see so much money wasted when I could not help all the poor people

I met as I drove about the country. But if I ventured to speak out about it, I only gave offense. The expenditure kept on increasing. Against my advice the King even demolished the first Trianon and rebuilt it on a more grandiose scale.

"I do not think my buildings are displeasing to God, Madame," he said. "Hunting and architecture are the only innocent pleasures kings can enjoy."

He was standing looking out of the window in my room, in a fine plum-colored silk suit trimmed with gold. He looked pensive.

"You are right, I haven't been thinking enough about my salvation in this connection. I am going to do something which I think will please you. I'm going to demolish the chapel here—it is too small, and unworthy both of God's glory and of my own—and build a bigger one over there."

He pointed to the other side of the courtyard.

"A much bigger one. I shan't stint on the money, either. God will be pleased, and so will you."

I could have thrown up my arms in despair.

It was the same with the Church. I did not approve of the declaration the Assembly of the clergy had made in 1682 with the object of reducing the authority of the Pope.† In my opinion a Christian king is undermining the foundations of his own authority if he allows any lack of respect for the supreme pontiff; and all discussions on the matter only encourage a spirit of rebellion and sedition from which the monarch is bound to suffer eventually. I thought the Pope should be regarded not as the imperfect man he may sometimes be but as the successor of Saint Peter, which he is always. So I preached reconciliation while the ministers, the bishops and the Parlement dreamed of leading the King in the other direction.

"It's true that if I listened to them, I'd be wearing a turban," the King conceded one day, laughing. But he would not yield an inch, preferring to leave thirty-five dioceses without bishops, since the Pope would not confirm their appointments.

This affair soon placed me in a very awkward position. The Pope knew of my marriage and of my feelings about the Gallican dispute. He tried to win me over still further by sending me some relics of Saint Candida, which he had formerly intended for the Queen, and a couple of very complimentary letters. The moment then came to approach me through the papal nuncio. This would have been a fatal step for me. The King could just bring himself to bear me disagreeing with him in private, but he would never have allowed this to appear publicly. For me to interfere in some negotiation in order to go against him would have been tantamount to digging my own grave. I had to use all my tact to get out of the proposed interview without offending the Pope, whose support might be useful to me in my uncertain situation at Court as the King's unacknowledged wife.

The nuncio approached me at the entrance to the chapel at Versailles, beginning with a few platitudes about the need for a good understanding between the Pope and the King. I answered that with such a saintly pontiff and such an excellent prince as we had, it certainly was desirable they should agree. The Pope knew, said the nuncio, how much I was doing to increase the King's piety; he was sure I would dissuade him from doing anything harmful to the public welfare in the present dispute. I said I was very distressed that things had come to their present pass but could not speak of it because such things were beyond a woman's wit.

The nuncio replied that everyone knew of my great talent, and it could not be better employed than in making the King aware that his advisers in this matter were scoundrels. I answered meekly that I would gladly give my life's blood for there to be no conflict between His Holiness and the King, but I did not see how I could do anything about it. Then I left him standing and shut myself up at home with a beating heart, thinking of the danger I had been in.

That evening I told the King everything. I was afraid he would learn about it anyway through his police spies, and I preferred to speak first. He was kind enough to congratulate me on what I had said, and not to blame me for the fact that anyone had dared to approach me on so delicate a subject. I was so relieved and grateful that I never spoke to him again about being reconciled with Rome.

The truth of the matter was that I trembled before the too great husband Heaven had bestowed on me. His least frown terrified me, and the basilisk looks he sometimes gave me when I expressed an opinion he did not like annihilated me completely.

I did come out of my shell whenever I thought it absolutely necessary for the public good. I first prayed to God for strength, then said what I had to say timidly but with resolution. Thus the first time I heard the King congratulating himself on having found an easy way to pay his debts, namely not to pay the last quarter's dues to the Hôtel de Ville, I was so outraged that anyone should have made such a pernicious suggestion to him that I said with an icy smile:

"In that case, Sire, you will be forbidding your judges to punish highwaymen."

The King pursed his lips as he always did when I surprised him, looked at me in silence for a while and then said calmly:

"No doubt you know more about finance than I do, Madame, but you're not going the right way about convincing me of it." We were estranged for three days, then everything went back to normal.

I also had some trouble over the Protestants. For a long time I had been trying to make the King mistrust counsels to harshness and violence, and to shrink from acts of arbitrary authority. Hence I was delighted at the gentle method he had chosen to convert the Huguenots when he established a Conversion Fund which gave money to every new convert. He paid their taxes and gave them missals. This had a remarkable effect on people who had always been told the Catholic Church did not want its members to know what the priest was saying. He wrote every day asking the bishops to send missions to instruct the new converts, and in short was always showering favors on them. I was sure this must be pleasing to God, and I rejoiced at it.

Before long Monsieur de Louvois persuaded him to change his tactics, advising him to put all the Calvinists under the jurisdiction of his own ministry. I do not know whether he was thinking of the glory of God, but he certainly was thinking of his own. We had been at peace for eight years, a vexatious state of affairs for a war minister, and Monsieur de Louvois could feel power slipping through his fingers.

The King asked me what I thought of his minister's plan. I said

I was not capable of giving advice on a matter of such importance and that the ministry officials were no doubt prudent enough for him to be able to rely on their recommendations, but for my part I had always considered kindness the best and most suitable method. I was speaking according to my conscience and my heart, which always led me to mistrust Louvois's proposals.

But the King gave way to his minister's urgent request, and Louvois, having thus extorted his master's permission, went on to exceed his instructions and incite his soldiers to terrible acts of cruelty, which the King punished severely when he found out about them.

It must be admitted, however, that military methods succeeded better than all the others put together. Every day Monsieur de Louvois brought the King news of thousands of conversions. One morning it would be the town of Montauban, which was converted by its own decree at the mere sight of the soldiers. The same evening it would be Saintes or Nîmes or a hundred thousand Huguenots from the region of Bordeaux. The King, who was being deceived as to both the scope and the manner of these conversions, was very pleased, and I was pleased for him, though I had my doubts about all these splendid victories.

These doubts increased when I heard from my cousin Philippe de Villette, who still clung to his religion, that in some places terrible means were being employed to obtain conversions. I wrote to Philippe expressing my indignation, saying those who abjured under constraint were placed in a dreadful position, and that hatred for Protestantism was being carried too far. This letter was read by the King, since his Post made copies of my correspondence just as it did of everyone else's.

"Madame," he said one evening as I was having my supper, "it seems we are carrying hatred of heretics too far in your opinion. I am not sure you are not carrying sympathy for your old religion too far. If so, it will not do you any good with me."

I was transfixed with my spoon in mid-air. The King said no more, just left the room in a very imperious manner. Until next day I was afraid he might never return. From that day on I wrote my letters in cipher or had them conveyed to my friends by secret means and under false names. From that day on, too, I ceased to speak out against the persecution.

When a little while later the question arose of whether to revoke the Edict of Nantes, the King did not consult "My Soundness." In any case, I would not have risked saying anything. I often heard him and his ministers talking about it in my room, and I soon saw he regarded it as a political rather than a religious matter.

He needed the support of the Pope in his relations with the Emperor, but he was then even deeper in the pontiff's bad graces because he had just refused to fight against the Turks, who were in the process of invading Austria. In those days the Turks were our great friends and the King's most necessary allies in his struggle against the Emperor. It could not be called a very Christian alliance, and the rest of Europe, including the Pope, loudly decried it. The King did not want to purchase the Pope's support by making any concessions in the Gallican affair, which had reached the excommunication stage, and he could see no other way of showing goodwill and obtaining the Pope's help than by revoking the Edict of Nantes and withdrawing the right of the Protestants to follow their own religion.

He thought it a cheap way of pleasing Rome because, believing Monsieur de Louvois's figures, he thought there was only a handful of heretics left in France. In this he was much mistaken, for in the years that followed more than two hundred thousand Calvinists left, taking with them more than two hundred million francs in cash.

When the Declaration was signed, I did the same as everyone else. I dismissed any of my people who were Calvinists and would not be converted, and I urged my brother to buy some of their lands in Poitou which were going cheap. I let my Sainte-Hermine cousins be shut up in the Bastille and the Nouvelles Catholiques;† they were still remarkable for their zeal and clearly aspired to martyrdom. I doubted whether they would soon be restored to reason, though, for I had learned for myself that you cannot rule consciences by force and that harshness repels people rather than winning them over. So while I rejoiced at the conversions I heard of and very much hoped my own people would be converted too, I could not praise the Declaration.

Even to be silent was a feat, when everyone in France, except the Huguenots, was extolling the King's virtues, and to some my silence appeared all too eloquent. "Nothing can exceed the beauty of the Declaration," wrote Madame de Sévigné. "No king has ever done or ever will do anything more memorable. The dragoons have been very good missionaries so far." Chancellor Le Tellier, Monsieur de Louvois's father, just had time to affix his seal to the decree before he died. As he closed his eyes, he said, "Now, Lord, Thou mayest recall Thy servant, for he has seen the triumph of Thy glory." In that family they were courtiers to the last gasp.

Not so in mine. I had to implore Philippe on my bended knees to be converted; he was as stubborn as the Sainte-Hermines, and I did not want to see him, too, shut up in some fortress.

"Humble yourself before God," I said, "and ask for enlightenment. Let yourself be converted by Him at sea, where you will not be suspected of opportunism. Be converted however you like, but be converted somehow, I beg. I cannot bear you to go on in your present position—which shows I am fonder of you than I thought."

In the end he gave in and abjured a year after the Revocation. He then came to Court, and when the King congratulated him on his conversion he replied dryly, "Sire, it was the only time in my life I was not seeking to please Your Majesty." He made as good a Catholic as he had a Huguenot, he would have been outstanding in any religion.

Once this affair was over I took no more interest in the Protestants and resigned myself entirely to the King's wishes. I could see politics was not my strong suit.

While I more or less gave up hope of getting affairs of state to be governed by the evangelical principles so dear to me and kept my feelings to myself, I did with time acquire some influence in the choice of the people concerned. Admittedly this is an easier matter. It can be approached gradually: you chat, you make jokes, you seem to be talking of quite different things, then you just slip in in passing an anecdote about X and a detail about Y. By little touches applied over months and years you can build up a portrait in black or white of those you want to help or to destroy. Besides, if I was to hold on to my position, it was absolutely necessary for me to exercise some influence, even an indirect one, over official appointments. I had no backing at Court and no family to support me outside it, and I could have been at the mercy of the first plot directed against me. I had to create a circle of people who were under some obligation to me so that they in turn might oblige me.

Two men above all I had to be wary of, because of their influence over the King. These were Monsieur de Louvois and Père de La Chaise; naturally, I chose my clients from among their enemies.

I was more than prejudiced against Monsieur de Louvois, whom I had never liked even in the Vaugirard days. Everything about him repelled me: his heavy, all too substantial body; his coarse red face; his rough yet false manners; and the way he bullied the humble and truckled to the great. There was not a trace of humanity in him. He was insatiably greedy and boundlessly cruel. Everything was permissible that served his ends or saved his face, whether it was unjust extortions, exorbitant taxes, the violation of God's law and man's, sacrilege, looting, arson, torture or devastation.

The aversion I had felt for him from the very first moment was greatly increased by the part he played in Madame de Montespan's plot against me and his comments to the King upon our marriage. I was not taken in by his stooping low now to try to please me: he even pretended to be interested in my embroidery, advising me on the choice of silks; he showered me with compliments at every opportunity; he strewed flowers at my feet, only to conceal his snares.

I was determined to get the better of him before he got the better of me. I had to act quickly, for Monsieur Colbert's sudden death and the subsequent collapse of his protégés had in a few months brought Monsieur de Louvois's influence to its height. His family, friends and creatures were in charge of everything, the ministries dealing with War, Finance, the Protestants, the Police, the Post, and even the Ministry of Works, which the King had taken away from Colbert's son Monsieur de Blainville and given to Louvois himself. All the Colbert family had left was the Admiralty, under Monsieur de Seignelay, Colbert's other son, and Foreign Affairs, still under Colbert de Croissi, his uncle. It was said the King was going to take away these too and put them in the hands of Monsieur de Louvois.

To counterbalance the influence and growing power of this dangerous man, I set out to restore the fallen fortunes of the Colbert family.

I had a high opinion of Monsieur de Croissi and knew Monsieur de Seignelay well. His sisters were married to the duc de Chevreuse and the duc de Beauvilliers, and I took steps to become better acquainted with those two ladies. This was not difficult, for they were women of such wisdom, piety and integrity that we became firm friends.

That done, I carefully advanced my pawns, at every opportunity skilfully pointing out the mistakes of the one and the merits of of the others. Two or three times, without dwelling unduly on the matter, I pointed out to the King that the marquis de Louvois's decisive manner and definite though impromptu answers were no guarantee against error. The King was impressed by the examples I quoted. He paid more attention and saw that indeed the minister often gave haughty and peremptory utterance to facts which on closer examination turned out to be untrue. The King soon had practical experience of this trait.

One day when he was inspecting the new buildings at the Trianon, accompanied by Monsieur de Louvois in his capacity of Minister of Works, he noticed that one window was several twelfths of an inch shorter than the others. The King had such a natural sense of proportion that he rarely made a mistake. Monsieur de Louvois, not wishing it to be thought he had been negligent in overseeing the work, answered airily but with assurance that the windows were all exactly alike. He thought the King would be satisfied with this and rely on his word as usual, but my husband, alerted by me to the minister's insolence, did not leave it at that. He sent for Monsieur Le Nôtre, and without telling him why, asked him to measure the windows there and then. It turned out that the King had been right. He gazed at Monsieur de Louvois for some moments and calmly instructed him to have the work in question undone and started again. Doubts began to revolve in the King's mind, and I did my best to sustain them.

I took care to contrast Monsieur de Louvois's presumption and audacity with the obligingness of Monsieur de Seignelay, the moderation and skill of Monsieur de Croissi, the duc de Chevreuse's benevolence and the duc de Beauvilliers's modesty. The King got used to seeing the two duchesses in my room often, and from time to time I also invited Madame de Seignelay, who was young and pretty and striking. The King was not immune to her charms. To lose no opportunity of sending up her husband's stock, I got him to invite the King and all the Court to a magnificent entertainment at his beautiful country house at Sceaux. On 30 June 1685 Monsieur de Louvois had given a similar party for the King at Meudon, but he had grudged either trouble or expense, and the fête was very dull. Rain completed the disaster.

I persuaded the marquis de Seignelay to spare no expense to eclipse his rival, and on 16 July he entertained the King to the most splendid party he had ever attended. Everything that could contribute to please, divert or surprise the senses was there in abundance: rare meats, exquisite liquors, fruits exotic or out of season; music which included an opera specially written by Lully; wonderful illuminations in the gardens and grottoes and on the artificial waterways, along which floated a couple of ships. In short, everything ingenuity and expense could provide was there to create a magnificent and unusual occasion. The King appreciated this attempt to please him right down to the smallest detail.

Monsieur de Louvois went on to complete his own destruction. The gods blind those they wish to undo, and the minister continued to behave in his former manner without suspecting the King's increasing distrust. His presumption grew until the King found it intolerable. One day when they were with the army, Monsieur de Louvois altered the position of a cavalry guard which the King had stationed there himself.

"But, Captain," said the King to the officer concerned, "didn't you tell Monsieur de Louvois it was I who had placed you there?"

"Yes, Sire," said the captain.

"Well," said the King, bridling and turning toward his retinue, "Monsieur de Louvois seems to think himself a great general. Better than anyone else." He found it hard to forgive this new offense. The hurt rankled, and I took care to remind him of it every so often.

But Louvois went even further. It was his disastrous advice which had led the King into the Palatinate war while Colbert de Croissi and I had pleaded in vain in defense of peace and treaty obligations. And now he was carrying out such terrible persecutions that Europe soon resounded to the cries of the unfortunate Palatines. The King did not like unnecessary violence: he feared the hatred which would rebound on him, and other dangerous consequences which might ensue. I took care to depict the cruelty involved in the arson in the Palatinate, invoking moral scruples as vehemently as I could, inspired at once by Christian charity and detestation of the minister.

Monsieur de Louvois, not noticing the King's growing ill-humor toward him, suggested burning down the city of Trier by way of a sequel to the terrible devastation in the Palatinate. This time the King could not be persuaded and said quite plainly that Trier was to be left unharmed.

A few days later Louvois, still not doubting that his stubbornness would carry the day, came as usual to work with the King in my room. When they had finished, he calmly told the King he quite understood it was moral scruples which had stopped him agreeing to the burning down of Trier. So he had done him the kindness of taking the sin on himself, and without troubling the King further he had sent a courier with orders that Trier should be burned down on his arrival.

The King was instantly, and most uncharacteristically, so transported with fury that he snatched up the fire-irons and was about to fall upon Louvois when I threw myself between them, crying "Sire, Sire, what are you doing? You are the King!" and tearing the tongs from his grasp.

Louvois, meanwhile, had made for the door. The King

shouted to him to come back and said with blazing eyes, "Send a courier at once with counterorders, and make sure he gets there in time. You will answer for it with your head if a single house is burned down."

Louvois, more dead than alive, vanished. As we discovered later, this was not because he was in a hurry to dispatch the counterorder, for he had taken good care not to send off the first courier. He had given him the dispatches and kept him ready and waiting in his own antechamber, to be sent away if the King showed the least spark of anger. Now all he had to do was take back his dispatches and tell the courier he could take his boots off. After this strange contretemps he was an easy prey, and I could have destroyed him completely if I had wished.

I did not do so because, much as I esteemed them, I did not want to hand the country over into the undisputed charge of the Colberts alone. I thought my own peace of mind and the good of the state would best be served if the ministers were equally balanced, so that their influences cancelled one another out. Besides, Louvois, who was very hardworking, was of some use to the King. I was satisfied when he cooled toward his war minister, made Monsieur de Seignelay minister of state and Monsieur de Beauvilliers head of the finance council and paid more attention to the opinions of Monsieur de Croissi and the duc de Chevreuse. I was then in a position to manipulate them all like weights in a scale.

Things were not so easy with Père de La Chaise. True, he was less of a nuisance, but when the occasion arose, it made me furious to see his dullness, lack of charity and general mediocrity. He was a typical Jesuit courtier—smooth, agreeable, artful and very accommodating to all the King's sins so long as he served the Society's interests. The influence this priest had acquired over the King derived not so much from his position as confessor as from his expert knowledge of medals. The King was fond of curios of all kinds. He had them sent from all over Europe and put them on display in specially made cabinets. Père de La Chaise helped him with advice on medals and procured for him some rare specimens. His usefulness in this respect soon lent him unlimited influence in the Church.

It was not long before he got in my way. To further his own interests he supported the most corrupt prelates, among them his confederate the archbishop of Paris, the names of whose mistresses were public knowledge, thus preventing me from having the chief positions in the Church filled by saintly men who would have enlightened the Huguenots and helped to reform the country's morals.

I was never able to quarrel openly with Père de La Chaise nor even point out quite frankly to the King the weak points in his teaching. Needing support from somewhere to help me keep my position, I claimed it from the Church, which was grateful to me for having put an end to the King's love affairs.

I limited myself to promoting whenever possible worthy priests who in their secret hearts were not favorable to the Jesuits. For this reason I got on friendly terms with Monsieur Bossuet,† whom I admired for his eloquence, his ardent and lively mind and the regularity of his conduct. Similarly, I made some moves in the direction of the archbishop of Rheims, even though he was Monsieur de Louvois's brother. Later on I made friends with the friars of the Foreign Missions, who opposed the Jesuits on the question of Chinese rites. At Saint-Cyr, and everywhere else I could, I placed Lazarists and priests trained at Saint-Sulpice.† I liked the simplicity of their manners, and as they had had nothing and owed everything to me, they were very ready to be useful to me.

I had thought this discreet way of edging aside the gentlemen of the Society would not attract attention, but eventually Père de La Chaise became suspicious and mentioned it to the King.

"You will not please me much, Madame," the latter said to me one day, "by disliking the Jesuits."

I assured him I was as fond of them as of the rest, but he was not taken in, for soon afterwards he sent Père Bourdaloue to tell me how distressed the Jesuits were because I seemed not to like them. I merely said I was ready to meet them part of the way.

I went on quietly trying to undermine Père de La Chaise's influence, though I never managed to eliminate him altogether. We kept each other in check, and to be on the safe side I contented myself with that.

After seven or eight years of such stratagems I was weary to death of plots and conspiracies and the Court. It seems all pleasures fade with use, and politics among the first. Besides, I was getting old.

The courtiers assured me I had not changed, and indeed I may have given an impression of youthfulness because of the slimness of my figure, the brightness of my eyes and my natural vivacity, together with a certain quickness and gaiety of manner which was in contrast to the reserve and gravity within. But I certainly was not getting prettier. Any shrewd observer who had seen me otherwise than in the heat of action or the cut-and-thrust of conversation would easily have noticed, as I did myself in my mirror when I was alone, the wrinkles drawing down my mouth and circling my eyes, the fold under my chin which spoiled the oval of my face, and the dullness of my complexion. Every day at my toilet I appraised the progress of the damage, and I spent longer and longer repairing its effects.

The King's love for me did not grow less despite the years; nor was it solely spiritual, as a friend of mine from Saintonge noted one day with surprise.

One evening at Fontainebleau, at about six o'clock, I was told a Monsieur Saint-Legier de Boisrond would like to be admitted. I had known him well in my youth, for he was a relative of one of my mother's uncles, so as I still had half an hour to myself before the King came, I decided I could not spend the time better than with an old acquaintance. I had not set eyes on him for thirty years and suspected he had come only because he had heard I was in favor, and out of curiosity. I saw him nevertheless, to amuse myself a little.

He was as rustic as ever in appearance, and his manners were rough and familiar. He was rather wily and cheerful for a Huguenot. He treated me to an earthy jest as he entered.

"I see you haven't changed, Saint-Legier," I laughed. "And I haven't changed toward you."

He had brought a whiff of the stable in with him too.

I sniffed.

"And I see you carry immutability so far as to be unkempt as ever. Do you remember that time at Montalembert's when you fell on to the dungheap and then came down to supper with old Madame La Tremoille? She held her nose and said someone must be hiding a horse under the table!"

We laughed and enjoyed ourselves, exchanging some other stories about old times. I apologized and sat down at my dressing-table to have my hair dressed, explaining that the King would soon be coming. He sat beside me astride a stool and made no bones about examining me closely.

"Well?" I said.

"Well, dear lady," he replied, "I wonder at the fact that though you must be all of fifty you haven't a single grey hair!"

"What sort of manners are these! Since when do people mention a lady's age?"

I put on some light make-up, sprayed myself with toilet water, rubbed some almond cream into my hands and put a few sachets of marjoram among my skirts.

Saint-Legier watched with eyes like saucers.

"Now what is it?" I said.

"It's that up till now I thought, like everyone else, that the King was interested only in your mind . . ."

"And?"

"And! And! And I think, to judge by the care you're taking, there must be something more material involved!"

I looked straight at him, smiling, and just said quietly:

"Can you keep a man just through the mind?"

He was taken aback, and I took advantage of this to change the subject. Remembering he was a Huguenot and stubborn, I turned the occasion to account and gave him some good advice about changing his religion.

He went out as much a heretic as he came in, and I never saw him again. But that "something more material" lingered in my mind.

_____

Whether his reasons were material or spiritual, the King grew increasingly attached to me. His ways were often rough and always demanding, but at least I could see I was not losing him.

During the ten months he was suffering such pain from the fistula, he would not let me leave his side. Apart from Monsieur de Louvois and the doctors, I was the only one who knew of the long operation he underwent on 18 November 1686. I was the only person in the room with them when the ulcer was excised by means of two attempts with lancets and eight with scissors. I stood at the foot of the bed. The King held Monsieur de Louvois's hand and looked at me. Just once he cried out, "My God!," and the rest of the time he did not so much as sigh. After the operation he was confined to bed for three weeks, suffering atrociously all the time. I left him only to go and pray to God to preserve him for me, and I was sometimes at his bedside for eight or nine hours at a stretch without a moment's respite. The pain made him bite his lips, he was drenched in sweat, but he never complained and still received the Court every evening in his bedroom.

"Madame," he said one day when I protested at this, "the health of kings is a matter of politics. They must never give their subjects the chance of hoping for their death. I want you to know, however, that as a private individual I would like just as well to hide myself away with you and suffer in peace."

When he was ill, he did not treat himself any better than he treated me when I was ailing. One must do him the justice of admitting that he was no easier on himself than on those he loved.

When he got better, he did two or three little things which showed the world how high I stood. First he elevated the estate at Maintenon into a marquisate and gave it out that I was to be known henceforward as its marquise. He also decreed that in chapel I should hear mass in one of the little gilded boxes which only the Queen used to occupy, and My Soundness was foolish enough to be delighted with this new honor.

If the constancy of the King's friendship surprised me, I was even more amazed by his fidelity. It is true that a little while after our marriage he had something of an affair with Mademoiselle de

Laval, one of the Dauphine's maids of honor. I was told on all sides that he found the young lady attractive and obtained from her all the happiness to be hoped for from a pretty woman. I did not know quite what to believe and how far things had gone, but soon afterwards the King came and said it was necessary to marry off Mademoiselle de Laval as soon as possible, and he entrusted the task to me. I would as soon have been spared, but as an obedient wife I did as required. I learned that only six or seven months after the marriage the young woman gave birth to a daughter, whose "father," hearing of her arrival, exclaimed, "Welcome, Mademoiselle, but I did not expect you so soon." I do not know how much truth there was in the story. The King never spoke of Mademoiselle de Laval again, and neither did I.

In the case of Madame de Montespan the situation was much clearer. The King did not wish there to be anything equivocal about their relations now. As early as 1684 he had taken back the apartment she had occupied next to his on the first floor at Versailles and given her one on the ground floor. He was even so scrupulous as to have the staircase between this set of rooms and his own removed, and the passage which led to it blocked.

The lovely marquise could not resign herself to her new situation and was always trying to win back a heart she had never got over losing. She thought the best way to do this was to imitate me, and so she attended all the processions and meetings in aid of charity. No one was taken in.

She made up for her dissatisfactions with caustic witticisms and bitter jests. For instance, she never got used to no longer riding in the King's coach. One day when we had taken her to Marly but she had had to ride in the third coach, she came up to the King when she arrived, curtsied to him in the middle of the salon, took up the attitude of a suppliant and said so that everyone could hear, "Sire, I beg Your Majesty to be good enough in future to let me entertain the hangers-on in the second coach."

Another time, at a gathering in my apartment, where the wealthy Court ladies met once a month to give alms for the poor of Versailles, she noticed as she came in that the priest was waiting outside, together with some Franciscan nuns and a few sacristans. She greeted me with an icy smile and said, "Madame, your antechamber is all ready for your funeral oration!"

As I am partial to wit and had not been spoiled in that respect being shut up with Marguerite de Montchevreuil, Nanon, the King and the Dauphin, I was amused by her sallies and the first to repeat them to everyone I met. As a matter of fact I would have loved to have the marquise de Montespan as my companion. No doubt this was not a suitable position for her, but for a long time there had been no suitable position for her anywhere at Court; and yet she could not make up her mind to leave. She was like one of the lost souls who haunt their earthly homes for ever to expiate their sins.

She gave me much food for thought on the fragility of greatness. When it does not end in disgrace, it ends in death.

"Tell me, where now are the masters and scholars you knew when they were living and in the flower of their learning? Others have taken their place . . . They seemed to be something; now they are heard of no more."

"Are you reading the *Imitation of Christ*?" said the maréchal de Villeroy one day, putting the book back on my table. "It's very banal, and one has read it a hundred times. These old things are so tedious."

He picked up another book and laid it down again.

"And 'Saint' François de Sales's *Introduction to a Devout Life*! A fine piece of work, and a nice 'saint'! I used to know Sales well— he was a great friend of my father's. And I can tell you, Madame, that he cheated at cards and told dirty stories just like anyone else!"

"It's no use, Monsieur le Maréchal," I said, laughing. "I mean to be devout and you are not going to stop me."

"You mean to be?" he answered, stroking his fair moustache doubtfully. "But I thought you were already!"

Villeroy was one of those splendid and gallant courtiers who know of nothing but what is said and done at Court and have no other ambition but to set the fashion in speech, manners and dress.

Still, I was always glad to see him because he was very close to the King, having been brought up with him as a child. Also, though his forte was bric-à-brac rather than brains, he was not ill-natured, or lacking in courage and sincerity.

"Monsieur le Maréchal," I said, smiling, "you are just the man for presiding over a ball, judging a tournament or singing the part of the hero at the Opera, but I don't think you're the right person to give advice about religion. You must admit you don't understand anything about it, and if I were to explain what I feel, you wouldn't be any the wiser. But I will tell you this: in the past I always loved God but rarely served Him—or at least I did not serve Him alone, and He is a jealous master. Now I have it in mind to do better, but it is not easy to attain to true piety without a guide. And the man you regard as a false saint is not a bad director of conscience.

"As for my reading," I said, pointing to a big pile of books on my table, "as you see I go from *The Life of Bayard* to *The History of England,* and from *The Finances of King Louis XIII* to the *Songs* of Coulanges. The *Pensées* of Pascal† are my bedside reading. In none of them do I find so many original thoughts as in the *Imitation* you find so wearisome. Every word of it moves me more than all the tragedies of Racine. I believe I shall end up by reading nothing else . . ."

Whether through distaste for Court intrigue, boredom from having too much time on my hands or lack of company, I was turning more and more to God. Perhaps I should never have thought of Him if I had not been disappointed by man—if I had not been surrounded by murder, rage, treachery and baseness, a mankind as full of corruption as the sea is full of water. Perhaps there was also an impure element in it all. When I think it over, I notice that all my advances in devotion have been in proportion to improvements in my fortune, and every increase in favor was followed by some progress in piety.

Was I really preparing for the future? Having achieved the highest of human ambitions, was my insatiable pride looking forward, as my brother suggested, to marrying God after having married the King?

All that is certain is that at Versailles, between my four walls of red damask; at Fontainebleau, amid the gold and white panelling of my little room; and in my dark chamber at Marly, hung with green brocade—wherever I was, I felt more and more strongly the sweet yet demanding presence of the living God. And I knew that to answer that call something more, and better, was needed than to give a few alms, endow some masses, found a school and try to save the King's soul. I must love God so much that I would renounce the love of myself, die to all self-interest and all friendship and surrender my soul entirely to Him.

But there was no one to help me. My spiritual director, whom admittedly I had often discouraged and snubbed in the past, had been turning into an out-and-out courtier since he learned of my marriage. I wrote him a long letter to recall him to his duties.

"I beg you to lay aside the style you have adopted with me, which does not please me and may do me harm. I am no more a great lady now than I was in the rue des Tournelles, where you used to tell me a few home truths quite plainly when necessary. If my present position makes everyone else fling themselves at my feet, it should not have that effect on the man who is in charge of my conscience, and whom I earnestly request to lead me irrespective of every other consideration along the path he thinks most conducive to my salvation. Where shall I find the truth if not in you, and to whom but you can I submit myself, since everyone else approaches me with respect, complaisance and adulation? Speak to me, write to me directly, without ceremony or circumspection, and above all, I beg, without respect. Look upon me as if I were divested of all that surrounds me, as someone desiring to give herself to God."

On receiving my letter, poor Gobelin, instead of giving me the help I asked for, began to tremble worse than before and sent me three pages of timid and confused respect, adding a request for help in some lawsuit. It seemed to me that at his age and as an ecclesiastic he would do better to be thinking of the Last Judgment, but I reassured him.

"As for your lawsuit," I said lightly, "trust to God, to the King or to me. The least of us three will suffice."

Then I left him to shut himself up for good and grow old in peace in the house in Saint-Cyr where I had installed him. That was how matters stood when one day, at the duchesse de Beauvilliers's, I met the abbé de Fénelon.†

For some months I had been going to dine with the duchesse or with her sister Madame de Chevreuse. The King did not object, because he knew from his own experience they were sensible, modest and not given to intrigue. I myself was more and more delighted with the wonderful understanding which existed between the two sisters, and with the still more extraordinary one between the two brothers-in-law. These four people were so united by lifelong habit and by a sober and noble faith that they shared one heart, one soul, one emotion.

As we often spoke of religion together, they began to invite some interesting prelates there to meet me. And that was how I met Monsieur de Fénelon, superior of the Nouvelles Catholiques in the faubourg Saint-Antoine.

He was tall, thin and pale, with eyes that blazed with spiritual fire and a countenance that was unforgettable. There was everything there, but in it the contrasts did not conflict, and gravity and gallantry, seriousness and gaiety coexisted quite naturally. It was the face at once of a scholar, a bishop and an aristocrat, but what shone out of it above all was subtlety, grace, wit and delicacy. It was difficult to take one's eyes off him.

I fell under his spell like everyone else. He had just published a little treatise on *The Education of Girls* and was very interested in what I was trying to do at Saint-Cyr. We spent hours debating, with equal pleasure on both sides, what girls should be taught, how to mix instruction with play, how to bring up infants and a thousand other things I would never have thought a man capable of discussing.

Then he spoke to me of God, and I was surprised to find his was like mine, a God of love and freedom, very different from the harsh God of the Huguenots and Jansenists, into whose hands we were told it was terrible to fall. I liked to think it must be wonderful to find oneself in God's hands, and to entrust oneself to Him like a child, and Monsieur de Fénelon did not correct me. In short, we agreed about everything.

Not long afterwards Monsieur de Fénelon, whom I had seen again every week at my friends' and who knew I was more or less without a director now, sent me at my request a letter clearly setting out the faults which in his opinion were preventing me from giving myself entirely to God. As it was the best description of myself I had ever seen, and all he said about my imperfections was absolutely correct, I copied the letter into one of my secret books and have always kept it by me. I cannot resist quoting it to you now, even though there is always a touch of vanity in speaking or causing others to speak about oneself.

"You were born with much of the kind of pride that is called proper, but which is all the more improper because we are not ashamed to refer to it thus. It is easier to correct obviously foolish vanity. Without realizing it, you still cling to this 'proper' pride: you value the esteem of respectable people and the approbation of good people, and you enjoy being moderate in your prosperity and seeming to be at heart above your position. The self of whom I have spoken to you so often is an idol you have not destroyed. You want to go to God with all your heart, but not through the loss of self. On the contrary, you seek for self in God. You are helped by a liking for prayer and the presence of God, but if you ever lost this taste, your liking for yourself and for the manifestations of your own virtue would place you in a dangerous situation . . . You must sacrifice self to God, and seek it no more, neither for the sake of reputation nor for the sake of the consolation one can get from contemplating one's own virtues . . .

"Again, it seems to me you have too much natural inclination for friendship, kindness and everything that holds society together. These are the best of qualities according to reason and human virtue; but they must be renounced for that very reason. All natural affections are refinements of self-love—more seductive, more flattering, more amiable and therefore more diabolical. If you no longer cared about yourself, you would no more want your friends to be fond of you than you would want them to be fond of the

Emperor of China. In a word, Madame, in God's eyes, to seek after friendship is as great a fault as to be lacking in it. Real love of God entails a magnanimous love of one's neighbor without any hope of return. One must be ready to be scorned, hated, decried and condemned by others, and to be condemned and troubled by oneself. This is a hard lesson for anyone who wants to enjoy his virtue for his own sake, but it is a sweet and consoling one for anyone who loves God enough to renounce his own self."

In all the twenty years that he was my director, the abbé Gobelin had never written me so penetrating and inspiring a letter as this man had sent me after six months' acquaintance. Nevertheless, I could not think of making Monsieur de Fénelon my director. I had no wish to cast off Gobelin: though he had not always been the guide I might have wished for, he had been a faithful friend in difficult times. Moreover, the prophetic authority Monsieur de Fénelon had acquired over all those about him had made him accustomed to exercise a domination which for all its mildness would brook no resistance. And I, not being by nature apt to be docile and admiring toward my pastors, was afraid that in practice the similarity of our two characters might produce a clash. So I just went on meeting him at the Chevreuses' and the Beauvilliers' and had him appointed tutor to the duc de Bourgogne, the eldest of the King's grandsons, when Monsieur de Beauvilliers, at my instance, was made his governor.

Time went by; one day was like another. I was getting to the age when everything begins to fade: gardens less luxuriant, flowers less vivid, colors less bright, meadows less verdant, water less clear. The landscape around me was changing. In 1691 it seemed to suffer an earthquake as all those I had known in my youth suddenly disappeared as if they had been swallowed up.

All at once the shadow of death lay over everything.

Monsieur de Villarceaux was the first to die. I had not seen him for fifteen years, though I had had him awarded the blue ribbon of the Order of the Holy Spirit. I did not mourn his death —he had already been dead to me for too long—but I did mourn my youth. I found I felt some emotion at the memory of the little yellow house in the rue des Trois-Pavillons, the country pleasures of the Vexin, the fair at Bezons and the lovely smooth face that I had over my dark muslin gowns and that he was carrying with him to the grave.

The abbé Gobelin was next, and with him another part of my past life crumbled away: the rue des Tournelles, Vaugirard and the scruples and agitations of my early life at Court.

Madame de Montespan left Versailles. The King had entrusted the education of her youngest daughter, Mademoiselle de Blois, to Madame de Montchevreuil, and she had protested loudly that her children were being taken away from her. The King let her know that he was tired of the scandals she created and needed her apartment for the duc du Maine. She went to live with her sister the abbesse de Fontevrault.

Then Monsieur de Louvois went. He had a horrible death, for it was sudden and he did not have time to confess his sins. He had been expecting to fall from favor for some time, and this tormented him greatly. One day he came and worked in my room, took leave very affably in the evening and went out into the gallery in good health, but as soon as he reached his own apartment, he collapsed on to a chair and died almost at once, without time to summon a priest or say farewell to his children.

He was soon followed into the grave by Seignelay, his rival and my protégé, who died the same year at the age of thirty-nine, just as he was about to attain power and greatness at last. So I had wasted my time as well as lost the semblance of friendship I flattered myself he felt for me. Vanity of vanities.

At about this time, too, the Dauphine died. She had never recovered from the birth of her third son. She was not yet thirty and had never seemed really alive, but with her passing there was no woman left in the King's family who was capable of holding Court or presiding over Court ceremonies. This did not add to our gaiety.

Everyone was growing old. Those who had been the King's early companions and created the brilliant and joyous Court of the beginning of his reign now began to shut themselves up at home, crippled with gout and rheumatism. If they still danced at all, it was with a limp.

The King no longer went to the wars. He captured Mons in 1691 and Namur in the following year, but as the years went by, the battles became less decisive and more deadly. France was being exhausted by the war into which Monsieur de Louvois had thrust us. The long-drawn-out campaigns and doubtful victories astonished Europe, so used to seeing the King of France cut swift and brilliant swathes through vanquished enemies. The varnish of the reign was flaking off.

Sometimes in the evening, when it had been closed to the public, I went into the Picture Room, which came just before the Curio Room and was almost opposite my apartment on the other side of the Cour de Marbre. I used to shut myself in there at nightfall and contemplate by the light of a candle Poussin's *The Ecstasy of Saint Paul,* which had hung for so long in Monsieur Scarron's room.

By a series of strange accidents of fate, the painting and I had followed the same path from the rue Neuve-Saint-Louis to the château of the King, by way of the hôtel de Richelieu. I had known it for forty years, and we had never lost sight of each other for more than very brief intervals. There was no human being about me of whom I could say as much, and I suspected I might some day be reduced to seeking friendship from that splash of color on canvas which at least had the appearance of an old acquaintance.

I used to wonder sadly what the future held for us both and how far our fates would continue alike. Of course I knew the answer. The picture was immortal.

Fifteen

The abbé de Fénelon prevented me from being engulfed in this melancholy.

I already had the help of pious friends in the little circle formed by the duchesses de Chevreuse and de Beauvilliers, together with their sister the duchesse de Mortemart and the duchesse de Béthune-Charost. To the pleasures of this little society Monsieur de Fénelon added the charm of regular teaching, and he soon convinced me that I might be absorbed into the immensity of divine love provided I yielded to God's call and accepted His choice of me.

Whenever I visited one of the private mansions which all these duchesses had in Versailles, I would find the new tutor to the King's grandsons. Our "little convent at Court," as we called it among ourselves, used to dine *à la clochette*: instead of having a servant standing behind each guest, we just rang a bell if anything was needed, and in that way we were able to converse freely.

My relationship with Monsieur de Fénelon was not that between a spiritual director and his charge. I already had a director in the person of Monsieur Godet-Desmarais, bishop of Chartres, whom I had chosen as successor to poor Gobelin. No, Monsieur de

Fénelon and I were rather in the position of two friends seeking salvation together and helping each other with advice and the fruit of their experience.

He maintained that it was eminently reasonable for us to sacrifice our reason to God, explaining with great eloquence that the kingdom of God is within us and we can attain it even in this life if we will become as little children, divesting ourselves of our wisdom and so forgetting ourselves that we are no longer conscious of the world around us.

I liked this way of talking and was attracted by these promises. I have always been more romantic than my rather serious manner suggests. I had never indulged, in my social life, in the sort of girlish naivety such leanings often involve; I had too much judgment not to know what men are like. In my religion, however, where I could rely on the infinite goodness of God, I thought I might safely abandon myself to folly and love. I devoted myself entirely to contemplation and resolved to change the robe of Martha for that of Mary.

A newcomer to our "convent" soon set me a practical example. This was a lady called Jeanne Guyon du Chesnoy, a wealthy widow from the provinces. My friends had interested me in her case in 1689, when she was imprisoned for over a year in Paris on the orders of archbishop Harlay de Champvallon, who accused her of heresy for some views she had put forward in public. The duchesse de Béthune, who had been a friend of Madame Guyon's late husband, told me that the archbishop, a man notorious for immorality and uncharitableness, was really after the Guyon fortune: by imprisoning Madame Guyon he hoped to force her to allow her daughter to marry his nephew. Moreover, Marie-Françoise de La Maisonfort, a girl I had admitted to the Institute at Saint-Cyr from its foundation, told me she was a close relation of Madame Guyon, whom she described as endowed with all the virtues, together with a great gift for communicating them to others. Her imprisonment, she said, was a dreadful injustice.

On the basis of all these representations I had Madame Guyon set at liberty, thus greatly scandalizing the archbishop of Paris. But I was not sorry to administer a rap on the knuckles to a man I did not respect and who was hand-in-glove with Père de La Chaise.

On her release Madame Guyon naturally enough came to Saint-Cyr to thank me. My visitor was a middle-aged woman of masculine physique, cross-eyed, with a pockmarked face. She spoke in a saintly manner of her imprisonment and seemed to me as ardently devoted to God as both her friends and her words had led me to expect. Several times, at my invitation, she came to Saint-Cyr; I even had her eat at my own table. Perhaps I found her bare arms and bosom unedifying in one who made such great professions of piety, but I reflected that with her appearance she was not likely to arouse lust, and I set her improprieties down to ignorance of the ways of our society. I was reassured on this score when a few months later she married her daughter to the comte de Vaux, Madame de Béthune's brother. I do not know whether it was the duchesse de Béthune, the duchesse de Beauvilliers or myself who first thought of including her in our dinner parties. She was soon coming regularly, and all the others liked her.

She called the love of God "Pure Love," and preached the abandonment of all self-interest, of will and even of thought. In God's hand we should be "a rag in the jaws of a dog." By continuous silent prayer she herself attained states of ecstasy in which she transmitted grace to all around her. Her doctrine was the same as that of Monsieur de Fénelon, but her practice went far beyond his. As soon as he met her, he was won over. Their spirits were pleasing to one another, their exaltations merged, they belonged to God together.

As for me, still immured in my coldness, barricaded by prudence and fettered with reason, I envied them but could not share all their bliss.

Madame Guyon told me to stop worrying so much about my faults and imperfections and give up tormenting myself about my salvation. To help me become a "fool of God" like herself she gave me a little book she had just published entitled *A Short and Easy Method for Prayer*. It began with an apostrophe which seemed to apply particularly to me: "Come to these living waters, all you who are thirsty; come, all you hungry hearts who find nothing to satisfy them, and you shall be filled." I did not read this, I drank it like a glass of clear water. From then on I carried the book about with me always, in the pocket of my skirt.

Madame Guyon afterwards gave me her *Explanation of the Song of Songs,* and then a long manuscript, as yet unpublished, called *The Torrents.* As I read all these writings I felt exalted longings which moved me to the bottom of my heart. One after the other my friends the duchesses experienced the ecstasy of the "new prayer," and found perfect spiritual peace in the practice advocated by Madame Guyon. The *Short Method* was soon part of the library of every pious lady and began to be made known at Court. One evening I tried to read some of it to the King. He listened for a few moments in silence, then shrugged his shoulders, looked at me pityingly and said, "Daydreams, Madame, daydreams!" I was neither surprised nor troubled, for I did not think him far enough advanced in spiritual exercises to understand the little book fully. My husband had only the husk of devotion.

Our little secret society, the "duchesses' cabal," the "convent," the "little flock" as we called it, was soon renamed the Sodality of Pure Love. We wrote to each other in cipher, adopted mysterious pseudonyms and indulged in other childish tricks. Monsieur de Fénelon and Madame Guyon encouraged us, saying one must die to ridicule as to everything else, and fear only the wisdom of the wise.

Although I was not very practiced in the "prayer of quietude," I was sure this was the only way I wanted to love God. I was thirsty for freedom and passion in religion, hungry for unreason and the absolute; I was tired of the Jansenist austerity which then prevailed, and I did not believe a person could come to God through excessive scruples and endless computation of his own good and bad actions. I wanted to be able to breathe in God.

I also found real pleasure in the company of my little "sodality," whose conversation had a warmth and artlessness I had almost forgotten in my long commerce with the Court and the King. For his part, Monsieur de Fénelon joined innocence and childlike simplicity to such extensive reading and ranging thought that every day I found his friendship more delightful. He wrote me very long letters, which I carefully copied out into my little secret books.

They were not really letters of spiritual guidance, but messages of pure and guileless friendship. Nevertheless, I did not mention them to Monsieur de Chartres, my director, for I feared he might take umbrage at a friendship which gave him a rival. I was old enough to know that some lady penitents constitute a useful capital for their directors.

Both my acknowledged and my hidden director agreed I ought to reform Saint-Cyr without more ado.

I must admit that during the early years of the Institute of Saint-Louis I had unwittingly passed on much of my own pride to the ladies and girls there. The whole place was so steeped in my vanities that my good intentions were stifled.

I had wanted my little girls to be witty, and they had adopted a mocking attitude to everything that was insufferable. I had wanted them to be spoiled a little and spared menial tasks, and they treated the lay sisters and even the mistresses like servants. In short, they had been shown such fondness and consideration that they had fallen into a haughty address, an over-refinement of manners and a smugness which would have been difficult to endure in the most illustrious princesses.

Madame de Brinon's policy as headmistress had only added to all this. She was virtue personified, but she was also a woman of the world. She wrote verses, corresponded with the philosopher Leibnitz and received members of the Court every day in an apartment hung with rare tapestries and full of unusual flowers. I sometimes wished she knew less of the world and more of the duties of her position. Furthermore, with her great lady's fastidiousness and her love of luxury, she could not keep the school's expenses within the agreed bounds, and the contingency account always contained several unauthorized items. All this gave rise to a conflict of authority: the teachers, trying to please both of us, were placed in such a difficult position that its effects were bound to be noticeable. And so, after many irritations and useless remonstrances, I resolved to dismiss Madame de Brinon.

Even this sacrifice was not enough to restore the school to

complete simplicity. The love of the theater which I out of foolish vanity had transmitted to the pupils completely turned their already giddy heads. The crowds of distinguished people who came to see *Esther,* and their thunderous applause, gave the girls such a ridiculously high opinion of themselves that they did not want to sing in church any more for fear of spoiling their voices.

Having been so poor myself as a girl, I had not wanted them to be stinted of ribbon and powder and pearls. But the result of this weakness combined with the play-acting to produce such a riot of rouge and frippery that the prescribed uniform and the modesty of well-bred young ladies were scarcely to be seen. Then came a few flirtations: notes were slipped to our young actresses, young pages from the château found their way inside the walls of the school . . .

The Jansenists said it was shameful that I should expose to the avid gaze of a Court audience these young girls come from all over France to receive a Christian education. Hébert, the curé of Versailles, publicly disowned me. My old friend Madame de La Fayette disapproved of me. Monsieur Bossuet himself objected to the performances and told the King. A universal plot was hatched by the bigots against the school. "Girls," they said, "are meant to live a retired life, and it is a virtue in them to be shy. Women can only ever half-know anything, and what little they do know makes them proud, scornful and talkative."

There was some justice in these criticisms, but I still thought I could remedy the excesses at Saint-Cyr without belying the educational principles I had laid down for it.

My first attempt at reform consisted in cutting down on ribbons and new clothes, abolishing the reading of certain worldly minded books and discouraging idle conversation, but this was not enough. I went on to impose more manual work and religious instruction; it was all of no use.

Saint-Cyr was slipping out of my control, and heading for shipwreck as surely as a ship without a pilot. An incident occurred which showed me that the trouble was more deep-seated than I had thought and could not be eradicated without changing the very form and rules of the Institute. Three of the Blues, annoyed because their teacher interfered with a secret correspondence they kept up between them, decided to poison her, and put hemlock in her soup and salad on two consecutive days. Fortunately the teacher did not eat much of what had been tampered with, and there were no fatal consequences. The use of the whip was brought back to punish this criminal act, however, and the culprits were expelled. I was very shocked by the episode. I said nothing about it outside the school, but could not keep it from my director, Monsieur Godet-Desmarais, who as bishop of Chartres was the Institute's diocesan superior.

"Your pupils have taken leave of their senses, Madame," he said. "You wanted to avoid the pettiness of convents, and God is punishing you for your pride."

He sat facing me in my little room at Trianon, wearing purple vestments trimmed with gold fringes and tassels. In his gloved hands he held the rolled-up manuscript containing the constitution of the House of Saint-Louis, as the Institute was called, and as he spoke he tapped the document against his knee.

"The trouble derives from the fact that you thought you could entrust the children's education to secular teachers. My dear daughter, one cannot give souls, especially such youthful souls, into the charge of lay instructors."

Through the open window behind him I could see the King's Garden, where my pretty niece Madame de Caylus was deep in amorous conversation with Monsieur d'Alincourt, the maréchal de Villeroy's son. Both the young people were married, yet they had reached the kissing stage. Esther had changed her role and become Mary Magdalen before her conversion.

"Permit me to say, Madame, as your director, that you have too great a liking for novelty. You must return to more ordinary principles and turn Saint-Cyr into a proper convent. You are pious yourself, and without meaning to, you have shown that education must be religious. The constitution of the Institute must be changed, and the mistresses must take religious vows."

"The King will be very upset, Monsieur."

The gold tassels were flourished.

"He would be even more so, Madame, if he found out what

has been going on in the school for which he has so much respect . . ."

"Please, Monsieur! He must never know . . ."

In the next room my other niece, Françoise d'Aubigné, was playing the harpsichord, or rather hammering at it, for she had no gift for music and her clangorous chords nearly drowned out our voices.

"No school in the world, Madame, calls for such humility as your school does," Monsieur de Chartres went on, warming to his subject. "Its situation so near the Court, its size, its wealth, its atmosphere of privilege and favor, its enjoyment of a great King's partiality and the help of an eminent lady—all these are dangerous snares and should move you to take quite different measures from those you have chosen so far. Let us thank God that He has at last opened your eyes!"

"Monseigneur," I said, "please do me the favor of giving me a little more time for consultation, and to prepare the King."

A glissando on the harpsichord put an end to the conversation.

As he left, the bishop of Chartres, not noticing a little china doll Françoise had left on the carpet, stepped on it and broke it.

As I had promised my director, I consulted my friends. Monsieur de Fénelon and all the members of the "little flock" agreed with the bishop. They thought I had given Saint-Cyr to the world, whereas it ought to be given to God.

"We all try hard to rediscover the true spirit of childhood," said the duc de Beauvilliers, "and at Saint-Cyr you have three hundred children who have that spirit naturally. And you would like to lead them out of that childlike simplicity! Give them back their innocence, Madame. Take away that hankering after wit instilled in them by teachers lacking in piety. Let them be foolish and ignorant in the eyes of the world, but perfect in the eyes of God. Your girls don't need to learn to be scholars or heroines; they need to learn to pray. Take Monsieur Desmarais's advice and turn Saint-Cyr into a convent."

On 30 September 1692 Saint-Cyr became a regular convent of the order of St. Augustine. The teachers, the ladies of Saint-Louis, wept. Some of them, who were interested in education but had no religious vocation, asked to be allowed to leave. Others began their novitiate; until they had taken their vows, they were replaced by nuns of the Order of the Visitation from Chaillot.

I prayed. I saw no one now except the King and my Pure Love friends. I devoted four hours every day to prayer and listened passionately to Madame Guyon in her ever more frequent visits to Saint-Cyr. She would sit at my feet in the room of her cousin, Mademoiselle de La Maisonfort, and preach a religion which filled me with happiness.

"When I pray," she said, "I can no longer either will or speak. My soul is like a drop of water lost and swallowed up in the sea. Pain and pleasure no longer exist. There is only a perfect peace, a void in which I am sometimes surprised to find assurance."

I had taken Mademoiselle de La Maisonfort to Court as my secretary. She was a passionate young woman with a lofty spirit and an intelligence equal to the finest of her sex, and I was very fond of her. Monsieur de Fénelon, her spiritual director, had just persuaded her to take vows, and I saw in her one of those distinguished souls who would one day lead a reformed House of Saint-Louis to a fulfilment pleasing to God. In the evening she and I used to read the *Short Method* and Monsieur de Fénelon's letters.

"There is no more winter for a soul that has come to God," Madame Guyon said. I myself could not yet see this spring, but I hoped for it. Sometimes I thought that life at Court and preoccupation with affairs of state were all that prevented me from attaining the plenitude I aspired to. I told my friends, perhaps quite sincerely, that I was going to abandon everything and go to America to devote myself entirely to God. Monsieur de Fénelon adjured me to do nothing of the kind. "God has placed you beside the King to be his guide," he said. "He wants you to be at Court and in the King's councils."

Poor Mary, sitting at the Lord's feet and waiting to hear His words, and before she has a chance to listen she is sent for to wash the dishes. The ducs and the abbé pointed out the great need for better housekeeping in the kingdom. The financial situation was deteriorating all the time. The national debt had doubled since Monsieur Colbert's death, and France spent two hundred million francs as against eighty millions in revenue. The poverty of the people was extreme, and spreading throughout the country like an epidemic. "France is like a devastated hospital without any supplies," Monsieur de Fénelon observed in private. Monsieur de Basville, my old friend from the Marais, whom I had helped to become a provincial administrator, sent the King ever more desperate reports about the Dauphiné, Provence, Languedoc, the Lyonnais and the Bourbonnais. The misery of the peasants, ruined by war and taxes, brought tears to Basville's eyes, and he saw no cure for it but the making of peace and the reform of the taxation system. The current method of farming out taxes was fraught with disaster, he wrote in a letter to the duc de Beauvilliers.

Meanwhile at Versailles we lacked for nothing. The only sign that the Treasury's coffers were low was the melting down of the magnificent silver furniture from the King's châteaux. In an access of austerity which struck the King himself as positively evangelical, we made do with wood instead and carried humility so far as to sit on chairs of walnut and write on tables of oak. The cabinet-makers soon found a way of embellishing this plainness, and after two or three years the furniture was so covered in tortoiseshell, mother-of-pearl, bronze and gold that no one could remember what it was really made of. At Court everything is disguised, even the wood.

Since the deaths of Monsieur de Louvois and Monsieur de Seignelay, the King had not appointed any men of importance as ministers. He had been too "relieved," as he said, by the decease of the other two. Since he was of the opinion that only he himself was necessary to the state, he was satisfied henceforward with a few very young ministers—not so much ministers, in fact, as beardless clerks, timid and without experience. Barbezieux, the new secretary of state for War and Monsieur de Louvois's own son, was scarcely more than twenty. "The King of France does everything the opposite of everyone else," said the Dutch pamphleteers. "He likes young ministers and old mistresses."

Monsieur de Pontchartrain, the new controller-general of Finance, who like Monsieur de Beauvilliers was a minister of state, was the only one of the group with any authority, but my friends thought his influence harmful to the country. The duc de Beauvilliers, whose position enabled him to judge, looked upon him as a "master of expediency."

"He changes nothing, Madame, though the whole machine is falling to pieces. He encourages the King in his love of expense, and invents some new Machiavellian trick every day to provide for it: today it's a lottery, tomorrow a delay in the paying off of arrears, the next day the creation of a new post as useless to the public good as it is costly to private individuals. And he is proud of it, Madame. He tells the King, 'Every time Your Majesty creates a post, God creates a fool to buy it.' You are too intelligent, Madame, not to know a country cannot be governed through 'amazing bargains' of this kind. In the end the supply will dry up or the people will get tired of it all." And indeed I and my Pure Love friends were astounded at the appearance one after the other of a right of control over wigs, a post of seller of oysters in their shells, and another office which gave its holder the right to hawk funerals. But I shrank from interfering openly.

"But you must," Monsieur de Beauvilliers kept telling me. "You are the only person who can tell the King certain truths. Remember he never makes up his mind on impulse, and his opinions can be modified by suggestion."

And so I ventured, under pressure, to say a word about the need for peace. I received but one short answer: "These are delicate matters." I tried, again under pressure, to raise the subject of the Huguenots and the desirability of treating them less harshly. The King merely said it would be difficult, and this was all the conversation we had that day. I made no further effort.

Meanwhile, memoranda were piling up on my desk at Saint-Cyr. Some were from Monsieur de Chamillart, a very honest man whom I employed to help with the finances of the House of Saint-Louis, and who showed me letters detailing the contrivances of Monsieur de Pontchartrain. Some memoranda were by the ducs de Chevreuse and de Beauvilliers, commenting on the forthcoming treaty with Savoy or on Sweden's mediation in the war. Lastly there were innumerable dissertations on every subject from Monsieur de Fénelon, enough to fill volumes. He set his arguments out in the form of question and answer, overcoming his own objections, stirring the whole brew up together, getting excited and mixing up cause and effect so thoroughly that I could not understand a word. His theology struck me as crystal clear compared with his politics.

At his request I passed one of these booklets on to the King, though without saying who had written it. The King read three pages and calmly tore the whole thing up. "Flights of fancy," he said disdainfully. After this I was even less keen to give him a letter which Monsieur de Fénelon had written him but which he wisely preferred to convey, anonymously, through me. It was meant as a warning, but it was more like a broadside.

"Your people are dying of hunger. Agriculture is almost abandoned; town and country are becoming depopulated . . . Trade has been destroyed . . . The people are beginning to lose goodwill, confidence and respect . . . They are full of bitterness and despair. Revolt is gradually kindling everywhere . . . While the people have no bread, you have no money yet will not see the extremity to which you are reduced. You must sue for peace, and through this humiliation expiate the glory you have made your idol . . . To save the country you must give back without delay conquests which you cannot keep without injustice."

The bearer of such a message would have been struck down on the spot. It was really too kind of Monsieur de Fénelon to entrust me with this sacrificial mission while he remained hidden. I kept his letter to myself, like most of his memoranda.

I was less skilful in concealing a very well-argued one by Monsieur Racine. In between some Christian verses, he had included something on the subject of national reform and the sufferings of the people, in the same style as the suggestions of Monsieur Vauban.† Ever since the King had been less than wholly victorious abroad, everyone at home had developed a mania for overhauling the machinery of state from top to bottom. Priests, military engineers, even poets joined in.

As I was reading the memorandum one evening in my room

at Marly, the King entered. I was not expecting him. I tried to hide the document, but he got hold of it, read a few lines and demanded to know the name of the author. I resisted as best I could. He grew angry.

"I see too many examples of this kind of composition about you these days, Madame. I am surprised people take the liberty to send them to you, and that you think it permissible to receive them. I have even been told you ask for them . . . In fact, I don't know what it is but for the last few months I have sensed in you a sort of opposition, something of the malcontent, the rebel. You are always trying to talk to me about affairs of state, and you make suggestions which are more like remonstrances. I don't like it."

"Sire, you cannot imagine . . ."

"I imagine nothing. So let us have done quickly with the present matter. Remember you owe me obedience both as your husband and as your King, and tell me the name of the great wit who wrote the masterpiece you find so interesting."

In the end I was forced to tell him it was Monsieur Racine. He seemed taken aback, was silent for a moment, then said:

"He was better as a poet."

When he met him the next day he did not greet him.

I wrote Monsieur Racine a letter, and sent it by Manseau, my steward, so that the Post should not see it. I gave him a rendezvous two days later in a wood at Versailles. I found him enveloped in a vast cloak and extremely agitated by what had happened. "I am lost," he said.

I tried to reassure him.

"Trust me—it will all come right," I said. "What are you afraid of? I am the cause of your misfortune, and for the sake of both my interests and my honor it is up to me to repair the damage. Your fate has become mine. Let the present cloud pass—I will bring back the sunshine. I know the King: he'll get over it."

"No, no, Madame, you won't ever get him to change his mind about me."

"Calm yourself, Monsieur, I beg. You're as pale as death. All we have to do is let a little time go by. Do you doubt my goodwill, or my influence?"

I suddenly heard the sound of a carriage driving at a great rate down the path. Grooms were shouting, riders brushing against the branches as they passed.

"Hide!" I said. "It's the King—he's coming this way!"

Monsieur Racine flung himself into a bush, tearing his cloak, and disappeared. I went back on to the path. The King, who was driving himself, pulled up when he saw me and gave me his hand to step into the carriage and stay beside him for the rest of his drive.

I wrote more letters to Monsieur Racine, pointing out that he still had his pension, his room in the château and his various functions. There was no formal sign of his having fallen from favor, but he was desolate, and I could not persuade him to hope.

"Madame," he wrote, "my present state deserves the compassion I know you have always shown for the unfortunate. I am deprived of the honor of seeing you, and hardly dare hope any longer that I may count on your protection, though it is the only one I have tried to earn."

In short, he buried himself in melancholy thoughts, fell ill and died soon afterwards. As he had the audacity to die a Jansenist, his death gave even more offense than his memorandum. Fortunately he was by then in a place where it is no longer a matter of concern whether the King raises his hat to you.

Somewhat against my will I was still a focus for all kinds of opposition against the government. My friends were always exhorting me in God's name not to be so timid. "Besiege the King, Madame, besiege him!" they cried. "This weakness does you no honor. If you are afraid to speak, at least bring your friends forward!" I grew a little bolder, and saw with astonishment that for all his fits of irritation and some humiliating rebuffs, the King seemed as fond of me as ever. It was about this time that he said something to the painter Mignard which gave the whole Court something to think about.

Mignard, whom I had known in my youth and who had painted several portraits of me, was then at work on the last, for he died soon afterwards. He was painting me as a "Roman Saint Frances" in an old-fashioned yellow gown and with a veil over my hair in the antique manner. One day while the King was watching him paint, my old friend turned to him and said, "Is it all right for me to give Madame de Maintenon an ermine cloak?" This was an ingenious way of asking about my rank. The King was silent for a moment, then said with a smile:

"Go ahead, Monsieur. Saint Frances richly deserves it."

I was far from displeased with this riposte, but was not left to gloat on it for long. God, to humble me, wanted me to find out for myself the truth of the old Roman proverb that the Tarpeian Rock is close to the Capitol. I spent the next three years in anguish and disgrace.

The "Affair" began in the most ordinary possible way.

While, as a result of the reform of the Institute, the ladies of Saint-Louis were all in their novitiate, I took charge for two years of the temporal side at Saint-Cyr. With the help of Nanon, appointed my deputy for the purpose, and of Manseau, my steward, I plunged among the pots and pans. I kept the accounts, enlarged the poultry-yard, inspected the wardrobes and supervised the menus, and all these things took me far away from the contemplation to which I aspired but for which I could see more and more clearly that God did not intend me yet. I consoled myself by reflecting that it was foolish to want to count the stars when one could not count the stitches in a tapestry or the apples in an orchard. Madame Guyon did not contradict me, but it was plain she felt some contempt as well as sorrow at my lack of progress in the "new prayer" and the exaggerated attention I paid to material occupations.

One day when I was putting some new linen away in the cupboards, I found a little girl sitting motionless in a cupboard as if in a daze. When I asked what she was doing there, she said she was in an ecstasy. I thought this very strange. Next day I found a whole troop of Yellows between fourteen and fifteen years old disposed along a corridor with their mouths open and upturned eyes. I had some difficulty in getting them back to normal, and the only explanation they had to offer was that they were "full of grace" and were "communicating in silence." I was very angry at this bizarre behavior.

As my duties at the school obliged me to spend more time there than I had in the past, and to go there every day, it was not long before I saw that during recreation the children talked of nothing but "pure love," "self-abandonment," "holy indifference" and "simplicity." This sort of talk was so common that it affected even the Reds, and children of six spoke to me like saints or illuminati. The craze for prayer soon reached such a pitch that the most essential duties were neglected. Instead of sweeping the floor, a girl would stand leaning nonchalantly on her broom. Another, instead of attending to the lessons of the young ladies, would go into a trance and abandon herself to the spirit. I was annoyed but not really alarmed by these extravagances. I begged them to change their tone, having soon got tired of such exchanges as "I have the gift of tears," "I am in a state of self-abandonment," "Were you really in ecstasy?" and other absurdities.

I found out that Mademoiselle de La Maisonfort had distributed her cousin's writings throughout the school, and that Madame Guyon herself, whenever she came, gathered a few of the junior mistresses together in some secret corner and taught them the new spirituality. I was not surprised that my little girls, deprived of the worldly amusements they had enjoyed so much, had turned so swiftly to spiritual distractions. Nothing is more likely to appeal to girls than the sort of piety which on the one hand removes all constraint and on the other encourages pride by telling them they are specially privileged souls. I believed I could easily overcome all this disorder and bring my flock quietly back to a more common piety.

But one of the mistresses, Madame du Pérou, anxious at the ravages the "new prayer" was making in the pupils' souls, and despairing of its being easily routed, told the bishop of Chartres without telling me. Monsieur de Chartres, after carrying out a brief inquiry in the school, asked to see me. I, realizing he took the matter more seriously than I did, began by saying that it was all childishness, that the girls were still play-acting in a way but would get over it eventually. He disagreed, said Madame Guyon was a dangerous woman and told me that three years ago the Holy Office had proscribed one of her books, *The Rule of the Associates of the Childhood of Jesus.* I had never heard of it and assured him it was not to be found at Saint-Cyr. I also told him that Monsieur de Fénelon, for whom his respect was equal to mine, guaranteed the purity of Madame Guyon's teaching.

I had some arguments with Mademoiselle de La Maisonfort when I tried to stop her handing out her cousin's books to the young ladies indiscriminately. After considerable resistance she gave in. Six months later, to make doubly sure, I forbade Madame Guyon to come to Saint-Cyr.

Some time afterwards Monsieur de Chartres told me how, six years before, Rome had condemned quietism and the writings of Molinos,† and said he saw a likeness between the ideas of the quietists and the extravagances of the girls at Saint-Cyr. Now I was definitely alarmed. Disorder and absurdity are one thing, heresy is quite another.

My anxiety deepened. One scene of rebellion followed another at Saint-Cyr. Mademoiselle de La Maisonfort led the most extreme of the hotheads, and she even had the audacity to oppose her bishop and myself publicly on the subject of the reform of the school. I then found out that despite my orders Madame Guyon was still coming to Saint-Cyr, and on 10 January 1694 I was obliged to repeat my prohibition.

The whole of Saint-Cyr had fallen into disobedience. The pupils were so "natural" they did not hesitate to insult their superiors, so "free" they could not bring themselves to obey their orders. A girl I reprimanded for making faces during mass said aloud to her companions, "How ridiculous!" and shrugged her shoulders. Such insolence and rebelliousness called for the sternest measures.

In December 1693 Monsieur de Chartres visited Saint-Cyr and made the ladies and young ladies hand over to him all the writings of Madame Guyon still in their possession. I had arranged this with him beforehand and was the first to set an example by producing the *Short Method* from my pocket. He then bade the whole community to "beware of false prophets."

My friends the ducs de Beauvilliers and de Chevreuse were

indignant at my having forbidden so saintly a woman as Madame Guyon to come to my school, but on 2 April 1694 the bishop issued an order making me superior for life of the new Saint-Cyr and excluding all other laywomen from it. This gave a clear and uncontestable justification for Madame Guyon's banishment.

It looked as though the rebels were resigning themselves to the new order. In May I wrote a letter to the sisters in the novitiate reminding them that they owed complete obedience to their superiors. "Be on your guard," I told them, "against the habit you have acquired of talking at length and raising questions and difficulties. This evil needs to be done away with in the young ladies; how much more in the nuns, who are supposed to die to all curiosity and subtlety."

Peace seemed to be returning gradually to the school.

Unfortunately Saint-Cyr was a subject of such interest to the whole Court that everyone always wanted to know what was going on there. Rumors of its internal disorders had spread outside its walls, and at the very moment when I was congratulating myself on having restored the community to obedience, these rumors reached Paris. It was immediately bruited about, untruly, that Madame Guyon was about to be arrested. The archbishop of Paris, who had not forgiven me for releasing her from his prisons five years earlier, was exultant, and the Jansenists were delighted at the difficulties the "prophetess" had got me into. Hébert, the parish priest at Versailles, came to see me.

He was a strange man. He had the uncouth bearing of a country priest, a horribly soiled cassock, dirty fingernails and big warts on his nose; but he was outspoken and possessed of certainties as strong as they were simple. The Court ladies were fond of making fun of his awkward speech, which once led him into such unintended double meanings that some of my friends would have choked with laughing if they had not been swiftly unlaced. Being what he was, he naturally loathed the subtleties of Madame Guyon.

"Just think, Madame," he said gravely. "She stole my female penitents from me. When she was at Versailles no one came to my sermons. Is not its outward attractiveness the very sign of heresy? That woman is possessed of the devil!" I was also told that when she was living in the provinces, Madame Guyon had committed offenses against morality.

The trances at Saint-Cyr, Mademoiselle de La Maisonfort's disobedience, my break with Madame Guyon—all these were as nothing compared with this. For the woman I personally had had released from prison to be publicly accused of heresy and infamy gave my enemies a Heaven-sent opportunity.

The pamphleteers were already saying Saint-Cyr was quietist, that Molinos's doctrine was openly taught there, and that all the pupils were "visionaries." Theologians claimed that Madame Guyon's books maintained that one could commit sins and still be innocent, and that damnation must be accepted if it is God's will.

To prevent scandal and forestall the critics, the only thing I could think of was to call together in secret some of my friends who were bishops, including Monsieur Bossuet, with Monsieur Fénelon, so that they might condemn Madame Guyon's works in unmistakable but moderate terms, thus demonstrating that I had been the first to perceive their dubiousness and to have them examined by theologians.

But while my friends the bishops were quietly considering Madame Guyon's writings at Issy, my enemy the archbishop of Paris, Monsieur de Harlay, found out our secret and in order to thwart it he himself condemned Madame Guyon's books as outright heresy. From then on there was nothing to be done and no hope of concealing the matter from the King.

Racked with anxiety, I told the King about the conference at Issy but passed it off as lightly as possible. I referred to Madame Guyon only as a relative of Madame de Béthune-Charost, carefully concealing her links both with Saint-Cyr and with my little "cabal of duchesses" and Messieurs de Fénelon and de Beauvilliers. As Harlay proposed to follow up his previous declaration by having Madame Guyon arrested and was already hoping to get her to admit publicly to her friendship with me and the members of the Sodality of Pure Love, I persuaded the King to write to the archbishop to quiet him down. I also asked Monsieur Bossuet, who was bishop of Meaux, to hide Madame Guyon in his diocese under a false name, to save her from arrest.

I could not sleep for worry about this affair, but I did not yet despair of putting a stop to it. I urged my ecclesiastical friends to issue the results of their consultations. After Monsieur de Harlay's declaration of heresy the Court would no longer be satisfied with a moderate condemnation: people would say we were protecting Madame Guyon. Now the condemnation would have to be unreserved and not hesitate if necessary to improve on that of the archbishop. Monsieur de Fénelon's signature at the foot of the page would be sufficient to show that he and his friends in the "little flock" had nothing in common with the fanatic he was condemning. Scandal would die down of its own accord.

But I was not reckoning with the blindness and obstinacy of Monsieur de Fénelon. The prelate I valued above all the rest put together, the man on whom I had bestowed my friendship and half of my heart, the little abbé who owed all his success to me, deliberately frustrated my strategy. He repeatedly told his colleagues he did not want to condemn Madame Guyon because she was his friend and in his opinion a saint. I did all I could to show him all the dangers involved in his attitude; I agreed Madame Guyon might be a saint, but that was not the point; whatever I said, he would not listen. "You are wrong to give way to panic, Madame," he said. "All this will clear up of its own accord."

All that came out of the "Issy Conversations" was what Monsieur de Fénelon was prepared to put his signature to, namely thirty-four very weak articles which did not mention Madame Guyon's name once.

The Jansenists exulted. Their chief author, Monsieur Nicole, wrote a book on the *Refutation of the Principal Errors of Quietism* in which he analyzed the heresies of Madame Guyon. Immediately there was fresh unrest at Saint-Cyr, and one of the confessors there had to be dismissed. Harlay was openly enjoying himself and said that if the "visionary's" acquaintance were examined, someone would be found who was among the highest in the land.

The accusation of quietism spread everywhere, just as accusations of witchcraft once had. I felt as if I were in a burning house, and when I tried to close doors to stop the flames reaching me, Monsieur de Fénelon did his best to hold them wide open.

Through an unfortunate combination of circumstances the see of Cambrai fell vacant at that point, and the King, who knew nothing about Monsieur de Fénelon's links with Madame Guyon or his recent differences with me, decided to reward his grandsons' tutor by appointing him to the post. I could not object, and when Monsieur de Fénelon asked to be consecrated at Saint-Cyr itself, by Monsieur Bossuet, bishop of Meaux, I had to accept that too. I must admit, though, that despite his dangerous obstinacy, Monsieur de Fénelon still had a place in my heart. I hoped he might be proved right after all, and that things would calm down of themselves.

While I was entertaining these vain hopes, Madame Guyon, who was still being hidden in Meaux, made a terrible mistake. Monsieur Bossuet had given her permission to go to Bourbon for her health, and she took the opportunity to escape. I learned that she had been helped in this by the duchesse de Mortemart, Madame de Beauvilliers's sister. The King was very displeased and allowed Monsieur de La Reynie, the Chief of the Paris Police, to institute a search. I was afraid she would implicate all her friends if she spoke. I hoped La Reynie would not find her, but in December 1695 he did. The foolish creature had been hiding right in Paris. Her arrest revived the whole affair.

Monsieur de La Reynie had no difficulty in establishing connections between his prisoner and the "little convent" of duchesses. He also learned that there had been disturbances at Saint-Cyr and wrote asking Monsieur de Pontchartrain, the minister of Justice, to make inquiries. Monsieur de Pontchartrain, who knew himself to be none too kindly treated by Monsieur de Beauvilliers's faction, decided both duty and self-interest required him to warn the King of the dimensions the affair was assuming. The fire was spreading to yet another room.

There was no way now of saving the Chevreuses, the Beauvilliers and the Mortemarts from scandal; and I seriously doubted whether I could save myself. The affair had become political. Rumor had it the duchesses had kept lists of vacant posts, and their husbands meant to transform the whole Court, with my help, by putting their own creatures in the highest positions. Under our pretended devotion to the King we sought only to control him . . .

I broke with my lady friends, who wanted to make martyrs of themselves for Madame Guyon. I publicly set a distance between myself and Monsieur de Beauvilliers, whom I began to suspect of having tried to make use of me for the past ten years under cover of Pure Love. When Monsieur de Pontchartrain and Monsieur de La Reynie, in my presence, showed the King a denunciation of quietist citizens in Paris and minor priests suspected to be of the same persuasion, I no longer even hesitated to give them the addresses of those I knew of, as evidence of my good faith.

In short, I put another door between myself and the fire and removed myself still further from the flames.

I shed tears of rage and grief at having lost all my friends. At least I still had God—the God Monsieur de Fénelon had taught me to love with childlike joy and self-abandonment. But apparently even this was too much. The worthy gentlemen resolved to take Him away from me too.

Madame Guyon's arrest had created animosity between Monsieur Bossuet, bishop of Meaux, and Monsieur Fénelon, now bishop of Cambrai. Monsieur de Meaux, furious that Madame Guyon had broken parole, was hurt that Monsieur de Cambrai should still defend her. They turned their quarrel into a theological battle. Monsieur de Meaux spent all 1696 writing a book in which he bracketed Madame Guyon and Monsieur de Cambrai together. This was precisely what I had been trying to avoid from the very beginning, but there was no stopping Monsieur Bossuet once he was launched. Monsieur de Cambrai, knowing what the other was preparing against him, was furbishing up his own arms: he was writing a book which was to defend some of Madame Guyon's ideas and show that Monsieur de Meaux understood nothing about the mystics.

I begged him for the last time to give up this project, which would inevitably mix up his own doctrine, which was good, with Madame Guyon's, which was not. But he refused. And so as not to be destroyed in the conflagration, I resigned myself to shutting the last door—the door which would cut me off for ever from Monsieur de Fénelon.

At Saint-Cyr all his books were sought out and confiscated. I myself agreed to hand over to the bishops of Meaux and of Chartres some of the letters of spiritual friendship he had written to me. I had to agree at last that mere love of God was insufficient, and only sorrow brings salvation.

In January 1697 Monsieur de Cambrai's *Explanation of the Maxims of the Saints* was published; in February Monsieur de Meaux's *Instruction on States of Prayer* appeared. It was like kicking an ant-hill. The courtiers ran in all directions. Hébert was in half a dozen places at once. Two main parties grew up in France overnight, and people declared themselves for or against quietism as they had for the Ancients or the Moderns ten years before.

The King had been surprised to see Monsieur de Fénelon taking part in a mêlée from which he had always seemed to him to stand aside. He spoke of the matter to Monsieur de Meaux, whose judgment he respected. Monsieur de Meaux threw himself at the monarch's feet like an actor, imploring forgiveness for not having warned him earlier about Monsieur de Cambrai's fatal heresy, implying that Monsieur de Fénelon had entertained the quietist error for years. The King indicated that he was surprised all this had been happening without my having told him anything about it.

Monsieur de Cambrai had informed Rome of the argument, so we had the edifying spectacle of the tutor to the King of France's son confronting the tutor to his grandson in full view of the Pope and the foreign courts, while the minister of Finance made covert war against the minister of state. Monsieur de Meaux even showed the Pope certain private letters from Monsieur de Cambrai to me, while Monsieur de Cambrai produced as evidence against Monsieur de Meaux some of the Latin compositions he had set the

Dauphin fifteen years before. As for Père de La Chaise, he jumped at the opportunity to harm me and openly declared his support for Monsieur de Cambrai, now that I had brought myself to declare myself against him. He tried to persuade the King that having long been imprudent I should soon be ridiculous.

All the prelates were tearing each other to pieces; the cabal grew larger and bolder every day; the most illustrious families in the kingdom were at one another's throats. And they all brought me into their quarrels.

Madame de Montespan had been destroyed for less. The Affair of the Poisons was nothing beside heresy combined with political scandal. It would be said how terrible it was for the King's grandsons to be entrusted to people who belonged to a new religion. As I contemplated the disaster in all its aspects, I was in torment.

The days I spent with the King were like being on hot coals. He did not tell me anything; he did not speak to me at all. His silence made me a prey to such violent attacks of nausea and anxiety I sometimes thought my body could not stand it. As I worked at my tapestry beside a husband as silent as the grave and as black as a thundercloud, I would stick my needle in my finger till I drew blood, just to feel I was still there and my flesh could still find the strength to contain my spirit a little while longer. I was so gnawed at from within, and I grew so thin and sallow that Madame, the King's sister-in-law, gave it out that I was suffering from cancer of the womb.

At last, after having restrained himself for a long while, the King let his wrath burst forth.

All the afternoon he had been pacing to and fro in my room. I was pretending to go through the Saint-Cyr accounts, but I could not see one figure. Suddenly he grew tired of this pretense and came and stood in front of me. Without taking his eyes off my face or raising his voice, he said:

"I cannot thank you, Madame, for making me choose a heretic to be an archbishop and the tutor of my grandsons, and a friend of his, another heretic, to be head of my finance council and minister of state. If they had been just heretics, I might perhaps have been able to overlook it, but it appears they were also ambitious, and with your help appointed their own creatures to all the official posts. And that too, Madame, would have been nothing, if on top of all the rest they had not been a couple of fantastical fools!"

As I had lowered my eyes, he took hold of my chin and made me look at him.

"I have read some of the memoranda on the present issue which Monsieur de Cambrai served up to Monsieur de Chévreuse and to yourself. Yes, you, Madame! Without exaggeration they are a tissue of absurdities! I don't know what his religion is, but his politics . . . ! And when I think, Madame, that on your advice I made this fanatic, this muddle-head, this dreamer, responsible for the education of a future king!"

I still had my account-book in my lap. He snatched it up and aimed it angrily at a table a few feet away. He missed, and it fell on the floor. I think this irritated him more than all the rest.

He began to shout right in my face:

"Did you think I hadn't enough trouble on the frontiers without being saddled with this division inside France and all this uproar?"

He grabbed the arms of my chair and shook them so hard I thought I should be overturned.

"And do you think that after fighting against the Pope's authority for twenty years, I like having to ask him to judge between my own children's tutors? I thought you were sound, I thought you had common sense, but you're like all the rest—presumptuous, a liar, an intriguer!"

He gave a bitter laugh.

"It's marvelous to see what a wit can do in affairs of state!"

I was expecting him to tell me where I was to retire to, for I had no doubt this conversation heralded the disgrace the whole Court had been buzzing with for the past two months. But he said no more, sat down, took up his papers again and worked in my room until the usual time. I remembered he was so concerned about appearances that he had continued going to see Madame de Montespan as if nothing had happened when already she meant nothing to him. I thought he might do the same in my case.

For weeks he went on coming to my apartment. He said nothing to me, I said nothing to him. Then he had me offered the title of duchesse, which from Mademoiselle de Fontanges's example I knew to be the first step toward exile. Not wishing to make it easy for him, I haughtily declined the "honor," saying it was too great for me.

Bonne d'Heudicourt told me everyone was saying I was to be succeeded by the comtesse de Gramont. She was an Englishwoman of forty, still good-looking and witty in the fashion of her country. The King had paid her special attention when she came to France with the Court of the exiled James II, and for the last few weeks his interest had been growing visibly.

"Françoise," said Bonne, "you can't let all this happen without putting up a fight!"

As she spoke she twisted her long grey hair, once so red, around her gaunt fingers. Her anxiety made her bare her yellow teeth in a forced smile; it also worsened the limp she had acquired a few years back. In days gone by she had been so pretty, but now she was exceptionally ugly. However, I had only to look at the brown spots on the hands that lay on my silk skirt to guess that I too was not changing for the better.

"What would be the good?" I answered. "It seems to me I've fought too much already over this business. I've been like someone who treads on the hem of a curtain and in struggling to extricate himself, pulls the whole thing down on his head, curtain-rod and all! I got myself entangled in quietism. Disgrace will give me a rest from it. Death even more!"

"Just the same," Marguerite de Montchevreuil said, "he did marry you!"

"What then? The marriage has never been acknowledged. He has only to shut me up in a nunnery—no one would say anything. Then he can take a mistress, and as no one knows anything about our marriage, there will be no scandal. Only Père de La Chaise could object, and you can imagine whether he would!"

"How can you contemplate such horrible things so calmly? Pull yourself together, Madame! Fight!"

"For whom? For myself?—or for you, Marguerite? What you're worried about is that if I fall, you fall too. That's it, isn't it?

But you believe in God. He'll console you in your retirement."

Madame de Montchevreuil burst into tears, and I reproached myself for being so cruel. Even so, I could not bring myself to ask her forgiveness.

I was turning vicious. I had doubts about the King's love, about friendship, about God Himself. I no longer knew how to pray to Him without being unorthodox. Saint-Cyr had been spoiled and was no longer a refuge. The only thing I hoped was that the Pope would condemn Monsieur de Cambrai's writings without delay, so that, on top of my other fears and troubles, all my betrayals would not turn out to have been for nothing. But I could see that every step I took was a false step, that I was spied on all the time, that I could not so much as blink without being observed. Sometimes slanderers accused me of still protecting heresy, out of obstinacy; sometimes they accused me of abandoning my friends, out of inconstancy.

I fell ill, with continuous fever and vomiting. I could neither eat nor sleep. It was generally said that I was dying, and I myself had high hopes of that cancer of the womb.

It may have been Monsieur Fagon who saved me. He told the King that to all appearances it was only sorrow I was dying of, but that this grief, combined with my American fevers and a weak constitution, would certainly carry me off. Monsieur de Chartres, my director, made so bold as to write the King a pleading letter.

"You have an excellent companion, Sire," he said, "full of the spirit of God and of affection and fidelity for yourself. I know the depths of her heart and can assure you no one could love you more tenderly and respectfully. She would never deceive you if she were not deceived herself."

One evening in October as I was dozing inside my curtains, my mind clouded by an unusually violent fever, the King, just returned from a ball, suddenly burst into the room, had the lamps lit and came straight over to the bed.

"Well, Madame," he said brusquely, "must we see you die of this business?"

He had a chair brought to my bedside, and then, when the footmen had left the room, he said:

"Do you not trust me any more? I don't want you to die . . . It's true no one else would have got off so lightly."

I was weeping copiously.

"Don't cry, Madame. I know you have been deceived, but I am going to set all that right in a way you will approve of."

To set the seal on our reconciliation he insisted I take some veal bouillon, and nothing would do but that I drink it in front of him. Then he flung all the windows wide open.

"Don't worry any more," he said. "I shall cut the evil right out."

I gave myself up to Nanon's tender care and Monsieur Fagon's medicines, and from my bed of convalescence saw Monsieur de Fénelon relieved of his tutorship and Monsieur de Fénelon's writings banned. The junior tutors were also dismissed. Monsieur de Beauvilliers had to repudiate Madame Guyon and Monsieur de Cambrai. The Pope was called upon to condemn the archbishop of Cambrai, whom he supported in secret, and to declare him a heretic. Mademoiselle de La Maisonfort and two of her friends were banished from Saint-Cyr by *lettres de cachet.* The King went there himself to recall the community to obedience.

My husband was marvelous. In a moment he cut all the knots which had been strangling me for three or four years. He was a king.

In a few weeks quietism was swept away, and I had no more open enemies.

I cannot pretend I came out of this affair the same as I went into it. A song that was popular then in Paris summed it up. It said that according to some, the French prelates' search for truth had only succeeded in destroying hope; that according to others the victim was charity. But what was really shattered, though no one thought of it, was faith.

The King, once his ill-humor had faded, was the same as ever.

"Well, that's over and done with," he said to me. "I hope it will have no more painful consequences for anyone."

His favors were restored to me in every sense of the word; in all respects he acted as if nothing had happened. His sensibility was never troubled by anything more than ripples; never by waves.

In the year when great theological tomes were being hurled at him from all sides, he wrote a book too. It was called *How to Display the Gardens at Versailles*.

Sixteen

On either side of the terrace at Marly there was a dense shrubbery clipped into a maze. Each of these "green apartments," as they were called, contained at its center a round pool and a fountain, one in honor of Arethusa and the other of Amphitrite.

When he first fell in love with carp, the King had them put in the four oblong pools along the sides of the château. Then others were put in the canal in the western shrubbery and in the round ponds in the "green apartments."

I often used to spend my afternoons there. I liked the arched bowers; the little trellis arbors; the rows of clipped yews. I especially liked the silence and the shade. Apart from such places I did not much care for the King's gardens. He designed them so that all you found in them was what he himself liked, above all sun and wind. He would not let a tree grow one leaf freely. Continual trimming, which he sometimes did himself, reduced all the elms and chestnuts to what he called the strait and narrow, in other words, to lines of geometrical regularity.

I used to avoid the great avenues, open to the elements, and take refuge inside the "green apartments," where I would sit on the edge of the pools and watch the carps.

The King regarded the carp as the royal fish par excellence, the only one which with its majestic movements and gorgeous appearance was worthy to swim in pools belonging to the Crown. So the pools had to be worthy of their inmates. Some were lined with pottery tiles from Holland or Nevers decorated with leaves of autumnal yellows and greens. Others were inlaid with semi-precious stones and mother-of-pearl. The carps which inhabited these splendid waters were of all colors, some like gold and silver, some a pinkish blue, others speckled with yellow and white or black and red. When their colors faded, the King had them repainted or had a pearl necklace hung around their necks. He used to feed them from his own hand, and he invented charming names for them. Apart from that he treated them like his courtiers, taking them about with him from place to place regardless of weather or season. They did not live long. The King used to wonder why.

I remember one of the afternoons I spent conversing in the shade with those mute favorites. I had dipped my hand in the water and was stroking the fish as they swam past—Golden Sun, Millefleurs, Dawn, Mirror. My two nieces were sitting behind me, prattling away to one another on a marble bench in a little arbor. Marguerite de Caylus was no longer at Court then, having been sent away for follies of which I shall speak later, but she sometimes came to see me at Marly when the King and his courtiers were out hunting.

Now and then I would turn away from Sunstone and Topaz to look with satisfaction at the two young women. Marguerite was wearing a formal dress of silver moiré which went perfectly with her fair curls and pale complexion. Françoise d'Aubigné, her arm affectionately around her cousin's waist, was confiding her girlish secrets. She looked older than her age with her full black velvet skirt, the rouge she put on her face and lips, the pearls on her bodice and her natural gravity. The smiling blonde and the shy brunette made a pretty picture sitting there side by side, the one amply revealing the rounded white shoulders of a woman, the other imprisoning a girl's imperceptible bosom in a black corselet and lace collars.

The splendid Marguerite left her dark cousin for a moment and came and stood beside me.

"The King is not very lucky with his carp," she said. "They don't live long. I heard Proserpine was dead . . ."

"It's true," I said. "The King is very upset. He says Proserpine used to obey him. But I don't regard that as anything unusual in this part of the world. At the most it may be a rare thing in carp."

"But what's the matter with them all, Aunt?"

"I'll tell you, Niece. They are like me: they miss their native mud."

Marguerite de Caylus's lips formed a little round "o" of surprise, then she spread out her wide skirt and sat down next to me. She leaned her head on my shoulder and looked at me with her characteristic mocking half-smile.

"Say rather, Madame, that you miss your lost youth."

I gently shook my head.

"Oh no . . . I shan't pretend that when I see you looking so pretty, I don't think sadly of what I looked like once. But I feel other things besides regret now that my youth is no more. Nothing makes a person happier than detachment, and since to attain that you have to have played a part in the world, you wear away your youth amassing a treasure of fame and pain. Then, one day, you find your soul is rich enough to have done with all those exaggerated feelings and vain strivings. The play is over, now you can be indifferent. Marvelous!"

I had resolved that the quietist affair would be my last heartbeat. After that I would be indifferent to the fate of the nation, the salvation of the King, the opinion of my friends and the question of how to serve God.

In any case, things were not going too badly and could well do without my advice. The plenipotentiaries had just signed the peace at Ryswick. People said it was not to our advantage, but the King was pleased to have shown that all the European powers put together could not get the better of France. The people were glad to go back to their crops. Credit, which had been cut off altogether at one point, was restored at once, and the King was offered money at six per cent, when six months earlier he had been unable to borrow any for twelve.

In order to demonstrate how wrong everyone had been to say

France was exhausted, the King had a magnificent camp set up at Compiègne in 1698. All the armies took part in twelve days of maneuvers. Fine linen tents and a specially built village welcomed the Court and the foreign ambassadors. The new uniforms, the splendid horses, the discipline of the regiments and the abundance of gold plate showed Europe it still had a Master. I was told all about it. I was pleased but told the King and his ministers I did not want to know any more.

In religion too I stood aloof from doctrinal quarrels and kept my sensibility in check. I read neither the *Answer to the Account of Quietism,* nor the *Remarks on the Answer,* nor the *Answer to the Remarks.* I resolutely confined my piety to resignation; if I still had faith, it was out of the remains of habit.

"I take communion only out of obedience," I wrote to my director. "I acquire no virtue, I do myself no violence for the love of God and I experience no union with Him. Prayer bores me; I cannot either keep it up or go back to it. But I do pray continually, if to groan to God is prayer."

Monsieur de Chartres pronounced himself very pleased with this attitude. He thought it less dangerous than enthusiasm. I agreed; he was my director.

I wanted to be an ordinary wife, concerned with nothing but amusing her husband and ruling over her family. My husband's triumphant emblem was the Sun. For my emblem I chose a lantern. My motto indicated my whole ambition. It said: "I shine only for him."

But the modesty of my new ambition could not hide the magnitude of my duty. As to family, the King was the father of eighteen legitimate, legitimized or publicly acknowledged children, not to mention the obscure bastards I also had to look after—marrying them off, giving them dowries, placing their daughters at Saint-Cyr and getting their sons into the cadet corps. Out of the eighteen acknowledged children many had died, but there were still enough left to occupy a responsible stepmother.

The first, both in age and in rank, was Monseigneur le Dauphin. Round as a barrel and sunk in his fat, he gave evidence of nothing resembling intelligence. He was timorous and trembling in the King's presence and my own, but he was incapable of malice because he was incapable of anything. "All I can say," he wrote to me at about this time, "is that I am doing all I can to become capable of something." But it was a lost cause.

My only concern was that he should not hinder his father by forming a party around himself as pretenders usually do. His feeblemindedness made him easy to maneuver by men who were ambitious and long-sighted. So I flattered and reassured him all the time in order to keep him as close as possible to his father. These efforts might also prove useful to me if the King should die before I did and leave me subject to the whims of his successor.

I therefore undertook to get the King to accept his son's remarriage. After the Dauphine's death, Monseigneur had fallen in love with a maid of honor attending on his half-sister the princesse de Conti, daughter of Mademoiselle de La Vallière. The lady in question was Mademoiselle de Choin, a dark, snubnosed, stocky young woman whose only wit was backstairs gossip. She had a horribly big bosom, but this must have attracted Monseigneur, for he was said to drum upon it with his fingers. For this or other reasons he was so fond of her that he married her in secret, after which he asked me to tell the King. It was not for me to cast aspersions on discreet misalliances, nor did I think the King in a position to do so. I persuaded him to tolerate amiably what he could not in conscience object to. He resigned himself to it on condition that Mademoiselle de Choin stay at Meudon, which the Dauphin had just bought from the children of Monsieur de Louvois, and that she never appear at Court. Once this treaty was concluded, father and son continued to rub along together.

But things were not so easy between the King and his daughters. He had three of them, by two different mothers, and none of them was turning out well. The fairies, instead of endowing them with all the gifts usually bestowed on story-book princesses, had divided the advantages up among them, leaving each of them lacking. The princesse de Conti, daughter of the duchesse de La Vallière, had received beauty and grace as her share, but nothing more. Mademoiselle de Nantes, Madame de Montespan's elder daughter and by marriage the duchesse de Bourbon, had all the wit of the

Mortemarts but no advantages of face or heart. Mademoiselle de Blois, by marriage first the duchesse de Chartres and then the duchesse d'Orléans, had inherited the marquise her mother's noble mien and general loftiness, acting like a "daughter of France" even on her close-stool; but that did not make her any prettier or more intelligent.

The princesse de Conti, a widow at nineteen and an out-and-out coquette, did not let her admirers languish in vain for her charms. But as she lacked both wit and kindness, her lovers were unfaithful and the Court made merry over her disappointments.

The duchesse de Bourbon, also known as Madame la Duchesse, was married at twelve years old to a grandson of the great Condé,† who looked more like a gnome than a man, and she made up for her conjugal dissatisfaction with intrigues and epigrams. I had been solely responsible for her upbringing from her birth until she was eight. I can truthfully say that while her wit corresponded exactly to her education, all she lacked apart from education was evident when you examined her heart.

As for the duchesse de Chartres, married at thirteen to the King's nephew, she lived in the clouds and had no feelings for anything but her own rank. I remember how, a few weeks before her marriage, when it was said that the young duc de Chartres, the future Regent, was so much in love with Mademoiselle de Blois, as she then was, that he was prepared to defy his mother's opposition to the match, I mentioned it to her, innocently supposing she would be pleased. She answered me in her usual sleepy manner: "I don't want him to love me, I want him to marry me." She was duly satisfied on both points.

There was no love lost between the three sisters. On the day of her marriage the duchesse de Chartres underlined the distance between herself and the other two by insisting they address her henceforward only as "Madame," to which they objected loudly. The duchesse de Bourbon spent all her time making fun of the princesse de Conti's love affairs and the duchesse de Chartres's fondness for strong liquor and drew ruthless portraits of them under fictitious names in what purported to be a history of the reign of Augustus. They all stole one another's purveyors and wig-makers, jostled one another at official ceremonies, and trod on one another's feet under the table. Their quarrels were quite public. One evening in the grand salon at Marly, the princesse de Conti referred to her sisters as "wine-sacks," to which the daughters of Madame de Montespan, suddenly reconciled by a common hatred, retaliated by calling her a "sack of refuse."

Whenever I could see the King was getting tired of their squabbles and excesses, I summoned them to my room to give them a dressing-down. The younger two were in awe of me, as their former governess; the eldest feared me as a person of wit. They came in trembling and went out sobbing. A month later they were back at their old tricks again.

It must be admitted that the only older woman in their family —Madame, the King's sister-in-law and their aunt—did not set them a good example. Unable to rule over a court, careless of other people's opinion and proud to the point of madness, she enjoyed spreading unrest and dissension among her family. From time to time, on the King's instructions, I called her to order too.

Thus I recall one evening, not long after Monsieur's death, when at the King's request I went to see her. She was sitting in an inner room drinking good German beer with one of her women and making a fuss over one of her dogs, which had just had five puppies on her gown. It was not a very appealing sight, but Madame regarded cleanliness as a fad. She reluctantly allowed me to take a seat, then launched into a speech about the indifference with which the King had treated her during her recent illness. I told her the King only wanted to have reason to be better pleased with her than he had had for some time. At this Madame protested she had never done or said anything displeasing and trotted out a list of complaints and excuses. I interrupted her by taking a letter out of my pocket and asking her if she knew the handwriting.

It was a letter from her to her aunt the duchesse of Hanover, in which, after some Court news, she expatiated at length on my living in sin with the King, referring to me as usual as the "pantocrat" and worse. She then went on to foreign and domestic affairs, describing the woes of France, from which she said the country could never recover, and severely criticizing the King's diplomacy.

The Post had opened this letter, as it opened almost all correspondence, but this one was too extreme just to send the King extracts, and they had sent him the original.

Madame was thunderstruck, as may be imagined. For a moment she froze like a statue, then she started to weep, while I calmly pointed out to her the enormity of every part of the letter, especially when sent to a foreign country. She cried out, confessed, asked forgiveness; she poured out repentance, promises, supplications. But as she was just as incorrigible as her nieces, she soon began to write the same sort of letters again. I, however, had learned enough detachment not to care.

To tell the truth, the only members of his entire family to whom the King might look for some satisfaction were his two illegitimate sons.

The younger one, the comte de Toulouse, grand admiral of France, was then scarcely twenty, but already as amiable as he was handsome. He was discreet, modest, diligent in business and obliging in personal relations, and had almost no enemies at Court. Moreover, he kept away from it as much as possible, living mostly in his house at Rambouillet when he was not roaming the seven seas to learn his trade. I could not claim credit for his virtues, for he had been brought up entirely by Madame de Montespan, his mother, to whom he was still very attached. I did not respect him any the less for that, and spoke in his favor to the King whenever the occasion arose.

As for the duc du Maine, my beloved child, I rejoiced to see all the good qualities I had divined in him as a child being confirmed as he grew older. No one could possess more wit of every kind than he. He had no dissolute habits, and just enough ambition to serve his own renown and that of the King. He was more affected by the harmony of a line of poetry than by the outcome of a battle between officials, and more inclined by nature to literature than to politics. In my view he was scornful enough of courtly vanities to be able to reach true greatness. Later on the duchesse his wife rebuked him, saying, "You are asleep, Monsieur, and you may wake up in the Academy. But your cousin of Orléans will wake up on the throne." I myself preferred this moderate ambition to an insatiable thirst for affairs of state which would have displeased the King.

I steadily guided this reasonable and measured aspiration toward the highest positions, only regretting that my "little prince" retained two embarrassing defects from the education I had given him. First, he was very shy, a relic of the excessive severity with which I had always repressed his pride; and second, he had an aversion to military matters which sometimes amounted to lack of courage in action. This latter trait undoubtedly derived from my own hatred of war and violence, though it may be that the inhibition owing to his own infirmity would of itself have prevented him from being a hero in the field.

In short, for his former governess her "darling" was what he had always been, a sensitive and affectionate child. No one in the world tried harder to please me; no one was so grieved if he caused me displeasure. Though I tried not to prefer him to his brothers, I always succumbed to his charms, which were increased for me by the pity he inspired. His delicate health and the dreadful lameness which deformed an otherwise handsome figure moved me as much as all his mental and spiritual virtues.

It was this compassion which made me resolve to intervene in the matter of his marriage. He saw no reason why being illegitimate and lame should deprive him of domestic happiness; but the King took a different view. When he was twenty-five, Monsieur du Maine begged me to tell his father he would be desperate if he was not allowed to marry. "I don't think men like him ever should marry," said the King to me curtly. When I pressed him a little, I was told it was not so much his deformity as his illegitimacy that the king held against him. He feared for the country if bastardy had offspring.

"When I married my daughters," he said, "their blood was lost in that of their husbands; their children are Condés and d'Orléans. But I see all too clearly the troubles that arise in a country out of the marriage of male bastards. Look at what my father the King had to suffer at the hands of the bastards of the King my grandfather . . . It is dangerous to have two royal lines. Tell Mon-

sieur du Maine I want to hear no more about it. And you, Madame
—please do not return to the subject, either for him or for Monsieur de Toulouse."

But I did return to it, and in the end I had my way.

For a wife for my "darling," the choice fell on a sister of the
duc de Bourbon. The Condés were only too pleased to redeem
their error in the Fronde by throwing all their children into the
arms of the King's bastards. The young lady, Bénédicte de Bourbon, was, like all her sisters, so small she looked almost like a dwarf.
On her wedding day her headdress was taller than she was.

I do not know if Monsieur du Maine was happy in his marriage, but I do know it was not long before his pocket duchesse was
giving me as much trouble as her tall sisters-in-law. I had been told
she was pious and well behaved; she turned out to be completely
lacking in devoutness, rebellious and a lover of intrigue. Soon she
and Madame la Duchesse and the princesse de Conti were tearing
one another's hair, disagreeing over precedence and over lovers.
When they became too turbulent, I used to scold them all and send
one to do penance at Chantilly and another to stand in the corner
at Clagny.

All this was not very amusing perhaps, but to me, in my state
of general lassitude, it was a sort of relaxation. The follies of this
family were entertaining enough once one no longer vested esteem
or friendship in its members. Sometimes I even laughed in private
at their extravagances and stupidities before I solemnly lectured
them. To tell the truth, the King's family was made up not so much
of real people as of ridiculous characters worthy of the Italian
theater, and as I was not trying to improve them, which was beyond
my capabilities, but only to avoid scandals which might upset the
King, I could afford to treat it all as a distraction.

When I was in good form I also did a little cleaning up nearer
home. My own family, though not so much in the public eye or so
spoiled as the King's, still had its quota of play-actors and fools.

My brother, Charles, who had got into increasingly low habits
as he grew older, had finally exhausted my patience. To keep him
out of the drinking-dens he frequented, I sent him into retreat at

Saint-Sulpice, where he told everyone I was trying to humbug him into thinking he was devout. "She surrounds me with priests—it will kill me!" he said, and escaped.

He was found living with a woman called Ulrich, who traded in her somewhat faded charms. I decided to provide him with a keeper. The man, Madot, clung to him like a leech and as often as possible kept him away from Paris. This did not stop him having yet another child with a woman named de La Brosse. It was a little girl, Charlotte, and I had to take charge of her for as long as I lived, as I had of her brothers and sisters before her. Charles died in 1703, taking the waters at Bourbon. I mourned the child he used to be but had no regrets for the debauched old man he had become. He was buried quietly, and the King would not let me wear mourning.

Philippe de Villette, whom I had made a lieutenant-general in the navy, was left a widower, and at over sixty decided to marry a girl from Saint-Cyr, Mademoiselle de Marsilly, who was eighteen. This marriage of January and May was the talk of the Court.

My nephew Mursay caused me a different kind of worry. He was brave, a good officer and an honest man, but he was extraordinarily stupid. A hundred stories were told at Court about him, his light-bay horse, his manservant, Marcassin, who mocked him and ruled him with a rod of iron and his exaggeratedly pious wife, who would not sleep with him on Sunday. People maliciously pretended to regard this great simpleton as the true representative of the d'Aubigné family.

His sister Marguerite de Caylus was completely different: she had beauty enough for four and wit enough for a hundred. She annihilated people at table, where she was at her most brilliant. As she was not very keen on her husband the comte de Caylus, the King obligingly left him on the frontiers all the year round. My niece did not make very virtuous use of her liberty.

She flaunted her relationship with the duc de Villeroy† more and more openly. No matter how much I begged her to be discreet about this double adultery, she thought her intelligence placed her above ordinary moral laws and Court gossip. What is more, despite my protests, she made friends with Madame la Duchesse, who was the same age and shared the same tastes. I told her one should only respect such people and never get fond of them, and that Madame la Duchesse's misdeeds would inevitably redound on Marguerite herself. But she did not believe me, followed her own inclination, gave herself up entirely to the duchesse de Bourbon and paid the price. There were epigrams about ministers, vivid portraits of ambassadors and slanderous jests about my friends and even about the King himself. He scolded his daughter and forgave her; he sent my niece away.

On learning she was requested to leave the Court, Madame de Caylus responded with a characteristic haughty witticism. "It is so boring here that this is the real exile," she said. After a week of Paris, however, she was crying. After two months she toyed with Jansenism by way of a little amusement. After a year she begged me to take her back into my good books and let her meet me sometimes by stealth. I agreed because I loved her, and we resumed a regular correspondence. But the King feared her wit, and left her in exile for twelve years to give her time to come to her senses.

If, as one grows older, one is willing to stop being an actor and become a spectator, life provides plenty of amusing surprises. The Villettes, father and children, whom I had always loved and cherished, gave me nothing in those days but trouble, whereas the Sainte-Hermines and the d'Aubignés, who had been millstones around my neck for twenty years, gave me several reasons for rejoicing.

My female cousin de Sainte-Hermine, the Huguenot and martyr, suddenly became a Catholic and emerged from prison. She behaved well and was given a pension; she became a comtesse and was made much of, dowered and promoted. Finally she pleased the King, and the comtesse de Mailly, as she was by her marriage, was appointed mistress of the wardrobe to the duchesse de Bourgogne and soon became our intimate companion.

My d'Aubigné niece, who I had feared would take after her father, had the good sense to bring the most charming of sons-in-law into the family and the wit to make him happy. In 1698 the King gave her in marriage to the comte d'Ayen, eldest son of the duc de Noailles, and the young man, who had been chosen only for his name, turned out to be perfect in every respect. He was gracious and affable in society, full of pleasing repartee, always ready to fall in amiably with other people's wishes, brave in war, a good writer and a rare speaker. He even flirted with me a little on occasion.

I gave the young couple my house at Maintenon, which was all I possessed in my own right. To this the King, of his own free will, added eight hundred thousand livres in cash and seventy thousand in jewelry.

I had had to wait until I was sixty to find out that a family can be a source of pleasure, at a time when one least expects it. I said as much to the King to cheer him up about his own family. But his afflictions, like his affections, were always merely superficial, and the troubles inflicted on him by his relatives were forgotten as soon as they were felt.

I was sitting in the big octagonal salon at Marly with a silver chocolate pot in front of me, watching night fall beyond the panes of the cupola.

My companions spoke to me in whispers, for Monsieur had died the previous day. Apart from its volume, the conversation was the same as ever, convent chitchat. The usual subject was clothes; the staple of the ladies' talk was shops, materials and the shape of caps. Today the theme was novel—they were discussing green peas. It was the fashionable topic: how eager one was to have some, or how delicious they tasted or how one looked forward to having some more. I thought back sadly on the conversation of Mademoiselle de Lenclos. But the great think their vision a beatific one, sufficient unto itself and able to take the place of wit.

The duc de Bourgogne, the elder of the King's grandsons, suddenly burst into the room, went up to Monsieur de Montfort, who was dozing in an armchair, and asked him if he would care for a game of brelan.

"Brelan!" said Monsieur de Montfort, astonished. "You must be forgetting, Monseigneur, that Monsieur's body is not yet cold!"

"Pardon me," answered the prince. "I am not forgetting. But the King does not want people to be bored at Marly. He has instructed me to make everyone play, and lest no one should dare to begin he has told me to set an example."

So they sat down to a game of brelan, and soon the salon was full of card-tables and the sound of voices and laughter.

That was how deep the King's sorrows went.

As I had resolved to be a better wife than in the past, and to do all I could to keep my husband amused, I at first thought it my duty to put in an appearance at more festivities. This was indeed devotion, for I could hardly endure these occasions.

With the return of peace there were magnificent balls, but I found them very tedious. The minuets were so long I thought they must have been danced at the request of the bigots, to make people think of eternity. Those who, like me, did not take part, but just sat in one place, watching, did nothing but yawn and exchange material for gossip.

Performances were given of old plays and operas. I made myself go and see *Le Bourgeois gentilhomme* for the fourth time, and was there in person for a production of Monsieur Scarron's *Jodelet, or the Master-Valet.* The whole Court flocked to this one, to please me, or to do the opposite.

As for gambling, that was a disgrace; the lansquenet tables looked as if some vile trade were being carried on at them rather than a game. I forced myself to follow the hunt in a calash, but it was still an ordeal. What can I do if the faces of the stags move me and I feel sorry for them? It made me cry, having to look on, and the King, pleased I had gone hunting with him at last, ordered the tearing of the quarry to pieces to take place by my carriage windows, "so that you can see the best of the show," he said.

Though I agreed with the Jansenist who said that "a king without diversions is a man who is bored," I could not bear Court etiquette and the round of entertainments any longer. I decided to provide amusement in my own apartment and to teach the King to enjoy in those two rooms all the pleasures that ordinary people find in their homes: the laughter of children, the company of chosen friends, new books and intellectual pastimes.

Despite his love of ceremony and the Court, the King fell in with my plan, for the gout from which he had been suffering since

1694 now occurred in acute attacks which tended to keep him from his usual pleasures. Moreover he was getting fat, letting himself go, apparently caving in. He looked smaller, and his face became more inexpressive every day.

As for his once beautiful mistress, the marquise de Montespan, she was said to be quite white-haired and as wrinkled as an old apple. Madame d'Heudicourt, who had been to see her in her château at Petit-Bourg, said she had found her sitting in her kitchen making a sauce, surrounded by pumpkins and cabbages. She was fatter than ever; but, said Bonne d'Heudicourt, "I think she is as wise as Cincinnatus."

I thought it my duty, for the King's sake, to put up a better fight against the ravages of time. I also had to struggle against possible rivals. These were the comtesse de Gramont, a flatterer and yet a backbiter too, whose company I put up with but whom I found more and more insufferable; and the Queen of England, Mary of Modena.† The latter, a refugee at Saint-Germain, had inherited the Italian charm of her mother, a "Mazarinette," and this touched a soft spot in the King's heart. Both these lovely ladies were twenty years younger than I.

Fortunately, because of good posture, I still had a supple and shapely figure. Bodies were no longer in fashion, but I would not have them forgotten, either by the young ladies of Saint-Cyr or by myself: I was of the opinion that physical laxness was soon followed by moral backsliding. I was also very careful to be always perfectly turned out, in thick rust-colored damask trimmed with silver braid, ample mauve or black velvets, gold brocades. I decked the actress while the player herself should have been thinking only of her shroud.

Since it had been decreed I should no longer occupy my mind with anything but trifles, I was quite proud to have brought ribbons back into fashion and to have given my name to the "Maintenon," a little cross set with four diamonds, worn round the neck.

As for my hair-style, I never went in for the "Fontanges" look, for the King loathed it, though he could do nothing to stop the other ladies adopting it. Kings are nothing beside fashion. Before she died, the King's last favorite, the duchesse de Fontanges, had given her name to a way of wearing the hair caught up in a ribbon on top of the head. It looked quite becoming on her, but as time went by, the Court ladies had modified and elaborated it to such a degree that they ended by wearing pyramids of hair two or three feet high, the whole edifice crowned with lace and jewels. Not liking to appear in public in a coiffure which the King did not like, but at the same time not wishing to be out of fashion, I covered the simple chignon in which I usually did my hair with long lace mantillas to match my gowns, or with large loose caps.

I was vexed, however, to see Madame de Gramont compete successfully with the fashion for "Fontanges." The favor she appeared to enjoy with the King, and the craze for imitating the Englishwomen at the Court of Saint-Germain in everything, brought back low hair-styles. But that was the only victory the comtesse won over me. I was still the King's only wife.

"The King has never loved any mistress as he does her," Madame used to say crossly to the duchesse de Ventadour, referring to me. "He really does love that woman," she would admit to her aunts, in between two scurrilous descriptions of me. It was true the King loved me, and I greatly appreciated the way he had shown it in the unfortunate affair of the quietists. He proved his affection energetically whenever we were alone. Even when I was seventy years old, he still performed his marital duties with the regularity of a young man, an assiduity worthy of astonishment rather than praise.

As I grew older, I could well have done without being honored so often. I was ashamed of my own gaunt, withered body and felt a revulsion from his. The encounter of the two struck me as ridiculous. I have never got any more pleasure from love than that one gets from the taste of a big white loaf when one is hungry, or from a cool dip in the river when the weather is hot. In my mind I could not separate the temptations of the flesh from the follies of youth. Even when they had been blessed by the Church, the pleasures of love seemed to me like childish games which it is proper to tire of as one grows older. I had no more desire now to go to bed with the King than I had to play hunt-the-slipper.

But it was no use trying to get out of it. When I consulted my director on the matter, he said very firmly:

"I pray to God, my beloved daughter, that you will not faint under the painful experiences you mention. It is a great purity in itself to preserve from possible impurity and scandal him who is entrusted to your care. You must persevere with the submission your vocation calls for, and be a refuge to a sinful man who would otherwise be lost. What a blessing, Madame, to be able to do out of pure virtue what other women do out of passion."

I learned my lesson, and I passed it on when I wrote to a young bride: "Satisfy your husband," I told her. "Do everything he asks and enter into all his fantasies."

The best marriages are those in which each partner suffers in turn at the hands of the other with kindness and patience. The King had suffered with good grace my political imprudences and my repugnance for Court life; surely I could suffer obediently his immodest appetites and constant tyranny, and swallow the pain inflicted on me by the clandestineness of our marriage.

"Do not weep, Madame," the bishop of Chartres wrote to me in this connection. "Your position is neither a temptation nor an accident, but a choice and intention of God." Nevertheless, foreign ambassadors went on regarding me as a courtesan, and certain pious ladies wrote and rebuked me for my equivocal situation.

"My bishop knows all about it," I replied to one of them, one day when I had had enough.

No matter. I was amply rewarded for all my pains when I saw the King free and cheerful in my apartment, relaxing from the anxiety of affairs of state.

He enjoyed the conversation of a little group of witty and virtuous young ladies whom I gathered together daily to amuse him: the gentle and lovely Sophie de Dangeau, who was born in Bavaria and whom I was fortunately able to get hold of before she was spoiled by the manners of the Court; the gallant Madame de Levis, daughter of the duchesse de Chevreuse and quick as mercury; my young cousin Madame de Mailly; and the highly romantic Madame d'O, daughter of my old friend and admirer Guilleragues.

These very young ladies were sometimes joined by two others, less young but more voluble than the most effusive among them. These were my old friend d'Heudicourt and Madame de Bracchiane. The latter was none other than the little comtesse de Chalais, with whom I had had such agreeable conversations at the hôtel d'Albret in the old days. Exiled with her husband thirty years ago, she had lived first for a while in Spain, and then in Italy, where Monsieur de Chalais had died. At first she was inconsolable, but then when she was thirty-two, she was consoled by marrying the first among the Roman princes, Monsieur de Bracchiane, otherwise known as Prince Orsini. She had been rich and honored and a great friend of the Pope, but one fine day, after some political quarrel or other with the prince her husband, she had decided to abandon all her palaces and come home. She had been living in France for eight years in proud poverty, without children or near relations, when I got wind of her return and rescued her.

Not having met for thirty years, we found each other much changed. Her little pointed face had put on so much flesh that at first I scarcely recognized it, and the slim body which once she used to dress in the height of Marais fashion was now swallowed up in fat and full Spanish skirts. Only her eyes had not changed. She still had the same mobile, keen, almost cruel glance that touched anyone she looked at to the quick; at most, the violet of her eyes, which used to be so acid, had acquired, with experience and the rings drawn round them by the years, more depth and softness. She was still always ravishingly dressed and painted with red and white, always on the alert, quick to make a point.

"How dare you say you're old!" she cried one day. "I'm only seven years younger than you and I'm quite young!"

The princesse Orsini had breeding and an incorrigible confidence in life; her energy and gaiety were irresistible.

She and Bonne d'Heudicourt met again in my apartment with the greatest possible joy. Among the three of us we could conjure up the wit of the salons in the old days. The only one missing was Madame de Montespan.

While we three laughed and told stories of the past, our young friends smiled and added their witticism to ours. Madame d'O, who was a very good reader, would sometimes give us an extract from

Perrault's *Tales* or Monsieur de La Bruyère's recently published *Characters*.

"Listen to this," she would say. " 'The Court is an edifice of marble: it is made up of men who are very hard but very polished!' Well put, is it not?"

The King laughed, and Madame de Dangeau took this as license to do one of the imitations at which she excelled. She would mimic Pontchartrain, grave and fat, or the lazy Barbezieux. Sometimes, at the subject's own request, she would take off the King himself as he walked through his gallery beset by crowds of spongers and petitioners: "I'll see, Monsieur." "It's possible, Monsieur." "It's impossible."

Then Madame de Levis would sit down at the harpsichord and the comtesse de Mailly would sing. My servants, more silent and invisible than ghosts, served every kind of delicious drink. I had laid it down once and for all that I wanted the King to be at his ease in my apartment, and no one, from the last of the footmen to the first of the ladies, ever asked him for anything there. Only Jeannette would sometimes dare to ask a favor, saying, "Monsieur, have you any sweeties?" and wiping her sticky fingers on the King's doublet. But Jeannette was only five years old. She was my latest discovery.

One winter on the way to Saint-Cyr I saw a woman on the road. She was tall, gaunt and in rags, but of good appearance, and before I could tell the coachman to stop she had flung herself in front of our wheels. We picked her up and found she had a child with her, quite a big girl and very frightened. We gave the woman something to eat and consoled the child; then we got them to talk. The woman was a member of the Breton nobility, but a widow and ruined. She had six children to feed and was desperate at having to watch them die of hunger. Having heard of my charities, she had not hesitated to come a hundred and fifty leagues, half by coach and half on foot, to see me and implore my help. She was burning with fever and covered with vermin and mud. I gave her all the money I had on me and promised to send her a small annual pension out of my own purse, through the provincial administrator of Brittany.

"Oh Madame, since you are so kind," she said, "won't you also take this little girl into Saint-Cyr?"

I considered the child for a moment, then said:

"No, Madame, I do not know if you could provide the necessary qualifications for her, and anyway Père de La Chaise is in charge of admissions. And I see your daughter here is more than twelve, and we do not take children as old as that."

"In that case, Madame," she answered, breathless with fever, "I have another daughter who would suit you. Oh yes! She is only two, she's my youngest. She is so pretty, Madame, it's a marvel— she's an angel of God. Hair like gold, skin whiter than milk, heavenly smiles, little hands made to be kissed! As for her intelligence, Madame, I have never seen anything like it . . ."

"Intelligence in a child of two . . ." said my secretary, with a scornful curl of her lip.

The poor lady seized my hands and crushed them in her anxiety.

"Oh yes, Madame, I assure you! She speaks like a book. Her sisters have started to teach her her letters—she'll soon know them. Do take her, Madame! Do! I beg you on my knees! I love her so, and she is lost if she stays with me. I'm ill, as you can see. I shall die, and my children will be thrown into the street. You can do anything. Save my little Jeannette. She's so young."

"Calm yourself, Madame," I said. "We don't take children of two at Saint-Cyr either . . . But I should like to do something. Send the little girl to me, and if she is as wonderful as you say, I'll take charge of her myself."

Six months later a messenger from the provincial administrator of Brittany brought me an untidy little package. It was Jeannette de Pincré, later comtesse d'Auxy, then a few pounds of pink and white flesh, a pair of blue eyes and a tongue that would have silenced a parrot. She was not shy: she threw herself straight into my arms, and a fortnight later was calling me "Mamma." I decided to bring her up myself. It seemed a long time since I had heard the prattle of children in my room, and I wondered how I had got on for so many years without it. I have always strewn my path with children, so that when I look back, it is them I see most clearly, like so many little white pebbles. The duchesse de Bourgogne is not the least precious among them.

The duc de Bourgogne, Monsieur le Dauphin's eldest son, was a strange child, with a face like an angry cat, a hunched back and a kind of pride that kept him aloof from the rest of humanity. Fortunately he was not without intelligence, and Monsieur de Fénelon, when he was his tutor, used to boast of having overcome his pupil's misanthropy by a judicious application of reason and piety.

What little I saw of him seemed to me to bode no good. The boy remained very attached to his tutor and appeared unwilling to forgive us for Fénelon's disgrace. When the King heard of the Curia's ruling on the *Maxims of the Saints* and said, "Monsieur de Cambrai's doctrine has been condemned," the young duc replied curtly, "What he taught me never will be." The King was surprised and hurt.

I myself was sometimes the victim of Monsieur de Bourgogne's moods. One day when he was in my room but was cold, dreamy and even absent-minded, I reproached him gently for it, saying he seemed not to know me. "Indeed, Madame," he replied severely, "I know you very well. And what's more I know the duc de Bourgogne is in your room." This brusque retort made me silent in my turn, and the princesse Orsini came over to me and whispered, "Time will tell, Madame, whom we have to deal with."

To impart some humanity to this ungracious grandson, the King decided to marry him off when he was fourteen, and he selected for him a daughter of the duc de Savoie, who through her mother was granddaughter to Monsieur, the King's brother, and his first wife, Henrietta of England.

Marie-Adelaïde de Savoie was not yet eleven years old when she came to France. The King went to Montargis to meet her and fell in love with her at first sight. I use the words deliberately, for it really was a passion—noble and purified no doubt, but absolute —that the aging man felt for the girl, who was already entirely feminine and a coquette. As a matter of fact we both loved the child beyond reason, I as a grandmother, for I had been old enough for such feelings for some time, and the King, who still felt like a young man, as a Platonic admirer, possessive and jealous.

The letter he sent me on the very evening of their first meeting at Montargis is, apart from two or three notes, the only one from him I have kept. It recalls so well my little princesse and the spell she cast all around her that I could not bring myself to burn it. It would have been like making her die a second time.

"I got here before five o'clock," wrote the King. "The princesse did not arrive till about six. I went to meet her coach. She let me speak first, and then answered me very well, but with a touch of shyness which you would have liked. I took her to her room through the crowd, having the torches brought close to her face now and then so that the people could see her, and she endured both the walk and the lights with grace and modesty. We finally reached her room, and I examined her in every possible way so as to be able to give you my impressions. She is more graceful and has a prettier figure than anyone I have ever seen. She was dressed like a picture, and her hair was also well arranged. She has very bright and beautiful eyes with lovely dark lids, a glowing complexion and great quantities of the most beautiful fair hair. She is thin like all girls of her age. Her mouth is very red, her teeth white, her hands shapely. She speaks little but is not awkward.

"We had supper, and she partook of everything with an amazing polish in all she did. She carried herself as you might have done, with a noble air and polite and agreeable manners . . . I almost forgot to tell you I saw her play spillikins with delightful skill. When the day comes for her to appear in public she will charm everyone with her graceful manner, dignity and composure."

The King loved feminine society, but he was very hard to please. I could see from his letter that it behooved me to be enthusiastic about the little girl from Piedmont.

I did not have to force myself: Marie-Adelaïde was more charming than I would have thought possible. When she came into my room at Fontainebleau with her doll under her arm, she did not strike me at first as being so pretty as the King had described her. Her figure was certainly pretty, but her face was not perfect. Only the huge, beautiful eyes were beyond dispute. But the way she combined vivaciousness with majesty, her mixture of childishness and gravity, were irresistible.

She threw her arms around me and called me "aunt," a pretty way of confusing rank with affection. I tried to stop her caresses; I was too old. "Not so very old!" she said, settling confidently on my lap.

"Mamma," she said, "told me to give you all her love and ask you to give me all yours. Please teach me all I need to know to be agreeable."

That was what she said, but the gaiety, sweetness and grace that went with the words cannot be conveyed in writing. In short, I at once loved the little princesse more than I ought. I knew it, but I could not help it.

As soon as I had seen her, I begged the King not to let her mix with the Court, which would corrupt that singular dignity of hers. He agreed, and the duchesse de Bourgogne spent all her time either in my apartment, or at Saint-Cyr, or with the animals she loved in the little château the King had built for her in the Menagerie. I was her governess, Nanon her friend.

"Nanon," I used to say. "When you lived in the impasse Saint-Roch did you ever think you'd one day have the future Queen of France sitting on your lap?"

As we were not sure how her husband would behave, we at first allowed the duchesse to see him only once a week. Her time was divided up between lessons, moral instruction and the innocent amusements proper to her age. When she arrived in France, she could scarcely read; I also got a master to teach her writing. She used to come to my room and together we would read the life of Saint Theresa or the memoirs of Joinville, which he called the *Life of Saint Louis;* then she would run about in my sitting-room with Jeannette or play at grown-up ladies until they came and fetched her for her dancing or harpsichord lesson. The education I gave her was free of all constraint. I used nothing but gentleness and patience, overlooking many little things so as to insist on the important ones. Admittedly I let her leave her room untidy, play in the gardens at night, jump about like a little monkey when riding in a coach, read my letters and sing during public ceremonies. I agree it took her two or three years to learn how to behave like a grown-up at table. At supper with the King she would fidget about on her chair, bow to everyone, make the most horrid faces, tear chickens and partridges apart with her fingers and dip them in all the sauces.

But table manners and suchlike come of themselves by virtue of example. I was more concerned with something deeper. I wanted the duchesse of Bourgogne to love greatness and pride herself on the honor of being a great princesse, to know where the welfare of the people resided and to want to serve God, to love the King and obey her husband.

The last was not the easiest. The duc de Bourgogne, who never took his nose out his books on physics and geography except to go to vespers, was not exactly lovable. "It is not to be expected," I told my little princesse, "that a husband will feel the same affection as one feels oneself. Men are usually less loving than women. They are tyrannical by nature and want pleasures and freedoms for themselves which they want women to renounce. But they are the masters, and the only thing to do is put up with things with good grace."

Adelaïde would listen gravely, laugh, kiss me and run off and dress up as a sultana, a milkmaid, a sorceress or a queen of clubs for the "masked balls" which the King arranged for her.

For her the King multiplied his "Marlys."

The château de Marly, where we used to go and spend nearly ten days every month, had always been greatly prized by the Court. As there was less room there than at Versailles, the King himself selected the fifty or so "chosen" from the thousand or so "called." Two or three days before we left, courtiers would throw themselves at his feet imploring, "Sire, Marly!" as if their lives depended on it. "Even the rain at Marly doesn't make you wet!" said one of the lucky ones.

After he became smitten with his granddaughter-in-law, the King made up his lists of guests for Marly with even more care than before. There were hunting Marlys, bringing together all the Court's best hunters, gambling Marlys, Marlys with plays, carnival Marlys, Marlys for frolicking. In summer the princesse bathed in the river with her ladies, played on the swing which the King had had put up on the terrace and invited me to midnight feasts in the "green apartments." In winter she reviewed the troops, sang opera with the duc de Chartres and skated on the "Great Mirror" with my niece Françoise de Noailles.

Everywhere and at all seasons her natural, simple manner charmed everyone, right down to the footmen. She was irresistible whether she was in a velvet bodice and cloth-of-gold skirt feeding the doves from her own mouth in the aviary at Trianon, or in a flame-colored gown, her hair braided with pearls, in the big refectory at Saint-Cyr, or in pale grey velvet embroidered with emeralds in the chapel at Versailles, or at a ball at Marly, wearing a coronet of rubies, or at Fontainebleau, in a red hunting doublet, her hair all loose from her ride.

I do not say she never did anything amiss as she was growing up. She had all the imprudence of youth and of a naturally lively temperament. At gaming she lost more than the allowance the King made her; she put snowballs down the princesse d'Harcourt's dress; she smoked pipes which she borrowed from the Switzers of the guard; she was too ready to listen to the compliments of Nangis or Maulevrier; and lastly, she took liberties with the King, like a spoiled child sure of being let off scot-free.

But she made him as happy as could be, and she loved me as tenderly as I could wish. I never knew anyone else in the King's family who could love as she did, like an ordinary person, not even my own duc du Maine. She was the only person I would take with me when I fled the Court and went to one of the refuges I had gradually made for myself in various places: my house in the town of Fontainebleau; the Carmelite nunnery at Compiègne; a secret apartment I called "peace," behind the chapel at Marly; the little hôtel de Maintenon in the town at Versailles; and at Meudon a cottage hidden away in the park.

By dint of argument, and of time spent with me or in enforced loneliness, the naughty little girl finally became all we could have hoped. When she was over twenty-two, and I left her free to do as she liked, running her own household and with her own circle of friends, she appeared at Court as she really was: a thorough princesse, able to hold a witty conversation, full of kindness toward the unfortunate, enamored of the greatness of France, never incommoded by the crowd or by having to appear in public, always respectful toward her husband. Nothing was so lively and brilliant, so gay and agreeable as her actions, nothing more sound than her heart and mind. The people loved her because she was always ready to let herself be seen. The Court delighted in her because she imparted more life to its pleasures than any queen had ever done. And her husband adored her with a passion which was almost embarrassing both for her and for onlookers.

After having had to endure many speeches about the wrong way I was bringing her up, after being criticized by everyone for the liberty with which she ran about from morn till night, after having seen her accused of being horribly false in her attachment to the King and her kindness to me, I could not but be happy when everyone suddenly began to sing her praises, to say she had a good heart and a great wit, and to agree that she knew how to keep the courtiers at a proper distance.

If our joys could be as complete as our sorrows, I would have been perfectly happy. But the sight of the woes which soon overwhelmed France made me so ashamed of being content that after a few years of perfect happiness I fell once more into a deep melancholy.

As long as the peace lasted, France had gradually returned to plenty. The King devoted himself to the task. Sometimes he would spend a whole day in my room doing accounts, going over them ten times without wearying, and never stopping until the work was done. "A king should never leave his work for his pleasures," he would say gently to the duchesse de Bourgogne when she came and plucked at his sleeve, gave him a kiss or tickled him under the chin. He kept the organization of his armies on his own shoulders alone, and knew the strength of all his regiments in detail. He held several councils a day, and knew all the skills of government better than anyone.

So he spent less and less time on his choice of ministers. When he took Finance away from Monsieur de Pontchartrain and gave it to my friend Chamillart, I did not know whether it was because I praised the honest gentleman or because he was good at billiards.

As the King grew older, he grew increasingly fond of the game. "Here lies the famous Chamillart," said a Paris song, "his King's chief clerk: at billiards a hero, at government a zero." It seems probable that at first Chamillart lost at billiards in a suitable manner, for in 1701, when Barbezieux died young, the King added the War portfolio to the Finance ministry which Chamillart had held for two years. Pontchartrain was now only chancellor, but still had the Navy ministry, where he continued to do harm.

However, I did not wish to be mixed up in affairs of state any more, and for several years the King, still cool from the quietist affair, no longer talked to me about them. Madame des Ursins, as the princesse Orsini was called, who was passionately interested in political intrigue, used to urge me to pay more attention.

"But you know very well, my dear," I told her, "I can hardly see"—I had taken to using spectacles a few years earlier—"and my hearing isn't much better."

"Not a very flattering portrait," she replied, "but it mustn't be taken too literally. You hear what pleases you, you see what doesn't displease you and you speak or are silent as you think fit."

To my great surprise, the King wanted to know my opinion about a matter which arose at that time. He was worried about the flight of so many people out of the country as a result of the revocation of the Edict of Nantes and the harsh treatment of the Huguenots. He had asked for reports on the subject from Daguesseau, Basville and other provincial administrators, and from a handful of bishops. The advice they gave was so varied, at first, that the King pretended he did not know which to take. Monsieur de Noailles, the new archbishop of Paris, together with Monsieur Daguesseau and the Intendants of the north, counselled moderation, liberty of conscience and even in some cases freedom of religion, through a revocation of the Revocation. The bishops of the south and all the coterie still secretly inspired by Monsieur de Fénelon advocated continuing the policy of repression: they thought the extent of the emigration was exaggerated and regarded it as a nuisance rather than a disaster.

I read all these memoranda and was no less confused than the King claimed to be. In doubt, I thought it wise to steer a middle

course, and on reflection this solution seemed to me most in keeping with the greatness of France. I too wrote a memorandum, of
which I have kept a copy. Here is part of it:

"It seems to me that the best thing would be, without issuing
any new declarations or revoking any of those already made, to
make the treatment of the newly converted less harsh. Above all,
not to force them to commit sacrilege by taking the sacrament
without faith or without being in the proper state of mind; not to
drag the bodies of those who refuse the last sacraments through the
streets on a hurdle; nor to seek out and buy cheaply property put
up for sale by those who have left the kingdom. Entertainments
representing executions should be forbidden . . . As for assemblies,
they constitute disobedience and should be punished, provided the
chastisement falls only on the guilty, and the innocent are not
confused with them . . . One might start by converting, without
severity, the poorest of the Huguenots: setting up hospices in every
province, where parents could voluntarily bring their children to
be treated and educated with great care; their relations would be
allowed to see them, and they would be softened by the happiness
of their little ones. Boys could be admitted to the cadet schools,
girls into convents. Money could not be better employed, whether
one looks at the project from the Christian or from the political
point of view. Moreover, the sound instruction that might thus be
given throughout the provinces would benefit the old Catholics as
well as the new converts . . ."

As I see from rereading this document, wherever I started out
from, I always came back to children and the education of the
people.

The King did not go quite so far. He said lack of money
prevented him. He did, however, listen to what I said about the
gentleness which should accompany such severity as was necessary
toward the *réunis* or new converts, and he did not dwell on difficulties there. If I had been as clearsighted as I was well intentioned,
I would have spoken out more strongly on this matter of religion.
But it was all so difficult, obscure and uncertain that I dared speak
only in general terms.

By a secret memorandum of 7 January 1699, addressed to the

bishops and Intendants, the King merely counselled moderation toward the new converts: "His Majesty does not wish any constraint to be used to make them receive the sacraments; no difference should be made in this respect between them and the old Catholics." He gave Calvinists who had left the country permission to return, provided they were converted before six months were up, and deprived the Intendants of the extraordinary powers they had been allowed in the matter for the past fifteen years.

But, for the rest, he did not change his policy. He did once admit to me that the revocation of the Edict of Nantes might have been a mistake, and that the way it had been interpreted in some places certainly was one. Still, he never wanted to turn back. "It's by going straight ahead that you get out of the wood," he said.

People calmed down, except in the south where they are naturally hotheaded. In 1702, fanatics broke out in revolt in the Languedoc, and the trouble spread to the Vivarais. Our troops were unable at first to stamp out these mountain rebellions. They hated fighting against elusive peasants; they were used to great sweeping movements on the plains and were afraid of these peaks and ravines. Neither the burning of villages nor the most cruel tortures could pacify the provinces where the trouble was. The authority of the state and the safety of the nation, then engaged in another war with Europe, were for two years in peril.

It was the maréchal de Villars, a great captain and the son of my handsome admirer in the Marais, Villars-Orondate, who, with the help of my friend Basville, overcame the rebels. Every week the maréchal sent me long accounts of his adventures so that I might pass the information on to the King and his ministers and, when the occasion arose, defend Villars himself against his numerous enemies at Court. He thought kindness was more likely to bring people round than force alone, and he even spoke to the people himself to try to turn them away from their foolish obstinacy, their miracles and their prophets. Finally he managed to win over one of the rebel chiefs and eight hundred of the principal Camisards† by promising that they might continue to sing their psalms and practice their religion in the midst of the King's armies. "Let's stop up our ears," he wrote, "and have done with all this if we can." It was quite easy for him, afterwards, to mop up all the brigands who were left in the mountains, burning all the cottages for seven leagues around and killing everyone he came across, including women and children.

I organized a great procession at Saint-Cyr to celebrate the crushing of the fanatics and the return of peace. I meant to organize a greater one still if ever the foreign war turned out as well as the civil strife had done. But that happiness seemed a long way off.

The peace signed at Ryswick, so necessary for the restoration of trade and agriculture, had lasted only four years when it was ended abruptly by the death of Charles II of Spain.

Charles died childless and had bequeathed the Crown to the young duc d'Anjou, the Dauphin's second son, as his nearest relative and the person he thought most capable, with France's help, of keeping his empire intact. Unfortunately, the archduke of Austria, almost as close a relative of the dead king as the duc d'Anjou, also claimed the succession.

The King my husband knew enough about politics to realize that Europe would not look with favor on an arrangement by which the monarchy of Spain would be subordinated to France, for three hundred years her rival. So in 1699 he had negotiated, with England, Austria and Holland, a division of the future Spanish succession and a series of exchanges. As he told me later, he had claimed only moderate gains for France: Lorraine, which we had lost again at Ryswick; Nice and Savoy, or Luxembourg; and perhaps the Spanish Basque country or the Two Sicilies.

"I hesitated for a long time," he told me, "weighing up the respective advantages of profiting by the Spaniards' liking for France or else accepting what seemed less but was in fact more substantial and ensured the peace of Europe. Proper considerations led me to treat with the King of England, and with him to take the measures necessary to preserve peace. It seemed to me nothing was more propitious to the general good of all Europe than to lessen further the power of the house of Austria."

A secret agreement was concluded with the English and the Dutch, but the emperor of Austria would never subscribe to the idea of a division and refused any accommodation. So the situation was embarrassing, as it well could be, when the King of Spain died. If France rejected the Spanish bequest, the kingdom of Spain would go in its entirety to the archduke of Austria as second legatee, and the restoration of the empire of Charles V, which France could not accept, would make war inevitable. But if France accepted the will, she would be breaking the treaty with England and Holland, and would, with Spain, represent so powerful a monarchy in Europe that again war would be unavoidable.

It was in November 1700, in my apartment at Fontainebleau, that the refusal or acceptance of the will was debated. Twice, on 9 November, the King met there with his ministers and the Dauphin. I was wearing my glasses and spinning wool in a corner of the room, my feet on a footwarmer and with mittens on my hands, for a very cold draft came from the tall window with its thirty-six panes. I would have liked to be just an old woman, chilly and tired, blind and deaf. I did not want to know what people would say or be persecuted by anxiety and remorse alternately. I wanted to be at Mursay looking after the turkeys.

The Dauphin spoke little, but emerged for a moment from his fat and his apathy to conclude without hesitation that the will should be accepted. Turning respectfully toward the King, he said he would take the liberty of "asking for his inheritance." Torcy, who at the first meeting of the Council had declared for the carrying out of the treaty, now advocated accepting the will: "Whatever we do we can no longer avoid war," he said, looking very pale. "And it is better to wage it with Spain rather than against her, and for all the succession rather than for a part."

Monsieur de Beauvilliers, on the other hand, pointed out the immediate advantages of the treaty of partition concluded with the English, and the need to keep one's word. Barbezieux only muttered a couple of words about the King's greatness and the glory of uniting two ancient monarchies within the same family. Pontchartrain rehearsed at length, in very high-flown language, all possible arguments for accepting and all possible arguments against. After making this useless contribution he said no more.

The King listened carefully to all his ministers, thanked them, and dismissed them. He stood in the doorway for a moment, talking to Torcy and Barbezieux. I feverishly went on with my spinning. At last the moment I had been dreading arrived: when he was the only one left in my room, the King asked me what I thought about all this.

I felt incapable of deciding on a question so far beyond my competence, and was in despair. If I had had to fasten on to something I would, like Monsieur de Beauvilliers, have fastened on to the need to keep our promises to England, but I felt that this naive idea, which resembled those Monsieur de Fénelon used to put in his memoranda, was not really a political one. "Madame de Maintenon knows as much about politics as my dog Titi," Madame used to say, and it was only too true.

I told the King I could not, in conscience, give him any advice: he had ruled for so long he knew better than anyone what was good for France and need not bother with the views of his ministers, the Dauphin or an old woman. He pressed me further, but I was evasive and did not give an opinion. He looked troubled and uncertain. "I'm sure many people will condemn me whatever I decide," he sighed. It was after ten o'clock and he could not make up his mind to go to supper. He had always hated taking risks and only liked betting on certainties. It was torture to him that this time fate was forcing him to wager. He walked round and round the room, opening and closing the window, gazing at the stars.

I felt a great pity for him and his solitude. If I had not been so shy, if he had not been the King, I would have embraced, caressed, consoled him; we would have wept together. But I did not dare do anything, and he only kissed my hand gently as he took his leave.

Next morning the duchesse de Bourgogne, who had spent the night at the ball and the opera, came into my room as I woke up. She had just come home.

"You don't look very cheerful, Aunt," she said, rubbing her little cold nose against my neck.

"The Spanish affair is going badly, my dear," I told her.

"What! Is the King rejecting the will?"

"No . . . He may accept it, but that won't make it any better . . ."

"Oh, Aunt!" she cried, laughing and shaking her fair curls, "you have too vivid an imagination. You see dangers everywhere. You should be pleased: nothing will be so great and powerful as France and Spain together."

It is said that the decision the King finally took, urged on by the enthusiasm of his Court and his family, was not the right one. Perhaps he was indeed wrong, but he was magnificent even in error.

"Messieurs," he said, throwing wide the doors of his room on to the gallery at Versailles and ushering his grandson, the duc d'Anjou, dazed, before him, "Messieurs, here is the King of Spain."

"How splendid!" cried the Spanish ambassador. "There are no more Pyrenees—they have melted, and we are one country henceforth."

"There are not many princes," said the Dauphin, delighted, "who can say both 'the King my father' and 'the King my son.'"

The courtiers applauded; there were many other witty remarks. It was a great day, perhaps the high point of the reign. We paid for it with thirteen years of war and despair.

The war, against Europe in coalition, was indeed dreadful, for France was in no position now to wage it, and Spain, which we had believed to be strong, collapsed at the first assault. It was a dead body, which did not put up a fight.

At first we carried the war into Germany and Italy. France was bled white by the effort of equipping two hundred thousand soldiers, but still we were lucky enough to be fighting on foreign soil, and our own countryside was spared.

But the negligence of our military leaders, all generals of whim and favor, prevented us from profiting from our early victories. Old Villeroy dreamed, Marcin withdrew, La Feuillade disobeyed and Vendôme never left his close-stool, not a very convenient position from which to command an army. Only Villars, bold to the point of temerity, skilled in execution and loved by the men, did wonders wherever he was sent, in Germany, Flanders and the Dauphiné. But he could not be everywhere at once. Pontchartrain had neglected the navy, and we sorely missed its support. Soon the infantry was not being fed because there was no more money: Monsieur de Chamillart, who was minister both for War and for the Treasury, turned out to be a better courtier than financier.

In 1704 thirty-five thousand of our foot soldiers and eighteen thousand cavalry were defeated at Blenheim on the Danube. Among them was the old regiment of Navarre of which the King was so fond, and which before it surrendered, tore up and buried its flags. Thirty thousand men of the army of the Rhine were killed or taken prisoner, their standards, guns and baggage all remained in enemy hands. When the terrible news reached Paris, no one dared inform the King, and it fell to me to tell him he was no longer invincible.

Then our troops yielded everywhere: Catalonia, Gibraltar, the provinces of Valencia and Murcia, Madrid itself, all fell into the hands of the enemy. We had got out of Germany; now we had to leave the Milanese, and Villeroy abandoned Flanders after the battle of Ramillies, in which he lost eight thousand men in a single day. At Court people no longer spoke of victories, but of "strategic withdrawals"; we were withdrawing everywhere, and thought ourselves lucky if it was not in disorder and carnage.

These routs left me dazed, appalled, stupid, but my worst suffering came from seeing the King suffer. He suffered in silence, but the words he did not say were written on his face in bitter wrinkles and lines. Villeroy, relieved of his command for incompetence, returned to Versailles: the King only said to him wearily, "Monsieur le Maréchal, we are past happiness at our age . . ." That was almost his sole comment on his defeats. Sometimes he would be overcome by tears which he could not master and which I wiped away. Only the duchesse de Bourgogne could still make him smile.

In 1708 we were reduced to defending France's own frontiers. Providence had chosen to support a profligate rather than a Christian king. The latter, not knowing which way to turn in this debacle, turned to me as the person in his Court most likely to be on good terms with God. So in spite of myself I was more and more involved in affairs of state—half-informed, half-consulted, half-listened to.

I managed to get Villars another command; he had been kept out of the army for several months through intrigues at Court. Once on the Rhine he carried out the most brilliant actions with an army that had been said to be beaten and demoralized. He even got as far as Stuttgart, but he could not maintain his advance for want of supplies. He openly accused Monsieur de Chamillart of being responsible for this.

Villars wrote to me once or twice a week for ten years, telling me his plans and his troubles, looking on me as his friend and most intimate adviser. I would have liked him to have a more important command, Flanders for example, where all was in great danger. "It is sometimes best," I said to the King, "to give the cards to a player who has good luck." But all I could get for my brave soldier then was the blue ribbon of the Order of the Holy Ghost, even though the King included me in several councils of war.

I also carried on a regular correspondence with the princesse Orsini and with Spain.

When the King married his grandson, the King of Spain, to a young sister of the duchesse de Bourgogne, the question had arisen of who was to be the new Queen's *camerera-mayor*. This post, usually not much more than that of a lady-in-waiting, could be far more important in the case of a queen of twelve and a king of seventeen, both foreigners in their own kingdom and alone in a country at war. "I make so bold as to say," wrote Anne-Marie des Ursins, who had gone back to Rome on the death of the prince her husband, "that I am more suitable than anyone for this position, because of all the friends I have in Spain and the fact that I am a 'grandee' there. Moreover I speak Spanish, and I am sure the whole country would be glad if I were chosen."

As I ventured my opinion more on matters concerning the ladies than on others, I suggested my friend, who in addition to her great good sense, integrity and cheerfulness, had as she said the advantage of possessing a perfect knowledge of Spanish ways. The King and the duc de Savoie accepted her. The little Queen soon let herself be led as expected, and King Philippe, in this resembling his brother the duc de Bourgogne, was so taken with his wife he did whatever she wanted. And so the princesse Orsini, the Queen's governess, ruled Spain as well.

She and I wrote to each other every week regularly for nine years. She told me the kind of news ambassadors could not know, the hidden thoughts of the King and Queen of Spain, the opinions of the grandees. I wrote to her of the rumors at Court, my opinions on the conduct of the war and those of the King. The two were not always the same.

In fact, Madame des Ursins held the Spanish monarchy in the palm of her hand, for the King was shy and incompetent and did not really reign. With the help of the duc d'Orléans and the French army, she retook Madrid, and the English were soon driven back into the mountains of Valencia and Barcelona. She even succeeded in rousing the Spaniards and in making the young King and Queen so loved and admired by them that they invented a thousand ways of murdering the Austrians. In short, Madame des Ursins was doing what she was born to do, and she rejoiced in the worst of difficulties. When I confided my fears to her she said I was "vaporish" and should be ashamed of giving way to anxiety.

"Never despair," she wrote. "Everything can change in a moment. Often, when you think you're about to fall down a precipice, some unexpected happiness occurs."

"We should do very well," I replied, "if we could find a middle way between your confidence and my despair."

I asked her to get all the Spanish convents to pray for Their Catholic Majesties. She answered that in her opinion soldiers cutting off hands and noses would be more to the point. She was seeing the authority of her masters growing daily in Spain, but in France I was seeing the authority of mine decreasing. Marlborough was on our northern frontiers, Prince Eugene and his Germans to the east, the duc de Savoie at the gates of the Dauphiné, while the English sailed up and down the Mediterranean as freely as the swans at Chantilly. The state hung in the balance on the hazards of a day. The people were complaining.

A strange prayer was being said in the streets of Paris: "Our

413

father who art at Versailles, thy name is no longer hallowed, thy kingdom is no longer so great, thy will is no longer done on land or sea. Give us our bread, which is lacking everywhere. Forgive our enemies who have beaten us, but not our generals who let them do so. Do not be led into all the temptations of La Maintenon, and deliver us from Chamillart."

I begged the King to seek peace on any conditions the enemies wished, even if it meant leaving Spain to look after itself or the recall of his grandson. Madame des Ursins, now more Spanish than French, called my advice "cowardice," and as we told each other everything, we thought our correspondence was by no means dull.

The King greeted my supplications with a chilly silence.

"One does not treat with one's back to the wall, Madame," he said at last. "We must wait and hope."

"But, Sire, supposing God wanted to change the boundaries of the kingdom—would it not be better to sacrifice something rather than expose all the rest?"

"If that is what God wants, Madame, very well. But if it is what the English want, allow me to disagree."

Every so often, however, he would get angry with Madame des Ursins, who was not obedient enough for his liking, and I had to smoothe matters over between the two politicians.

But the national woes did not stop people from dancing at Versailles. In that year of 1708 there was a ball every other day. The King did it to show his enemies he was not afraid of them. So the duchesse de Bourgogne danced, but many of the courtiers who had been wounded in the fighting no longer attended the balls. Madame de Dangeau's son had lost a leg. The plays called forth only mechanical laughter. Debauchery was veiled with sadness, and the most enchanting haunts seemed faded. The whole kingdom was gradually being overcome by a strange lassitude. Beneath the still splendid appearances, illness and death were everywhere. My own life was becoming like a vast graveyard, desolate and empty.

Marguerite de Montchevreuil had died, and Nanon, and, the same year, my old friend Ninon de Lenclos; also kind Henri de Montchevreuil, who had witnessed my marriage and my rise, and my cousin Philippe. Then the abbé Testu went, and Madame de

Montgon, whom I had fed on my lap at Vaugirard when she was still only little Louise d'Heudicourt.

In May 1707 Madame de Montespan too left this world. I could not be unmoved by her death, for at no time was she ever a matter of indifference to me. But the King ordered the mourning to be brief.

The young duc de Bretagne, the duchesse de Bourgogne's first son, gave up his little soul to God, and after a short illness Madame d'Heudicourt gave up hers, though it was not so young and hopeful. Her *occupées*— the servants she and Madame de Montespan had to watch over them as they slept, so as to avoid a solitary death— had not done their job well.

I stayed by my friend's bedside for the five days her illness lasted and prepared her gently for her end. I now played a very peculiar role at Court, only telling people of what they did not want to hear, namely defeat and death. When Madame d'Heudicourt's soul had quitted her gaunt yellow body I kept vigil over her myself. My niece de Caylus, then back in favor, sat beside me, but she was frightened by the ugliness of the corpse and soon took refuge in the antechamber. I forced her to come back and contemplate for a moment that sunken face, that gaping mouth, that skeletal body.

"That is what you will be like one day, my dear, and what you will see about you before you get there yourself. So get used to looking at it."

I kept a list in my pocket of the people of quality who had died in the past two years. It was like the "list for Marly."

It is not true that one cannot look directly at the sun or upon death. One can look straight at them and feel nothing, after a moment, but a slight burning sensation. But you must be careful to turn your eyes away from time to time, so as not to become blind to everything else.

So my thoughts ran one evening in 1708, when by some chance or other I was alone at Versailles, looking out of a window in the Great Gallery and watching the sun go down.

It sank almost directly over the Grand Canal, spreading more gold over the mirror of the water and the mirrors in the Gallery than all the plate the King had had melted down. There is something splendid about the dying of the sun. The whole Gallery was bathed in a full yellow light which lit up the crystal of the chandeliers and the jewels in the epergnes more brightly than candles on the gayest evening. The flaming blues and ochers in the sky over the gardens reminded me of the mural of "The Chariot of the Sun Disappearing into the Waves" on one of the walls of the Trianon. In the painting of the god plunging into the depths I now recognized the features of the great King, just as I had recognized them long ago in the young "Apollo Served by the Nymphs" of one of the fountains.

Unable to take my eyes off the sight of the dying sun, I stayed there until its last ray was swallowed up by the canal and the shadows. Only then did I feel the darkness close in on me.

Seventeen

"The Almighty troubleth me," said Job. "The days of affliction have taken hold upon me." The King of France could soon say the same, so plain was it that God was against him and to punish his pride wanted to reduce him to dust and ashes.

It had been decided to give a command to the duc de Bourgogne, whom the King his grandfather considered intelligent and whom for several years he had included in his Councils rather than Monseigneur, his son. So he was appointed to share the command of Flanders with Monsieur de Vendôme. I had long wanted this post to go to the maréchal de Villars, but since my little duchesse was glad to see her husband given this distinction, I rejoiced with her when the duc de Bourgogne left the Court for Mons, where eighty thousand men were already quartered.

The campaign turned out worse than badly.

There was nothing in common between Vendôme, fat, lustful, presumptuous and always surrounded by scullions and minions, and the young prince, thin, timid and pious, who left his books for only a moment to follow the procession when the army went through a town. There was no possibility of their getting on together.

Moreover it may have been rash to send the duc de Bourgogne to the front at all, when he had never concealed the fact that he regarded the art of war as the scourge of the human race.

"To make war on unarmed peasants," he said one day in the King's presence, "to burn their houses and tear down their vines, fell their trees and set fire to their buildings is cowardice and banditry."

I think he would even have hated to rule. Monsieur de Fénelon, with whom he remained in close contact in spite of the distance separating them, had made him so sensitive to the injustices of government that he did not wish to have it on his conscience.

Vendôme wanted to fight; the duc de Bourgogne did not—but he was too unsure of himself to impose his will on his cousin. The army was divided between Vendômists and Bourgignons. While they were quarrelling, their enemies joined together. Vendôme attacked at Oudenaarde, alone. The duc de Bourgogne declined to take part in an operation he regarded as reckless, and his troops looked on at the battle like spectators at the opera. Then, against Vendôme's advice, the prince ordered a retreat, which because no one was in command, turned into a rout. We lost twenty-five thousand men, Marlborough ravaged Artois, and Prince Eugene laid siege to Lille.

Monsieur de Vendôme and the duc de Bourgogne could not agree about saving the city. This time it was Vendôme who did not want to attack, saying the siege was only a feint to trap the prince.

Old maréchal de Boufflers came to Versailles and offered to go to Lille's defense, and the King accepted his offer. He set out at once without baggage, using Post horses and not even going home first. No one had ever seen such zeal and virtue combined with such great age. But although he conducted a most vigorous and skilful defense, after weeks of heroic resistance he was obliged to capitulate for want of relief.

The King was very much affected by the loss of Lille, so French and so beautiful a city and one of the first conquests of his reign.

He was touched on the raw by the humiliation of our army, which had done nothing to come to Lille's support. And he was more than grieved that the Court imputed most of our misfortunes to his own grandson. Some people even alleged that the duc de Bourgogne was playing battledore and shuttlecock when he heard of the capitulation of Lille, and that he did not interrupt the game.

I myself did not cast all the blame on the young duc. I knew Vendôme was lazy and over-confident and mistakenly scornful of the enemy. I thought the prince, who was new to military matters, had been right in his judgment about Lille. And I sympathized with the sorrow of my little princesse. I would never have believed she loved her husband so much. Until then she had let herself be adored without returning his affection; the prince, who knew the influence I had over her, used to lament this fact to me in letters full of wit and sadness. But now she showed him a real and delicate love. She was distressed that the first action in which he had ever been involved should have been so unsuccessful. She shared his sorrow and anxiety, hoping for and yet dreading a battle. Every time the Post arrived, her heart beat faster. She feared for her husband's life; she feared for his reputation. She could no longer endure the stories told about him and the insolent criticisms. In a few weeks she had become one of the unhappiest creatures in the world.

I was just as distressed as she was. The courtiers murmured that the King had been mistaken in this campaign, and that army commands should not be shared between generals and princes. Freedom of speech has always been excessive in France, and now, at a time of defeat, it was becoming intolerable. If I had been in charge of things, all those fine talkers would have been in the army or in their homes in the provinces, and only indispensable officials would have been left at Court.

"But why so large a Court, Sire?" I asked. "All these useless people whom you support and who bite the hand that feeds them!"

"I have my reasons, Madame," replied the King, immovable amid the storms.

Once Lille had fallen, I imagined the enemy in France, in Paris.

Fear was written on every face at Court. It was shameful: every time a horse rode by more quickly than usual, people fled they knew not where. The churches were full of supplicants.

The fortress of Exile in the Dauphiné surrendered to the duc de Savoie without even putting up a fight. The King said some strange things were happening these days, and he could scarcely understand the French any more.

To sum up, our strongholds were abandoned, our frontiers exposed and our enemies stood between our armies and ourselves. All the north of the kingdom was suddenly invested and looted. The Germans even had the impudence to send a detachment of twenty officers as far as the outskirts of Versailles, where they were supposed to capture some princes of the blood but succeeded only in catching some people of no importance.

The King never despaired. He could not give me a particle of his courage, nor could I infect him with the least of my fears. He was determined not to treat for peace. He relieved Vendôme of his command, recalled his grandson to Court and replaced the pair of them with Villars, with instructions to rally the troops.

Then God, vexed by such resistance, struck harder. Famine was added to war.

Such cold as is not seen once a century spread all over the country. In the cupboards even of heated rooms, toilet waters and liqueurs froze and split their bottles. The sea and all the rivers froze too. The earth was solid: no fruits could grow, and all the trees died—the olive trees in Provence and Languedoc, the chestnuts in Limousin, the walnuts all over France. Theaters and schools were closed; artisans no longer worked; trade was at a standstill. Wolves grew bold enough to lurk on the outskirts of the towns, where they devoured such couriers and merchants as still dared to go about their business. The people died of cold like flies.

The worst was still to come. By February 1709 we knew we were threatened with the most terrible famine, for the entire wheat crop for the year had been destroyed by frost. In March the price of wheat began to rise, and thereafter doubled every day. By April there were cases of scurvy at the Invalides and the Hôtel-Dieu; this was said to be the prelude to the plague. The mills stopped working, and those who were lucky started to eat bread made of oats. The army in Flanders lived from hand to mouth, finding barley where it could. At Court, all I had to eat was barley bread and eggs, for all the vegetables, even the roots, had been killed by the cold. But the poor had nothing at all. They were black with hunger; some of them threw dying children into my coach.

A painful story was told at Court of a woman who stole a loaf from a baker's shop in Paris. The baker wanted to have her arrested, but she wept and said, "If you knew my plight you would not want to take the loaf away from me. I have three young children, and they have no clothes." The police officer before whom she had been brought told her to take him to where she lived, and there he found three infants huddled up in rags in a corner, trembling with cold as if in a fever. He asked the oldest where their father was, and the child said, "Behind the door." The policeman looked to see what the father could be doing behind the door and fell back in horror. The poor wretch had hanged himself in despair. Such things happened every day.

Soon there were riots every market day. The lesser towns rebelled when they were asked for wheat for Paris: there were revolts in Rouen, Clermont, Bayonne and in the Languedoc. Paris itself grew more and more difficult to control: bread was dearer every day.

The coming of warmer weather only brought new woes. Several cantons were ruined by hail, and floods caused by the melting of the ice carried away the crops in the few provinces where there had still been some hope left. Some began to predict there would not even be seed for the following year.

One day when the King, by way of conversation, asked président de Harlay if there was anything new happening in Paris, he answered laconically, "Sire, the poor are dying, but the rich are becoming poor and taking their places." What was really new was that all the poor, new and old, had ceased to suffer in silence.

Everywhere people were being maddened by want. It got to the point where we could not go out in safety. As soon as the princes left the château they were assailed by peasants crying for bread; stones were thrown at their coaches; even the King, driving through Versailles, heard some unpleasant things from the people shouting in the streets. Famine was making the whole population restless, and our enemies were stirring them up. The market women of Paris even gathered together to come to Versailles and demand a reduction in the tax on bread, but the King's soldiers stopped them on the pont de Sèvres, and the sight of the loaded muskets deterred them from crossing the river.

In August all Paris rose up in revolt. For some days the poor had been engaged in levelling a big mound of earth between the porte Saint-Denis and the porte Saint-Martin, with bread their only wages. Then one day there was not enough bread. Immediately they all rushed through the streets looting the bakeries. By degrees all the shops shut, and the crowd spread through every parish, yelling "Bread! Bread!" and taking it wherever they found it. By chance the elderly maréchal de Boufflers was in Paris. As brave in a riot as he was in battle, he walked alone into the furious mob, asking them what all the noise was about and telling them that was not the way to ask for bread. The people recognized him and listened; there were several cries of "Vive Monsieur le Maréchal!" Finally he quieted them all down, and that evening when he arrived at Versailles, he came straight to my apartment to see the King. He explained why he had come and ventured to speak in favor of peace. The King heard what he had to say, thanked him, stationed troops in Paris and sent eight thousand muskets to the Bastille. But he did not change his policy.

When you face rebellion, insults are unimportant in comparison. I had my share of them, however. One ditty that was sung in the streets held me responsible for the people's poverty. Crowds tried to stone me because I was supposed never to say anything disagreeable to the King for fear of annoying him. Every day I received anonymous letters asking "if I wasn't tired of getting fat by sucking the blood of the poor," and, being so old, what did I mean to do with all the wealth I was amassing. Some said I ought to be burned as a witch. I consoled myself with the thought that my conscience had nothing to reproach me with as regards avarice: I hadn't a penny left to bless myself with, and I had just sold a ring the King had given me in order to pay for my charities.

Nor was the King spared. There were complaints about all the money he spent. They wanted to deprive him of his horses, his dogs, his servants; they criticized his furniture; and all this at his very door. Some songs published in Holland even incited the people to violence: one listed the faults of the French royal family and told their subjects they would do well to follow England's example.

The King had a few booksellers, accused of printing or selling such disgraceful lampoons, hanged in the place de Grève. But I knew he could not punish those behind most of the scurrilous epigrams and verses which were always coming out, for to do so he would have had to make inroads into his own family.

For famine and defeat had caused a large party to grow up around the Dauphin, and there was talk at Court of the "Meudon faction." Weariness and impatience continually swelled the numbers of those who thought they could influence Monseigneur and who were waiting for the King to die. The princesse de Conti and her sister the duchesse de Bourbon, both very close to their brother and Mademoiselle Choin, were always with Monseigneur, plotting openly. Monsieur de Vendôme, angry because he had been relieved of his command and because the duchesse de Bourgogne would no longer speak to him, was the great warrior of the Dauphin's little court, while Monsieur de Chamillart, who had just lost the ministry of Finance to Monsieur Desmarets, was its treasurer.

These people all made a great to-do, and already the shrewdest courtiers intermingled "Marlys" with "Meudons."

The enemy was taking one French town after another. In the autumn they captured Tournai, and talked of burning down Versailles. Maréchal de Boufflers, who had gone to serve as a volunteer under maréchal de Villars, had to withdraw beyond Le Quesnoy; Villars was wounded in the battle. The allies offered their soldiers double pay and clothing in the hope of making our men desert. Whoever predicted the worst catastrophes was always proved to be right.

Yet, apart from the oaten bread on our tables and the mourning many ladies wore for their husbands or sons, nothing seemed different at Court. We still went to Fontainebleau and Trianon, and we had Marlys of war and mourning just as we used to have them for carnivals or plays. The King, thinking it best not to give the world too accurate an impression of France's despondency, gave a number of balls and twenty-two plays in three months. Some great noblemen attended these festivities between campaigns, and they looked magnificent. Their crutches were somewhat out of place, but you can carry anything off with the right air. At the same time, tradesmen refused to deliver any more sheets or other linen for the King's use until they were paid. There was an atmosphere of ruin everywhere.

"Our King was too glorious," I said one day to my niece de Caylus. "God wants to humiliate him in order to save him. And France expanded too far, perhaps unjustly, and God wants to confine her again within narrower bounds. Our country too was proud, and He means to humble her. God's will be done."

"Don't talk like that, Aunt," she said. "Do something about it all yourself, I implore you, and give us peace."

Marguerite's beautiful eyes were full of tears. She had a son of sixteen who had just distinguished himself at Le Quesnoy, but she was afraid of what might happen to him if the campaign continued.

"We must have peace, Madame," said the maréchal de Villars, who was being treated for his wound. "At any price. I cannot lead an army which has no bread."

"Monsieur," I answered, "God has not placed me where I am to persecute the man to whom I want to give rest. Besides, I am very unlucky in politics."

Nevertheless, a party gradually grew up around me of its own accord as a counterweight to the Meudon faction; its object was to persuade the King to make peace in order to save his greatness and authority. This group was soon referred to at Court as the "nobles' party."

It included Villars, Harcourt and Boufflers, our most illustrious generals; Voysin, who had recently succeeded Chamillart as secretary of state for War; chancellor Pontchartrain; Desmarets, nephew of the great Colbert and the new controller of Finance; the duc du Maine; my nephew de Noailles; and the duchesse de Bourgogne. When I saw that this party had public opinion behind it and was lent much luster by the popularity of Boufflers, I finally let myself be persuaded to speak out to the King.

Taking advantage of a friendly moment, I made my voice and attitude as ingratiating as I could, and said:

"Sire, I know you think one should die rather than surrender. And princesse Orsini agrees with you. Still, I cannot help thinking one should yield to superior force and to the arm of God which is so evidently against us. A King owes more to his people than to himself, and see what you are reducing them to . . . I do not like opposing your feelings, but I cannot disguise my own. We have suffered a series of misfortunes from which France can only recover through a long peace."

He did not answer.

"I know my opinions will not bring about either peace or war," I went on, "and I only utter them so freely because I know they are worthless. But I am too good a Frenchwoman to think we must lose France to save Spain."

"A lot of discussion goes on around you, Madame," said he.

I went pale at this reproach, for I had neither inspired nor encouraged the party he referred to, and since the quietist affair, I had given up all indirect methods.

"Sire," I answered indignantly, "you know quite well that my attitude toward the great is very unusual. In private I tell them the most severe home truths, both about affairs of state and about their own behavior. But in public I support them in everything, and I shall go on doing so till my last breath. Is that what you are accusing me of? Would you maintain I have ever said a single word to anyone against what you decide? . . . I ask your pardon, Sire," I went on more quietly, letting fall a tear or two. "I am ashamed to speak to you of matters of which I know nothing, but my own share of France's sufferings make me so unhappy . . ."

The King was sometimes more moved by my tears than by the woes of his people. After a few days he said to me:

"I shall ask for peace, Madame. As you've been wanting me to do for a long time . . . But I doubt if we shall get it."

Plenipotentiaries were sent to Holland. Madame des Ursins reviled me and warned me that Their Catholic Majesties would never agree to leave the country they had ruled for nine years.

The King was ready to sacrifice anything for France, but his enemies, drunk with success, were not content with taking away some of our territory. They also wanted the King of France to go to war to remove his grandson from the throne of Spain, where Philip V's subjects wished him to remain. In exchange for all this, they offered no more than a two-month truce. They did not want to treat for a real peace yet, as they hoped to gain more advantages out of a further campaign.

I, like all the ministers in the Council, was outraged when I learned of these proposals. The King told Monsieur de Torcy that since the war must go on, he would rather fight his enemies than his children.

He put his own jewelry up for sale, to give foreigners a chance to make some contribution; sent what remained of his silver plate to the Mint to be melted down; and requested his courtiers to do the same. Apart from Boufflers and myself, who sent the equivalent of fourteen thousand francs, they were in no hurry to oblige. But by such devices and the unexpected arrival of the Mexican fleet bearing more than twenty millions' worth of gold, we scraped together enough to buy wheat abroad, feed the people and avoid unrest. Monsieur Desmarets did all he could to restore credit, and in this cause the King did not hesitate to do the honors of Marly to the rich financier Samuel Bernard: the soldiers had to be fed. Monsieur Bernard, basking in royal smiles, paid up. And then went bankrupt.

"Monsieur le Maréchal," said the King to the duc de Villars as he was returning to his command, "I wish you success. But if fortune is unkind to you, I request the honor, as the oldest French soldier, of serving under you until death."

Another time he told the Council:

"I shall go and fight for the remains of my kingdom at the head of my nobility. I shall fight for every stream and every city, and we shall see what that can do."

Not wishing to be outdone in magnanimity, I told the King I should now be as steadfast in war as I had been for peace, and that he would always find me by his side, whether beyond the Loire or in the middle of the Pyrenees. "Even though at my age," I added with a smile, "I am not so keen on travelling as I once was."

The King's proud bearing in defeat, and through famine and rebellion, had made a great impression, and when the conditions offered by the enemy were made known to the people, the whole kingdom rang with a chorus of indignation and a demand for vengeance. The French, urged on either by honor or by hunger, enlisted en masse.

"In order to give bread to the brigades on the move," wrote Villars, "I make the ones who are left behind go without. I walk through the ranks and cajole the men; I talk to them and exhort them to be patient, and I have the consolation of hearing some say, 'Monsieur le Maréchal is right—you have to suffer sometimes.' "

At the end of the year our troops, now reinforced, confronted Marlborough and Prince Eugene at Malplaquet, and although inferior in men and guns killed twice as many of the enemy as they lost themselves. They left the battlefield in such good order, without losing a horse or a flag, that this semi-defeat seemed a complete victory. The country's courage was restored; it seemed that France was saved.

Then God sent the King the third affliction.

It began with an illness which for a while made us fear for the life of the King himself. Overwork, imminent danger and, according to Monsieur Fagon, the amount of food he ate, brought on another abscess, and the accompanying fever was immediately so severe I was thrown into great alarm. The King was very surprised when I said what ruin the country would fall into if he were to die then.

"Positions such as mine, Madame," he said, "never remain vacant for want of candidates to fill them."

True, he considered he had the largest family in all the courts of Europe. It was an astonishing sight to see him some evenings, sitting in his room with his son Monseigneur, his grandson the duc de Bourgogne, and his great-grandson the young duc de Bretagne, then aged four. Painters never tired of depicting this magnificent dynasty, a just object of admiration for the whole world. The succession seemed all the more assured in that the King had a third grandson, the duc de Berry, in addition to the duc de Bourgogne and the King of Spain, and besides the little duc de Bretagne, another great-grandson, the duc d'Anjou, whom my pretty princesse had just brought into the world. In all, the King stood at the head of thirty princes and princesses of the royal blood.

But God smote him even in this last pride and consolation.

On 9 April 1711 Monseigneur le Dauphin, getting up to go wolf-hunting, turned faint and fell off his commode. The King, when told of this on his return from Marly, went straight to Meudon, intending to stay there as long as his son's illness, whatever it was, lasted.

The King saw Monseigneur every morning and evening and several times in the afternoon, spending the rest of the time working with his ministers as usual. Mademoiselle Choin did not budge from her attic; she went to Monseigneur's room only when the King was not there. The princesse de Conti, on the other hand, never left her brother's bedside, and looked after him with great affection.

After three days, smallpox declared itself. We were immediately anxious about how it would come out. Monseigneur himself was worried about his age and kept saying, "I've got smallpox, and I'm fifty."

On the Tuesday the King came into my room, followed by Monsieur Fagon, and said, "I have just seen my son, and I felt so sorry for him I thought I should weep. His face has swelled up enormously in the last three or four hours. He is almost unrecognizable, and his eyes are starting to close up. But they tell me it's always like that with smallpox."

And he sat down to work with Monsieur Voysin and Monsieur Desmarets.

At eleven o'clock they sent for him, saying Monseigneur was in a very bad way. He found the Dauphin in convulsions and unconscious. The curé of Meudon, who called every evening for news, happened to drop in, and seeing from the servants' agitation how matters stood, called to him from the doorway:

"Monseigneur, are you not very sorry for having offended against God?"

The surgeon Maréchal, who was holding the Dauphin, said he had answered yes, and the priest went on, at the top of his voice:

"If you were able to confess, you would do so, would you not?"

Maréchal said the prince had said yes again and had even pressed his hand. Then Père Le Tellier, the King's new confessor, who had got dressed again in haste, came in and gave the Dauphin absolution.

What a sight met my eyes when, summoned from my bed, I entered Monseigneur's outer room: the King sitting on a day-bed, dry-eyed but shivering and shaking from head to foot; Madame la Duchesse in despair; the princesse de Conti prostrate; and all the courtiers standing about in a silence broken only by the cries and sobs which came from the bedroom whenever the dying man was thought to be giving up the ghost. At last the King's coaches drove into the courtyard. He got into the first, and I at once took my place beside him; Madame la Duchesse and the princesse de Conti sat on the seat in front. Just as we were leaving, the King noticed Pont-chartrain in the dark and called to him to tell the other ministers to be at Marly the next morning for the usual Wednesday Council of State.

As we drove along, the two ladies begged the King to let himself go, and weep; they feared the shock would be too much for him otherwise. But he never could give way to his feelings.

After stopping for a moment at Versailles to see the duchesse de Bourgogne and tell her of the death which made her husband the Dauphin, we arrived at Marly. They were not expecting us and had none of the necessary things ready, not even a sheet or a nightshirt. The house was freezing cold, for no fires had been lit. The keys of the apartments could not be found, nor even an inch of candle. We waited with the King in an antechamber until four in the morning, when he could at last go to bed.

When Monseigneur died, his body was already blue all over, so he had to be buried without ceremony. The corpse was put in a coach, and, accompanied by a chaplain, twelve guards and twelve torches, it was driven to Saint-Denis and put in the vault. So ends all greatness.

I was not unduly afflicted by the death of a man who when he was alive had inspired, almost without knowing it, a party so inimical to the King's authority, and who in himself I had always regarded as insignificant. For the first few days, however, I was alarmed by the King's appearance. His face made me think he at last felt the hand of God weighing heavy upon him. But I did not take care, thinking my Dauphine would soon be able to cure his grief, which with him never lasted long.

And, indeed, now more than ever, grace emanated from the little princesse's every step, from all her ways and from her most ordinary words. She had an inexhaustible faculty for happiness.

Everything seemed to promise it to her: the situation on the frontiers had improved and Villars was holding the borders intact; the Spanish monarchy was stronger and the whole country, with the exception of Barcelona, was back under the authority of the King; it was rumored that the English were tired of war and that Queen Anne had turned against Marlborough and sincerely wanted peace; and the death of Monseigneur and the collapse of the little court so hostile to both her and her husband gave her a sudden new freedom.

Light as a nymph, swift as a whirlwind, she seemed to be in several places at once, and in each she radiated movement and life. She was the ornament of all entertainments, the soul of all fêtes and balls. The King began to smile again.

She was with us all day, chatting, jumping about, flitting from one thing to another, now perched on the arm of a chair, now throwing her arms around us, rummaging about on tables and through documents and letters. One evening when she heard me talking to the King about the English court, she began: "In England, Aunt, the queens are better rulers than the kings, and do you know why?" She skipped about some more, then added: "Because with the kings it's the women who rule, and with the queens it's the men!" The King laughed, and said she was right.

One evening when she had been chattering a gibberish of all sorts of languages at supper and indulging in a hundred childish pranks to amuse the King, she noticed that Madame la Duchesse and the princesse de Conti—the daughters of Madame de Montespan and Mademoiselle de La Vallière—were exchanging signs and glances with each other and shrugging their shoulders scornfully. When the King left the table and as usual went into a further room to feed his dogs, the Dauphine pointed to the two half-sisters, who were only a few feet away, and said to me:

"Did you see them? Did you see them? I know as well as they do that what I was saying and doing was silly and foolish, but he needs plenty of noise around him and that sort of thing amuses him."

Then she suddenly started to hop up and down and sing: "Ha ha, what do I care? I'll be their queen! I don't have to bother about them, now or ever, but they'll have to bother about me! Ha ha, I'll be their queen!" And she went on singing and leaping about. She believed she was going to be their queen, and, alas!, who would have believed otherwise?

On 6 February 1712, at Versailles, she fell ill of a fever. It was an inflammation which caused a constant pain between the ear and the upper part of the jaw. The place was so small you could have covered it with your fingernail. She had convulsions and cried out like a woman in labor, and with the same intervals. She was bled twice a day, and four times took opium and tobacco. When the pain left her for a moment, she still found the strength to jest. "I shouldn't mind dying just to see what happens," she said to me. "I'm sure the Dauphin would marry a Franciscan nun or a portress of the Daughters of Saint Mary."

On the ninth a rash appeared on her skin, which made us hope her illness was only measles. The fever was still very high and her conscious moments very brief and confused. The doctors bled her. But things got worse during the night of Tuesday to Wednesday the tenth; the hope that it was only measles faded, or else the disease turned inward. The fever increased, and the emetic she was being given no longer had any effect.

Suddenly she said to me: "I have a feeling peace will be made and I shan't be there to see it."

Then the next minute she was telling me in detail what she would do when the first peace treaty was signed, and how she would pile one pleasure upon another and go to the ball and the opera all in one night.

At nine o'clock on the morning of 11 February, the King came into her room, which I now almost never left. The Dauphin, who had been there for three days, racked with anxiety, had at last yielded to his doctors, who, wishing to spare him from witnessing the horrors they foresaw, made him keep to his own apartment. The princesse was so ill when the King came that he asked me to speak to her about receiving the sacraments. I did so as lightly as I could, still hoping she might recover. Although she was in a very low state, she was surprised at my suggestion and asked me questions about how she was. I answered as reassuringly as I could, not wishing to frighten her. At last she decided to confess.

I then suggested she should take the last sacrament. The viaticum was brought from the chapel, and the King came with it, in tears. The Dauphine was given extreme unction. I was still with her.

"Aunt," she said to me after a moment. "I feel different. It's as if I had changed."

"You have come close to God, and He is consoling you," I said gently.

"I don't feel any pain," she said, "except that of having offended against God."

"That is enough for your sins to be forgiven, provided you are firmly resolved to commit them no more if God restores you to health."

"There is only one thing that worries me, Aunt," she said. "My debts."

"You have always trusted me before," I said. "Won't you trust me with them? I promise that if you get better, I shall never mention them again."

I was not unaware that the Dauphine had accumulated gambling debts. She sent for a casket, which she opened herself. She fingered some of the papers inside but had not the strength to go on. She shut the box and had it placed at the foot of the bed. After that, whenever she was conscious, she kept her eyes fixed on the casket, as if afraid of the poor secrets which might escape from it.

Seven doctors had been sent for, from the Court and from Paris, to treat her. They held a consultation in a neighboring salon in the presence of the King and myself. They were unanimous in deciding on bleeding her through the foot before the fever increased. It was done at seven in the evening, but brought no relief.

The Dauphine sent for the duchesse de Guiche to say goodbye.

"My pretty duchesse," she said, "I am going to die."

"No, no," said the duchesse. "God will answer the prayers of Monsieur le Dauphin and give you back to him."

"I do not agree," said the princesse bitterly. "I think God will send the Dauphin this affliction because He loves him."

After this she said to me and the few other people around the bed:

"Today a princesse; tomorrow nothing."

I could not help weeping.

"Oh, Aunt," she said, "I feel so sorry for you."

The King looked in almost hourly. The reliquary of Saint Genevieve was exposed in Paris, and he ordered public prayers.

It was a dreadful night. Toward six in the morning on the twelfth, the death agony began and she lost consciousness. I left the room briefly to attend a service for her in the chapel. While I was absent, a nobleman came with a powder said to be wonderful in its effects, and as the case was desperate, the doctors gave it to their patient. It roused her a little and she regained consciousness enough to say, "Oh, it's bitter!"

They sent for me and I went at once.

"It's Madame de Maintenon," one of her maids said to her. "Don't you recognize her?"

"Yes," she said.

They had just dressed her for the last time. She wore a long white shift without any lace; two pale hands, folded and motionless, were its only ornament. My eyes filled with tears as I thought of the pink satins and the diamond-studded skirts she had delighted in only a few days ago.

I could see she would not come back to us. Her eyes showed only the whites. I took her hand and said quietly:

"Madame, you are going to God."

"So soon, Aunt?" she sighed.

Those were her last words.

I kissed her tenderly, and withdrew, so as to give vent to my tears. She died at eight that evening.

The King got into his coach at the foot of the grand staircase. I went with him to Marly, accompanied by Madame de Caylus. We were both sunk in the most bitter grief. The King was torn by great tearless sobs, and I was too stunned by my own loss to be able to comfort him. We had not the strength to go to see the Dauphin, and he had not the strength to come to see us in the coach. He fainted away as he was coming down to do so.

He did not rejoin the King until the following morning. I went at once to his apartment, meaning to give him the Dauphine's casket and go through it with him, but he looked so wild and altered I did not think it appropriate to give him the papers then. Since the beginning of his wife's illness, the Dauphin had had two or three mild attacks of fever, which had been put down to sorrow and anxiety. "A fever resulting from pressure on the heart," said the doctors. But I feared it was something else. The King in turn saw his grandson, embracing him long and tenderly several times. At first they could only exchange a few words interspersed with tears and sobs, but then the King noticed the Dauphin's face and was alarmed, as I was. The doctors then told the prince he ought to go to bed.

On the evening of 15 February the Dauphin contracted the same kind of measles as had carried off his wife, but as his fever was slight and he appeared to have no untoward symptoms, no remedies were applied: the doctors feared they might have been too zealous in the case of the Dauphine. They were reassuring, and we, wrapped up in our grief for the princesse, did not go out of our way to worry about the Dauphin.

But on the seventeenth he suddenly felt so ill he asked for the last sacrament. Those about him did not know what to make of this, for he did not seem to be in extremity. They told him there was no hurry. Then, at two or three in the morning, he became violently agitated and asked for extreme unction. His confessor said he was not ill enough. "If you wait," the Dauphin said, "I shall have to receive it unconscious." He felt a great internal heat and kept repeating, "I am burning, but it will be much worse in Purgatory." He had spots all over his body but complained only of the devouring heat. Externally, however, there appeared to be no fever, and it was not thought necessary to waken the King. I spent the night quite ignorant of what was going on.

Toward six o'clock, death suddenly became imminent. The Dauphin suffered a stroke and was hastily given extreme unction —unconscious, as he had predicted.

His relations hurried to his bedside, and the unfortunate prince died a dreadful death before their very eyes. He struggled and tossed and clung to the bed, shrieking meaningless words in which oaths alternated with the holy name of Jesus. It was hard to believe he was going to God: he seemed to be fighting against the Devil and all the demons of Hell. He died at Marly at half past eight in the morning, and the King ordered his body to be taken to Versailles to lie beside that of the Dauphine.

The King's despair and my own stupefaction it is impossible to describe. Neither of us knew what to say, and when we tried to exchange a few words about matters of indifference the words stuck in our throats. The comtesse de Caylus never left my side; she even answered letters for me, as for several weeks I could not hold a pen. The King, choking back his tears, presided over the usual Council meetings, which discussed nothing but the peace that both the Dauphin and the Dauphine had so ardently desired.

The courtiers, who had run from Monseigneur to the duc de Bourgogne, now ran to the duc de Berry: it seemed pointless to try to curry favor with the new Dauphin, the duc de Bretagne, who was only five years old. He was said to be already a victim of the same fever as his parents, and his governess, my friend Madame de Ventadour, wrote and told me that when she informed him that he was now the Dauphin, he protested gently. "Don't call me that, Mamma," he said. "It's too sad."

He in turn was seized with great fits of sweating, and often asked to be put to bed during the day. Measles declared itself in him and in his brother the duc d'Anjou at the same time, but the disease did not come right out, though the fever was extremely high and accompanied by great thirst.

The two young princes had not been baptized, so the King hastily made arrangements for the ceremony, using such godparents as happened to be at hand. A few days went by. The children were bled. I dared not speak to the King about the young Dauphin's illness, although Madame de Ventadour kept me informed about it every day. She loved the child passionately, and indeed he was a well-made, intelligent child with charming manners, just like his mother in every way.

"Mamma," he said to his governess between bouts of fever, "I dreamed last night I was in heaven, and I was too hot, but all the little angels fanned me with their wings." The fever mounted daily, the complications grew worse. "Mamma," said the little Dauphin, "the journey to Saint-Denis isn't pleasant." He made that journey, but in good company. His father and mother were with him, and all three bodies were buried the same day in the same grave. The oldest was not yet twenty-nine.

The death of the Dauphine had grieved everyone; that of the Dauphin stunned them; the passing of the little duc de Bretagne gave rise to suspicions and some deplorable incidents.

There was talk of poisonings. The people attributed them to the duc d'Orléans, who by the recent deaths was brought so much closer to the throne. When he and Madame his mother went to sprinkle holy water, the mob shouted the most dreadful insults at him. As the procession passed the Palais Royal, where he lived, the shouting and booing was so loud that the situation seemed very dangerous for a few minutes. At Court not only did everyone avoid him but even in the King's apartments and the salons people removed themselves from his vicinity with unseemly ostentation.

Madame de Ventadour, inconsolable for the loss of the duc de Bretagne and alarmed by the rumors circulating everywhere, took the duc d'Anjou, the last surviving heir of the decimated family, and shut herself up in her room with him alone. Not even the doctors were allowed to enter. She gave him an antidote against poison, and as he was not yet completely weaned she called back his wet-nurse and let him have nothing but her milk. Their food was passed to them through a hatch, and the governess tasted everything before the nurse ate it. These precautions, or perhaps the absence of the doctors, saved the child. The fever abated and the rash disappeared.

So against all expectation he lived, while his uncle the duc de Berry, full of life, flown with hopes and courted by hangers-on and minor nobles, died suddenly without offspring as the result of an ordinary riding accident.

The succession to the Crown of France, which two years ago had seemed so well assured, now rested on the delicate head of a two-year-old Dauphin. Many thought this a very fragile bulwark against the ambitions of his cousin of Orléans.

As I had no wish to bring up any other child whatsoever and could not hope to live long enough to grow to love this one, I gave him up entirely to Madame de Ventadour. Besides, although the young prince showed every sign of being able to survive, with regular teeth and a good complexion, a child's life is so precarious we could not assume he would ever grow up to be a man, poison or no poison.

"I have nothing left, Madame," the King said to me. "What has happened to me is unexampled."

"God's will be done."

"Yes," he answered. "We must be grateful to Him for having afflicted me so much in this world that He will spare me worse sufferings in the next."

To him the deaths of the duchesse de Bourgogne and the other three were never anything but a private affair between him and God. He was so used to having people live for him he could not imagine they might die for themselves.

To tell the truth, that long struggle against the wrath of God left him tired rather than really downhearted. He was already think-ing all these events called for changes and new decisions in the future, and he did not exclude the possibility that he might live to be a hundred in order to straighten everything out.

One winter morning as I was going to Saint-Cyr with Jeannette, whom I had just married to the comte d'Auxy, the calash drove by the Enceladus fountain as we were driving through the park. The statue depicts the most illustrious of the Titans crushed beneath the rocks Jupiter has hurled down upon him in his fury. His body is buried, his face, imprisoned between two blocks of stone, no more than an agonized cry. But one hand emerges from the mass, trying to take hold, and this hand is so strong and robust it is as if one could see the giant move, as if he were already getting up and shaking off the rocks like snowflakes.

Jeannette, who had been tossing her muff in the air and playing with it to amuse me, stopped and fell silent. Her gaze followed mine.

"Mamma," she said, suddenly serious, "I know what you're thinking."

"Don't say it, child," I answered.

Eighteen

With the Dauphine gone, my world was bare and empty. I had no occupation, took no pleasure in anything. My eyes were moist, my heart dried up. I went about in a daze, not knowing if I was still alive. People said I was brave; but if I understood the courage which enables one to endure misfortune, disgrace or human injustice and ingratitude, I was helpless when it came to the affections.

One evening, shut up in my room, I made myself go through my poor princesse's casket. I sorted through the little secrets which had so obsessed her as she was departing this world, and found they were only what we all leave behind: hastily scribbled receipts and acknowledgments of debt, a page of naive jottings which she had taken for philosophical reflections, three or four withered flowers, a book of moral maxims I had given her when she was eleven, a miniature of the little duc de Bretagne, and some long, passionate letters from Monsieur de Nangis which showed she had been too kind to him when she was alive, and that, dead, she would be forgotten. I paid the debts and burned the rest. As the flames devoured this meager treasure, they took away the last phantom of my beloved girl.

There was no Court left. Madame was ill, the duchesse d'Or-léans, her daughter-in-law, did not like appearing in public, and the duchesse de Berry, her granddaughter, never left Paris now. Madame la Duchesse, the former Mademoiselle de Nantes, Madame de Montespan's daughter, spent all her time on lawsuits and quibbles. The princesse de Conti, Mademoiselle de La Vallière's daughter, was lazy, and gave piety as an excuse for never getting dressed. As for the duchesse du Maine, she was always at Sceaux, which she had bought fifteen years earlier. All the Court ladies now had their own little houses in the country for themselves and their friends. Versailles was like the palace of the Sleeping Beauty.

Only the efforts of the enemy sometimes stirred it into life. The situation of our armies on the frontiers caused us fresh alarms. The fortress of Landrecies was not expected to hold out under the repeated assaults of Prince Eugene, and it was thought Villars would be defeated in the first battle. There was some question of the King retiring from Versailles to Chambord.

"I know what the courtiers are thinking," he said to me one day. "They all want me to withdraw to the Loire and not wait for the enemy army to approach Paris, as it might do if my army was beaten. But I know by experience that armies as big as mine are never beaten so completely that a part of them cannot extricate themselves. I know the river Somme. It is very difficult to cross, and there are positions on it that can be fortified. If necessary I mean to go to Péronne or Saint-Quentin, assemble all the troops I have left, and join Villars in a last effort, to save France or die with him. I shall never allow the enemy to approach my capital."

"Sire," I said, "the most glorious decisions are sometimes the wisest. I know of none more noble than the one Your Majesty is thinking of."

He was as great a man as he was a king, even more admirable in misfortune than in prosperity.

I admired him. But just as great woes do not prevent us from feeling small inconveniences, so I was becoming more and more impatient of his private tyranny. The more resistance he met with in great matters, the less he was inclined to put up with in small ones. Unable to extend his rule further over Europe, he tightened his iron grip on me, using trifles as pretexts for reducing me to slavery.

I had never been allowed to arrange my apartments as I wished. For thirty years I had lived amid red and green furniture, when I like only blue. In summer I slept with no protection from the light, for my windows were without shutters or frames so as not to spoil the symmetry of the architecture. In winter my teeth chattered with cold because the windows had to be kept open to let out the smoke from the fire. "My Soundness" and my health had long suffered from having to live with people who wanted to live and to seem like gods. But although I knew the King was interested only in grandeur and magnificence, and drafts must be endured so that all the doors might be in line with one another, I was surprised to see him in his latter years indulge in more whims of this sort than ever.

Having had the audacity to put screens in front of my main window at Fontainebleau to protect myself a little against the air, I was asked to remove them immediately; they spoiled the look of the room. Curtains were forbidden, my alcove was taken away, in short, I was shown I must resign myself to perishing symmetrically. Madame des Ursins sent me a very pretty lacquerwood tray; it had to be thrown away because the japanning was supposed to have a disagreeable smell. I had put up portraits I was fond of on the walls; they were replaced by battle pieces by Van der Meulen, more suitable for the repose of a great warrior. I was not allowed to have one of the new cabinets called commodes. All my carpets were changed, against my wishes. No doubt all this was to remind me that I was not in my own home.

But the tyrant, preferring to kill his slave by inches rather than at a blow, was prepared to tolerate the "niche" I invented in order to survive. This was a kind of large cupboard without doors or floor, only sides and a roof. These were lined with wadding and damask, and the front was half-closed with thick curtains. A sofa, a chair and a little table could be placed inside, as could Madame de Maintenon and her lady friends, if the Master permitted. They were thus protected, if only for a moment, from the cold and wind prevailing in the room. The "niche" could easily be dismantled and was thus transportable, like its occupant. So both were freely driven to and fro over all the roads of the Ile-de-France, from Marly to Rambouillet, from Versailles to Compiègne.

My time, like my movements, was regulated from on high. I had always been on call; now I was at heel like a shepherd's dog. Just as I was getting ready to leave for Saint-Cyr, I would be told I should be receiving a visit in my room within the hour. I took off my cloak. Two hours later a groom would bring me a note saying the writer had finally decided to go hunting but would come and take refreshments with me at five, and that between now and then I must not receive anyone. I waited. At five, another note, telling me to be at once with such-and-such a lady on the other side of the park, to be picked up in a calash. I hastened to the spot. At nightfall, as we were walking up and down to keep warm, a servant would come and tell me there had been a change of plan: I was awaited in my room, where we were to have an evening of music, and I was to be ready then to leave for Marly. All these orders and counterorders were very civilly accompanied by an "if you please," or an "if it is no trouble," or a "your wishes are my commands." How often have I got out of my bed in the morning at Versailles, taken an afternoon rest on a couch at Trianon and gone to bed again the same evening at Fontainebleau!

Between whiles I toiled to amuse a man who was no longer amusable. He had never been a great talker, but he came in the end to have no conversation at all: not a smile, not a wish, just a mask of gravity and an image of boredom beneath a magnificent wig.

As I alone was not up to the task, I got the maréchal de Villeroy back into favor so that he could help me with his laughter, repartee and memories. He had been with the King when they were both children and knew more tales about the monarch's youth and more old stories about the Court than I did. As nothing amuses age more than recalling youth, the two men would entertain one another at the expense of people who had been dead for fifty years. It passed the time.

Music was a great resource too, I found. The King still loved music passionately, and although gout now prevented him from playing the guitar, he liked joining in when I had the little girls from Saint-Cyr, or Madame d'O, to my room to sing songs from the operas to him. For some time I had had a secretary called Mademoiselle d'Aumale, who in addition to her talent for writing also had a beautiful voice. I had her taught to play the harpsichord, so that she could accompany herself and divert the King with her songs, which were often drinking songs. Two or three evenings a week I had the King's violinists and oboists to my room to play the music of Lully, Couperin and Charpentier, which the King never tired of hearing over and over again.

For the rest I counted on the ladies of our circle, who brought to my apartment the pretty faces and the atmosphere of gallantry the King could not do without. The pranks of Jeannette d'Auxy, the mischievous tricks of Madame de Levis, Marguerite de Caylus's witticisms and Madame de Dangeau's mimicry could always make the King smile, however sad and bored he might be. Even if they were ill, the ladies would come and spend the afternoon in my apartment, spreading around them the loose ribbons and rumpled laces of their dishabille. The duc du Maine used to slip in by the back way to chat with them and egg them on. He was better than anyone at consoling his father for his afflictions and making me forget my sadness by reminding me of the days of Vaugirard and Barège. He was our child, and we were grateful to him for his kindness.

When, however, the entertainment was over and my little flock dispersed, I was overcome once more with melancholy and somber reveries. "I am alone in the world," I wrote to the princesse de Vaudémont. "I have broken off with it completely since I lost the duchesse de Bourgogne, who was the only person in it who interested me. I do all I can to amuse the King . . . My only consolation is the hope that I shall not last much longer. I only wish I desired death for the love of God instead of out of hatred of the world."

"What are people reading in Paris?" I sometimes asked my niece de Caylus, who still had a house there.

"Well, Madame, they're reading Chardin's *Travels in Persia,* Newton's mathematics, *The Slough* by someone called Arouet,† the quips of Swift, an Englishman, and they are talking about the burlesque Monsieur de Marivaux is writing on *Télémaque.*"

"Oh. And what's on at the theater?"

"Lesage . . . Crébillon . . ."

"I don't know the names . . . Tell me, don't people read my friends Madame de La Fayette and La Rochefoucauld any more? Don't they perform Scarron, Racine, Lully . . . ?"

"Madame," answered Madame de Caylus with a look of consternation, "they've all been dead a long time."

"You are right, child. Everyone's dead except the King and myself. Perhaps we're dead too and no one dares tell us."

Only my keen reaction to insults made me think I was still alive. The letters and pamphlets still came. One set of verses represented the King as saying that if he had sinned with La Montespan, he was now doing penance with La Maintenon. The penance seemed long to both of us.

I lived like a hermit in the midst of the Court, and the princesse Orsini was really my only company. She at least had known the things of my youth, the same faces, now long gone. The bonds between us had grown stronger during the few months she spent at Versailles and Marly in 1705, after a quarrel with the French ambassador and a brief fall from favor. We spent whole days chatting in my room. She shared my bed, and lightened my cares with her laughter. I found her energy as amazing as ever. Her letters were written without reserve and I awaited them eagerly; it was also a great pleasure for me to send her the news of the Court. But we did not like the same things. She had a passion for politics; I loved only children. But since God often helps us save our souls by making us play roles that are alien to us, it was she who rocked cradles and gossiped with nurses, while I conversed gravely with ministers and ambassadors.

We exchanged useful advice. I worked out fine projects for her children's upbringing, for as the King said, I always had a mania for education. I wanted her to make the experiment of rearing her princes as they do in England, where the children are all tall and well made. There they are not wrapped up in tight swaddling clothes and corsets, but just wear a loose shift and diaper with a

444

frock over them. In this way they can be changed easily as soon as they are at all soiled, and do not have to remain, like our infants, all bound up in their own dirt. This method spares them much crying and chafing and avoids crooked legs. I was eloquent on the subject, but the princesse was not interested in such domestic details, and did not want to know how one should sit to rock a cradle. She answered my educational projects with talk about European politics, and it was always her desire, there in Madrid, to reform our government in France.

Her point of view about the war never varied. She would not hear of the King of Spain's claims being scaled down, or of negotiation. She believed the success of our armies would restore her king to possession of all his lands and give France back all her territories. It was true that the unhoped for victory my maréchal de Villars had won in capturing Denain, the retreat of our enemies in disorder and Prince Eugene's weariness did change the aspect of the war somewhat. In a few months our troops recovered Douai, Bouchain, Le Quesnoy and most of the strongholds in the north which had been lost in previous years. I hoped for an honorable peace at last. My dear *camerera-mayor* hoped for a fight to the finish.

The King and his ministers came round to my way of thinking. This did not surprise me: my advice now prevailed more and more often. The whole ministry was made up of my creatures or friends. Voysin, war minister and chancellor, had helped me in the management of Saint-Cyr eighteen years before he became a minister. Torcy and Desmarets, ministers for Foreign Affairs and Finance, belonged to the Colbert clan I had once done so much to promote. Villeroy, whom the King had just made a minister, owed his restoration to favor to me. All of them did their best to please me, and few matters came before the King without my having approved of them beforehand. At seventy-seven years old I had become the channel through which everything must pass.

Thirty years of married life and forty of daily converse had taught me to know my husband's character. You had to let him get used to things gradually, never surprise him, speak naturally and without vehemence and never seem to care about what you most wanted to obtain. In the last period of our marriage it had become the simplest thing in the world to me to make him do what I wished; I no longer had any fear of the terrible humiliations of the early days. Then, and then only, did I come close to power. I wielded it all the more easily because the King, whom I knew inside out, was less alert mentally and less resolute than he had been. Time was doing its work.

Certainly his health seemed better than ever, and he appeared to have no more infirmities at seventy-four than he had had at forty. He ate enough for ten, was a most elegant shot at pheasant, and would hunt stag for six or seven hours at a stretch. But at our age we could not do everything, and I could see that the King's really extraordinary activity, hunting and driving, left him tired, drowsing over his papers when it was time to examine affairs of state. I husbanded my strength by frugality and a cloistered existence, and by now, I realized, my mind was the more agile of the two.

But I did not want to rule France. To the indignation of the princesse Orsini, I confined my counsels and my influence to the pursuit of peace.

Peace was concluded in the spring of 1713 at Utrecht, with the English, the Dutch and Savoy. The conditions were not dishonorable. France had to dismantle the fortifications at Dunkirk and hand over to England some of her smaller colonies, including the island of Saint-Christophe, where I had spent some months in my childhood. There was an exchange of territory with the duc de Savoie, but France did not lose by it. The King recognized the elector of Brandenburg as King of Prussia, and agreed to cease giving asylum to the pretender to the English Crown. He also agreed to give up supporting the claims of his grandson the King of Spain to the Low Countries and Sardinia. In exchange for these trifles, we recovered Lille, Béthune and our northern provinces. And we had the glory, after waging war for fifteen years against all Europe and undergoing every possible misfortune, to see the struggle end with a peace which kept the Spanish monarchy in the family of the King of France for ever.

Apart from the peace negotiations and the bestowing of favors, I did not interfere. The ministers often told me some abuse or other ought to be remedied, but does a monarch easily change a method of government he has followed for sixty years? And was it easy for me, at my age, to change the face of a whole kingdom? I answered that they could change everything just as they liked when we were dead. They had only to be patient.

Nor did I dabble in the affairs of the Church, although Monsieur de Chartres often urged me to. "Defend truth against novelty always," he had written to me some years earlier. "It is one of your duties. The decisions of the Church authorize you to speak with perfect confidence against Jansenism and Calvinism. Suggest suitable ways of destroying these two sects." But another time he had told me: "Too much zeal for good can do great harm in your position: put off the better to another day." I was struck by this last observation, which corresponded to my experience.

I wrote to my nephew: "The Jansenists and the Jesuits, Monsieur le Cardinal de Noailles and Monsieur de Cambrai, all make a good deal of noise. But if you want my opinion, they are all much in the wrong." I would have treated all this agitation with indifference, since I had an equal hatred of the Jansenists and of their enemies the Jesuits and would not have cared about the outcome of their conflict, if the King himself had not come to be so troubled by the controversy.

Where I still saw only seekers after novelty, such as will always be with us, he saw and was horrified by a spirit of dementia and disorder which was spreading everywhere and neutralizing his authority. One day Père Massillon had the audacity to tell him, "It is not the sovereign, Sire, but the law which should reign over the people. You are only its chief minister. It is the people who, by God's command, have created all kings."

"But when I say I wish such and such a thing," cried the King in a rage, "I had better be obeyed!"

On another occasion I heard him tell the advocate-general of the Parlement, which refused to take cognizance of the Pope's and the King's wishes, "It is not a question of Gallican liberties. It is a question of religion. I will have only one religion in my kingdom, and if liberties are used as a pretext to introduce others, I shall begin by destroying those liberties."

He even told Daguesseau, the procurator-general, and the

chief président of the Parlement that he was ready for them, and that if the Parlement hesitated he would trample all over it. It was not far from his room to the Bastille, and he did not care if he was accused of tyranny!

But after getting carried away he came to himself, and when we were alone he wept and lamented: "These people will be the death of me!" He was pale and looked a hundred years old.

I did not like to see my King weeping, but there was nothing I could do but add my tears to his and help him to bear this new cross. Though we could not be happy with one another any more, we still managed to be unhappy together.

When I had dried the King's tears and wiped away my own, I hastened to Saint-Cyr, where I found little girls laughing and happy, pure and innocent souls, simple faith and order and cleanliness both in the inmates' rooms and in their minds. I had at last succeeded in making the place correspond more or less to my original intention.

I suppose I must admit that the House of Saint-Louis, as I have shaped it, is not entirely beyond all criticism. The education it affords wavers rather too much between worldliness and renunciation, between retreat and the attractions of society. The pupils go, often without any transition, from God to a teacher of accomplishments, from meditation to a lesson in curtsying. But it is a woman's lot to be obliged all the time to go from prayer to her saucepans and from her saucepans to the trivialities of conversation. I thought it healthy, after all, that my girls should be prepared for the life that was awaiting them in the world, and I never tired of observing the fulfilment of my efforts in their faces—soulful in chapel, attentive in class, roguish at recreation.

The girls, the mistresses and the lay sisters all revered me: there alone I was queen. My wishes were anticipated, my smiles hailed with delight, my every word treasured. And I returned their love. Nothing I might do for them was repugnant to me. When I spent the day with them, I did everything that needed to be done, picking flowers to decorate the chapel, ironing their linen, replacing a mistress who was ill or helping the doctor with his examinations. Soeur du Pérou would sometimes say with surprise, "Most great folk find this sort of task disgusting."

"But I am not great," I whispered in reply, "I have only been raised to greatness."

One day I spent the afternoon in the kitchen helping the lay sisters prepare supper, and from there I had to go straight to a ceremony at Versailles where there would be crowds of people. "But Madame," cried the scullery maids, "you'll smell of fat!" "Yes," I said, "but no one will dare think it's me!"

When I was not helping in the House, I used to rest a little in my room there, where I liked to entertain Madame de Glapion, now our superior.

"Madame," said the gentle Glapion shyly, "in spite of our faults, are you a little bit happy among us?"

"As happy as one must be when surrounded with frank faces and kind looks. I count it no little advantage that here I do not meet with ladies with their noses crammed with snuff and openly carrying grey handkerchiefs in their pockets, as is now the fashion. Outside Saint-Cyr the younger generation has become as intolerable to me as I am to myself, which is saying something. No, you who do not know the Court cannot know what charms one encounters here."

Monsieur de Meaux was dead, and so were Monsieur de Fénelon and Monsieur de Beauvilliers. Monsieur de Vendôme was dead, followed by Monsieur de Boufflers. Monsieur de Chartres, my director, was dead, and so was Bontemps, the King's chief valet, and Bourdaloue, and Mansart. Everyone was departing; I remained —but living so retired a life that people scarcely knew I was still there. The courtiers never saw me now, except perhaps for a glimpse caught as I got out of a chair or went up a staircase when we went on one of our journeys. I was a living skeleton, which, though it often walked about, was like a ghost and did not seek company.

My only consolation for living so long was seeing the country gradually return to peace and plenty.

The emperor had refused to sign the treaties of Utrecht because he would not abandon his claims to the Spanish throne, and Villars, as if transported with rage, had carried the war beyond the Rhine, taken Landau and Freiburg and reduced Charles V to unconditional surrender. Peace was signed at Rastadt in March 1714. Alsace, including Strasbourg, remained part of France, which also gained the citadel of Landau. Philip V was confirmed in his possession of Spain. The following year, when the last Germans left Catalonia and Barcelona was retaken, he at last ruled in peace over all the territory accorded to him by the treaties.

When Villars returned, I embraced him with all the eagerness and pride of a mother. He proved I was not always wrong in my judgment of men.

The winters became mild again, the harvests more abundant, trade picked up. Only the national debt was still a source of anxiety. We had borrowed so much to fight the war that we now owed four hundred and thirty-two million francs. Payment of the interest left the Treasury with only seventy-five million, while our current expenditure amounted to a hundred and nineteen. Every year the debt increased by the difference; it seemed impossible ever to pay it off. Monsieur Desmarets liquidated everything he could, and often spoke to me of "bankruptcy." The mere mention of the word filled me with horror. I sent him on to the King, not wishing to know what he thought or to burden my conscience with the matter.

Apart from that preoccupation, which seemed small enough to us compared with what we had gone through these last few years, the crisis which had threatened the destruction of the country was well and truly over. The King had behaved with admirable firmness, not changing any of his ways in matters concerning government. The blows of fate appeared to touch him as little as the rigors of the weather: never did a tougher body contain so imperturbable a soul.

But that body, worn out by so many trials and fatigues, was beginning to fail. For some months the King had been declining visibly. His attacks of gout were more severe, so that some days he could not walk and had to go through the rooms of the château in a wheelchair. At night he sweated so much that his valets had to rub him down from head to foot and change his shift every morning. He was getting thin. Only his face remained incomparable.

I thought grief might be the cause of this deterioration: the King, like me, had never got over the death of the Dauphine. Without meaning to be, he was secretly bitter about it, and this resentment was gnawing at him from within. So more than ever he tried to anesthetize himself with hunting and ceremony, and to stupefy himself with interminable suppers.

"But this is childish," I said to him. "You'll ruin your health. Could you not give up hunting and cut down a little on what you eat?"

"If I do not hunt, Madame, I suffer from the vapors."

"Pooh! I suffer from them myself, but I shan't die of it. The vapors make people feel depressed but they don't make their hearts stop beating any more than headaches prevent them from thinking. And what about those suppers? Four soups, six roasts, ices, salads, stewed fruit, sweets—is it reasonable at your age? Monsieur Fagon often tells me how worried he is about it."

"Monsieur Fagon is the doctor, not the King. He does his job, I do mine. A king has to be seen, he has to have a good appetite. Anyhow, I don't wish to make any changes in Court etiquette."

As he grew older, this grandson of Henri IV grew increasingly attached to the principles of his Spanish ancestor Philip II.† Madame des Ursins said he was becoming amazingly like him.

"But if you were really ill, Court etiquette would have to be changed . . ."

"Not at all, Madame. Kings are not ill. They just die."

"Oh, Sire—could you not be less of a king sometimes?"

"Perhaps occasionally with you, Madame. But nowadays, you don't want . . ."

"I assure you," I said, laughing, "that on those occasions you were as much a king as always."

Maréchal, the chief surgeon, asked to see me and said the obvious decline in the King's health was causing him great alarm. I replied that Monsieur Fagon, whom I saw every day, explained the King's increasingly frequent fevers as the consequence of overeating and an irregular way of life. Maréchal shook his head. "I respect Monsieur Fagon's opinion, Madame," he said, "but I must point out that His Majesty's chief doctor is himself growing old. His sight is failing, his hands shake, as you know. I cannot have complete confidence in a doctor who is in no better health than his patient."

"Monsieur," I said, "please show no disrespect either to your master or to your King. Moreover, the King's health is a matter of politics, as he has often told me himself. So I do not advise you to let the courtiers think he may be ill, or even not so well as usual. Anyhow, I try not to deceive myself, but I am hopeful. Please try to be hopeful too. And in any case, do not say anything."

Monsieur Maréchal emerged very dissatisfied from this interview, and I expected him, like so many others, to complain to all the Court of my coldness and discourtesy.

A few weeks later it was the turn of the duc du Maine to come and talk to me. He was always with us in private, wrote music to amuse his father, made our ladies laugh, showered me with little presents and often delighted us by bringing his two children, the prince de Dombes and the comte d'Eu, both very handsome and well-brought-up, to visit. The King was so fond of them that he had recently, by an edict of July 1714, decreed that they, like the duc du Maine and the comte de Toulouse, should be heirs to the throne in the absence of legitimate princes, of whom there were now only three or four. Of course, according to public opinion a King of France could father princes of the blood only with the Queen, but this King was above public opinion, and the people, who had no objection to our bastards, accepted this decision even though it provoked veiled hostility at Court.

Monsieur du Maine, a loved and loving son, sat in my "niche," curled up in a corner, and told me plainly that he was worried by the change in the King's looks. He begged me to think about the possible consequences, and after shrinking for a while from doing so, I agreed at last to contemplate the worst, provided it was with him.

The Dauphin was only five years old, and the duc d'Orléans would inevitably become Regent.

"The life of the Dauphin is very vulnerable," said the duc du

Maine," and you know what they said about the duc de Bourgogne three years ago."

"Yes," I answered, "but they all died of measles. The duc d'Orléans leads a life of debauchery, I agree, but I cannot think him capable of murder. The King himself calls his nephew a mere bragger of crimes."

"Perhaps, Madame," replied my "darling," "but supposing the Dauphin, who is very delicate, were to die a natural death. Could the duc d'Orléans then reign undisturbed? You know what the King of Spain feels about him. There'd be a war."

I was well aware that the King of Spain, the King's only surviving legitimate grandson, had hated his cousin of Orléans implacably since 1709, when the latter, after his successful campaigns in Spain, concluded a secret peace with the English. This was when the war was at its worst, and the future regent had cold-bloodedly planned to dethrone the French King's grandson and, with the help of our enemies, to take his place. Madame des Ursins had foiled this plot, and the prince's agents were arrested, their papers seized and the proofs of his treachery sent to Versailles. Philippe d'Orléans, once my hero, was recalled to France and excluded from all military command for the rest of the war.

The King had briefly contemplated putting his nephew in the Bastille, where he would have time to reflect on the duties of princes, but he was afraid of the scandal that would cause, and the matter was dropped. But the King of Spain, who had more memory than wit, did not forget, and he did not conceal the fact that, rather than let the duc d'Orléans reign if the young Dauphin should die, he himself would unite the crown of Spain to the crown of France, which he had never explicitly renounced.

"So then," said I, "it would mean war straight away with the whole of Europe. My God, how I hope I'll be dead before all the upheavals you will see, my poor child. But the King will live. He must."

"But, Madame, wouldn't it be possible . . .?"

"No, it would not. Nor would it be possible to take the regency away from the duc d'Orléans. Monsieur Voysin tells me that in order to do that the States General would have to be convened, and that would belie the whole reign. Let us say no more of it. Besides, the duc d'Orléans may not be such a bad regent. He is intelligent . . ."

"Are you serious, Madame? If he were merely a traitor to his country I might agree with you, but he is irreligious and a cause of scandal in every way. His daughter, who has learned from him to flaunt her impiety, is said to have an unnatural relationship with him, and knowing these rumors he still chooses to spend all his time with her. His irreligion, his contempt for slander, his dependence on so outrageous a person as his daughter, all tempt one to believe what is almost incredible. This being so, how could he promote the proper education of the Dauphin and the order necessary to the state?"

"I know, Monsieur," I answered, "that the duchesse de Berry behaves in a shocking manner toward her father; her own mother is jealous. But do we really have to imagine it is as bad as they say? Perhaps she is only a woman of her time, and all of them are insufferable, with their ridiculous clothes, their snuff, their wine, their coarseness, their idleness and their loose ways. All the things I most deplore . . ."

The duc du Maine then attacked me on my weak spot, pointing out that, everything else apart, his cousin of Orléans was clearly not the best person to be in charge of a child's education. I had to agree.

During the weeks that followed the comte de Toulouse also spoke to me on this matter when we were staying with him at Rambouillet. Then the duchesse d'Orléans, like him a child of the King and Madame de Montespan, and wife to the future Regent, came to see me.

She usually did so merely out of politeness. She appeared to have nothing to say and would sit down and play piquet with me in silence. After an hour or two of this she would go away again, with a short farewell which was civil but cool. This time, however, the "sleepyhead" spoke with some vivacity, and the haughty Mortemart made an effort to be warm and ingratiating. With the same wit as her mother would have used in her place, she gave me a swift but vivid description of her husband's vices and begged me to have his brothers given the power to prevent him doing harm to the

Dauphin and to France. She spoke as an unhappy and jealous wife, and was all the more eloquent for that.

The next day the duchesse du Maine, whom I never saw, invaded my room on the pretext of wishing to thank me on behalf of her children for the decree issued in July. The tiny "Doña Salpetria," as she was called, prickly, muddle-headed and restless, practically filled the room, stunning me with a flood of words from which it emerged that in the opinion of the whole Court the duc d'Orléans was the king of poisoners and the poisoner of kings.

Finally, torn asunder by four princes as others had been by four horses, I yielded to the bastards' entreaties, partly through reason, partly out of affection and partly out of weariness. I ventured to speak quietly to the King, and I was amazed to find I carried the day at the first attempt. In August 1714 the King made his will, and the regency was entrusted not to one man but to a council of fourteen, including the duc du Maine and the comte de Toulouse; the duc d'Orléans was only the chairman of the council.

"Well," said the King to me, once the document was sealed and sent to the representatives of the Parlement, "I have purchased some peace, but I know how useless and powerless that will is. We kings all do as we like while we live, but afterwards we can do less than commoners. You have only to look at what became of my father's will as soon as he died, and there are many other examples. Mine will have to take its chance . . ."

And having done all he could to ensure the safety of the Dauphin and set his own conscience at rest, he gave himself up entirely to his ailments and his woes.

I thought I ought to prepare him for the last battle of all. A few days before he died, Monsieur de Chartres had reminded me for the last time of the duties belonging to my position: to console the King, obey him and save him. I considered I had done my best, for forty years, to lighten my husband's troubles, and my room had always been his refuge. Nor had I ever, whatever it cost me, been lacking in obedience. But when it came to salvation, I knew I had not altogether reached the goal which Providence had set before me, and could only throw both the King and myself, who had been entrusted with his soul, on the mercy of God. I prayed to the Lord to forgive both of us our imperfections; I knew my own sins, though more hidden, were not less reprehensible than those of the King.

I could see that despite sixty years of piety I had made no real progress in the matter of pride. I was still surprised sometimes by the violence of its attacks, but at least I was no longer entirely consumed by it. As for the rest, I knew I was only lukewarm. I wanted too much to be loved to be able to practice self-renunciation. I was frequently quick-tempered, moody, impatient, too confident in good times and too downcast in bad. Nor did I find consolation for these defects in prayer, in which I let my imagination stray. I felt no beneficial effects from communion and was even repelled sometimes by the sacraments. In short, to me great piety was dreary. I had honored God out of obedience when I was a child; out of defiance when I was eighteen; out of idleness at thirty, self-interest at forty and error at fifty. Now, at seventy-seven, I was afraid I could love Him only out of weariness.

And yet often, when I least expected it, I would be filled to overflowing by the love of God. In the evening I could be in tears, in the morning wake up full of grace. But once the ecstasy was over, I was not sure if such plenitude, lost as soon as glimpsed, was not harder to bear than emptiness. A distant sight of God seemed more unbearable than His absence. "Thou shalt eat and not be satisfied," it says in the Scriptures. I, who have never been able to set bounds to my desires, experienced every day the bitter truth of those words.

In the summer of 1715 the King's health gave such great cause for anxiety that the English, we heard, were wagering in London that he would not last until the winter. This made the King less willing than ever to make any change in his habits.

"If I go on eating with my present good appetite," he told me one evening at supper, "all the Englishmen who have laid large bets that I'll be dead by the first of September will lose their money."

At the beginning of August he received an ambassador from the King of Persia, looking magnificent in a black and gold coat embroidered with diamonds worth two million five hundred thousand livres. A few days later he began to complain of a pain in his left leg when he walked or moved. Monsieur Fagon said it was a kind of gout cramp, but the King seemed to me very cast down for such a minor ailment. On the evening of our return from Marly, he was so weak he had difficulty in getting to his prie-dieu. He was also terribly thin; his flesh seemed to have melted away in the space of four or five days.

He spent several afternoons in my room, emerging from his lethargy only to listen to music. Madame de Dangeau and Madame de Caylus came in to help with the conversation. On 21 August, when he was to have reviewed some of his troops from his windows, he put it off to the following week, but he held the Council of State after dinner. On the twenty-second he was worse, and Monsieur Fagon began to give him quinine in water and ass's milk. He seemed better on the twenty-third, when he ate, slept and worked with Monsieur Voysin. On the twenty-fourth he was up for supper, which he ate in his dressing gown, among his courtiers; but it was for the last time. I was told he could swallow nothing but liquids, and was embarrassed at being seen. He went to bed and his leg was examined; it had black spots on it. The doctors were thrown into confusion, and stopped the milk and quinine, though they did not know what to prescribe instead.

The same day the King ordered a room to be prepared so that I could spend the night near him. It had only a day-bed in it, and from then to the last day of his life I passed every night but one there, sometimes alone and sometimes with my secretary, Mademoiselle d'Aumale.

The twenty-fifth was the feast of Saint Louis, the King's saint's day. The drums came and greeted him with aubades as usual, and he had them stand under the balcony so as to hear them better from his bed. While he dined, his twenty-four violins and oboes played in the antechamber; he had the door left open to listen. Then he fell asleep during a conversation we were having with our circle of ladies, and when he woke up, his pulse was so weak and his mind so confused I suggested he receive the sacrament without further ado.

The curé of Versailles and the chief chaplain of France brought it by the secret stairs, with no more accompaniment than seven or eight torches carried by some of the château's floor-polishers and one of my servants. While the King made his confession, I helped him remember his sins, reminding him of some actions of his which I had witnessed.

"You are doing me a service," he said. "Thank you."

He received extreme unction with great devotion, repeating several times in a loud voice, "Father, have pity on me." All the Court was waiting in the Galerie des Glaces; not one courtier had left since the day the King was confined to his apartment.

After he had received the sacraments, the King remained admirably calm, as if he were merely about to set out on a journey. He asked me to leave his bedside for a moment so that he could add a codicil to his will, entrusting the care and education of the young King to the duc du Maine; Monsieur de Villeroy was to be his governor. I took advantage of this interval to cry my eyes out in the antechamber, for try as I might to emulate the King's steadfastness, I could feel my tears welling up all the time. When I returned, the King received, one after the other, at length and in my presence, Monsieur de Villeroy, Monsieur Desmarets, the duc d'Orléans and the duc du Maine.

He then bade farewell to Madame, very kindly, saying he had always loved her. He told the princesses his daughters, smiling, to live in harmony with one another. He ordered Monsieur de Pontchartrain to take his heart to the house of the Jesuits as tranquilly as, when he was well, he had ordered a fountain for Versailles or Marly. He also gave orders that as soon as he was dead, the Dauphin should be taken to Vincennes to be in the good air; as the Court had not been there for fifty years, he ordered some alterations to be done immediately, and had the plans sent to the minister of Works.

In the evening Monsieur Fagon came and whispered to me that there was gangrene in the leg, that it had penetrated to the bone, and there was no hope. I spent the night at the King's bedside. Though he had no fever, he was extremely thirsty, and I gave him a drink three times.

On 26 August the doctors, seeing his resolution, considered

amputation. Monsieur Fagon did not want to suggest it; I said I would.

"Do you think it would save my life?" he asked them.

Maréchal said it was not likely.

"In that case," said the King, "there is no point in making me suffer."

At that he turned to the maréchal de Villeroy, held out his hand and said: "Goodbye, my friend. We must part."

He dined in bed in the presence of those who had the *entrée*. As the meal was being cleared away, he had the courtiers come nearer.

"Messieurs," I was told he said, "I ask your forgiveness for the bad example I have set you. I owe you much thanks for the way you have served me and the attachment you have shown me. I ask you to bestow on my grandson the same diligence and fidelity you have given to me. He is a child who may encounter many difficulties. I hope you will all work toward unity, and that if anyone departs from it you will help to bring him back . . . But I find I am upsetting myself, and you too. I ask your pardon. Adieu, Messieurs. I hope you will think of me sometimes."

Some time later he asked Madame de Ventadour to bring the Dauphin.

I was alone at his side, except for the necessary servants.

"My child," he said to the fair little boy, frightened by this impressive scene, "you are going to be a great king. Do not be like me in my love of building or my love of war. Try to be at peace with your neighbors and to succor your people, which I, alas, was never able to do. Do not forget the gratitude you owe to Madame de Ventadour."

Then, embracing the boy, he said: "My dear child, I give you my blessing with all my heart."

When the little prince had been taken off his bed, he asked for him again, and kissed and blessed him once more. Madame de Ventadour quickly took him away; he was on the brink of tears.

Afterwards, as the King leaned on his pillows, looking weary and about to lose consciousness, I asked him if he was in great pain.

"No," he said. "That's what troubles me. I'd like to suffer

more to expiate my sins." Then, after a short silence, "I am going. But France remains."

Sometimes he would let fall a phrase like "When I was King," or refer to the Dauphin as "the young King." If he noticed some movement around him, he would say, "I wonder why it doesn't hurt."

Absorbed already in the great future he knew he was so soon to enter, with a detachment devoid of regret, a humility devoid of self-abasement, a scorn for all that was now for him no more and a kindness and self-possession which consoled all those at his bed-side, he was a most touching sight: always intact, always the same, completely superior and completely Christian.

Right up to the end, everything happened with the same outward propriety, gravity and majesty that had accompanied all the actions of his life, but now there was at the same time a naturalness, an air of truth and simplicity which had not always been so evident.

In short, he died like a hero and a saint.

On 27 August he finished ordering his earthly affairs by seeing the duc du Maine and the comte de Toulouse for the last time, and by going through his two private caskets with me. He made me burn many of the papers they contained and gave me his instructions about what to do with the rest. He laughed when he came on the lists for Marly, and said: "We can burn all this—we shan't be needing it any more." Then he asked me to bring his pouches, which he went through himself to see what had to be got rid of. He found his rosary and gave it to me, saying with a smile, "Not as a relic—as a souvenir."

He said he had heard it was difficult to resign oneself to death, but having arrived at the dread moment himself, he was not finding it hard. I replied gently that it was very hard for someone who was attached to the inhabitants of this world, who had hatred in his heart or who had reparations to make. "Oh," he answered, "as to reparations, I owe nothing to any individual. For what I owe to France, I trust to the mercy of God."

The next night was very disturbed, with the fever very high. In the morning of 28 August he bade me farewell for the first time, saying as he woke that "his only regret was leaving me, but we should meet again soon." I begged him to think only of God. But he went on thinking of me, more than he had ever done before. "I have not made you happy," he said with a sigh, "but I have always loved you. And I assure you you are all I regret in this world. You can believe what I say," he added, smiling. "This is not the moment for gallantries."

He said goodbye to me again in the afternoon, asking my forgiveness for not having lived with me as satisfactorily as he ought, but assuring me he had always loved and respected me. He wept, and asked if anyone else was there. I said no. He said, "But no one will be surprised when they hear I wept with you."

At the third farewell, on the evening of the twenty-eighth, he suddenly said, "But what will become of you, Madame? You have nothing."

"I am nothing," I answered. "Do not think of anything but God."

And I went away so as not to disturb him further.

Then, reflecting that I did not know how the princes would behave toward me and that indeed I possessed no house or furniture in my own right, I retraced my steps and asked him to recommend me to the duc d'Orléans. The King sent for him at once and said: "Nephew, I recommend Madame de Maintenon to you. You know the esteem and consideration I have always had for her. She has never given me anything but good advice, and I only regret I did not always follow it. Do all she asks, either for herself or for her friends and relations. She will not take advantage. Let her deal directly with you."

Then, while they were changing his dressings, the King asked me to leave and not to come back because my presence affected him too much. He said there was nothing more to be done, and he wanted to be left to die in peace. Soon after that he lost consciousness and everyone thought he was dead. Maréchal de Villeroy told me to go to Saint-Cyr without waiting any longer. He sent some of the King's guard to see that the road was safe and lent me his coach so that I should not be recognized.

Next day, the twenty-ninth, in the afternoon, the King emerged from his torpor and showed a small flicker of life. He ate two biscuits steeped in wine and sent for me. I was told at once, and returned. I spent the whole day at his bedside, but without hope. He recognized me, however, and said, "I admire your courage and your friendship, Madame—being present all the time at such a sorry scene."

At about eleven that night his leg was examined, and the gangrene was found to have spread to the knee and the whole of the foot; the thigh was very swollen. The King fainted during the examination.

The day of the thirtieth was as troubled as the previous night, with deep torpor and confusion in the intervals of consciousness. The King swallowed nothing but plain water. I was the only other person in the room apart from the doctors and the most indispensable servants. The King was easily brought round to the subject of religion in his clearer moments, but these were becoming rarer and more brief. By evening he was no more than a machine, aware of nothing. Monsieur Briderey, superior of the priests of Saint-Lazare and my confessor, came to the bedside, looked at the King and said to me:

"You may go. He no longer needs you."

Seeing I could be of no further use, I went to my own apartment, gave my servants such stuffs and other trifles as I had there and made ready to go to Saint-Cyr. However earnestly I bowed to the will of God, I was very much afraid I should not be mistress of myself when the King actually died. I was also afraid that when he was gone, I should not know what attitude to take during the funeral ceremonies, because as far as Court etiquette and public opinion were concerned, I had no rightful place. I even feared I might be insulted in the streets, and treated as I knew from experience those in favor often were treated after they had lost everything. So I left during the night with Mademoiselle d'Aumale, escorted by the duc de Villeroy's men, to stay at Saint-Cyr.

The King was still alive on the thirty-first, and Monsieur de Villeroy kept me constantly informed. I was told that late that evening, when they were saying the prayers for the dying, the King had returned to a semblance of consciousness, and said several times: "O God, make haste to help me."

On 1 September at eight in the morning Mademoiselle d'Au-male came into my room and told me that the whole House was in church, praying. I knew what this meant. That day I was present at the office for the dead, and the next day I went to a service attended by the whole of the community.

The King's body was scarcely cold when, on 2 September, the duc d'Orléans assembled the Parlement and had them overturn both his will and the codicil, just as he had predicted. D'Orléans, having excluded the duc du Maine from the powers assigned to him, assumed the whole of the regency. The same day Monsieur Voysin, the chancellor, came to see me. "Look at all those fatherless children," I said to him, sadly pointing to the little girls out in the courtyard. I had reason to fear the worst for them and for myself, for I knew the duc d'Orléans was aware of the part I had played in the drawing up of the will.

On the sixth I was told the Regent was at the gate asking to see me. When he was admitted to my apartment, he said he had come to assure me of all the consideration I could wish for. When I began to thank him, he interrupted me coldly and said he was only doing his duty, and that I knew what had been required of him. I answered mildly that I was indeed glad to see the gesture of respect he was making toward the late King in coming to see me.

He said he had taken measures to ensure that I received exactly what the King gave me out of his own purse. And he kept his word, even going so far as to say in the citation of my pension that it was my disinterestedness which made such a grant necessary. I thanked him very humbly, saying it was too much in the present state of the country's finances and that I did not want so much. "It is only a trifle," he answered, "but it is true the finances are in a bad way." I said I would pray to God for the help he needed. "Please do so," he answered. "I am beginning to feel the weight of the burden entrusted to me." I assured him with a smile that he would feel it more and more as time went on.

He protested that he would do all he could to put the affairs of the country in order, that this was his only ambition, and that he would esteem himself happy if he could hand the kingdom over to the young King in a few years' time in a better condition than it was now.

"No one has a greater interest than I in the preservation of the young King," he added, "for if we lose him, I should not be able to reign in peace and we should have war with Spain."

I answered, with the gentleness of a mother and the suavity of someone with forty years of Court life behind her, that if he was not insatiably ambitious to reign, as had always been said, his present plan was a thousand times more glorious.

In short, it was a cat-and-mouse conversation, after which we separated on the politest possible terms. We had daggers in our hearts but flowers on our lips; we both had intelligence enough to keep within bounds. As soon as the Regent had gone, I hurried to my desk to write down an exact account of what had been said. I mean to leave this record to the ladies of Saint-Cyr, together with my will, in case when I am gone, the duc's memory should become a little hazy about the promises he made to me.

This was the last of my political labors. I had resolved that the misfortunes threatening France should spare the House of Saint-Louis, that the storms of the age should leave a clear sky over these few acres.

I shut my door to princes and courtiers and let them know I did not wish to see or hear of the world any more.

On 9 September the King was interred at Saint-Denis, without any pomp or circumstance.

For forty years I had been nothing but the hero's shadow. When he disappeared, I vanished from the sight of men, and from their memories.

Nineteen

"And the evening and the morning were another day . . ."

It is four years now since I shut myself up in Saint-Cyr, but for the last three months I have been suffering from a slight low fever which will soon set me free. I am being treated with poppy juice, quinine and Bordeaux wine, but either in spite or because of this diligent care I am dizzy all the time and the pen keeps slipping from my hand. The last doctor to examine me thought I was better.

"I am better," I said to my nephew de Noailles, when he asked how I was. "I am better, but I am going."

I have wished for death for so many years I can have no fear of illness. All I fear is this cold which chills me to the bone, numbs both my fingers and my brain and persecutes me even when I am in bed.

All my life I have been cold. Some babies are dedicated to the Virgin or some other saint. I was dedicated to the cold one November day in an unheated cell in Niort prison, and my patron has never deserted me since. He was with me at Mursay in that little

465

bedroom which never had a fire so that I should not get used to comforts above my station. He caught up with me at La Rochelle, that rainy autumn when I went through the streets barefoot in search of bread. He enshrouded me one winter evening when they were burying my brother's coffin. He wooed me in Paris when, with holes in my shoes, I tried not to slip on the pavement. He wedded me at Versailles, when the wind swept through the wide-flung windows of my room.

I have been cold in cotton frocks that were too thin and too short. I have been cold in full ceremonial dress, beneath a carapace of gold and jewels. And I am cold today, muffled up in black cloaks and huddling behind the curtains of my bed. It seems to me not all the fur capes in the world, not the thickest feather beds, nor the hottest braziers could overcome that cold. I can still warm the outer husk, but the soul inside is frozen at last. It is hard for me to keep even a little corner warm for you, my child.

But I do not want to abandon a book undertaken for your instruction without giving, as at the end of a novel, a brief account of what became of the survivors of my story, or without drawing its moral.

The maréchal de Villeroy is still the young King's governor, and the old courtier takes his role so seriously that he sees threats everywhere and is becoming sadder than all Monsieur Racine's tragedies put together. When he comes to see me, which he does despite my prohibitions, he talks of nothing but attempted poisonings, rumors of assassination and semblances of murder. Nevertheless, our King is getting on for ten years old, and in such good health that despite all this drama they are thinking of getting him married.

Monsieur du Maine has not been so fortunate. After having deprived him of his powers, the Regent had his titles taken away from him one after the other. I urged on him the necessity for resignation, and he agreed sufficiently to have begun an excellent translation of Lucretius. But his little duchesse was unable to adapt herself to Latin verses and the reverses of fortune. She started to plot with the Spanish ambassador and got mixed up in a conspiracy. The Regent had everyone imprisoned, including even the servants. My little prince was put in solitary confinement. The family was ruined; my child was lost.

Madame de Caylus tries to distract me from my sorrow by telling me of her follies. Since becoming a widow, she has been living with the duc de Villeroy. They eat, drink and live in great style, but her health is very poor, and I doubt if she will make old bones. But she is always cheerful. Only her son, the chevalier, worries her, talking of nothing but poetry and travel. They thought he was going to be an officer, but he wanted to be a versifier. He is also rather a good-for-nothing, gambling, losing, borrowing and getting his mother to pay his debts. At present he is thinking of going to Constantinople to restore his fortunes. That sounds familiar. Blood will out. The young chevalier is a true d'Aubigné.

Monsieur de Noailles is the only one of my relations who is not out of favor. The Regent has recognized his merits and made him chairman of the council for finance. Luckily his duties do not prevent him from begetting children on his wife, and as that is what she does best, they will soon have a dozen of them.

I am told my cousin Madame de Villette is the mistress of a great English lord, Lord Bolingbroke, and that my other cousin, Madame de Mailly, is one of the most fashionable members of the new Paris society. Nothing remains to remind anyone of her former principles, whether Calvinist or moral.

The abbé de Choisy is getting on for a hundred and has at last been made a member of the Academy, where no one in skirts had ever been seen before. I thought he was going to write the Memoirs of the reign, but it was Monsieur de Dangeau who did so. He gave me the manuscript before sending it to the printer, and I read his eighty notebooks in three weeks. Princes, ministers, favorites, palaces, hunts, fêtes, battles . . . I had forgotten how heady that liquor was until I tasted it for the last time.

But when you have emptied the cup, you must know how to drain the dregs with the same good grace. Such is the case of my friend the princesse Orsini, who has just fallen from the heights of fortune into the depths of disgrace. She had ruled the Queen of

Spain, who had ruled the King. But the Queen, being mortal, died. The princesse herself was too old to aspire to the Crown. The choice of a new queen needed to be made with the utmost deliberation, but she was carried away and lost by the same enthusiasm which had so often saved her. She took it into her head to vest her authority in a little Italian priest called Alberoni. I knew him for an intriguer who had lived for a long while at Anet, sponging off Monsieur de Vendôme, whose minion he became in circumstances worthy of them both. The priest had made his fortune by flinging himself upon Vendôme as he rose from his commode and kissing him in full view of all on the most exposed part of his person. Try as I might to warn Madame des Ursins against so shabby a character, she would not listen. She had confidence in herself in everything, except morals.

Alberoni, armed with the powers of the *camerera-mayor*, chose the new Queen in his own country, and took long enough on the journey from Italy to Spain to indoctrinate her thoroughly. Madame des Ursins went to meet her, and no sooner had she knelt before the new Queen than the latter, on her mentor's instructions, had her arrested, flung into a carriage and driven to the frontier out of hand. I saw the princesse when she was in Paris; she bore the collapse of her power, the loss of her fortune and the ingratitude of kings with her usual good health and spirits. Besides, nothing has really changed: today, as yesterday, the Queen of Spain commands the King, but now it is Cardinal Alberoni who commands the Queen. What is greatness when such a man rules a kingdom?

As things are now, one hardly wants to hear the inside story of events. You cannot survive your own epoch and not pay the price. I congratulate myself every day on not being in the know about politics any more. I could believe myself as much forgotten outside of here as the great men and politicians I no longer think of, were it not for an occasional proof that people remember I once existed, even though they do not know I exist still. The other day Czar Peter of Muscovy asked to see me, as he might ask to be shown a historical monument.

He arrived at about seven in the evening, setting the whole house in an uproar. I was in bed. Out of politeness I attempted a scrap of conversation, but I soon perceived his interpreter could not understand what I was saying. The Czar then stood up, and in the silence that followed flung aside my bed-curtains to look at me properly. Then he left without a backward glance, with what satisfaction you may imagine. For what is there in common between the woman who won the love of the King of France and the bag of bones on this mattress, except for the long brown hair which by some embarrassing freak has never shown a trace of white? And what link is there between the little Françoise of the past and the old Marquise de Maintenon, apart perhaps for the emotional hunger which nothing has ever satisfied, the impatience which has never been appeased?

"If you do not know what you want," my worthy aunt de Villette used to say to me, "you will assuredly never get it." I suppose I did not know what I wanted, for I did not get it.

Even as a child I was determined not to seek for happiness. Already it seemed wisest to me to aim only at what neither war, illness nor death could take away from me. I chose glory: it seemed a very reliable possession. By the time I was forty, I had attained it. But then my life, until then so concentrated in pursuit of that goal, began to come undone like a badly wound ball of wool. I realized with surprise that I was not completely satisfied with what I had and that I still felt a vague spiritual restlessness which nothing but another quest could dispel. I did not know what other goal to choose: I was tempted in turn by love, power and renunciation, and tried, for fear of missing something in the short time I had left, to aim at all three at once. I missed them all.

I missed with the King because I never succeeded in loving him or making him love me in the way I would have liked. In the last years of his life, although I respected him as a hero, I had come to hate him so much as a man that I waited eagerly either to die or to be made a widow. Now that he is no more, I look tenderly on the rosary he gave me and have Mademoiselle d'Aumale play the pieces he liked on the harpsichord. The only books I really enjoy reading are those which speak to me of him. In short, I like whatever brings me near my husband as much as I used to like what kept us apart. But it is too late to repair the misunderstanding.

I feel less regret for the loss of power, which I sought only out of imitation. It takes more strength than I possess, or less greed, not to run toward the spot to which you see everyone else running: you want to have your share, even if you throw it away afterwards. I ran with the crowd, but my heart was not in it. My lack of ardor is probably the reason I attained only a shadow of influence, and then so late that it was more of a pain than a pleasure. For this half-victory it is fair I should feel only half a regret.

I feel more bitter at having missed with God, though to tell the truth I did not miss by much. I do not deny I was called, and I confess I heard the call quite clearly. But I had other worries and other desires, and frankly the sacred virtues had less appeal for me than those consecrated by opinion.

"You are called to another kingdom than that in which you reign," my director wrote to me, "do not forget the place where you are going and where the King awaits you." Coming and going between the kingdom of France and the kingdom of Heaven, I got stranded on the way somewhere between the two. Like the princesses of legend, who are found in the morning bereft of their kingdoms, their clothes and their memories because when they reached their goal, they could not say the right word or produce the magic key, I have seen my hopes melt away and my possessions disappear like snow in the sun.

It is too late now to lament. We live only once, and the only conclusions I want to draw from my own faults are such as may be useful to you. If you will believe one who has tasted all the fruits of this deceitful world, you will not leave Saint-Cyr for the vanities outside and the pursuit of nothingness. When you are twenty years old and have spent a few days going through this account of a whole life, burn these Memoirs and my memory together; do not waste a glance on the iron grille which separates our House from the palace of kings, but go to our chapel and take the black veil of the ladies of Saint-Louis. Those who have read travellers' accounts of journeys around the world may stay at home.

If you do not take my advice, I shall console myself with the thought of you wearing close-fitting dresses of pink, your hair braided with diamonds, with bracelets on your arms and your little feet shod with figured silk . . . I am not really sure I know what I want for you any better than I knew what I wanted for myself. Anyhow, whatever follies you commit, I shall not be there to grieve over them.

So now I leave you, as I have already left the fountain and foliage of the Green Courtyard, the dormitory of the Reds and the classroom of the Blues. I shall stroll no more through the grove of elms at sunset, nor go along any of the walks and alleys whose names were chosen by the King: Solitude Walk, the Way of the Heart, the Path of Thought. I shall not sit any more in the Games Room and hear the laughter of your friends, nor go up the King's Way, at the end of which he was so often waiting for me. A week ago, for the last time, I looked out of my window over the gardens and saw the grey sky of the Ile-de-France, which I shall never see again. My bed is too far from the window for me to hope for a glimpse of one last cloud.

When everything else has been taken away from me, I still have you. But it is time to bid you adieu. I say it in silence so as not to frighten you, and the tender words I should like to say will not cross my lips. Farewell, my joy and comfort; farewell, delightful companion; farewell, last pleasure of my life; farewell, my only consolation in my sorrows . . .

Once, among the Mursay papers, I came across a letter telling the Villettes about the last moments of my grandfather d'Aubigné. It seems that on the morning of the day he died, when he opened his eyes on his last sun, he said to those who had been watching by his bed: "Behold the happy day which God has made for our desires! To Him be glory, and in it let us take pleasure." Agrippa d'Aubigné was a poet and an incorrigible boaster. I shall not go so far as to claim that my last day will give me pleasure.

It is not that I am very much afraid of being dead. The void of the atheists is not a state in which one could feel much discomfort, and if my own faith has not misled me and God has mercy on my sins, I shall meet with eternal felicity when I reach the other side.

But though I do not fear being dead, I am very much afraid of dying. It is not so much the new state in store for me as the transition to it that I dread, and my last day makes me tremble more than all the ages after. I am afraid of suffering, and pray to God every day to heed my impatience and spare me great pain. I am afraid of this chill already spreading through my flesh and mind, and of the darkness into which I shall fall. Even if it lasts only a moment, it must seem long. Going through that infinite second, I dread being alone, being in doubt, struggling like a woman drowning.

Lord, help this old woman with no further part to play and no one to watch her go. Help this proud one, whose pride can no longer come to her aid, to make in silence and in secret an end worthy of him who was her husband. And let me enjoy for a few more days the feel of that little hand in mine, and the singing of the children that sounds to me like angel music.

"We are the red ribbons, red ribbons, red ribbons, And we want the green ribbons, the greens for our friends . . ."

Poor Marie, as soon as you stop singing, Mademoiselle d'Aumale or Madame de Glapion sends you away, saying you tire me. They know I am going to die, and you do not. But your ignorance helps me, and the light cool kiss you drop on my hand is more to me than the prayers of your elder sisters.

I only regret I cannot pay you back. Perhaps I shall be with you when your last hour comes, but I doubt that in my future state I shall have a hand or lips to offer.

To give you back some of the comfort you give me, I can only teach you some words I thought I had forgotten, but which have kept coming back to me in the last few days. They are from an old hymn I used to sing in church at Niort as a child, among the Poitou Protestants. If you learn them from me as I learned them from

Madame de Villette and say them again in your last moments, perhaps you will not be quite alone. They are from the Gospel of Saint Luke.

"Abide with us: for it is toward evening, and the day is far spent."

Sources

The main source for this book is Madame de Maintenon's Correspondence.

When she died in 1719, Françoise de Maintenon left behind nearly eighty volumes of letters. In the late eighteenth century, forty volumes were still preserved at Saint-Cyr. Since then, because of bequests and political upheavals, the Correspondence has been scattered and even partly destroyed. Still, more than four thousand letters have survived.

An important element is missing, for the letters written by Madame de Maintenon to the King and to her closest woman intimates are absent. We still have the many she addressed to her relatives and friends, her spiritual directors, her stewards and servants, the superiors and pupils at Saint-Cyr and various political figures of the age.

Also at our disposal are a large number of letters written to Madame de Maintenon. These include one from the King, which together with several short notes escaped when, before her death, the marquise systematically destroyed the correspondence between herself and her husband.

A further source—Madame de Maintenon's instructions to the

pupils and teachers of Saint-Cyr—survives more or less in its entirety. It includes, besides accounts of one-sided conversations in which the marquise spoke (often about her own experiences) and the young ladies took notes, a number of one-act plays written by Madame de Maintenon as aids to moral and civic instruction.

Throughout the book, wherever possible, Madame de Maintenon's own words have been used. They have been taken not only from her own letters and other writings but also from the memoirs of Madame de Caylus, her niece, and of Mademoiselle d'Aumale, her secretary, which claim to reproduce Madame de Maintenon's own accounts of such events as the King's death and the visit of the Regent.

Madame de Maintenon did not need to describe people well known to her correspondents, and such descriptions the author has generally supplied from contemporary memorialists such as Saint-Simon, Madame de Sévigné and the Princesse Palatine, where their views on the person in question are likely to have resembled those of the marquise herself. Throughout, the author has striven at the greatest possible accuracy through meticulous documentation.

Of the enormous general Correspondence, no complete edition exists. For details of attempts to compile complete editions and the material of individual correspondences, as well as for information on numerous other sources published and unpublished, the reader of this translation is referred to pages 523–526 of the French edition, and to its comprehensive chapter-by-chapter notes on sources.

The French edition's careful chapter-by-chapter distinctions between the entirely documented and the partly invented passages in the narrative are reproduced in abridged form below.

CHAPTER ONE

All the facts and details recorded in this chapter are authentic. Madame de Maintenon's feelings are such as emerge from the confidences she made to those near her. The only invented element is her decision to write her memoirs. Although, after reading Dangeau's Memoirs she may have felt tempted to write her own, she had the strength to remain silent to the end. One day she said to Mademoiselle d'Aumale, "I shan't write my memoirs. Nothing ought to be left out . . . and once again I can't tell all."

CHAPTER TWO

All the information in this chapter is documented, except for the following.

1. Constant d'Aubigné's place of detention. The Conciergerie in the hôtel Chaumont has been chosen as the most likely of three traditional alternatives.

2. Madame d'Aubigné's place of residence in Niort. It is not known whether she spent the three years before she left Niort within the precincts of the prison or in some other lodging. In Poitiers she had chosen to live with her children outside the prison, and this fact, together with some IOUs after 1636 which give her domicile as Niort instead of the Conciergerie at Niort, made the author opt for the same arrangement now. The Regratterie quarter was chosen to show what the popular districts of Niort were like at that time.

3. Françoise's nurse. Tradition holds that Françoise had the same nurse as one of her girl cousins, but other biographers have disagreed as to whether the cousin in question was Aimée or Madeleine. The character of Louise Appercé is invented, but documents show that the farm at Mursay was let to a family of that name.

CHAPTER THREE

All the facts here are exact. There has been some confusion as to whether the guarding of the turkeys belongs to Françoise's stay with her aunt de Villette at Mursay or to a later period with her aunt de Neuillan in Niort. The uncertainty probably arises from inefficient note-taking on the part of the young ladies of Saint-Cyr, and Mursay has been chosen as more probable.

Madame de Maintenon never concealed her indifference and even resentment toward her parents, and her great love and admiration for her aunt de Villette. Every year, on the anniversary of her aunt's death, the marquise retired alone to her oratory and spent the whole day there in meditation and prayer. The ladies of Saint-Cyr say that whenever she mentioned Arthémise de Villette her eyes filled with tears.

CHAPTER FOUR

The first sojourn in La Rochelle, the crossing of the Atlantic on the *Isabelle,* the visits to Guadeloupe, Marie-Galante, Martinique and Saint-Christophe, together with the return to France are all copiously documented (in particular with the help of a biography of Constant d'Aubigné published in 1971) so as to give an unusually full picture of this period of Madame de Maintenon's life. The exact dates of her family's peregrinations are difficult to determine, and the author sometimes had to use her own judgment in surmising which incident took place on which island.

The character of Zabeth Dieu is invented, though both her name and her song are authentic. Biam Coco is also imaginary. Their habits and fates are drawn from contemporary accounts. The cruel punishment inflicted on Françoise was a real event, though the reason for it is unknown. Tesseron too is real, though we do not know whether this strange servant, who followed Constant from prison to prison, was the same as the one who went with him to America.

There was a real Jean Marquet who sailed as a "volunteer" on the same ship as Françoise, though their meeting is invented.

A choice had to be made among several accounts of the period between Françoise's return to La Rochelle and her second stay at Mursay. Several families claimed in the eighteenth century that their forebears had taken her in; one tradition even has her left with a merchant as surety for one of her mother's debts. The author has simplified the tribulations of a few months which must have been even more disturbing and humiliating for the young Françoise than they appear in this book.

CHAPTER FIVE

The facts about Françoise's life with Madame de Neuillan and with the Ursulines, and about her meeting with Scarron, are well known and documented, but little is available about her second stay at Mursay. Even its length is uncertain.

The death of Françoise's elder brother has been given an importance she may not have accorded it herself. The exact circumstances of his death remain mysterious: some contemporaries wrongly attributed it to a duel, though it now seems established that he was drowned. The theory of suicide is a hypothesis of the author, not of Madame de Maintenon.

CHAPTER SIX

Françoise's marriage and her life with Scarron are copiously documented as to the visible facts. Like most historians, the author has decided to view their marital relations as a *mariage gris,* though she does not entirely exclude the possibility that the marriage was consummated. Concerning their feelings for one another, while Françoise seems to have entertained nothing more than polite indifference and sometimes even discreet disdain for him, Scarron, though irreverent enough in his public allusions to her, expresses considerable affection and respect in his private correspondence. They seem to have been a genuine if odd couple, linked by their love for the matters of the mind and by their social ambition.

The author has adopted the theory that the love of Françoise for the maréchal d'Albret remained unfulfilled, and was followed by a long *amitié amoureuse.* No doubt there was such a loving friendship between them, but many contemporaries, including Saint-Simon, believed it had been preceded by a real liaison. The present author, while considering a genuine affair possible and even probable, decided to treat their relations entirely as an *amitié amoureuse* so as to have the pleasure of describing a situation and feelings different from those which apparently existed between Françoise and Louis de Villarceaux.

CHAPTER SEVEN

Again all the facts, even down to minor details of dress, are amply documented from many contemporary and later sources.

The conversations between Françoise and Ninon de Lenclos are mostly imaginary, though they make use of sayings attributed to Ninon. Those between Françoise and Villarceaux are either transposed from conversations and love-letters attributed to contemporary free-thinking wits, or else invented.

Though Villarceaux's family and fortune are well known, and the nude portrait he painted of Madame Scarron can still be seen in the château at Villarceaux, little is recorded about his personality. Nor do we know where the two first met. The meeting certainly took place in 1658, and a year later the marquis was so smitten that his love was the talk of Paris. All this being so, the author has attributed to Villarceaux some of the words and actions Madame de Maintenon related in her "conversations" at Saint-Cyr without specifying to which of her former "gallants" they could be ascribed.

Whether Françoise "yielded" to the marquis during Scarron's lifetime or only after his death is a mystery. The author let herself be guided by psychological probability and Scarron's own conviction.

CHAPTER EIGHT

The affair between Françoise and Villarceaux gave rise to countless stories and insinuations, all the more significant because some of them belong to the period when she was still young Madame Scarron, when there was as yet nothing to foretell her future greatness and she was a relatively unrewarding subject for slander. In the face of so much evidence and presumption of guilt, it is hard for a biographer to argue in favor of her heroine's virtue.

There was no need to invent anything about the existence, the public manifestations or the duration of the liaison, but the author did have to imagine the feelings which might have brought together two such apparently contrasting characters. For this she relied to some extent on the relations between Valmont and Madame de Tourvel in *Les Liaisons dangereuses.*

We do not know who paid Madame Scarron's bills at La Charité Notre-Dame after the break with the duchesse d'Aumont. It has been hinted that Villarceaux might have done so, but the author preferred to think it was some pious lady friend of Françoise; despite what Saint-Simon may have said, Madame Scarron never accepted money from any of her admirers and bore her poverty proudly.

The description of the little house in the rue des Trois-Pavillons is due to the author, though both its location and its rent are known.

Contrary to tradition, Nanon Balbien is represented as a young woman, probably younger than her mistress. This difference from previous historians is based on various calculations, including one derived from the fact that when in 1691 Nanon was made *surveillante générale* or senior mistress at Saint-Cyr, her mother was still alive and came to Saint-Cyr for a while to assist her in her new duties. Little is known of Nanon's social origins, but a number of clues suggest that she came from a family of masons belonging either to the common people or to the slightly better-off class of small artisans. The author chose the first of these alternatives because it gave her the opportunity to show what life was like among the lower classes in the famine year of 1661.

CHAPTER NINE

Nothing in this chapter is invented except the conversations between Madame Scarron and the maréchal d'Albret, and the exchange between her and Madame de Scudéry.

On the available evidence it is impossible to decide whether the abbé Gobelin became Madame Scarron's spiritual director in 1669, just before she entered the service of Madame de Montespan, or in 1670, just after she had taken charge of the "child of sin."

As for Louis XIV's height, the author hesitated between medium and tall, despite the modern tendency to say that the "great king" was really quite small. Even the most critical of contemporaries, such as the foreign ambassadors, never described him as short. He was usually said to be of medium height, and sometimes even very tall. Hébert, the curé of Versailles, who saw him every week for eighteen years, said in his Memoirs that the King was "six feet tall." While the author did not want to go that far, she did not feel she had to represent the Sun King as just a little fellow.

CHAPTER TEN

Here once again the facts and feelings are all authentic, though sometimes slightly rearranged, with the exception of the conversation between Madame Scarron and Madame de Montespan beside the pool at Genitoy, which is imaginary.

No one knows whether little Toscan was really the son of Charles d'Aubigné. Madame Scarron, with the abbé Gobelin's approval, looked after him like a mother until he died at about the age of seven, and one of her biographers has hinted that he might have been her own child. She could certainly have had an illegitimate child either by Villarceaux or by d'Albret, and would have been quite capable of concealing its existence without actually abandoning it. But it seems more probable that this was the first of the many bastard nephews of whom her brother, as she said, made her a present.

CHAPTER ELEVEN

While the Correspondence shows the main outlines of the King's conquest of Madame Scarron, it does not reveal the details of the process, and the author had to rely on her imagination for the intimate scenes between them. Some biographers have placed Madame Scarron's final surrender in 1678, but the present author, like most modern historians, considers 1674 more likely. As well as adducing some factual evidence, she points out that it was heroic enough for Madame Scarron to resist the King's advances for two years; to have held out for six or seven, when she saw him every day, would have been an almost incredible exploit.

CHAPTER TWELVE

The records are not clear as to whether there were one or two breaks in the relationship between Madame de Montespan and the King before the final rupture in 1678–79.

The conversation between the two Françoises in 1675 is based on one placed in 1676 by Mademoiselle d'Aumale.

The scene between Madame de Maintenon and the maréchal d'Albret at Bordeaux is invented, as is that between Madame de Maintenon and the dying Mademoiselle de Fontanges.

CHAPTER THIRTEEN

Here only the two conversations between Madame de Maintenon and the King are invented, and these make use of certain authentic phrases.

The marriage between the King and Madame de Maintenon is no longer in doubt. As to its date, the author adopts the all but universal modern opinion, which is confirmed by the Correspondence and challenged by only one recent biographer, whose arguments the author finds interesting but unconvincing. He places the marriage after 1697.

CHAPTER FOURTEEN

The facts and opinions recorded here are all accurate, though some have been slightly rearranged or reattributed. The author thinks it unlikely that Louis XIV, so celebrated for his polished manners, would, when indulging in one of his well-known sallies at his wife's expense, have chosen so facile a means of attack as her modest origins; but this was a way, in the book, of emphasizing the doubtfulness of the d'Aubignés' claims to nobility. Madame de Maintenon herself, once informed of the dubiousness of these claims, wished to know no more on the subject. Late-nineteenth-century studies showed that Agrippa d'Aubigné ennobled himself and that his father, Jean, succeeded in entering the entourage of the d'Albret family straight from the lower classes, without the usual detour by way of the bourgeoisie.

As for the legend about Madame de Maintenon's role in the revocation of the Edict of Nantes, no modern historian believes she played any part at all. The myth was started by the Princesse Palatine thirty years after the event, elaborated by Saint-Simon, who was only ten at the time of the Revocation and taken up again a century later by Michelet, but it does not stand up against the evidence of modern documentation.

Another apparently indestructible legend was created by Michelet in the nineteenth century: that of the alleged influence of the Jesuits upon Madame de Maintenon. The Correspondence, however, is full of hostile remarks on the subject, and contains only one that is even neutral, let alone favorable.

CHAPTER FIFTEEN

This chapter goes unusually deeply into the political aspects of the quietist "cabal." Even though they are irrelevant to Madame Guyon's doctrine and behavior, they are essential to the understanding of Madame de Maintenon's attitude.

The account of Racine's fall from grace favors the version of his son Louis over the implausible explanation put forward by Saint-Simon. The latter says Racine was disgraced for having inadvertently mentioned the name of Scarron in the King's presence—but the King regularly had Scarron's plays performed at Court.

Monsieur de Beauvilliers's views on the reform of Saint-Cyr are invented, but based on his known convictions. The physical portrait of Hébert is also imaginary, though his personality and views are clear from his Memoirs and other evidence. The scene in which the King reproaches his wife actually took place, as both the Correspondence and Hébert's Memoirs show, but the King's words have been imagined by the author.

CHAPTER SIXTEEN

Unlike the legend created by Saint-Simon about Madame de Maintenon's position on the Spanish succession, this chapter draws on the accounts of two of the main witnesses: Torcy, minister of Foreign Affairs, and Louville, the King's envoy extraordinary to the young King of Spain. Both these men were present at the discussion on the subject which occupied the King and his Council for several days. Torcy says Madame de Maintenon gave no opinion. Louville says indignantly that she, like Beauvilliers, was in favor of rejecting the will. The author adopted the Torcy hypothesis as the less improbable; in any case, it is impossible to maintain that Madame de Maintenon urged the King to accept the succession, even though as usual she refrained from disagreeing when he made his position officially known.

This chapter also offers an opportunity to correct the caricature of Madame de Maintenon as a frigid "lady in black."

It was only rarely that she wore black. She did so regularly only in the two or three years when she actually discharged the duties of mistress of the robes to the Dauphine (as she said in a letter, it was the dress that went with the job), and then again thirty years later, right at the end of her life, after the death of the duchesse de Bourgogne, and especially after the death of the King. Apart from this, though at the age of about thirty-five she gave up wearing "colors" (which meant, according to contemporary usage, giving up garish reds, pinks and greens)—she never dressed in black, which the King disliked and which she herself could not bear unless it was ornamented, for example with gold braid.

In 1707, a year taken at random (when she was seventy-two), the orders she gave her niece de Caylus for the purchase of materials included requests for white lace and satin, a grey-brown damask, some slate-blue cloth, a purple watered moiré with a gold belt and some "black and gold stuff." The last is the only item in the whole year which recalls the legendary black. Many of the portraits currently put forward as portraits of Madame de Maintenon (some of them identified as such only because they depict an "old lady in black") are thought by experts to be of doubtful authenticity.

As for Madame de Maintenon's alleged frigidity, this legend is based entirely on the letter to her from Godet-Desmarais concerning "painful occasions"; but what is omitted is that the letter dates to the year 1705, when its recipient was seventy. Can the marquise's reaction at that age to the appetites of her indefatigable husband really tell us what her attitude and aptitudes might have been when she was twenty-five, or forty? The present author is inclined to agree with those who think it was not just by her soundness that Madame de Maintenon was able to attract, and to keep, a king still young and of an amorous temperament.

CHAPTER SEVENTEEN

None of the events in this chapter are invented.

However, Madame de Maintenon's sale of the ring given her by the King is placed in 1709 instead of 1694, which was also a year of great famine; Mademoiselle d'Aumale shows in detail that Madame de Maintenon's charities were even greater in 1709–10 than at the earlier period, and the change avoids a break in the rhythm of the narrative. Similarly, the King's illness is placed several years later in time here than in reality. The death of the duc de Berry is also brought closer to that of his brother and that of his nephew, though in fact it occurred nearly two years later: the impression made on people at the time was of a tragedy which struck down all the members of the family at once.

CHAPTER EIGHTEEN

Historical truth has been observed throughout in this chapter, apart from some very minor rearrangements.

As regards what was in the Dauphine's casket, the author was reduced to hypotheses: while it is almost certain that Madame de Maintenon did in fact find in it the little anthology of maxims she had written out for the duchesse de Bourgogne when she was a child, and which on her death she passed on to the ladies of Saint-Cyr, we do not know what those other discoveries were "which would have been painful to us if the Dauphine had lived."

The apologists for the duchesse de Bourgogne claim that this refers to gambling debts, but this is unlikely because the correspondence between the young duchesse and the elderly marquise shows that Madame de Maintenon had known all about them for years. The Dauphine's detractors, on the other hand, have said that the unwelcome discovery related to a secret correspondence between the young princesse and her father, the duc de Savoie, in whose interest she would have been ready to betray the King of France. But this does not square with the duchesse's character as we know it. Above all, if this hypothesis is true, it is hard to see how Louis XIV and Madame de Maintenon would have been able, as they did, to remember the princesse always with love and sorrow. The present author adopted the most likely theory—that what Madame de Maintenon found were love-letters, probably from the marquis de Nangis. Saint-Simon maintains that Madame de Maintenon was told by the duchesse about her flirtations, but the Correspondence shows that this was not the case: in the duchesse's latter years, the marquise thought she was in love with her husband. This probably explains her surprise and sadness when she opened the casket.

As for the Jansenist quarrel, the author sticks to Madame de Maintenon's own "official version," according to which she "did not meddle" or get involved. But the truth was certainly more complex, for her correspondence with chancellor Voysin shows that she was well informed on these matters, sometimes before the King himself, and that the ministers consulted her about what and what not to tell or ask him. While she certainly did not back the King in this quarrel—Père Tellier and the Bourgogne and Beauvilliers faction were much more influential—and while once again the political aspects of the question were beyond her, still she did not play the moderating role which her position at the time would have allowed her to play.

Thus, on the debit side of Madame de Maintenon's political influence must be ranged the two great quarrels of Louis XIV's reign: first the quietist affair, in which she began by being imprudent and afterwards showed a certain degree of cowardice; then the Jansenist question, in which she either could not or would not act as a restraint upon the King.

On the credit side we must list the following: her unqualified condemnation of the war in the Palatinate; her advice that the Spanish succession should be refused; her constant advocacy of peace; her unwavering support of Villars, the only great captain in the latter part of the reign; her disapproval of Court extravagance; her desire to promote the education of the disadvantaged, including women and the common people; and the degree of moderation she showed in matters concerning the Protestants.

Regarding the choice of administrative and political officials, where Madame de Maintenon's influence was seen earlier and more clearly than in other matters, modern historians tend to think that the appointments for which she was responsible were not so unworthy of their great predecessors Louvois and Colbert as nineteenth-century commentators contended. As revealed in both their writings and their actions, such men as Beauvilliers, Chamillart, Pontchartrain and Torcy were hardworking, honest and intelligent, though these may not be political virtues. In any case, whatever their degree of competence, they probably confronted an economic, diplomatic and military situation radically different from the one their predecessors were fortunate enough to have to deal with. Lean years rarely bring forth great finance ministers, and it may be that the art of government consists in coming on the scene at the right time.

CHAPTER NINETEEN

This chapter is based directly on the Correspondence as it relates to the marquise's years of retirement. The only change is that the author has addressed to little Marie de La Tour the fond farewell which Madame de Maintenon really addressed to Madame de Dangeau.

Madame de Maintenon died on 15 April 1719 and was buried at Saint-Cyr. In 1793 the revolutionaries profaned her grave, dragging the body through the mud and scattering her bones, while noticing that even in her coffin she had no white hairs. "That day," writes one of her biographers, "she was at last treated like a queen."

Notes

CHAPTER ONE

3   François Michel Le Tellier, marquis de Louvois (1641–1691), Louis XIV's war minister and the reorganizer of the French army. He encouraged war, instigated religious persecution and was largely responsible for the devastation of the Palatinate in 1689.

CHAPTER TWO

5   Agrippa d'Aubigné (1552–1630), poet and ardent Protestant. His chief work, *Les Tragiques,* the "epic of Calvinism," helped to establish the alexandrine as the vehicle of serious French poetry.
The *Marais poitevin* was a marshy area, part of the old province of Poitou.

CHAPTER THREE

17 The Parlement of Paris was the oldest of the ten French parlements or judicial assemblies. It consisted of two hundred magistrates who sat in general assembly to consider important matters of state and register royal edicts. Separate benches dealt with civil suits and criminal cases. The parlements had control of the police. Official posts of their officials were hereditary and could be bought and sold.

CHAPTER FIVE

40 Anne of Austria (1602–1666), wife of Louis XIII, mother of Louis XIV and Regent during his minority.
A *lettre de cachet* was a letter sealed with the King's privy seal, usually to command arbitrary imprisonment or exile for the person named in it.

52 Madeleine de Scudéry (1607–1701), author of the popular romans à clef *Le Grand Cyrus* and *Clélie,* about the writer's contemporaries. Her *samedis* or Saturday receptions were among the earliest of the literary salons.

53 Antoine Baudeau, sieur de Somaize (b. 1630), who took up the defense of the *précieuses* after Molière had satirized them in *Les Précieuses ridicules* (1659). The *précieuses* were ladies who sought after the fashionable *esprit précieux,* originally a cult of elegance and distinction in manners and language, which tended to degenerate into affectation.

CHAPTER SIX

59 The Fronde (the name derives from a boys' game in which *frondes* or slings were used) was a revolt against the absolutism of the Crown which took place in two phases during the minority of Louis XIV. Its immediate cause was the unpopular financial policy of Cardinal Mazarin. The First Fronde (1648–49), led by the Parlement of Paris, was inspired partly

by constitutional principle. In the Second Fronde (1651–53), which began after Mazarin imprisoned the prince de Condé, commander of the Regent's army in the First Fronde, the revolt degenerated into general turmoil. The Court was driven from Paris, and the monarchy was nearly destroyed by a rebellious nobility in league with Spain. The disorders of the Fronde probably inspired Louis XIV's personal style of government.

59 *Mazarinade* was a general name given to the many pamphlets and satires written against Cardinal Mazarin during the Fronde. Scarron's was the most famous.

59 Paul de Gondi (1649–1679), archbishop of Paris and later Cardinal de Retz. First an opponent of Mazarin and the Regent during the Fronde, he went over to the Court in return for the promise of a Cardinal's hat.

60 Jean Regnault de Segrais (1624–1701), a man of letters who was secretary to the duchesse de Montpensier and a friend of Madame de La Fayette, both of whom published novels under his name.

63 The Marais is an old quarter of Paris on the Right Bank of the Seine, an originally marshy area that was drained in the late Middle Ages. It became a fashionable area for noblemen's town houses after Charles V went to live there in the second half of the fourteenth century, and especially after the construction of the place Royale (now the place des Vosges) in the early seventeenth century.

65 Nicolas Fouquet (1615–1680), surintendant des Finances from 1653, who amassed a huge fortune enabling him to act as a patron to writers and build the château of Vaux-le-Vicomte. Colbert, who was to succeed him as finance minister, denounced him to the King for embezzlement. He was arrested in 1661 and spent the last nineteen years of his life in prison at Pignerol.

69 The Louvre was formerly a royal palace.

81 Louise d'Orléans, duchesse de Montpensier (1627–1693), niece of Louis XIII, generally known as "la Grande Made-

moiselle." She took an active part on Condé's side in the Second Fronde, ordering the cannon of the Bastille to be fired on the royal troops.

82 In 1616 Marie de Médicis (Regent, 1610–17) had the ancient path leading out of Paris along the Right Bank of the Seine transformed into a magnificent promenade, the Cours-la-Reine, which still exists.

82 *Les Italiens* were a company of Italian actors authorized to perform commedia dell' arte in Paris, but they gradually introduced more and more scenes in French. They were expelled from Paris in 1697 after ridiculing Madame de Maintenon in *La Fausse Prude,* but returned in 1716 after Louis XIV's death.

82 Cardinal Mazarin had many Italian nieces—among them five Mancinis—whom he brought to Paris to make advantageous marriages. Louis XIV had a youthful affection for Olympe Mancini, later the mother of the great general Prince Eugene. Louis also fell deeply in love with Marie Mancini, but Mazarin would not agree to their marriage.

82 The Palais-Royal was originally the Palais-Cardinal, built by Richelieu about 1636. Its gardens were open to the public, and it was a popular meeting place. Richelieu bequeathed it to Louis XIII and his heirs, and the young Louis XIV lived there for some years from 1643 on.

85 The Hôtel-Dieu was a hospital for the poor.
La Salpêtrière was the women's section of a general hospital for vagrants and beggars, part hospice and part prison, founded by Louis XIV in 1656 on the site of a former arsenal.

85 Homosexuality was punishable by death at the stake.

CHAPTER SEVEN

87 The hôtel de Bourgogne was the oldest permanent theater in Paris. In 1656 it was occupied by the *Comédiens du Roi* (the King's Players), who in 1680 combined with Molière's company to form what now survives as the Comédie-Française.

The hôtel de Bourgogne was then taken over by the *Les Italiens* company.

92 The Company of the Holy Sacrament was a powerful secret society for the promotion of faith and good works, a "congregation" of lay and clerical members founded in 1627. Its methods were unscrupulous, and its hypocrisy was satirized in Molière's *Tartuffe.*

93 Marie de Rabutin-Chantal, marquise de Sévigné (1626–1696), famous for her *Letters,* written mostly to her daughter.

99 The Hôpital de la Charité was founded by five friars of the order of Saint John of God, whom Marie de Médicis brought from Florence in 1602.

110 This Congress was a public trial of a husband's ability to consummate a marriage, in a suit brought to dissolve the union.

CHAPTER EIGHT

122 Val-de-Grâce was a Benedictine nunnery set up by Anne of Austria largely as a personal retreat for herself and transformed into a great abbey after the birth of her son the future Louis XIV.

124 Hospice des Quinze-Vingts was a hospital for blind paupers and beggars, founded by Saint Louis about 1260.

126 The Grève (or strand) was a stretch of sand on the Right Bank of the Seine which in the Middle Ages became the center of the capital's water-borne trade. The Port-de-Grève dealt in grain and wine. The various other specialized ports along the Right Bank included the Port-au-Foin, for hay.

CHAPTER TEN

157 Jean-Baptiste Colbert (1619–1683), Louis XIV's finance minister, successor to Fouquet and a great and enlightened administrator. He founded the academies of science, architecture and inscriptions.

161 The hôtel de Rambouillet was the town house of Catherine de Vivonne, marquise de Rambouillet (1588–1665). It

was the intellectual center of Paris society in the first half of the seventeenth century, and made *préciosité* fashionable.

162 *Histoire amoureuse des Gaules* (1665) is a scandalous account of Court intrigues under fictitious names by Roger de Rabutin, comte de Bussy, cousin of Madame de Sévigné. For publishing this satire he was banished to his estates.

173 Saint François de Sales (1567–1622), founder of the Order of the Visitation and author of the *Introduction à la vie dévote* (Introduction to the Devout Life), intended to reconcile the Christian life with the life of the world.

177 Charles Perrault (1628–1703), a poet and critic employed by Colbert as artistic and literary adviser. He is chiefly remembered for his collection of fairy tales, some of which were published separately before the edition of 1697.

184 *Imitation of Christ* is a translation of *De Imitatione Christi,* a widely popular devotional work by Thomas à Kempis (1380–1471), a German Augustinian monk.

CHAPTER ELEVEN

194 Marie-Madeleine, comtesse de La Fayette (1634–1693), author of *La Princesse de Clèves* (1678) and other studies of married life, including the shorter novel *La Princesse de Montpensier.*

202 From the thirteenth century on, certain indirect taxes were farmed out in France for fixed periods to private persons (*fermiers-généraux* or farmers-general) who had the right to exploit them, often making large fortunes.

209 The Val was a small château built in the park at Saint-Germain-en-Laye.

CHAPTER TWELVE

221 Louis Bourdaloue (1632–1674), a renowned Jesuit preacher. He was considered the greatest preacher of his day, rational, penetrating and severe.

221 Jules Mascaron (1634–1703), a noted Oratorian preacher. He was named bishop of Tulle, and later of Agen.

226 "He doesn't take after his mother . . . He takes after his father. He's got a nice face . . . How I hate that female devil! I tell you, that whore . . . You'll see. Just you wait and remember what I say!"

252 Cour des Princes was the courtyard of the special wing at Versailles built to house the Princes of the Blood.

253 Hocca was a game resembling roulette, which gave rise to so much cheating and such huge losses that La Reynie, the Paris Chief of Police, had banned it. The King had previously allowed it at Court, and even played it himself.

265 The duc de Saint-Aignan, the father of Monsieur de Beauvilliers, later a friend of Madame de Maintenon and one of Louis XIV's ministers.

CHAPTER THIRTEEN

277 Chambre Ardente was a special court of the Paris Parlement which tried cases of heresy and other exceptional crimes such as poisoning. The room was draped in black and lit by torches even in the daytime.

278 Catherine Monvoisin (La Voisin), chief suspect in the Affair of the Poisons.

279 The place de Grève was an open space used as a place of execution (now the place de l'Hôtel-de-Ville).

288 By the Edict of Nantes (1598), Henri IV granted the Protestants freedom of conscience and certain political rights, including the right to live in safety in certain towns. By the Edict of Alès (1629), Richelieu allowed the Protestants to retain their liberty of conscience but took away their political rights.

CHAPTER FOURTEEN

319 Madame de Brinon's words are still sung as the English national anthem—"God Save the King/Queen"—though to a different tune, composer uncertain.

324 The truce of Ratisbon was a twenty-year armistice signed by Louis XIV and Leopold I of Austria in 1684. In 1690 Louis sent his army into the Palatinate, a stronghold of Calvinism, in an attempt to embarrass William of Orange, recently made William III of England.

325 In 1682 the Assembly of the Church of France, presided over by Bishop Bossuet, supported the doctrine of Gallicanism by declaring in favor of the sovereign's independence of the Pope in temporal matters.

329 The Convent of the New Catholics was founded in 1634 to give religious instruction to female Protestant converts.

336 Jacques-Bénigne Bossuet (1627–1704), famous for his sermons and funeral orations, and previously tutor to the Dauphin. In 1681 he became bishop of Meaux.

336 The Lazarists were a congregation founded in 1625 by Saint Vincent de Paul to train missionaries.
Saint-Sulpice was a seminary built in 1645 to train secular priests.

342 Pierre du Terrail, chevalier de Bayard (1473–1524), was the brave knight whose exploits earned him the title of "chevalier sans peur et sans reproche."
Philippe-Emmanuel, marquis de Coulanges (1633–1716), a writer of light verse, cousin and friend of Madame de Sévigné.
Blaise Pascal (1623–1662), a philosopher, physicist and great prose stylist who in 1654 was converted to a religious life and in 1655 went to live among the Jansenists of Port-Royal. His *Pensées,* fragments of an unfinished apology for the Christian religion, was first published in 1670. His *Lettres provinciales* (1656–57) was banned and burned in 1660.

344 François de Salignac de la Mothe-Fénelon (1651–1715), a disciple of Bossuet, a writer as well as a prelate, consecrated archbishop of Cambrai in 1695. His *Aventures de Télémaque,* an indirect critique of the policies of Louis XIV, was published in 1699.

CHAPTER FIFTEEN

360 Sébastien Le Prestre, seigneur de Vauban (1633–1707), military engineer and maréchal de France. In 1707 he published a *Projet de dîme royale,* which advocated an egalitarian form of taxation.

365 Miguel de Molinos (1628–1696), a Spanish theologian whose *Spiritual Guide* initiated the doctrine of quietism.

CHAPTER SIXTEEN

383 Louis II de Bourbon, prince de Condé (1621–1686), known as "le grand Condé." A great captain who joined the enemies of the Court during the Fronde, he was later pardoned and restored to high command.

388 The maréchal de Villeroy transferred his ducal title to his son in 1696.

392 Mary of Modena, the daughter of Laure Martinozzi, one of the nieces Mazarin brought to Paris to make an advantageous marriage.

406 Camisards were rebel Calvinists in the Cévennes, so called because they wore white canvas shirts (*camisa* in Old Provençal) over their other clothes.

CHAPTER EIGHTEEN

443 François-Marie Arouet, the real name of Voltaire (1694–1778).

451 Philip II of Spain (who married Mary Tudor), well known for his inflexibility and his unremitting devotion to affairs of state.